THE
MONEY
WOLVES

THE MONEY WOLVES

PAUL ERIKSON

WILLIAM MORROW AND COMPANY, INC.
NEW YORK   1978

Library of Congress Cataloging in Publication Data

Erikson, Paul.
    The money wolves.

    I. Title.
PZ4.E67Mo   [PS3555.R46]   813'.5'4   78-17730
ISBN 0-688-03378-4

BOOK DESIGN   CARL WEISS

Printed in the United States of America.

First Edition

1   2   3   4   5   6   7   8   9   10

With love to

My dearest Cyn, who knows the whole story

My children, who know only a part

My late mother, in belated recognition for her remarkable prescience

And to Harold Matson, who made it all happen

. . . This was a game these wolves knew how to play. They knew how to stalk, how to wait, and how to move in for the kill when they sensed vulnerability . . .

THE
MONEY
WOLVES

E LLIOT THOMPSON SMOKED A NERVOUS CIGARETTE AND stared out of the window of the fiftieth floor of 140 Broadway. It was a gray day with a low mist that completely shut off any view of uptown Manhattan.

The investment research report that he was reviewing on Computer Ecolog looked as if someone had hemorrhaged on it. In fact, Elliot had. He had slashed furious red underlines. Questions annotated in margins. Barbed comments that cut and thrust at the analyst's facts and premises.

Who the hell told him to write this shit? When I hired him, that presumptuous little prick was good. He's still good, but he's a phony.

Elliot stubbed out the cigarette and saw his phone light up. He had told Mary to hold his calls. How can you read this kind of semitechnical crap and answer every damn phone call?

He saw the smoke curl from the squashed cigarette, the last one from the first of two packs he would smoke that day.

He was so goddamned tired. He leaned back and let his mind wander and all he could see was the apartment. The stupid damned apartment, where Marge would have left the kitchen in chaos. With last night's cigarettes and liquor bottles all over the place and her damn bras and pantyhose in the bathtub.

The report stared up at him, slick, gimmicked, fraudulent. He could see the heads nodding in investment offices around the country as they read this tripe. He saw the overcoated and furred bodies sitting mesmerized in front of flashing electronic numbers and symbols. He saw it all.

The gunslingers swapping one-hundred-thousand-share blocks. The traders and the big producers with the phones to their mouths, not daring to break for lunch for fear of missing one pulsebeat of the market.

And here in front of him, written by that little shit of a computer analyst Bob Friedman, a so-called real *know* guy in computer stocks, and one of the top analysts in the business—he had to pay $75,000 a year and a piece of the firm's profits to get him—here, hidden behind all the catch-words and technical jargon, was a con job. This report, this polished piece of stylized introspection, was a fucking fraud.

He had come out of the investment research depart-ment's meeting with his pale face and large dark-brown eyes smoldering. The research committee had spent the whole morning on Computer Ecolog. The net result was that they all looked at him, with that hidden needle that he knew was behind the faces that stared at him. Masked. Complacent. Sardonic.

"Well, doesn't anybody here feel the thing is blown sky-high? Don't any of you smug bastards feel that a stock that is selling at a hundred and twenty times earnings, with one genius running the fucking company who can't balance his own checkbook, and one kooky promoter mak-ing acquisitions with Chinese paper, and no guy in that whole company who is a real manager—doesn't someone here agree with me that we ought to blow the whistle on Computer?"

There was a shuffling of chairs and a few hands stubbed cigarettes into round stainless-steel ashtrays.

"Elliot." The voice was low and controlled. The eyes of Bob Friedman did not meet Elliot's.

"Are you willing to tell Sullivan that our number one baby that this firm underwrote, whose customers bought four hundred thousand shares of stock at eighteen, which is now forty-six after two stock splits; are you going to tell Sullivan that we should blow the whistle?"

Elliot glared at Friedman.

"Look, Elliot, I know my report is at variance with your views on the company." Friedman was in shirt sleeves. A vertically striped blue and white shirt with white collar and cuffs. Four small round gold balls served as cuff links. A Sulka tie draped loosely over Friedman's narrow chest.

"But that's how I see Computer, Elliot; and though I bow to your authority as director of research of this firm, I don't waive my expertise in my own area—" and Friedman held up his hand. With his high forehead and receding red hairline, his light-blue eyes and slightly flattened freckled nose, Friedman was aloof, furtive; somewhat deferential, but unintimidated. Hand still held in a gesture of abeyance.

"Elliot, spare us your vocabulary, please. Just in clear declarative sentences tell us—tell me—what there is about my analysis of Computer that bugs you so much."

Everyone in the room watched Elliot make a massive effort at self-control. His facial muscles seemed to be having individual spasms. "All right, Friedman"—dropping the "Bob" was particularly abrasive to Friedman—"do you want me to sit here and delineate—I should rather use the verb vivisect—what I consider to be the inadequacies of this report? Do you wish me to give you my"—Elliot bowed and waved his hand in broad salute to Friedman—"my criticism regarding your interpretation of Computer's accounting practices? Your analysis of their competition and the effect of IC technology on Computer's main product lines? Do you . . ." Elliot could contain himself no longer.

"Oh, for Christ's sake, Friedman, stop jerking me off. Who told you to write the goddamn report?"

Friedman's face burned in anger beneath a newly acquired Caribbean tan.

"I don't like your implications, Elliot."

Friedman was trying hard to fight the impulse to attack Elliot with all the explosive enmity that each held for the other. "You know that the report on Computer is my normal follow-up." Friedman's voice became very low. "No one other than you, Elliot, can ever tell me when or what to write about."

"That's a lot of shit." The mist was breaking up and re-forming. The cigarette smoke swirled slowly toward the air-conditioning vents. Muffled traffic sounds arose from the streets far below. The heartbeat of the room was almost audible.

"This report, if it goes out at all, which I seriously doubt —at least not with my approval—will move Computer another ten points at least."

Elliot was tilted back in his chair. "Isn't there one shred of integrity among any of you? I hired every son of a bitch in this room after interviewing the sweat off your balls. I probed and twisted to find out if you really were any good —if you had the kind of talent to back up the money this august firm is willing to pay you. I know at least some of you have that kind of talent. But what I didn't think to look for was guts. Just plain old-fashioned moxie. Maybe you might call it the ability to resist arm twisting."

Elliot got to his feet and pointed at them all. "While I am director of research at Sullivan, no one—*no one*—not from management, not from sales, not from corporate finance—not even Frank Sullivan is going to tell me or my analysts to write some goddamn slick tout sheet disguised as a professional institutional research report." He looked squarely at Friedman, who was thinking about the Renoir hanging in Sullivan's office, about Elliot's ulcer, and the fog that kept opening and closing about the windows of the conference room like some lazy giant fish feeding in slow motion.

Elliot turned to Bob Friedman.

"Friedman. How's your schedule for lunch today?"

"I have a date uptown with Grant of Winston Fund."

"Cancel it. You're my guest. The small dining room's free. They had a cancellation. I'll tell Mary to book the two of us. Gentlemen, this meeting is adjourned. I'll call for you again when we get a chance to settle some things around here."

There was visible relief at his departure, as if an infected wound had burst its tissue. Everyone looked at Friedman, who had pushed his chair back and was doodling on the yellow lined pad in front of him. He never raised his head to look at any of his fellow senior security analysts, but his voice, although he spoke very quietly, was heard clearly by everyone.

"It is my suggestion that this little scene just played by our favorite impresario stay right here in this room." He looked about him, his light-blue eyes seeking everyone. "My further suggestion, and I imply that it is more than a suggestion, is that not one word of negative implication concerning good old Computer get to the Street. I know that company better than anyone in this shop and I think its price is justified by the potential for its product lines." His eyes tested each of them, and he saw his warning reflected in a variety of faces in different ways. But he saw that it was understood.

Elliot had been thinking about Marge. How much he would like to have her all over him right now. How empty, stupid, and useless he would feel when it was over.

The console on his desk buzzed. He almost jumped. "It's twelve thirty, Mr. Thompson." Elliot grunted a reply. He squashed another cigarette and walked out of his office to the small dining room on the forty-ninth floor.

Friedman was waiting for him in the anteroom. Several of Elliot's partners greeted him as they escorted their guests. He nodded strained smiles with an occasional "Chuck,

Jack, Flint." He motioned Friedman into the paneled room with the circular Regency table, the Sheraton chairs and the brass chandelier with its small shades—the corner cupboards softly lit, showing to advantage the Chinese export porcelain. Friedman was in his dark-blue suit with those flared trousers that Elliot couldn't stand. He motioned Friedman to a seat. At that moment the door opened and Dean Faulkner poked his head in. His face feigned congeniality. "Could you two use a third, or are you going to force me to go to the DTA?"

"Sorry, Dean. But Bob and I have things we want to talk about that we wish to keep from you corporate finance types." Elliot caught the tiny glanced signal from Friedman to Faulkner.

Faulkner smiled thinly and shut the heavy walnut door.

Elliot pressed the buzzer underneath the table, and Goulet came in. His swarthy face and bright dark eyes were alert. He could take the particular drink requirements of fifteen guests without a pencil, and deliver each drink to each guest exactly as requested. It was truly a remarkable skill that never failed to impress everyone.

"You know mine, Goulet."

"I'll have some Chivas and water, please."

Goulet passed silently through the swinging door and into the kitchen.

Friedman's habit of sitting and bringing the fingers of both his hands together, lips compressed, eyes focused on whomever he was talking to, with a slight hunch to his posture was characteristic of him when he was intent.

Goulet brought the drinks.

Elliot sighed as he downed his first martini much too quickly.

Friedman sipped at his scotch.

Elliot pressed the buzzer again and Goulet appeared with another drink automatically. He knew Elliot.

Friedman waved a pass and Goulet went back to the kitchen.

One thing about these Jews, Elliot thought. They didn't drink enough. He took about a quarter of his second martini and felt more relaxed. "Now, Friedman"—still no Bob, which Elliot meant to be deprecating, insulting— "just tell Uncle Elliot what the hell you are trying to pull."

Friedman's eyes were not on Elliot. His mind was on Dean Faulkner and Frank Sullivan.

"I asked you a question, Friedman."

Friedman came back to Elliot. "I would prefer you calling me Robert or Bob. Not Friedman, Elliot. Or I am going to start addressing you as Thompson."

"Score one for the tiny man in the bell-bottom pants." Elliot waved a compromising bow.

"Elliot, if we can cut the theatrics and sarcasm, I'll be glad to tell you what is *up*, as you put it, because nothing is *up*." Elliot put down his glass and was about to speak but Friedman held him off.

"I don't know what the hell is bugging you about this report, other than the fact that we have a winner in this firm for a change and it happens to be in my area."

"Horseshit."

"It's not horseshit. We've got a company that has found a way to take impregnated microwafers, turn them into the world's cheapest restricted-function computer, and couple that to monitoring devices that can monitor forty different pollution effluents. Which is just about combining the two hottest items on Wall Street—*computers* and *pollution.* Every steel mill, every chemical plant, every damn industry that is dumping garbage into the rivers, the earth, the sky, will have to buy one of these things to comply with government regulations."

"That's for the hucksters and con artists, Bob. Not for pros like you and Uncle Elliot. What I am responsible for in this firm is to keep the *con* off the *cob*, if you will pardon

18 /

a very bad pun. I'm not responsible for helping this firm kite stocks that I don't believe merit investor support. Now Computer Ecolog—just the name of the goddamn company is enough to make you retch—is in my opinion one of the *supreme* con jobs of all time. Those bastards have raised all kinds of money from institutions, through people like ourselves. They have set themselves up in a palatial manufacturing facility. They have produced to my knowledge exactly one hundred Computer Ecologs, all of which have been giving test problems in the field. Karkov the mad scientist keeps telling everyone that they are just a few months from working the bugs out, and Fletcher Court- ney, the white-shoe boy that Karkov has holding the hands of all the banks, insurance companies, and silly pricks like us, has been oozing slop over the country about what a fabulous company Computer is." Elliot's jaw mus- cles began to work again and Friedman saw him reach for the buzzer. Everyone who knew Elliot knew that it was two martinis before you ordered, and a third while you ate.

They both took pencils and checked off on the menu what they wanted for lunch.

"Bob"—Elliot was now alcoholically magnanimous— "have you been doing any quiet trading in Computer?" He cocked a sardonic eyebrow at Friedman.

"You know I haven't. That's against firm policy."

"I know that, young man. I created that policy. I in- sisted on it." Elliot's speech was now blurred. He's a god- damned liar, Elliot thought.

"Why did you write that report, Bob? Now don't horse- shit me, damn it. I've been around too long and I can smell a bomb farther away than any guy on Wall Street, and Computer, dear boy, is a bomb. Now give. Who and why the report? Did Dean ask you to do it? That crooked bastard is on the board of Computer. Did Frank? No, Frank wouldn't talk to little Bobby, would he." This was Elliot at his abrasive best. A three-martini lunch and his stream-of-consciousness dialogue could be appreciated only by his analyst.

The light from the chandelier cast its soft reflection off the shining tanned skull of Bob Friedman. He had picked at his lunch, avoiding Elliot's eyes. His thoughts were on the money he had made trading Computer in his brother's account. He thought about Dean Faulkner and Frank Sullivan, the firm's senior partner.

"Give to Uncle Elliot, Bobby boy."

Friedman rose, looked at Elliot.

"My suggestion is that you speak to Dean about all this. And now, if you will excuse me, I'd like to get uptown. I was able to postpone that fund meeting until three." Bob Friedman left the room.

The triumph that Elliot felt as he watched the smoke curl from his cigarette was dampened by the pain from his ulcer. A part of his mind urged caution, but he knew he would veto caution in favor of bravado. An inner voice told him he would end up a loser.

Bob Friedman stopped in the lobby of 140 Broadway and put in a call to Dean Faulkner. Dean was tied up in a meeting, but Bob insisted on his being called to the phone.

"Sorry to interrupt, Dean."

"That's okay."

"Thought you had better know that Elliot's going to call you. At least that's my guess. And soon."

"Oh? Anything in particular?"

Bob had to smile at the practiced calm.

"Not particularly." That ought to hold him, Friedman thought. He held the pause just long enough.

"Elliot seems to be less than enthusiastic about my report on Computer."

"I see."

Friedman smiled again as he could visualize the practiced lack of any change of expression crossing Dean's face.

"Well, that's not so earth-shaking is it?"

Friedman really had to hand it to this barracuda. You would have had to know Dean very well to catch just the slightest change in pitch and inflection in his voice to discern that they were talking about anything other than the weather.

"Just thought I'd let you know. I've got to run."

"Thank you, Bob."

They both clicked off.

Dean Faulkner paused for only a moment and turned toward the five men in his office whose meeting he had interrupted to take Bob's call. He heard the drone of their voices and feigned interest in their proceedings, but his mind was on Bob's warning call; on Frank Sullivan, and on Dina, Sullivan's wife. But most of all Dean looked past the five faces sitting before him and thought of Elliot. Pale, nervous, caustic, explosive, gifted Elliot. What cyclonic winds would that hard-drinking neurotic cause to blow?

The meeting was over. The fog had disappeared into the early-January night. The lights of the city seemed to melt into the drops of rain running erratic patterns down Dean's windows. The phone rang. It was Elliot.

Elliot's long lunch had left its alcoholic glow, easing his normal threshold of hostility.

"Dear boy. Sorry we couldn't let you in for lunch. Had to have a talk with Bob." Pause and a chuckle. "Matter of fact, old boy . . ." This was Elliot's speech pattern after the martinis had left their glow. Like many heavy drinkers, Elliot couldn't hold his liquor, and its effect lasted far longer than it would have with most people. "Matter of fact, old boy"—pause—"want to talk to you. Got a minute?"

"It's a little late, Elliot, and Chris is giving a dinner party. Anything that can't wait?"

"Oh, no." Elliot now broadly sarcastic. "Oh, no, dear boy. Nothing important enough to break up your wife's

evening. Wouldn't dream of it. One of those trifling matters that could affect the firm somewhat."

Dean was exactly five feet nine inches tall. He was taut
and muscular with dark closely cropped hair, a sharp
face, and darting black eyes. His face, usually pale, was lean
and narrowed to a small but firm chin, which gave him a
look of sharpness. His movements were quick and well
coordinated, like those of a fencer, and his voice, high in
pitch, often became irritating as he tongue-lashed a sub-
ordinate with total disregard for anyone else present. Compassion and tact were not the long suits of Dean Faulkner.

He reminded Elliot and others of a ferret, one of the
most savage vertebrates pound for pound. But Dean's ruthlessness was well covered by layers of surface gentility which
he had polished to a high gloss over the years.

"Believe you've heard of the company." Elliot had to
chuckle. He couldn't help it. He could see the ferret eyes
narrow at the other end of the line.

"Elliot, I would appreciate it if you would come to the
point." Just the hint of a strain in Dean's voice.

"The point, dear Dean"—that was marvelous, Elliot
thought: dear Dean—"The point is that I think we have
the makings of a little catastrophe before us. But"—and
Elliot paused to let the effect sink in—"really no need to
spoil Chris's evening over anything minutely catastrophic."

At this moment Dean felt more hostility toward Elliot
than he would care to admit even to himself. His reaction
was simply training and there was no betrayal in his voice.

"Elliot. If it's not mere melodrama, and I have enough
respect for your capabilities not to accuse you of over-
dramatizing, I think I can always find time for a catastrophe or two."

"Monico's in about fifteen minutes?"

Dean hated Monico's. It was the haven at this time of
night for those seeking refuge from the murderous pressures of a day on Wall Street. Men who wanted to delay

going home. Its scarlet walls and dark furniture. Its waiters, who managed to be both obsequious and insolent simultaneously, always left him with the impression that the place was an ancient bordello from which all the women had fled.

"See you in fifteen minutes." Dean hung up.

The meeting with Elliot lasted for almost an hour. He had to call Chris and tell her he would be late. This was nothing new to Chris, who never expected Dean to be on time for anything. Dean was now totally preoccupied with thoughts about his meeting with Elliot.

As the cab passed through the darkened streets of lower Manhattan and made its way to the East River Drive, Dean watched the lights reflected in the dark swirls of the river and the drifts of mist beginning to form into low cumulus scud. He thought of Dina, and Frank Sullivan, his senior partner. Frank would be there tonight, and they would have to find time to be alone. Dean could still hear Elliot's voice as the cab pulled up to his apartment at Sixty-second and Park.

"Dear boy, we've got a bomb on our hands." He could see the neurotic delight in Elliot's eyes and in the twitching of the facial muscles that contorted into a smirking grin.

"Dear Dean, we've got an eighteen-million-dollar bomb on our hands."

Dean slammed the cab door and strode into the lobby of his apartment building. He didn't acknowledge the doorman's salute or the elevator operator's greeting.

The elevator opened at his door. His apartment occupied the floor. He could hear the laughter and the noisy babble as he inserted his key.

Dean's living room was off the foyer. He put his coat and hat in the hall closet. His nostrils picked up the scent of burning logs, and his eyes caught the soft glow of his living room where the fire burned and the air conditioners were hidden behind beige silk draped windows that never opened, summer or winter.

His whole apartment was literally an investment in good taste. From the authenticated English and French period furniture, to the signed oils that were hung unobtrusively against walls covered with dark-green silk. Exquisitely painted Chinese screens separated the living room from the dining room. Only the muted blare of horns from the street with the wail of an occasional siren, that anguished cry of the city, could reach up to soil his seclusion in this sanctuary that his money and his wife's taste had created.

"Hi, Dean, sweetie. We had almost given you up." Cissy Cartwright, in short hair, had been the first to see him; she extended a jeweled arm. "Come here with me, sweetie, Chris has you all the time."

Cissy pulled him close to her and squeezed his arm. "Dean." It was Henry Cartwright, laughing at the sight of his wife nuzzling an old friend. "Well, so the host finally showed up."

Chris had invited four couples, all old friends. They had been through the hors d'oeuvres and most of them were on their third or fourth drink. It was as if they had all made a pact to enjoy this dinner party and say to hell with everything, at least until tomorrow morning. Another curse of New York: midweek socializing that lasted until nearly midnight, when experienced wives made excuses to drag their overworked husbands home for some rest before the pressures of a new working day would begin.

Dean's eyes first sought out Chris. She signaled the butler to take away the last of the hors d'oeuvres, then turned to him and flashed a warm smile that disguised the fact that she was watching the way Cissy's left breast rubbed ever so gently against Dean's arm.

Dean winked at Chris, who came over and kissed him.

She was about to talk to her husband when she saw Frank Sullivan leave Dina, who was at the far corner of the room, and move toward Dean.

Dean's eyes had searched for Dina from the moment he entered the room. In the back of his mind the warning lights were lit. He knew his wife's ability to sense any interest he might have in another woman, and Dina's sexual presence was so evident that he was sure Chris had long ago sensed her husband's strong physical attraction for the wife of his senior partner.

Dina moved to talk to Carl Graham. Dina was tall with sleek hips. Her eyes were large, almost violet in color. Her streaked blond hair, parted in the middle, hung loose to her shoulders, and she was wearing a long-sleeved blue silk blouse, cut very low, and a dark velvet skirt. The outlines of her tanned breasts were accentuated by a double strand of long pearls that lay in her cleavage; her nipples pressed discreetly against the silk of her blouse. Dina cradled a glass of champagne as she turned her head ever so slightly, following her husband as he approached Dean. Only the most meticulous observer could have seen the change of expression in her eyes as she saw Dean with Cissy still clinging to him, and watched her husband rescue his partner with welcoming banter and small talk.

The dinner moved through its ritualized ballet. The table had been cleared, and Sajie the butler was offering cigars to the men, who were contentedly sipping their brandy.

Dean caught Frank Sullivan's eye and stood up.

"I wonder if all you beautiful people will excuse Frank and myself." Feigned protestations and cries of lament.

"Don't you guys get enough at the office? You're going to be there again in twelve hours." It was Carl Twining, senior partner of Twining, Davis, one of Wall Street's most expensive and respected law firms.

"Carl, truly I'm sorry. Frank and I won't be long. Just a little bit of catching up to do. Frank and I don't get much of a chance to see each other at the office. Please excuse us."

Frank Sullivan stood up, took his cigar and brandy, smiled at his friends, and chuckled. "These young fellows are just too eager. Nothing can ever seem to wait until morning." He shrugged and followed Dean into the living room and through the door that led to the library and Dean's study.

Frank couldn't help thinking as his eyes surveyed the room how far his partner had come in what seemed to Frank such a short time. It had taken Frank much longer, and there had been a lot of jolts along the way. When you lived in the material jungle in which both Frank and Dean daily fought for survival and success, you learned to develop instincts like an animal who is both the hunter and the hunted.

For some reason, in the recesses of Frank Sullivan's mind, he knew that tonight was beginning a train of circumstances that would end God knows where. He sensed what Dean wanted to talk to him about and he felt a small knot of anxiety begin to form.

They settled themselves in Dean's study with its black walls lined with books, the deep leather chairs that flanked a glass-topped desk, the aluminum swivel balled lamps that gave a utilitarian look to this room that the rest of the apartment lacked. This was Dean's room, without pretense. It was, like its owner, dark, functional, and without warmth.

Dean put out his cigar and took a long pull at his brandy. He looked at his senior partner, who was rolling his own brandy glass between two tanned, well-formed hands.

Frank Sullivan was sixty years old. His face was burned tan from the sun of Nassau. His hair was full and a pepper-and-salt gray. He viewed life through narrow horn-rimmed glasses that framed light-gray eyes which could shine with irony one minute and turn cold as a winter's sea the next. He had heavy gray brows that seemed to make the tan of his face more pronounced.

He was tall and very erect; always immaculately groomed. He took special pains regarding his weight and muscle tone. Frank Sullivan was vain about his appearance.

He evoked, especially among women, an air of seasoned masculinity. He was a man of recognizably strong character. His manner was at once commanding, congenial, appraising, wary. He spoke quietly in a low husky voice that had an instant authority to it. Frank Sullivan was in his own mind a WASP Catholic who had fought his way into the desired acceptance of the WASP Protestants. If Frank could have been born as he wished, he would have chosen to be a moneyed Irish nobleman—a titled landowner who could spend his time pursuing his passions, which were the game of success, and following the sun with people who were attractive, rich, and powerful.

Frank Sullivan had worked like a tiger to achieve what he had. Like many men whose inner security was in the visible objects of their achievements, Frank had always stretched himself very thin, both socially and financially.

"You seem to be a little wrought up tonight, Dean, my boy." He was looking at the amber liquid that he kept slowly turning in his brandy glass.

"You mean it shows." Dean laughed.

"Only to an old hunter like me."

Dean watched Frank carefully.

"I had a meeting with Elliot today."

He saw the frown form ever so slightly.

"How is our peripatetic director of research?"

"He's the same talented arrogant bastard we all know and regret."

"What did you talk about?"

"Computer."

Dean watched Frank carefully, but there was no change in expression. Frank was an old hand.

"Do you think you could be a little more informative?"

Dean sighed at the tired sarcasm. He was tired himself. His mind saw Dina and those nipples, and her long tanned legs.

"Elliot doesn't want to okay Friedman's report on Computer. He thinks the whole company has become a con job and we ought to publish a sell recommendation to our institutional and retail customers."

Dean stared intently at Frank. This time there was a slight compression of Frank's lips, but that was all.

"Is Elliot aware of the firm's total position in Computer?"

"Elliot may be abrasive, but he's anything but stupid."

"You're on the board of Computer." Frank never looked up. He kept slowly swirling his brandy. "What is your opinion of the company?"

Dean began tapping his foot absentmindedly.

"Frank, the stock is selling at an out-of-sight multiple; there's no doubt about that"—he paused—"but if Karkov is right and he can get those impregnated chips to work in that computer of his, the stock is dirt-cheap."

"Is Karkov right?"

"How the hell should I know, Frank? I majored in finance and law, not physics. That's the trouble with these damn high-technology companies. The boys who put up the money can never understand the guys who spend it."

The room began to get stuffy and Dean reached over and flicked on the air conditioner.

"Who wrote the report?"

"Friedman."

Pause. Frank drank his brandy in one swallow and put down the glass. He began to cough. "Isn't Friedman supposed to be one of the best computer analysts on the Street?"

"He'd better be. We're paying him enough."

"Well, what does Friedman think?"

Dean lit another cigar. "Friedman has been trading that

stock in someone's account. I'd bet my life on that. I don't think Friedman's objectivity is something we can rely on at this point. That's just a guess, Frank. I could be dead wrong."

"What does Elliot want to do, blow the whistle?"

"That's what he wants to do."

The room was quiet except for the hum of the air conditioner.

"Have you been doing any diddling in Computer?"

Frank did not look at Dean as he asked the question. Dean's face went white.

"For Christ's sake, Frank, I'm a director. I have to report every—"

Frank held up his hand.

"I'm aware of your obligations as a board member." He repeated the question.

"Have you in one way or another been trading in Computer stock?"

Dean's dark eyes flashed anger but the knife of fear cut deeply.

He could feel it twist inside him. He knew what he had done and was still doing. He had made a small fortune trading Computer in his attorney's account. He had used his position as a director in the company to gain the advantage of inside information that was denied to anyone but the officers and directors of Computer. Not even Frank knew what he did about that crazy little company that was about to have an impact on all their lives.

Dean's stomach felt the ice spear of fear as he remembered Charlie Birdwell.

The best lawyers in New York couldn't save Charlie from the wrath of a hostile jury; from a judge who chose to make an example of Charlie for using his position as a director on the board of Forest City Mining to make money in the stock without reporting his trading activities as he was required to do by law. A little extra greed had ruined Charlie Birdwell.

When he came out of prison after serving fourteen months he was through in the securities business. He had become plaintive, gray and gaunt. His friends smiled and nodded to him briefly and hurried on. It had broken him.

Dean could still see the wide luminous eyes and thin narrow gray face of Charlie, whom he had happened to run into on the street. It was the devastation and hopelessness that hung about Charlie that Dean remembered. Dean never even broke stride.

"Charlie." He waved an index finger in a brief niggardly salute as he swiftly walked by in the late-afternoon rain. He could feel even now those twin pools of desolation focusing on him as he hurried away from the human disaster that stood staring at him; little rivulets of rain trickling down the face of Charlie Birdwell, who long ago had used up all his own tears.

But he was no Charlie Birdwell. He wasn't a loser. He'd been smart enough to cover his tracks. How the hell could they touch him? Even his instructions to buy and sell were given in code. He brushed the thoughts from his mind and faced the quietly appraising gray eyes of Frank Sullivan.

"Frank, you're my senior partner and a guest in my house. That's a hell of a question to ask me."

"Forget it. I was just wondering. Let's get back to Elliot. Does he absolutely refuse to authorize the report?"

"Yes."

"And I suppose he's discussed this in his usual calm manner with the senior research group?"

"He has. He also had lunch today with Friedman, who called me. My guess is he bawled the hell out of Friedman. My bet is that tomorrow you'll be getting a call from Elliot."

Frank sighed and stood up.

"It's late. Let's talk about this tomorrow. You had better get back to your guests."

* * *

The clouds now ran before a cold front that promised a clear gusty day. Occasionally a star's light pierced the swiftly moving cloud cover.

Eight blocks north, at Seventieth and Park, Dina watched the night rush by and looked at the form of Frank Sullivan as he lay in drugged sleep. God, how she wanted to be loved tonight. Not just sex. She wanted to lie in the arms of a man who would hold her, whose warmth and tenderness would envelop her, protect her. Perhaps with such a man she could have the one overriding desire of her life: a child.

She lay quietly, staring at the ceiling, her mind recalling the men in her life who had brought her so little joy.

She was only six. She had reached back in her mind thirty-two years.

It was a warm summer night, when the breeze that normally swept silently across the lawn from the sea to rustle the heavy green leaves of the ancient maple outside her window was absent. She was restless. She couldn't sleep. She had on a mauve summer nightgown, as diaphanous as the wings of a butterfly. It made her feel silky and grown up. She got out of bed and pirouetted, flaring her nightgown, pretending she was a very beautiful lady at a great ball.

The sounds of the summer night insects called her to the window and she leaned against the sill looking out at the great curved galaxy of stars that arched over the shadowed lawn toward the quiet moonlit ocean.

Beneath the darkness of the great maple tree she saw a shaft of light from the screened porch define and then lose itself in the vastness of the darkened grass.

She decided to investigate. Silently, on long slender summer-tanned legs she moved down the stairs, across the sprawling living room to the front porch.

Her father was sitting there, a decanter of whiskey and a half-filled glass beside him. He was lost in thought.

He kept pushing back his fair hair, which had started to turn the color of sand mixed with gray; his eyes, that violet blue which was the color of her own, seemed lost in thought. His face had an expression of such absorbed melancholy that her heart broke for him.

He was and would always be the handsomest man she would ever know. There was such an affinity between these two that as lost as he was in his own thoughts, he became aware of her presence.

He saw her and smiled. "What are you doing up this time of night, sweetheart?"

She ran to him and climbed into his lap, kissing him hard, her slender arms squeezing his neck with all her strength.

She smelled the alcohol on his breath, and she became aware of her father's silent torment. *And then she knew.* At the age of six she sensed his weaknesses, his vulnerability, and she knew that as she grew up *it would be she who would have to take care of him.* And that's the way it turned out; that's why she had let herself be manipulated into a marriage with her first husband, Peter; into an empty bed with an impotent husband whose money had saved them all; had saved the one man she really loved, her hapless, ineffectual, well-intentioned father.

Peter had given her one thing only: financial independence. The settlement he had agreed to was generous. Frank had shrewdly managed those funds for Dina until now, by most standards, she was a wealthy woman in her own right; but she almost never thought about her money. It was unimportant to her. Most of the time she even forgot it was there.

Frank loved her, and in her own way she loved him. But still there was no child. The doctors couldn't tell her why. Physiologically there were no reasons why she couldn't conceive. Frank was not a problem and neither, so they said, was she. It had become the overwhelming preoccupation of her life. It was driving her crazy, *and she had to resolve it.* One way or another she would not be denied a child upon whom she could lavish the love that had been suppressed within her for so long—a love she would not manipulate or reject. She reached over to her night table, took two sleeping pills, and buried her head in her pillow. A siren wailed from the streets below.

The chauffeur picked up Frank and two of his partners each morning for the drive downtown. Frank always sat in front reading the *Wall Street Journal*. The conversation was usually light, often pointing toward things Frank wanted someone to do that day.

This morning as they crossed town and edged into the flow of southbound traffic on the East River Drive, Frank Sullivan was silent, deep in thought. Frank held the largest piece of Computer and had ridden the stock to its present level. It was one of the biggest winners of his career. At current market his holdings were worth nearly five million dollars. But what bothered Frank more than his current position in Computer was the lockup deals he was in and couldn't unload, and the interest he was paying the banks to finance those investments. But even more was his constant need for cash to support his life-style. He had a home in Connecticut, heavily mortgaged, that had cost him half a million. True, he had two hundred and fifty feet of prime shore frontage. At a thousand dollars a foot it should be prime.

This house was Frank's pride, and it was the place he thought of as home. He spent far less time there than he would have liked, lately not even getting away for an occasional weekend. This house did not bring him peace of mind; he had to bring that with him. Its solitude could be enjoyed only when things were going well, and at this particular juncture his life was anything but tranquil.

He owned a large country house in Ireland where he bred and trained racehorses. This house, really a small castle, cost him $125,000 American, and the stables and staff, even though cheap by U.S. standards, were expensive to maintain. As a matter of fact, Frank was right now boarding and selling horses to lighten the load a little. In addition, he owned a cooperative apartment at Seventieth and Park Avenue that he paid over $185,000 for four years ago, and whose maintenance costs had risen every year. The apartment today was worth perhaps $250,000 now that Manhattan real estate was coming back.

Frank also belonged to several exclusive clubs, one on a cay off Nassau. He had paid handsomely for the privilege of picking his neighbors and ensuring their mutual exclusivity.

All these domiciles were liquid investments, at least relatively so, but the sale of any or all might indicate to Frank's peers a serious financial problem.

The properties themselves were not nearly as demanding as the cash drain for their maintenance, the money needed to meet the expenses of living up to the public image that Frank Sullivan had laboriously created for himself.

His firm was just now recovering from the last stock market debacle, and though the firm's operations were profitable, Frank's share of the partnership after taxes, which went into his capital account and could not be touched, left him with his tax-paid salary of two hundred thousand a year, which for someone with a more modest life-style would be enormous. But to Frank Sullivan it covered less than half of his yearly expenditures. The rest he manipulated by speculations in marketable securities or in lockup deals that he hoped he could eventually sell and end up with a handsome long-term capital gain. He was deep into the banks with collateral loans and right now the biggest piece of collateral he had was his investment in Computer. Should that collapse, the banks would begin calling, which was an old story to Frank, and they would ask him to put up more collateral. If Computer really hit the fan, Frank would have to sell almost everything he owned to meet his obligations, and that calamitous thought was more than his Irish pride could swallow. In a sense, he would be cleaned except for his interest in the partnership, and the damage such a debacle would bring to his own prestige and that of the firm he had so laboriously built was incalculable. The New York Stock Exchange would bring pressure on the firm to increase its capital. His partners, whose own capital would be jeopardized, would be tearing at him like wolves on an old bull elk caught in the snow.

These were the thoughts that were going through his mind as he walked past his secretary and asked her to have Elliot Thompson see him.

Frank's office took up one enormous corner facing north. He could look from his walnut-paneled aerie up the Hudson, which was white with chunks of floating ice. On a day as clear as this he could see past the George Washington Bridge to the curve in the river where the jutting Palisades cut off the view. He could see all of Manhattan, whose steel and concrete buildings rose like irregular teeth in some giant mouth gaping at the sky. He watched briefly as pieces of paper flew about, blown upward by the erratic physics of the wind that swirled the grime and debris of lower Manhattan into the eyes of those on the street, hunched against the cold, hurrying toward the warmth of their particular tower.

"Good morning, Frank."

"Good morning, Elliot."

Frank looked at his director of research. Elliot was as usual neatly and conservatively dressed; his face pale and haggard, his perpetual cigarette either clenched in his mouth or waving nervously between the fingers of a hand never at rest.

"Care for a cup of coffee?"

"Tea, sir, if you have it."

Frank pressed the signal button on his desk console. "Miss Finley. Two cups of tea, please." He turned to Elliot. "Milk or lemon?"

"Just tea, sir." Elliot in saying "sir" was not being sarcastic or deferential. He had a deep admiration for Frank Sullivan. He admired the acquired style that was never pretentious, the natural graciousness, and the undeniable guts that it took to claw his way up to an office like this.

"Elliot, let's talk about Computer."

Elliot liked the direct way Frank came to the point. No bullshit. Right out on the line.

"I understand you're disturbed by our favorite company."

Elliot smiled.

"Let's say, sir, that I am paid to be a cynic and a critical observer, and I simply want you to get your money's worth."

Frank thought there was something attractive about the integrity of this abrasive personality. He drank too much and talked too much, but had some hard streak of honesty that Frank could find in so few of his other partners.

"What is there about Computer that makes you nervous, Elliot, aside from the obvious price of the stock in relation to the company's earnings?"

The door opened and Miss Finley came in with tea steaming from two Meissen china cups on a small silver tray.

Frank let his tea cool.

"I had dinner with Dean last night"—he saw Elliot's face smile sardonically—"and asked him in his capacity as a director if he shared your views on Computer." Frank paused.

"And what did he say, sir?"

"He said"—Frank sipped his tea—"that he did not have the technical knowledge to give a valid opinion."

Elliot stopped smiling.

"That's a frank answer, sir, in my opinion."

"Yes, I believe it is, too." Frank looked at Elliot with the light from the north windows playing on the left side of his face. "But what interests me, Elliot, is why you feel more qualified than Dean, or your own senior analyst Bob Friedman, who is an acknowledged expert in this field, to pass judgment on Computer?"

"I don't, sir."

Frank sipped more tea. His voice was now very quiet.

"Then I'm afraid I don't understand."

Elliot lit another cigarette, and Frank watched the muscles of his face tighten as he flipped the burned match into an ashtray.

"Have you ever heard of Dr. Gerson Eisenstadt, sir?"

Frank shook his head.

"Dr. Eisenstadt is at MIT. He is one of the world's leading authorities on impregnated chip microcircuitry."

Frank felt the old knot return to his stomach.

"I spent last Sunday with Dr. Eisenstadt playing chess, at which he is very good and I am very bad. He has a charming little house in Cambridge."

"And how did you come to know Dr. Eisenstadt?"

"Simple. I called him. Told him of our interest in Computer and asked him if I could come up and see him. The only time he could see me was on Sunday. Since I had a mercantile interest in his field of knowledge, he agreed to see me provided that we play chess."

"It must be difficult to glean information from a man playing chess."

"It is. But Dr. Eisenstadt seemed to have some respect for my mission, if you will, sir."

"And what mission was that?"

"To find the truth. After all, Dr. Eisenstadt is a scientist. Searching for the scientific truth, if you will, sir, is what his life is all about."

"I see. And what did Dr. Eisenstadt have to say about Computer?"

Elliot put down his tea and stubbed his cigarette out. His facial muscles began to work and he could feel his ulcer begin the pain.

"He said, sir, that Karkov of Computer was a brilliant

fraud. That impregnated microcircuitry was at least two to three years away from the type of computer functions Karkov is trying to build into his Computer Ecolog monitoring devices."

Frank looked hard at Elliot.

"Did you feel you had the authority to talk to Dr. Eisenstadt without my permission?"

Elliot's face stiffened.

"Not only the authority as head of research for this firm, but the duty on behalf of my fellow partners and the customers, both retail and institutional, that we put into the stock."

Frank swiveled in his chair to look at Manhattan gleaming in the cold morning light. His back was to Elliot. Elliot watched his hand reach for the humidor and select a cigar. He saw the blue-gray smoke rise slowly in the room.

"I assume, Elliot, that you have some proposal to make regarding Computer."

Elliot hesitated.

"Yes, sir, I have."

"And . . ."

"An interoffice flash to sell, sir."

Frank swiveled slowly around to face Elliot. His tanned face betrayed the flush of his anger. The light-gray eyes were merciless, but the husky low-pitched voice was under control.

"What makes you think that Eisenstadt is more knowledgeable than Karkov?"

"His reputation among his colleagues."

"And Karkov?"

"He is held in somewhat less esteem, sir. And that is the understatement of the age."

"Am I to understand that on the basis of one scientist's opinion you would put out a sell flash on Computer?"

Elliot could feel the trap.

"Well?"

"I would, sir."

"Well, I wouldn't, and neither will you." It was a shot, not a sentence. The controlled force of Frank's anger cut at Elliot like a laser.

"What do you suggest, sir?"

"I'll tell you what I suggest, Elliot, when I'm ready. And until then, you sit tight on Computer, or you're through."

Elliot didn't need to be told that the interview was over. Frank had reached for some papers on his desk, which was his cue to anyone who knew him that it was time to leave.

In Boston they were getting the weather that New York had gotten the day before. Only in Boston it was wet snow.

The windshield wipers of Martin Karkov's Cadillac clicked hypnotically. Beside him sat Fletcher Courtney. They were stuck in midday traffic on Storrow Drive as they struggled to make their way to a luncheon date at the Ritz Carlton. On their right the dull ribbon of the Charles River wound its way toward Cambridge, and to their left, the soot-covered red brick apartments stared at them behind wide-paned curtained windows.

The two men were silent.

Fletcher Courtney sat with his thoughts. His mind had a death's grip on their luncheon meeting. It seemed that he had waited all his adult life for this particular moment and he was sitting here stuck on Storrow Drive unable to move because of the idiotic way human beings transport themselves in major cities.

For some reason he was thinking of that last board meeting almost six years ago at Universal American when he knew he was through. He had spent fifteen years with that company, and when the old man died he knew that it was only a matter of time. When he resigned he vowed to himself that he was through with Big Board companies and their internecine politics where you spent half your time playing the power lines and half your time doing your job. But he had been shrewd. He had lived fairly modestly for an executive vice-president of finance who earned $110,000 a year before taxes. And he had speculated carefully in the market so that when the time came, he could tell them behind his frozen set smile to go to hell.

He was born and bred in Missouri. He had studied finance not at one of the name schools, but in his home state. He had used an appraising, tough, quiet, persistent ability to climb consistently up the corporate cliffs until he had become the chief financial officer and director of a billion-dollar company.

Six years ago he had had a luncheon date with his old friend Gordon Palmer at one of the major Boston banks. He even remembered the call from Gordon because the circumstances that call initiated had changed his life.

"Fletch, I'm really embarrassed. How long are you going to be in Boston? Well, to be perfectly candid, Fletch, I got my signals crossed. I have to lunch with the chairman of one of our client companies who is trying to raise some money for a little computer outfit up on 128." Fletcher remembered the pause on the phone as if it were today. "Say, Fletch, this fellow is a regular guy, awfully bright and interesting. He's got a hot little company that's manufacturing computer peripheral products. If I call him and tell him about my goof and if he doesn't mind your joining us, you might enjoy meeting him. It will give me a chance to see you. It's been a while."

And that's how Fletcher Courtney met Dr. Martin Karkov. That luncheon nearly six years ago had been the precursor of the one to be held today. Only after today's repast, Mr. Fletcher Courtney, that spare, flat-bellied, wry opportunist from St. Louis, would add to his net worth approximately $1,715,000 before taxes. For Fletch Courtney was playing the odds in a crapshooter's game. He didn't know a thing about the complicated physics that Karkov was always talking about. But he did understand money and he was a shrewd judge of greed and timing. In fact, it might be said that Fletcher saw life as an insane carrousel out of sync, and as this mad device rotated he would wait his turn, and reach to pluck a reward without ever having to get on and ride himself.

In the stalled traffic, Fletcher's mind returned to their luncheon. After months of persuasion he had finally talked Karkov into selling 200,000 shares of Computer Ecolog out of the 1,800,000 shares Karkov held. The price of the stock had moved steadily upward to its present peak of forty-nine after two stock splits. Fletcher would join in the sale with 50,000 shares of his stock that he had realized through the exercise of a portion of his options, and though his tax consequences were not as favorable as Karkov's, his old "country boy" instincts told him to get some hard cash while everyone was hungry.

Horns blared as snow started to gather on the corners of the windshield.

Fletcher chuckled inwardly as he thought of his negotiations with the institutions. He and Karkov would sell their stock for a discount from current market of 30 percent with an investment letter. The board of Computer Ecolog was offered a chance to participate in the sale, but nobody would budge. They thought Fletcher and Karkov were crazy. For it was generally assumed by the seers of the marketplace that if Karkov could get his impregnated IC's working properly, that just the computer applications alone, without the pollution-monitoring devices, should triple the present price of the stock. Such are the dreams that fortune spins, and it's a rare man who is able to walk away. But Fletcher Courtney was such a man.

The line of cars began to move slowly.

Karkov thought that Fletcher was a shrewd financial manager but a nag. He wasn't interested in selling his stock or anything else; he only wanted to solve the problems of those goddamned impregnated chips. His drive was not money. So Karkov let Fletcher handle the details, which Fletcher did, which was why they were on their way to the Ritz in this miserable New England weather instead of back at the plant, where Karkov really wanted to be.

The traffic was moving now. Karkov stalled the Cadillac. He swore. Started it again; lurched forward as he pressed too hard on the accelerator, and jammed on the brakes to keep from hitting the car in front of them.

Fletcher turned a strained smile toward Karkov. "Let's not splash us all over the drive now, Karky. Not, at least, until we've signed this deal."

Karkov was the world's lousiest driver. His mind was always preoccupied. He never really saw what was physically taking place around him as he drove, but he always insisted on driving. Fletcher put up with this eccentricity only because he had to. Most of the time when they drove together Fletcher wondered whether they would wind up in some emergency ward.

Fletcher watched the gulls soar over the river.

Karkov was a very difficult man to read. Even now, after six years of close association, Fletcher didn't know whether he was a genuine genius or a fraud. He seemed to be attractive to financial types because of his honest disregard for money. To those whose lives were its pursuit, it was a psychological fascination to meet a man who had inadvertently made a fortune and couldn't care less. It was perhaps this freedom of spirit that they envied, even while they snickered at Karkov's eccentricities. But none would snicker after this day ended.

The Ritz in Boston to those who know it is one of the few civilized oases left in America. Its air is one of sober propriety. A quiet understated luxury.

In these surroundings two men would dine: one, who didn't care, would receive a check totaling $6,860,000 before taxes and after a 30 percent discount from the current market, and one, who cared passionately, would be $1,715,-000 richer. The laughter would sound, and the ice in the glasses would tinkle and the waiters would clear the roast beef from the table in the double suite that Fletcher had reserved, and an early January dusk would descend upon Boston, and events would begin that would shatter lives.

There is probably no environment as sensitive to the flow of information as the stock market. Millions of dollars invested in the most sophisticated kinds of communications equipment link vast networks of people together in the interest of obtaining information and translating that information into action—profitable action, hopefully, with as much speed as possible. All phases of the Street's activities eventually find their reward or doom in the marketplace. And the marketplace is the screen upon which is played the collective neurosis of mercantile man.

With the growth of institutions participating ever more heavily in the stock market, investment banking and brokerage firms like Frank Sullivan's and the institutions themselves have had to retain skilled analysts who specialized in various areas of business activity. Some of them are good, but as in most vocations, true talent with the necessary courage to back up intelligent opinion is in as short supply on Wall Street as in most other areas of activity.

But regardless of the attempts made by institutions to divine the fluctuations in the stock market, regardless of the improvement in telecommunications and computer applications, the marketplace is today what it has always been, a creature of rumor—a testimony to the deep-rooted insecurities of men.

The very sophistication of its communications network and the close association of the financial community made the news of the sale of 250,000 shares of Computer Ecolog by Karkov and Fletcher widely known within hours of its having taken place—known only within a small circle of professionals but known nevertheless.

And why not? It was a perfectly legal move. It would be reported to the Securities and Exchange Commission, and soon would be reported in the nation's major financial papers. It was not earth-shattering news except to those whose lives were tied tightly to Computer. And one of those lives was Frank Sullivan's.

Oddly enough, the sale of the stock created among the professionals a positive reaction. Some large brokerage houses learning of the news, and knowing the buyers of the stock to be highly respected and sophisticated financial institutions with great resources, made the Street even more buoyant about Computer. The stock moved in five business days to fifty-two dollars a share.

It was the custom of Frank's New York partners to hold brief meetings after the close of the market. The firm's activities of the day would be reviewed, perhaps a brief talk by the firm's economist and a general discussion of the firm's inventory. Special meetings were scheduled on a regular basis by the various department heads: sales, syndicate, corporate finance, research. Policy of the firm was made by its board of directing partners, of which Frank was the chief executive partner. Today's directors' meeting was held in an atmosphere that was strained by the sensitivity of the firm's investment in Computer. The stock now at its current level comprised an equity position that constituted a significant percentage of the firm's capital. The general mood among the five men who sat around the table in the senior partners' conference room was mixed.

Dean Faulkner was speaking:

"Frank, my feeling is that we should give some thought to lightening up on Computer." There was a nod from Bill Davis, head of syndicate.

"The market's strong, Frank. It will take the stock."

Frank moved his lips slightly and pressed the tips of his fingers together. The recessed lighting in the room fell on the circular walnut table. The hands of the numberless clock behind Frank's chair pointed to four thirty.

Frank removed his glasses and poured some water from the carafe in front of him. He drank slowly. When he spoke he toyed with his horn-rimmed glasses. His voice was husky, more throaty, than usual. He was looking at no one. His eyes seemed to be focused on the yellow pad in front of him.

"Elliot seems to feel that the firm should put out a sell flash on Computer, isn't that right, Elliot?"

Elliot's face was frozen; his mouth appeared to be a slit cut into it. He nodded.

There was a general shuffling of chairs. The room was now filled with anxiety.

"Jesus Christ, Elliot." It was Glen Farrell, managing partner of sales, his wide shoulders hunched in concentration toward Elliot. "An internal sell, Elliot. Christ, that will be internal for about as long as it takes my men to start making their calls. They'll kick the shit out of this stock in a day."

Farrell began to puff nervously on his cigar. In the windowless room with its subdued lighting, blue-gray smoke climbed toward the ventilation ducts.

"Elliot, why? What the hell's the reason? Everyone's talking about the stock going to a hundred and being split again."

The room was now focused on Elliot.

Elliot began to speak quietly in clipped tight sentences. He told them of his conversation with Eisenstadt. Farrell's dark hair glistened under the lights. His face was white with tiny drops of perspiration at his hairline.

"But, Jesus, Elliot. Those guys who just bought Computer are one of the sharpest groups around. They must have had competent technical advice . . ."

"They did." Elliot stubbed his cigarette and blew the smoke first from his nostrils and then from his mouth. "They had Tittle as management consultants, and they had Eisenstadt from MIT—"

Frank interrupted. "Eisenstadt?"

"Right."

"But I thought you told me Eisenstadt was very negative on Karkov and Computer."

"He is."

Frank took another drink of water. His eyes fixed on Elliot like a wolf's.

"I am afraid," he said in very even tones, "that you've lost me somewhere."

Elliot sighed. Jesus, he thought. Why the hell didn't I teach school or become a plumber? What the hell was the use in beating your body and your brain out day after day like this? "It's really not very complicated, Frank. When they heard Eisenstadt's views, Tittle's group called in Paul Nichols from the Nichols Institute. Paul's views are much milder than Eisenstadt's. He admits to possible delays in the technology but he thinks Karkov's going to make it. Simple, Frank. They bought Nichols and rejected Eisenstadt."

There was an undercurrent of rumbling in the room.

Dean Faulkner looked at Frank.

"Shouldn't we consider not sending out any report for the moment and kiting the stock, but just lighten up the firm's position . . ."

Elliot was seething. "I'm sure that you realize, Dean, that lightening the firm's position could also have a negative effect on the market, although I agree, at this point in time, slight. But as the investment bankers for Computer we have an obligation to our customers—"

"For what?" snapped Farrell. "To kill a market when we don't even know which one of these geniuses is right? What the hell kind of an obligation is that? For that matter, Elliot, Dean tells me you want to kill a research report by Friedman, who should know more about Computer than anyone here—"

"That's correct," snapped Elliot.

"Well, why, for God's sake?" Farrell was now flushed. Like most of the partners sitting around the table, he had no love for Elliot.

"Because"—Elliot's voice was a choked whisper—"that goddamned report is a fraud . . ."

Dean's face was controlled fury.

"In whose opinion . . ."

"In my opinion, God damn it. I am the director of research of this firm and what my analysts write and publish comes after I have authorized both the project and its publication. That is the research policy of this firm, established by this board."

Frank broke it up. "Now let's not all get carried away. There are definite conflicts of views here which we lack the knowledge, the technical knowledge, to understand.

"Elliot's feeling is that the stock is overpriced and it is—"

"But, Frank," Farrell interrupted. "This thing could go to two hundred."

"Or it could hit the fan."

Farrell glowered at Elliot.

"What I don't want to do is throw it at the fan, Elliot." Glen paused. "Look at Avon. Do you know how many times those guys across the Street met like we are meeting here to talk about selling Avon? And each time they decided not to sell. And they parlayed a two-hundred-thousand-dollar investment into sixty-five million."

Elliot laughed. "They were betting on cosmetics, not impregnated silicon wafers. For Christ's sake, women have been painting themselves since the Egyptians, and probably long before that.

"But to get back to the point, gentlemen, if we lighten up ourselves, I believe we have a moral obligation to suggest that our customers do likewise—"

"That's moralizing nonsense," Dean flashed at Elliot. "We have no obligation to tell our customers to get out of a security unless we think there is something wrong with the company . . . and so far, Elliot, the only ones who think there is something wrong with the company are you and this Dr. Eisenstadt."

"That's correct."

It was Frank's voice that interrupted. "I don't think we can base any moves on the information we have now. It's too nebulous. I don't agree with Elliot on a sell flash at this time. That would be premature." Frank put his glasses in his pocket and looked at his watch. "I don't want to challenge Elliot's authority in his own department . . ." Frank looked at Elliot. "I do want to see you for a moment, Elliot, after this meeting. For now, gentlemen, I suggest we sit tight for a few days. I'm going to the Coast over the weekend and expect to be back Monday or Tuesday. We can take this up again when I get back."

The meeting was over. The rush to make late trains, to return exhausted to impatient wives and children that saw them all too infrequently had begun.

Elliot stayed behind.

Frank walked to his office and motioned Elliot to follow him.

"Have you any plans for this evening?" It was Friday night.

Elliot was completely surprised.

"Nothing that can't wait, sir." He thought of Marge, who would scream and curse and kick furniture when he told her he might not be home as expected. The hell with her, he thought.

"I would like to ask you to join Dina and myself for dinner. I have a few things I want to talk to you about."

Frank pushed the button on his private line and called his wife.

Elliot had heard about Dina and had met her only briefly once or twice at Frank's annual Christmas buffet for his partners. He knew that she was at thirty-eight a strikingly beautiful woman. And it had been rumored that Dina's taste for men extended beyond Frank.

Frank put down the phone.

"It's fine. She'd be delighted to see you. Say about eight thirty. I have a few calls to make."

"Eight thirty is fine with me, sir. I've got a lot to do and I can get some work done before I meet you uptown."

Frank smiled. "Look forward to it, Elliot."

When Elliot left, Frank sat back in his chair and looked out at Manhattan lit up for the night. The city is like no other in the world at dark. Its dirt and grime are covered by darkness while its lights flash excitement even to those accustomed to work and live on that overcrowded island.

When Frank married Dina about two years after his first wife died, he married her for many reasons that he knew. The more important ones, unknown to him, lay deep in his unconscious.

Dina was twenty-two years younger than Frank. They had been married for ten years. They had no children. Dina had been divorced from her first husband for whom she had borne no child, and had met Frank at a party—one of those endless, mindless New York cocktail parties that are a modern form of social penance.

He remembered that she was easily the most beautiful woman he had ever seen. But her beauty was a physical statement of fact. She knew it and accepted it and was completely unaffected by it. This was her most attractive initial appeal to Frank. A beautiful woman who didn't give a damn about her beauty. She didn't have to.

When they first started to see each other he found her quiet, charming, and bright. She came from an old Newport family whose fortune had long been dissipated; had gone to the right schools and had the necessary social graces to be the hostess and wife that Frank saw himself needing for the role his ambitions had outlined.

As the years began to pass, he noted in his wife a peculiar melancholy which, though it seemed to make her more distant, had also developed her sexual appetites so that Frank found her more exciting than any woman he had ever known. But the old hunter knew the game and realized that this kind of passion could not be maintained by one man. This knowledge did not affect Frank as it would most men, and this was the reason that Dina had stayed married to him. From the beginning she had found him attractive and protective and able to provide her with the material things that made life more tolerable for her. At first, he was able to satisfy her in bed. But as she changed with that inner silent sadness which grew from the knowledge that she would be childless, Frank was not enough. He couldn't be.

So they had made a tacit compromise; a silent bargain to exchange an initial attraction for a current warmth and understanding. Each knew the boundaries of the other, and they respected these restricted areas. They agreed to look the other way. Dina yearned for what she could not have: a child. And this self-preoccupation precluded love, for love is in large part an act of giving, and neither Frank nor Dina was capable of that. Both used each other and others for their special purposes and tonight, willfully and with full knowledge, Frank was going to use Dina. For uppermost in Frank's mind was Elliot's implied threat to Computer with his desire to have the firm announce a sell recommendation for the stock before Frank had a chance to unload his shares.

He could of course fire Elliot, but if Elliot turned out to be correct in his forebodings then Frank would face serious criticism from his partners. On the other hand, if Elliot was wrong and they helped to kill the market for the stock prematurely before Frank was able to get out, his whole financial structure, his life-style, the approval and acknowledgments of his friends—Frank's reason for being—could be destroyed.

As he walked through the empty executive offices to the elevators, Frank's sole purpose was concentrated in two areas: to keep Elliot from doing anything about Computer until he could talk to Nichols on the coast, and to dump his stock at the first sign that Elliot's suspicions were accurate. But this old hunter knew that to unload his position he would have to do it while the market was hungry for the stock. A crack in the general euphoria that the market presently felt for Computer could be ruinous to him.

Elliot was erratic; unpredictable. Even if he fired him, Elliot could still be as dangerous to Frank out of the firm as he presently was in it. What Frank needed for Elliot was a trap—a leash—and with a wry smile as he watched the flashing numbers of the elevator descend, he knew that Dina could buy him the time he had to have.

The dinner was intimate and cordial. Although Frank was somewhat self-absorbed, Dina discovered in Elliot a responsive guest who had mellowed with the wine and the brandy and the conversation that had turned mainly to art.

Frank had bought several very valuable paintings as investments, and Elliot's surprise at seeing a Renoir, a Matisse, and several less well-known artists had given Dina and Elliot a common ground of interest which Frank did not share.

Elliot was completely captivated by Dina's almost physical force. She was quiet in her speech. Very unaffected. But her presence for Elliot was overwhelming. She looked at him steadily with those violet-blue eyes. She was dressed in a simple black cashmere long-sleeved sweater with a small diamond brooch pinned above her right breast. Her skirt was long and black. Her blond hair, parted in the middle, fell casually to her shoulders. It framed her exquisite tanned face and offset it like a jewel displayed on velvet. Her lips were full and sensual, and when she spoke to Elliot she seemed to be looking right through him. Her eyes, though discreet, made Elliot feel as if she were already making love to him.

Frank excused himself to make some calls and went into

his study. Elliot was alone with Dina. She sat beside him with a half-empty glass of champagne and turned slowly toward him, never saying a word. As she did so her sweater pulled just a little tighter and her carefully contrived bra, which gently lifted her breasts from underneath, but did not cover her nipples, outlined them beneath the dark cashmere. She sat silently regarding Elliot, who was having difficulty just breathing. As she watched him she crossed her legs and slowly stroked the inside of her thigh in so sexual a gesture that Elliot had an instant erection. Since Elliot's penis was rather large, this sudden bulge in Elliot's trousers made Dina smile. She continued stroking her inner thigh. Elliot felt that he was going to have an orgasm in seconds if something didn't happen pretty damn soon.

Dina kept looking at Elliot. She spoke very quietly. "Frank is going to be away for the weekend, maybe longer. I want you to pick me up at eight o'clock Saturday night." It was a command, not an invitation. "We'll go out to the Island, a little place I know. It's right by the sea, so bring some warm things. I like to walk on the beach if it's not too cold."

This didn't surprise Elliot, because he had become so overpowered by her physically that he would now have committed murder for her. He just prayed to God she wouldn't touch him, or he would ejaculate right in his pants. And there was still Frank. He had to say good night to his senior partner, whose wife was going to drive him mad. He was actually quivering.

Dina never moved. Never took her eyes off him. She herself was aroused by the passion and energy she saw locked inside Elliot and if he was panting in expectation of Saturday night, so was she. She knew that with Elliot, this highly strung emotional man, she could arouse passions in them both which would sear their souls.

Elliot could only mumble and nod his head. He'd be there—God almighty would he be there.

* * *

In his study Frank had managed to locate Dr. Nichols. He had explained why he wanted to see him and Nichols agreed. He told Nichols that if he could get Eisenstadt to come with him he would like to bring him along. Nichols sounded unenthusiastic about the latter suggestion, but he agreed to this as well. They would meet at the Bon Air Hotel tomorrow night for dinner with or without Eisenstadt. This meant that Nichols would have to fly down from San Francisco, but when Frank assured him that he would send his own jet to pick Nichols up and bring him down to Los Angeles, Paul Nichols agreed.

Frank had been lucky. He was able to locate Eisenstadt in Cambridge. When he had told him what he was trying to accomplish, that he had arranged the date with Nichols, the opportunity to meet an eminent fellow scientist whose views Eisenstadt disagreed with, but whose work and reputation he respected, appealed to him. Eisenstadt agreed to come. Frank told him that he would pick him up in the firm's private jet at Butler Aviation, Logan Airport in Boston, at noon tomorrow. The authority in Frank's voice, the chance to jet privately across the country on some important mission of high finance appealed to Eisenstadt as Frank guessed it would. The arrangements were set.

The door of the study opened and Frank, seeing Dina in quiet conversation with Elliot, knew that his Venus's flytrap had done her work. He felt a flash of jealousy which he quickly repressed.

The drive out on the Island was tedious until they had left the traffic of western Long Island behind and began to move past the small towns on the expressway toward Riverhead, and then northeast past Peconic Bay. Just before Southold, Dina told Elliot to turn down a narrow asphalt road which led toward the ocean. The road twisted and turned until he could sense that they were near the sea. With the windows rolled up he couldn't as yet hear the surf, but as the road wound past a few scattered houses closed for the summer with boarded doors and shuttered windows, Elliot could begin to see the white outline of surf through the scrub trees on his right.

About two hundred yards ahead on the right was a well-lit inn with a weathered painted sign that blew in the wind that said JOLLY ROGER. Elliot turned to Dina. "Is that it?" She nodded her head. Elliot smiled to himself as they got out of the car. "Jolly Roger, eh. Jolly Elliot, rather." He took the bags and pushed open the heavy door.

The Jolly Roger was as good as its name. In summer it was a swinging place that served good seafood and drinks and rented its few rooms to those aficionados of pleasure who could afford the prices and wanted the action of the evening, with the quiet of the sun and beach during the day. In winter, it was a cozy offbeat hideaway for those who wanted to get away from New York for a variety of reasons, none of which were ever questioned by the management.

The desk clerk in a woolen open-neck shirt took their two overnight bags up the carpeted steps to the corner of the second floor and opened the door of a spacious suite in which a fire was burning in an old stone hearth. A table was set facing a wide window that viewed the sweep of surf-battered beach and the windblown sky of this January night. There was a bucket chilling a bottle of Dom Pérignon champagne beside the table set for two with candles lit. A pitcher of martinis stood on a small bar in the corner of the room.

The man in the wool shirt looked at Elliot and then at Dina. He spoke to Dina. "We'll have the scallops up whenever you ring." He started to leave and Elliot attempted to hand him a bill. He waved it away and left.

Elliot had never before been so dominated by a woman. This hideaway. The arrangements. How many men had she brought here? He pushed the thought out of his head. She was unpacking and he stood there watching her.

"I'm starving, Elliot. Would you push that buzzer on the table? You must be hungry too." She turned to look at him as he walked toward her, but she was too experienced a woman to begin things now. She would orchestrate this evening move by move.

They dined. Talked. Had the table removed. Turned down the lights. They started with champagne. She excused herself. When she returned Elliot nearly fainted. She stood near the bed looking at him. She had oiled her body so that it glistened in the firelight of the room. She had rouged her nipples and was holding her breasts cupped in each hand so that the nipples were like lances. She stood that way while she moved her hips in undulating invitation.

Elliot almost screamed. He tore off his clothes, ripping buttons, throwing socks and shoes. He leaped at her, forcing her to the bed. Her tongue was all over him, licking him. She whimpered in ecstasy. Suddenly she was on top of him, teeth, nails, raking his body. She forced his penis inside her and thrust herself upon him again and again. Sighing. Sobbing.

Elliot's mind had exploded. His passion had burst the limits of his sanity. With one massive upthrust of his body he drove deep into her, and in that searing blinding explosive orgasm his body spasticized. His face contorted into a mask of pain which Dina in her own abandon didn't notice. He quivered like a spent animal and then he died.

Dina lay on top of him pumping her passion upon his dead body until her series of orgasms had spent all her strength. She lay stretched upon Elliot's corpse, unknowing, gasping for breath. Elliot had been dead for almost five minutes before Dina began to realize the horror of what lay beneath her.

In his last orgasm on earth, Elliot had succumbed to a massive coronary occlusion. He died as if shot by a gun.

Dina, not comprehending—a part of her mind refusing to grasp the fact that Elliot was dead—slowly raised her body from his. She was in a trance. Her lips kept moving without sound, but her mind repeated over and over. No! Oh, my God, no! No! No! No!

She wrapped her dressing gown around her and poured herself a drink. She brushed back her hair. Looked at herself in the mirror. Her eyes really didn't see anything.

She turned to Elliot's corpse and began to sob; slowly, quietly, the tears streaming down her face. She knew she had to approach that bed and she knew she had to cover Elliot's body. Something told her that she could not give way. If she lost control she was finished.

She moved to the bed and covered Elliot. She couldn't bear to look at that face, whose expression still wore the reflection of the pain of that last tearing thirty seconds.

A part of her mind now began to function—slowly. It grasped to find something to hold on to. A course of action. A direction. Something to do. Her whole body was shaking so that she had to hold the drink with both hands. She had some tranquilizers in her handbag and she fumbled for them and swallowed one with water. She knew that the combination of Librium and the amount of alcohol she had for dinner that night was dangerous but she didn't give a damn. By reflex she forced herself to the phone. It rang for an interminable time before the sleeping desk clerk became conscious of the buzzer on his switchboard. He looked at his watch. Jesus Christ, he thought. These goddamn people who have to make phone calls at nearly three o'clock in the morning.

Dina tried to control her voice as she asked for the outside operator. She choked back the sobs that were racking her body.

"Would you please call New York . . . 212-288-4390." She waited what seemed a lifetime. She could almost see the hand of Dr. Whitney Fraser reach for his phone.

"Whit. Oh, Whit. Thank God you're home."

"Who is this?"

"Dina."

"Dina!" Whitney sat straight up in bed. He was one of those people who could come out of a deep sleep almost instantly awake.

"Dina, what's wrong?"

He heard her voice break. "Oh, God, Whit, it's so terrible. Oh, Whit, please help me . . . please."

"Dina, get hold of yourself. What's wrong? Where are you?"

"He's dead," Dina sobbed. "He's dead."

"Frank's dead?" Whit pulled back the covers and stood up.

For a moment Dina only sobbed.

"Dina. Is Frank dead?"

The cries of anguish hit Whitney like spears.

"Not Frank? Where's Frank?"

"On the Coast."

"Then, Dina, for God's sake, who is dead? Where are you . . . ?"

"Oh, Whit, please, please help me."

"I will. I will. Just tell me where you are . . . and who is dead."

She choked out to him the directions for finding the Jolly Roger. She felt herself going and she fought to hold on. "It's one of Frank's partners. He—he just— Oh, God, Whit—he just died. He simply died. I killed him. I must have. Oh, Whit, please."

His voice grew stern. He had to.

"Now look, Dina. I don't know what the hell is going on there but it sounds—well, forget how it sounds—but until I get there, you stay in that room and don't make any more calls to anyone. Do you understand?"

She sobbed a whimpered assent.

"Listen, Dina. Pay attention. Do you have any Librium with you?"

"I took one."

"Have you had a lot to drink?"

"Yes."

He pursed his lips. "When did you take the last one?"

"Just a few minutes ago." Her sobbing seemed more under control as he talked.

"I want you to take half of one more. Just half of one, and pour the others down the toilet. Do you understand?"

"Yes, Whit."

"I will be leaving as soon as I get dressed. I'm going to bring a Cabulance. I should be there before dawn."

"Oh, Whit. Oh, Whit. Thank you. Thank you."

"Hang on now, Dina . . ." He paused. His voice lowered. "You owe it to Frank."

She hung up.

Dr. Whitney Fraser awakened his nurse and instructed her to call the hospital and get the chief resident to cover for him.

As the Cabulance drove out the Island toward Southold where Dina awaited him, he tried to organize the details of his life that led him to this night.

He was Dina's physician. He knew Dina before her divorce. After his own wife died and his two boys were in college—one in medical school—he simply let his work absorb his life. With the exception of Dina.

When she needed him medically, he would come. He knew her better, he felt, than her husband. For one thing he knew that there was no physical reason that Dina could not have a child. Why she bore no child to two men he didn't know, but that she was capable of doing so he was certain. Perhaps there were psychosomatic reasons for her wanting a child so desperately and not having one. But he was not a psychiatrist. He was a specialist in internal medicine on the staff of one of New York's leading hospitals.

The sky began to lighten in the east, the outlines of homes first in clusters, then more scattered between the low scrub trees. The driver left him alone with his thoughts as they drove at seventy miles an hour through light snow showers.

Each time he had seen Dina, he had to remind himself that she was Frank's wife. For though Whit had no monopoly on virtue he had a peculiar code of his own which kept him away from other men's wives. There was something that could grow between the two of them. He felt it. And he knew that she felt it. That was the reason she called him tonight. In his own way, without ever expressing it to her, he had grown to love her. Even, God help him, before Sue had passed away. Never by word or by touch had he ever let Dina know. But she knew. And sometimes he could read silently in her eyes the plea for the warmth and understanding, for the compassion that he could give her that she had never had. The love that she had never had. All her life Dina had been used by men. By her father, who promoted her first marriage to save himself from bankruptcy. By Frank, who used her and who also loved her as much as he was capable of loving anyone, but whose kind of love never answered her deep-rooted psychological needs. She had never really been loved except by Whit, and there Frank stood in the way.

The Cabulance stumbled around the back roads following Dina's sketchy directions until they finally found the Jolly Roger.

Whit banged on the door until the desk clerk shuffled to open it. His eyes blinked as he saw the Cabulance.

Whit had been thinking that Dina must be here under an assumed name and he had to be very careful.

"I'm sorry to trouble you so early in the morning. But I'm Dr. Whitney Fraser. One of your guests is a patient of mine and her husband is ill and has to be taken back to the city."

"You mean Mrs. Thompson."

Whit inwardly sighed in relief.

"Yes, that's right. If you'll give me a key to her room, I would like to go right up."

The desk clerk was now wide awake and watched the Cabulance driver light a cigarette.

"I'll take you up, Doc."

"No, that won't be necessary." There was authority in Whit's voice. "I don't want Mrs. Thompson disturbed any more than she has to be." He held out his hand and smiled. The desk clerk walked over to the mail slots behind the desk where the keys were hung and picked up a straight old-fashioned notched key attached to a large circular brass plate which said 2A and handed it to Whit.

"It's up the stairs to the left. Corner suite on the right."

"Thank you."

Whit hurried up the stairs.

When he entered the suite he saw Dina seated before the window watching the dawn's light bathe the ocean. She seemed asleep. As he shut the door quietly she turned around slowly and stared at him. The anguish of that beautiful face broke out into a sob of relief.

"Oh, Whit. Oh, God bless you, Whit." She rushed to him and put her arms around him and sobbed against his chest. He felt the softness of her breasts press against him and he found his arms around her and his lips kissing her hair.

It just happened. He tried to push her gently away from him but she wouldn't let him go.

"Darling, you must let me do what has to be done." He heard himself call her darling. "Darling, you must."

He unclasped her hands from the back of his neck and sat her down in a chair. Then he turned to the figure on the bed. He briefly examined Elliot and initially diagnosed his death as a coronary occlusion. He wrapped Elliot's body in a blanket so that his head and face were partially covered.

The Cabulance driver brought up a stretcher and Whit told him that he had given the patient a sedative to make him sleep until they arrived at the hospital.

He quickly packed Elliot's bag and helped Dina to pack and dress. He helped her as she walked shakily down the narrow steps to the Cabulance. He paid the bill and left.

As the driver started the engine the sun had just edged its way over the eastern edge of the Atlantic to begin a new day.

Earlier that same day Frank had left the house before Dina was awake. He was out in front of his apartment, where his chauffeur waited, at 8 A.M. The drive to La Guardia in the Saturday morning traffic was easy.

They left Park Avenue, crossed over to the East River Drive, and went across the Triboro Bridge. They turned off the expressway and wound their way around to the general aviation section, where the firm's plane waited to take him to Boston.

Frank greeted the pilot and the co-pilot and stepped into the Sabre Liner.

They got clearance from ground control and as traffic was light Frank soon felt the rush of power from the engines as the jet hustled down the runway and lifted off into a wide climbing turn that put them over the middle of Long Island Sound. When they left La Guardia's control zone the pilot pushed the throttles to full climbing speed and Frank looked out his window and saw the coast of Connecticut slip by. They climbed to nineteen thousand feet and leveled off and soon Frank was looking at the sun glisten as its light reflected off the low overcast of clouds that was spilling intermittent wet snow over eastern New England. The whole flight lasted thirty-five minutes before they touched down at Logan and taxied over to Butler Aviation, where Frank was to meet Eisenstadt.

Frank walked into Butler. He looked around and saw no one who answered Eisenstadt's description, so he sat at the refreshment counter and drank an unwanted cup of coffee.

This whole trip might just possibly turn out to be a waste of time. For what Frank was trying to discern was the validity of Eisenstadt's opinions on Computer versus those of Nichols. He was well aware that he would not be able to understand any highly technical discussions the two physicists might get into once he had them together in California, but he was a good judge of men. He hoped to be able to uncover in the relaxed environment of the Bon Air Hotel some clue as to what he should do with his holdings in Computer. For the one thing Frank could not risk was the market for the stock being negatively affected by some unfortunate disclosure before he had a chance to unload his position.

"Would you be Mr. Sullivan?"

Frank turned and saw a man of medium height carrying a plastic overnight bag which had Pan Am stenciled on its side. He had on a Persian lamb fur hat, a wrinkled tweed overcoat and rubbers. His face was smiling. He had an olive complexion and in his brown eyes there was a twinkle of merriment that made his manner almost instantly appealing.

Frank put out his hand.

"Dr. Eisenstadt?"

"Yes."

"It's my pleasure to see you, Doctor. I certainly appreciate your making this trip on such short notice."

The brown eyes twinkled and his face smiled.

"I am really looking forward to it. You know, Mr. Sullivan, even with the amount of consulting work we college professors do nowadays, to spend a weekend like this is most exciting. It is I, sir, who am in your debt."

Frank liked the cheery little physicist immediately, as did almost everyone else. Eisenstadt was one of the most popular lecturers in the physics department at MIT.

"Well, shall we be going, Doctor?"

"Certainly."

They walked out into the now heavily falling wet snow to where the jet was parked. As the pilots saw them coming they opened the ramp door with its extended steps and both men entered the Sabre Liner.

In a few minutes they were climbing high above the

overcast to reach their assigned cruising altitude of thirty-eight thousand feet.

Their route of flight would take them from New England across Pennsylvania, Ohio, Indiana, Missouri, and into Wichita, Kansas, where they would stop to refuel. Then across the lower corner of Colorado, over New Mexico and Arizona and finally into Los Angeles, where they would arrive about 3 P.M. Pacific standard time.

During the trip Frank and Eisenstadt got to know each other better. Over drinks from the walnut bar, they discussed a variety of subjects.

To the physicist's surprise, Frank was well informed about a wide range of topics. His knowledge of history and government, economics, and international politics surprised Eisenstadt.

As Frank poured the professor another drink Eisenstadt smiled.

"Perhaps I chose the wrong field, Mr. Sullivan." Eisenstadt did not go in for first names easily. "You Wall Street fellows certainly know how to lead the good life. Just think of it"—his eyes twinkled—"little old Eisenstadt at forty thousand feet drinking your magnificent scotch at five hundred and forty miles an hour. That's what your pilot said, I believe—five hundred and forty miles an hour." Eisenstadt broke into a belly laugh. "Please don't tell them back at the university, Mr. Sullivan, that Dr. Eisenstadt consumes scotch at the rate of five hundred and forty miles per hour."

They both laughed.

After leaving Kansas, where they had refueled and had a quick bite to eat, Frank thought the time had come when he might do a little quiet probing. They were over the moon surface of New Mexico with its twisted, empty, red-surfaced mountains; its landscape sculptured into gargoyles of rock and canyons cut by lances of running rivers, swift blowing winds, and the passage of geologic time.

"Tell me, Doctor, why don't you agree with Dr. Nichols and Dr. Karkov on Karkov's belief in the soundness of Computer Ecolog's technology?"

Eisenstadt flashed a wide grin. Frank could almost read the physicist's mind. He knew that Eisenstadt recognized that the time had begun when the little guy was going to start paying for his lunch.

"Well, Mr. Sullivan, it is just a matter of degree. It's not that I don't believe in Karkov's technology. I just think he's rushing things a bit. I think impregnated chips will find their way into computer applications, but it is my belief, from the present state of the art, that this is at least two years or more away."

Frank looked out of the windows and then back at Eisenstadt. "But Karkov's producing these things now, Doctor—"

"I don't like to disagree, Mr. Sullivan, but in my opinion what Karkov's producing is a number of prototype models that are giving him problems in the field—and he will continue to have problems for some time. After all, there are companies with far greater resources than Computer Ecolog that have hesitated to bring to market a competitive device—"

"Doesn't Karkov's patent position protect him from this kind of competition?"

"In my judgment it does not."

Frank opened a humidor and offered the professor a cigar.

Eisenstadt grinned. "Thank you." He sniffed the cigar and pressed it between his fingers.

"Havana?"

Frank smiled. "They'd better be. I go to a lot of trouble to get them."

Frank let the heavy blue smoke hang in the air before he spoke again.

"If what you say is correct, Professor, then why did

Tittle's firm and Dr. Nichols advise a group of investors that Karkov's technology was more perfected than you suggest?"

Eisenstadt hugely enjoyed the cigar. His eyes laughed as he looked at Frank. "I really haven't the faintest idea; but then"—he paused and laughed—"I suppose that is why we are on this very expensive voyage to see Dr. Nichols, is it not?"

Frank nodded reflectively.

They had been losing altitude for some time and were now being vectored by Los Angeles approach control. The mountains rimming the City of Angels cupped the air pollution effectively. It formed a flat gray layer that hung over the city like a pall.

As the Sabre Liner let down through this emphesymatic man-made fog, Frank Sullivan felt a vague sense of uneasiness. The jolly little professor who was enjoying himself immensely was an honest man. Frank was sure of that. But was he correct in his assumptions? Frank's lips tightened into a silent smile. Well, he thought, as the little guy said, that's what we're here to find out.

The Bon Air at night always reminded Frank of a Caribbean resort—or, perhaps more accurately, a private club in the tropics. Its cottages, its flowered landscaping lit artfully to create soft shadows, made it seem unreal, especially since it was not more than a long cab ride from downtown Los Angeles.

They had met Nichols in the bar, which had a fire crackling in the hearth. They had a chance to relax and mellow a bit in the warm firelight.

Frank appraised Nichols carefully. No two men could be more contrasting than Eisenstadt and Nichols. Nichols was tall, stooped, with a slightly balding gray head, rimless glasses, and a nervous tense manner. He spoke so rapidly that it gave Frank the impression that his thought patterns could not keep pace with his ability to verbalize them. It made him stutter, which caused him private agonies.

They had dinner and then moved to a comfortable table in the bar, not too near the fire.

Throughout dinner the two scientists, who had never spent any time together, kept breaking into long technical discussion on various phases of research in their respective fields, and were continually apologizing to Frank, who listened politely and told them to continue.

Now, in the glow of the firelight with several drinks behind them, Frank thought it was time to get what he came for.

"Dr. Nichols. It is my understanding that your views on the development of the technology of Computer Ecolog are at variance with Dr. Eisenstadt's. Is that correct?"

Nichols toyed with his glass.

"I guess that is a fair statement, yes."

"Is it just your differing interpretations of Karkov's technology or do you have information that Dr. Eisenstadt is not aware of?"

Nichols kept looking at his drink.

"Dr. Eisenstadt is an authority in the field of impregnated wafer chips and microcircuitry. I wouldn't presume a knowledge greater than his own."

"You must have some reasons for feeling Karkov is on target, Doctor, or else why would you have advised Tittle and his crowd that he was?"

Nichols reached for some peanuts.

"Science, Mr. Sullivan, is many times not as clear-cut as laymen believe. Facts are always open to differing interpretations. Dr. Eisenstadt has his views and I have mine."

Frank thought he was back on the Street listening to those goddamn economists who talk out of three sides of their mouth.

They sat in silence as Frank thought.

"Dr. Nichols, have you been to see Computer's operation on Route 128?"

"Oh, yes."

"Has Karkov been here to consult with you?"

"Yes, he has. On several occasions."

"I see."

Frank began to find a direction that was making Nichols uncomfortable.

"Has Fletcher Courtney ever been here to see you?"

Nichols chewed some more peanuts and asked for another drink.

"Yes, Courtney has been here."

Eisenstadt popped up. "I'll have another drink too, Mr. Sullivan, if you don't mind." He laughed. "You see how you capitalists corrupt us." He thought for a moment. "Speaking of capitalists, Mr. Sullivan, old Nichols here is one of our best. You know we are all starving for government-sponsored research grants, but not Nick. He seems to be able to come up with money every time to fund the projects his boys are working on." Eisenstadt looked at Nichols admiringly. "I don't know how you do it, Dr. Nichols."

The old hunter was beginning to scent spoor.

"Well, Dr. Nichols, that's a game I know a little something about. Tell me, how do you account for your success?"

Nichols smiled nervously. He took off his glasses and wiped them.

"Just luck, I guess."

Frank watched him carefully. "Raising money, Doctor, is never easy, and rarely does luck have anything to do with it."

The logs snapped in the fireplace.

"Dr. Nichols, tell me something. When was the last time Fletcher Courtney came out to see you?"

Frank watched Nichols' face like a wolf.

Nichols' eyes focused on his drink, then on the table, then on his hands. He spoke very softly. "About a month ago."

Eisenstadt watched them both.

Frank's face was a taut mask. It was just a hunch, but his whole career was based on intuitive guesses that on average were more often right than wrong.

Could it be that Fletcher Courtney had promised some large anonymous grant to have Nichols say the right things to Tittle and the investor group that had just bought into Computer?

Frank ordered another drink.

"Tell me, Doctor, this facility of yours for finding research funds. Are your largest contributors well-known foundations or philanthropies?"

"Some."

"I don't wish to pry, but are any of your significant admirers anonymous?"

"A few."

The fire snapped. It had been a long day. Frank thanked both his guests and suggested that if they wished to continue talking by all means to do so. He was tired and wanted to go to bed. Besides, he had what he came for. For as sure as the sun would rise tomorrow, there was a connection between Fletcher Courtney and Nichols. And the jovial little scientist Frank had brought across the country was probably right about Computer. And this lanky stooped bastard with the stuttering speech was probably a whore in the temple.

Frank was to rise tomorrow to receive one phone call, and to make two calls himself. Those calls would shroud him in catastrophe.

Frank never slept well on the Coast the first night. The time change bothered him. He made it a habit to take some sedatives with him so that he could get some rest.

He awoke and looked at his watch. He kept it set on New York time. It was six o'clock in New York. Christ, he thought, it's only three in the morning here.

He got up to get a glass of water and swallowed a Dalmane. What had disturbed his sleep in addition to the time change was what he planned to do tomorrow. He felt now a growing fear for the future of Computer's stock. The years had shown him what rumor and a change in psychology could do, not only to a particular stock, but to the whole market.

He rationalized that what he was about to do was still based on no positive proof; just an educated guess. It was an individual decision, based on intuition, not facts, that he would apply to his own holdings, no one else's. But perhaps something else was harder to rationalize. He intended to have the research department publish Bob Friedman's report on Computer as soon as it could be released. Then he would sell. And why not? He had uncovered two schools of thought regarding Computer, and he was technically not knowledgeable enough to discern between the two. Friedman liked the company, and he knew a lot more about it than Frank did.

But behind all that psychological self-justification, Frank was the old hunter. His instincts told him there was trouble ahead, and he had to be sure he was the first one out. The hell with the rest of them. They would feed on his bones if they could, all of them; his partners, his friends. For in truth, a truth which Frank recognized, he had no friends. Only people that he used and who used him. This is the way the Street had molded him.

The hell with friends, he thought, and returned to bed.

He slept fitfully. His sleep was interrupted by the ringing of the bedside phone.

"Have a call for you, Mr. Sullivan, from New York."

Frank rubbed his eyes and looked at his watch. It was noon in New York—9 A.M. here.

"Put it through." His voice was husky and he coughed as he spoke.

"Go ahead, New York."

"Frank?"

"Yes."

"This is Whit."

At the mention of his doctor's name, Frank was alert. "Whit. Good to hear your voice. Is there—is something wrong?"

Whit paused before he spoke. "Frank, I am afraid there is."

"Is it Dina? Is she all right?"

"Frank, Dina is all right physically. She's had a severe shock. I have her home under sedation with a private nurse. I thought under the circumstances that would be preferable."

"Circumstances?" Frank's mind raced. "What are you trying to tell me, Whit?" Frank was up now sitting on the edge of his bed. "Stop playing footsie with me and tell me what the hell is going on."

"It's one of your partners, Frank. He's dead."

Frank didn't understand. "Who is dead?"

The reply was so slow in coming it spoke volumes to Frank when it came.

"Elliot Thompson."

"Oh, my God. How? When did it happen?"

"Last night. He had a heart attack. Frank . . ." Whit paused. "I don't think it advisable to go into the details of this over the phone. Dina is fine physically, but she is going to need a lot of rest and care. I believe I can help her. What I want to do now is to notify Thompson's family or anyone else who can take care of the funeral arrangements."

Frank's mind was touching all the bases. This could be ruinous if what he thought had occurred became known publicly.

"Where was Elliot when it happened?"

Whit didn't want to do it this way. "Frank. That's not important."

"Was Dina with him?"

"Frank."

"God damn it. Was Dina with him?"

"Yes, Frank, she was."

Frank held onto the phone without speaking. God, he thought, if the papers ever got this.

"Frank. Are you there? Frank?"

His voice was almost inaudible. "I'm here."

"Listen, Frank. No one knows about this. Elliot is in my hospital. If things are carefully handled, no one need ever know. I am told he has parents living in St. Louis. I'll get in touch with them."

"He is also living with some woman at his apartment. I don't know anything about her."

"Don't worry, Frank, I'll handle everything. I think I know what this could mean to you."

"It would be mortifying."

"I know, Frank. I know. Just get back here as soon as you can. I'll handle everything as discreetly as possible."

"Whit, I'm glad you're there. For God's sake, keep a lid on this thing."

"Don't worry, I understand. I'm terribly sorry to have been the one to tell you all this."

"Whit, I'm depending on you." The tone was husky now.

"Don't be too upset, Frank. It will come out all right."

"I'll be back as soon as I can. Thanks, Whit. I can't tell you how grateful I am." He hung up the phone.

He sat there stunned for a moment. Jesus. He had put the two of them together. What the hell had happened to Elliot? That son of a bitch picked a hell of a time to drop dead.

As he walked to the bathroom to get a tranquilizer, the spirit of the old hunter began to return. He swallowed the Librium and felt the cool water at the back of his throat.

He walked to the bed and lay down for a moment staring up at the ceiling. It never ceased to amaze him how the events of life moved on the waves of circum-stance.

He reached for the phone and told the desk operator to locate a Mr. Robert Friedman in New York.

In about ten minutes the call was put through.

"Hello—Bob? Frank. Bob, first thing Monday morning I want you to release that report of yours on Computer to the full institutional and retail list."

"But, Frank, Elliot—"

"Elliot's dead."

There was a long silence at the other end of the phone.

"Elliot's dead?"

"That's right. Died of a heart attack yesterday."

"Jesus Christ, sir, that's awful."

"It is very unfortunate, Bob. Elliot was a good man."

Frank hung up.

He lay back in bed for a while and then put through another call to Brooklyn Heights. This one he placed him-self. He distinctly told the operator not to mention where the call was coming from.

"Mr. Charles Fox is on the line, sir."

"Charlie, is that you?"

"Frank?"

"Charlie—you son of a gun, how are you?"

"Frank, where the hell are you? What are you doing working on a Sunday? Don't you ever relax?"

Frank managed a chuckle in his voice. "Sometimes, Charlie.

"Charlie, I want you to line up a few buyers for some Computer Ecolog stock."

Frank could see the fat face, its slit furtive eyes narrow-ing, as his old friend Charlie Fox heard the order.

"Whose stock is it?"

"Mine."

"Yours? Hell, I thought your firm was bullish on Com-puter."

"We are. As a matter of fact, we have an institutional research report coming out this week recommending the stock."

"Then I don't understand."

Frank made his voice sound affable.

"I need some money, Charlie, and I don't want this to go through our firm. You understand."

"Sure, Frank. Sure. How many shares do you want to sell?"

"Seventy-five thousand."

"That's a lot of meat and potatoes."

"I'm a heavy eater."

Fox laughed.

"One thing, Charlie." The authority was back in Frank's voice in the form of a warning. "I don't want this leaked to anyone . . . do you understand that?"

"Sure, Frank, I understand."

Frank paused. "I'll leave it up to you."

Frank leaned back in his chair, his mouth compressed, his eyes hardened, as he reviewed what he had just done. Was he clean? He had sold stock which he had a perfect right to sell. Unlike Dean, he wasn't legally connected with the company. Dean was on the board of Computer, and if Frank's hunch was right, he'd bet a thousand dollars that the little weasel had been trading in Computer without reporting it as he was required to do by law. That could really get his tit in a wringer, Frank thought, because as a director, Dean was legally presumed to have "inside" information on Computer that wasn't available to the general public.

Frank thought carefully. He wasn't a director like Dean. He wasn't required to report his buying and selling of the stock, and furthermore—he reached for a cigar from the humidor on the desk and cut off the end—and furthermore, the key point was that he didn't have any real inside information. That's what they really grabbed you for—profiting by knowledge that was denied the general public.

Did he have such knowledge? He thought hard about that. He decided he didn't. He really didn't understand the technical differences between Eisenstadt's and Nichols' opinions. All he had to go on was his own hunch that Nichols was a whore in the temple; that he had been had. He didn't even know that for certain.

He lit the cigar slowly and blew the heavy smoke into the room. He smiled to himself. No, he was covered. He was clean. The only thing they could criticize him for was not selling his stock through his own firm. That was a moral question: whether or not he wanted his partners to know what he was doing. He smiled as he thought of that. If they knew he was selling the majority of his position they would all join him and it would kill the market for the stock; the partners of the major under-writing firm for Computer bailing out.

Frank thought for a moment longer, and the humor disappeared from the strong lined face. The hell with them, he thought. He'd been around too long and had too much tied up in this little company not to get out when the market was still hungry. Especially when his instincts were sending him warning signals.

He was convinced he could not be criticized, at least by the authorities. He reached for the phone to call Rose Finley. A look of humorous cynicism came back into the cold gray eyes.

Charles Fox was one of two partners of the firm of Fox and Bohlen, whose offices were located in a small suite at 72 Wall.

Fox and Frank had started out as messenger boys back in the Depression. They worked for different firms and their careers had certainly taken different roads. Frank had built a powerful and successful firm—one of the major houses on the Street. Fox had scraped along as a small trading company whose principal asset was its seat on the New York Stock Exchange—which as of now was a well-depreciated asset, much to Fox's regret.

As computerization and specialized services grew with the demands for an ever-increasing need for capital to finance a growing American industrial base and an expanding government—as more institutions became responsible for an increasingly higher percentage of daily stock market activity—firms like Fox and Bohlen had no reason to exist. They could not compete effectively with the larger houses, nor could they offer the specialty services of the successful smaller ones. They hung on, if they did at all, by trading securities for a few small institutions and private customers; for old friends who out of a sense of loyalty gave their commission business to the Charlie Foxes.

As their capital slowly increased they also traded for their own account. But the stock market debacle of May 1970 changed things for Messrs. Fox and Bohlen. With the worst crack in the market since 1929, the firm found itself in violation of the capital requirements of the New York Stock Exchange. Simply put, they needed more money. But since their operations were blatantly archaic, they not only couldn't find anyone to merge with, or buy out their business, they couldn't borrow a dime to increase their capital—that is, not until July of 1970, when Charlie Fox got a call from a Mr. Angelo Vittorio.

Charlie remembered as if it were yesterday. So did Angi.

Angi was sitting in the living room of a small two-bedroom apartment in a six-story brick building, not far from La Guardia Airport. Angi Vittorio was fifty-five years old. He was tall, with that full dark head of hair that many Italians are blessed with, and his sideburns were only slightly gray. His complexion was very dark; his olive skin was further tanned by the sun of the New Jersey shore at Deal, where he rented a small apartment in a converted old house.

Angi's whole life was a carefully contrived fraud to present to the Internal Revenue Service a man who lived modestly, filed his tax returns promptly, and declared an income of forty thousand a year. What Angi, of course, did not declare was his cash receipts from various enterprises such as loan sharking, bookmaking, and investments in legitimate businesses that ran through a network of complex corporations whose shareholders always turned out to be people who were owned by Angi Vittorio.

Now, Angi thought that he might like to try the stock market. He saw all those sucker deals that had gone public through small firms which the recent crash had wiped out. Hundreds of thousands of people who had speculated their greed in hot little stocks found themselves with pieces of paper that had little value.

There was no market for that kind of operation any more, so Angi thought that now was a good time to get in —cheap. For Angi was a student of human nature. And he knew that sooner or later the suckers for the hot stocks would be back. And when they came, Angi wanted a vehicle to milk them. That's why on this unbearably hot afternoon in July of 1970 Charlie Fox was sitting in Angi's air-conditioned living room in Queens, drinking cold beer and eating little Ritz cracker hors d'oeuvres covered with Russian caviar.

Angi looked at Fox closely. He saw a fat little man about his own age with sharp slit eyes set in a jowled face, whose fingers were thick and whose belt closed over a broad belly.

To Fox, Angi seemed like a nice sort of fellow, but his native shrewdness knew that his Sicilian host was a barracuda who would eat your ears off if you crossed him.

"So tell me, Charlie—I hear you're a little tight."

"You have big ears."

Angi laughed. "Yeh. I got a few friends."

And the conversation went on. And other meetings were held, and before the summer ended, one of Angi's legitimate companies lent Fox and Bohlen a considerable sum of money to meet the capital requirements of the Exchange. Fox and Bohlen were on the hook, and when you were hooked by Angi Vittorio, you stayed hooked.

All of this of course was completely unknown to Frank Sullivan when he placed that call to his old friend Charlie Fox, giving him instructions to sell a large block of his Computer Ecolog stock.

Frank looked at his wife with Whit Fraser holding her wrist, taking her pulse. Dina's face was white as death. The dark circles under her eyes resulted from endless weeping.

On occasion, she would awaken and cry out as if in a nightmare, "I killed him, oh, my God, I must have killed him!"

When Frank first heard her say that, his stomach felt as if it had been struck by an iron bar.

"Whit, what if someone hears her? The nurse, anyone . . ."

"The nurse has been told that Mrs. Sullivan has had a nervous breakdown, that she is irrational and not to pay any attention to what she says. The nurse was also very carefully selected by me and is costing you one hell of a lot of money."

Frank looked at his wife for a long time without visible emotion. "To hell with the money. Just get her well again."

In Dina's sedated mind whirled the torment of guilt that left her helpless in depression and despair. She had always been aware of the power of her sex, and in her wild abandon she more than once thought that Frank would not survive her passion. Frank on several occasions thought the same thing. Now, Dina tormented herself that she had actually killed a man with her body. It was not too far from the truth.

For the size of their firm, Fox and Bohlen had acquired a large position in Computer due to Charlie's past friendship with Frank. They had bought into the stock early, and on Frank's suggestion doubled their position. At this point in time, Fox and Bohlen had holdings of approximately two million in Computer at current market prices, and they had one hell of a profit. Angi watched the stock like a hawk and called Charlie at least once a day concerning it. It was for this reason that Charlie Fox, who had a unique appreciation for the necessity of keeping Angi informed about Computer, put through a call to the brick apartment house in Queens on Monday morning at about 11 A.M.

"Angi. I thought there is something we ought to give some thought to. It's about Computer." Charlie sensed Angi's increased attention on the phone.

"I'm listenin'."

"I got a call from Frank Sullivan yesterday at home."

"Yeh."

"He asked me to round up some buyers for seventy-five thousand shares of Computer."

Angi hunched over the phone.

"He wants to sell?"

"That's right."

"Is it his stock?" Angi was now a coiled spring.

"It is."

Angi's voice was a hoarse rumble. "I thought that fucker was hot on the company."

"He says he is. He says his firm is putting out an institutional report on the stock this week."

"So why's he sellin'?"

"He says he's short of cash."

"Sullivan's short on cash? Don't jerk me off, Charlie."

"I'm only telling you what he told me."

"Look, Charlie—cut out all this horseshit Wall Street crap and tell me what you think is goin' on. We got a hell of a lot of dough wrapped up in that stock and"—he lowered his voice to a harsh growl—"you know, Charlie, I ain't a great one for losin' money."

"Angi, now don't get your Irish up." It was a little joke between them. "I figure if Frank's firm is putting out an institutional report on Computer it's got to be good for the stock. If Frank is selling a part of his position that's his business. He's giving us the commissions. I should be able to round up a few buyers easily."

"That's how you figure it, Charlie?"

"Yes."

"Well, I figure that this prick Sullivan could know somethin' we don't. And he could be gettin' his ass out while we stay put like suckers."

Charlie paused. "You want to sell, Angi?"

Angi reflected. "Where you think the stock is goin'?"

"How the hell do I know, Angi? We've got a good profit in the stock. On Frank's recommendations, I might add, and if he thinks it's still a buy I would be inclined to hold it awhile. But," he hurriedly answered, "I'll do whatever you say, Angi."

Angi thought some more. "You call that prick up and ask him what you should do. Then we'll do what he suggests. But if that cocksucker is tryin' to screw us, I'll take his eyes out."

Needless to say, Charlie Fox was about to call his old friend Frank Sullivan.

Frank's phone rang on his private line. He swiveled his chair around to answer it.

"Charlie?"

"Yes, Frank." Charlie hesitated. "Frank. This call is important so I would appreciate your leveling with me." Charlie paused. "It's important to all of us, Frank."

The old hunter was sniffing the wind. He had known Charlie since the late thirties and he knew him to be shrewd and intuitive. He wouldn't want to have to bank too heavily on Charlie's integrity, but then that was just a surmise. Over the years they had done each other quiet favors, and outside of feelings of vague caution, Frank had no reasons to fault Charles Fox.

"You there, Frank?"

"Yes, Charlie. What have you got? It sounds ominous." Frank chuckled.

"Frank, level with me. Is there anything sour on Computer that you know and I don't?" He paused. "I've got a guy who is pretty heavily into the stock and I wouldn't want to see him take a beating." Charlie's voice took on more urgency. "Frank, this guy doesn't play around."

Frank began to understand.

"Charlie, there are some conflicting technical opinions regarding Computer, but Dr. Paul Nichols and the Tittle group in Boston think Karkov is going to do what he says he can do. You know those Yankee traders; they would never have put eight and a half million into Computer if they thought Karkov wasn't going to come through."

Frank could hear the wheels spinning inside of Charlie's skull.

"Eight and a half million, Frank, that's a pretty convincing argument."

"It seems that way to me."

"You still want me to sell your stock, Frank?"

"I do."

"Well, you're a big boy. I appreciate the information." Then Charlie added, "For both our sakes, Frank, I hope you're right."

Charlie hung up and called Angi. He repeated his conversation with Frank.

"I don't like it, Charlie." The Sicilian sensed something like a jungle animal. "I don't trust that Sullivan bastard."

"You want to sell, Angi . . . ?"

There was a long silence on the other end of the line. "We'll stay put for a while. But if that Irish prick is pulling a fast one, it will be the last jerk-off he ever pulls. Nobody gives it to Angi Vittorio."

Charlie hung up the phone and looked out of his window, which faced a soot-stained brick wall. He ought to get the hell out of this business, he thought—retire. He wasn't wealthy, but he could manage. Sell out to Vittorio. Get away from that dago bastard. He sat with his hands folded across his belly and sighed. Nobody gets away from Angi.

The week ticked by. The report jumped the stock to fifty-seven dollars a share. Frank's shares were sold at an average price of forty-nine. Frank didn't complain.

Large investment banking and brokerage firms are too busy for empathy. The swiftly moving pace of the marketplace doesn't allow the kind of personal relationships that exist in less demanding environments.

Elliot's death rated only a small announcement in the *Journal*. Besides his mistress, who mourned his passing, there was his family in St. Louis—and there was Dina. His partners after hearing of his death had gone on to other business with the shake of a few heads and expressions of various forms of surprise.

February came and Dina began to improve. Frank noticed that her doctor was spending a lot of time with his wife. But Frank's own feelings of guilt were such that he hadn't the heart to intervene.

Whit's love for Dina was making her well. It was a quiet love that expressed itself in compassion and understanding.

As Dina began to respond she was able to understand how Elliot's death was really an accident. It could have

happened in the subway, on a plane, in the shower, anywhere. And as Whit slowly began to assuage her guilt, he
began to build up her confidence.

They had discussed at length her desire for a child and
it began to occur to Dina that Whit might be right. There
was something in her mind, not her body, that prevented
conception. And she began to believe him.

February in New York is for those who can't afford to
leave, and for those who think they can't afford to leave.
Normally, Whit would have been sailing for ten days with
his friends, gunkholing around the Virgin Islands. This
February, and on this day, he paid his usual visit at noon
to Frank's apartment to visit his favorite patient. When
he rang the nurse let him in; he noticed that Frank's
butler and maid were not in the apartment. Frank had
that morning given them both the day off.

Whit sensed what was going to happen and seemed to
feel himself incapable of stopping it. He told the nurse
to come back at two and went into Dina's room.

She was sitting up in a lavender bed jacket; her hair
had regained its luster. Her eyes were bright and filled
with the warmth of the love she felt for him. He moved
toward her, feeling as if he were in some underwater
ballet that was choreographed by a power greater than
his own.

She held out her arms to him and he bent to kiss her.
He slowly started to undress.

It was the kind of lovemaking Dina had never known
before, because it was the first time she had really been
able to give herself to a man that she felt deeply for—and
a man who felt the same about her. It was slow, rapturous,
miraculous lovemaking that probed the inner souls of
each of them. For Dina, it was the beginning of a new
life. For Whit it was the fulfillment of his middle age.
For Frank it would turn out to be the trial of his life.

* * *

In the middle of February the government's estimated budget deficit was announced, and it totaled nearly sixty billion dollars. Unemployment figures were estimated to be 7.5 percent.

The stock market had reached record levels on the Dow.

Computer was now close to seventy dollars a share, and to those who held its stock all seemed right with the world.

But what the suckers who hold highly overvalued securities never seem to learn is, that the further you go out on a limb, the better chance you have of breaking your neck.

What the suckers also never learn is that for things to blow up on Wall Street doesn't mean that things have to blow up on Main Street. For one of the peculiarities of the market is how a very small number of men can have their general fears affect millions of people's lives and at times precipitate economic havoc.

The market had begun a sharp decline. Nothing tragic —just precipitous. And it was during this general period of uncertainty that one of the most respected financial writers on Wall Street had a full-length feature article on Computer which in detail and with conviction labeled the stock terribly overvalued at best, and a rank (meaning "to smell") speculation at least. All this came under the byline of Stirling Livermore—the Dean of Seers.

Livermore had called the turn on the May 1970 debacle nearly six months before it happened. He also had a reputation for reading the footnotes of complex annual reports and prospectuses—for being able to take the numbers presented by prestigious accounting firms and translate them into a comprehensive analysis. That, combined with years of watching the eccentricities of the market, gave him an outstanding record for taking the lift out of some of the highest of flyers, and in addition coming up with overlooked companies that were clearly unrecognized values.

In short, he was a self-opinionated authority with a wide following and his recommendations were taken very seriously by many professionals as well as the ordinary tape watcher. His recommendation on Computer was a loud SELL.

The general market sentiment, which was wary to begin with, reacted strongly to Livermore's article. In three days the stock had dropped from seventy-six to thirty-five dollars a share. A hasty meeting was called by the board of directing partners of Sullivan & Co.

In Boston a similar meeting was being called by one of Boston's most powerful banks, which had formed the investor group that had bought privately and at a 30 percent discount a block of Computer Ecolog from Karkov and Courtney.

The bank was summoning Tittle's firm, whom it had retained as technical advisers, and Karkov and Courtney to find out what was going on.

Nothing fundamental had changed in regard to Computer Ecolog. Karkov was still having trouble getting the impregnated chips to give him the consistency of performance necessary for his new small and inexpensive computer, and this was giving him field problems with his equipment. But that was nothing new. Everyone who knew anything about the company was familiar with these difficulties, and the general consensus (before Livermore's article) was that Karkov would overcome them. That's what pushed the stock, with a little help from the firm of Sullivan & Co., to seventy-nine.

But today's stock market is largely the opinion of a few powerful financial institutions and major Wall Street brokerage firms. When they get scared their fears can create havoc with the fortunes of millions of shareholders who join in the crises these men initiate. Simply put, a very few men can affect what the market does—and their reactions need be based on nothing more than their own reasoning, which leads them either to collective optimism or collective panic. At this point, it was the latter that was driving Computer's price downward.

They sat in the senior partners' conference room, which was electric with anxiety. Glen Farrell's phone had been ringing almost steadily since Computer had started its slide. So had Dean Faulkner's and Bill Davis'. So had Bob Friedman's; he was not a member of the board of directing partners, but he had been invited to attend this meeting.

Frank sat underneath the numberless clock, his face concerned, but his thoughts somewhat mollified by the fact that unknown to the men in the room, he had made a killing in the stock while the firm's position had suffered drastically. Dean Faulkner's own holdings, which were public knowledge as a director of Computer, had suffered badly in the decline of the stock. His private account, which was held in the name of an attorney who traded the stock on Dean's coded instructions, fared much better. Dean had felt the stock to be overpriced and had sold well over half his clandestine position, which helped ease his losses. But Dean was never a good loser: He went for the jugular. As they sat down to discuss Computer, Dean was hostile, impatient, and vibrating with anxiety.

He needed a release from the pressures that surged within him. Dean needed power as he needed air to breathe, and as he looked at his senior partner, who always seemed in control, who exuded a certain contagious masculine charm that Dean knew concealed a tough Irish gut fighter, he resolved with even more covert dedication that when his opportunity came he would do what had to be done.

Porter Conrad, the firm's trading partner, had sold Computer for the firm on Dean's advice. He had reduced the firm's holdings, but not enough. When Computer hit the fan, Glen Farrell, the firm's sales partner, had all he could do to placate the three hundred brokers scattered throughout his retail and institutional sales organization who had only recently called their customers in response to the report on Computer that Frank had ordered released. But it was the institutions that were driving Glen up the wall. As Computer's investment bankers, they were clamoring for information from Sullivan & Co. about the stock. Several were raising hell about the institutional report that Bob Friedman had written.

The six men in the room counting Bob Friedman were concerned mostly about the *firm's* investment in Computer. Though it was still highly profitable on an initial investment basis, they were seeing this margin reduced almost hourly. There were no block buyers around for the size position the firm held and since they were all partners, they suffered according to their partnership interest in the losses as well as the profits of the firm. If they took a bath in Computer, it wouldn't be fatal for the firm, but it would eat into each of their personal accounts, and this touched the nerves of everyone in the room.

Since Frank held the largest position in the firm, he would appear to have suffered the biggest loss. But the old hunter had taken quite good care of that. As they sat there waiting for Frank to open the meeting only Dean Faulkner had any vague suspicion that his senior partner might have pulled a fast one.

Frank smiled inwardly as he looked around the room. It's lucky, he thought, that when they designed this room it had no windows. Some of these birds looked to Frank as if they might jump.

Frank lit a cigar. All attention was riveted on him. He finally spoke. "It seems that our friend Livermore has given us something of a problem."

"That smug son of a bitch." It was Glen Farrell. "I've got every institution on both coasts calling me including the ones in the middle. What they are all screaming about is that goddamn report." He turned toward Bob Friedman. "I thought Elliot didn't want that report released, Bob." Glen paused. "Jesus. That poor bastard was certainly right about Computer."

Dean's face was taut. "Bob, how did that report get re-released?" Friedman felt uncomfortable as the black eyes bored into him.

Frank's face betrayed nothing.

"The report had been ready for two weeks, Dean." Friedman was doodling on a yellow pad not looking at Dean. Friedman had quietly shorted the stock and had still not covered, but no one in the room knew this—not even Frank. Both Dean and Frank would not have been surprised. What Friedman had done was very simple. He had sold Computer stock at very near its high, suspecting it would decline in price, and he would cover or buy back the stock he had sold at a much lower price. The difference would be his profit. The Livermore article on Computer was a blessing to Bob Friedman.

Dean's eyes were black coals. "You haven't answered my question, Bob. Did you release the report on your own authority? It was my impression that Elliot violently opposed such a release."

Bob Friedman had made so much money in shorting the stock that he could afford to tell them all to go to hell. But Friedman was a professional product of the Street. He knew how to play the game. "As a matter of fact, Dean"—Bob still avoided looking at Dean—"I released the report on Frank's authority."

Frank's partners felt as if they had been hit by a live grenade.

"Is that true, Frank?" Dean's voice was incredulous.

Frank sat unmoved. He had taken off his glasses and wiped the lenses with his handkerchief and made some penciled notes on the pad in front of him.

"That's correct."

They were all stunned. Dean's voice was now high-pitched as was characteristic when he became excited.

"But why, Frank—Elliot warned me, you—all of us—he thought the stock was overvalued."

Frank's style under pressure was always something to watch. His face remained impassive. His whole demeanor was controlled. Only those who knew him well—and these men did—could recognize the increased huskiness in his voice, its slightly lower pitch, and none of these characteristics went unnoticed by Dean.

"I think we all have to keep some perspective on this. In the first place, Bob's report, which he had repeatedly asked Elliot to release, was a thorough professional report written by our senior analyst covering this company. With due respect to all of you here, including myself, and including Elliot, Bob is supposed to know more about Computer than anyone else." Frank tipped the ashes of his cigar into the tray in front of him. "With Elliot's death, I saw no reason for holding up this report any longer." Now the old hunter was showing his mettle. "If you recall, in a meeting held in this room last month, you, Glen, were most indignant that Elliot was unwilling to authorize the release of this report and you vehemently opposed his release of a sell flash. I believe your reason was that it would kill the market for the stock."

Skillfully, Frank had taken some of the pressure off. But Dean was not to be assuaged so easily. "You recall, Frank, that I stated in that meeting that I felt the stock was overpriced and we should sell. I told you that privately as well."

Frank tapped his cigar. The room was hushed. Bill Davis, head of syndicate, was usually fairly quiet during these meetings. He remained so now. But he watched Dean closely.

"Yes, I recall your advice. In retrospect it was good advice." Dean relaxed slightly. "But let's look at this situation as it really is. There are divergent points of view regarding this stock; there have been from the beginning.

That has not changed. The company has not changed. The interest in Computer was recently strengthened, as you all know, by a Boston syndicate of investors who on the advice of Tittle's firm bought a large private block of the stock. We all know this group. They are as smart a bunch of Yankee traders as there is around. They would not have moved into the stock without excellent technical advice. It was this that largely influenced my decision to let Bob publish his report. I thought then, as I do now, that those fellows in Boston, sitting almost on top of the company, and surrounded by all the technical research groups that they could rely on for opinions, simply would not have put up eight and a half million unless they had solid reasons for believing in the validity of the stock."

Frank had defused the meeting. Bob Friedman breathed an inward sigh of relief. Dean lit a cigarette and then quickly snubbed it.

"Frank—what about Elliot's report on Dr. Eisenstadt's views about Computer? As I remember, Elliot distinctly told us that Eisenstadt thought that Karkov's technology was at least two years away."

"That too is correct. But Elliot also told you that the Boston group didn't buy Eisenstadt—they bought Nichols. It seems to me, as I mentioned earlier, there are differing technical points of view. As of now, Eisenstadt still seems to be in the minority."

The telephone rang. It was Porter Conrad, the firm's trading partner.

"Frank?"

"Yes, Porter."

"Market's off six points. Volume on the big board is heavy, about seven million at eleven thirty. French finance minister calling for meeting of Common Market countries to ask president to support dollar again. Last sale on Computer was fifteen hundred shares at twenty-three and three quarters. Volume in the stock about seventy-five thousand shares."

"Thanks, Porter." Frank hung up. He looked at his watch; it was eleven forty. The stock was continuing to be heavily traded.

Frank repeated Porter's information to his partners.

"It seems to me, gentlemen, what we should be deciding is what we are going to do about the stock."

Glen Farrell had been exceptionally quiet. "Do about the stock? You guys must be kidding. We've got a falling stock market and a security everyone's afraid to touch. Our only prayer is that we get a turn in this market and some institutional buying steps in. But I certainly don't expect that."

Frank turned to Bob Friedman. "Bob, have your feelings changed any about Computer?"

Friedman had been an almost silent observer up to now. His mind had been focused not on the conversation but on the masterful way in which Frank had controlled the meeting, how he had parried Dean, who Bob had sensed was the real threat to Frank in this group. His mind also dwelled on how soon he should cover his short position in Computer. His instincts told him to wait.

Friedman spoke in a low professorial tone that had just the right flavor—scholarly, knowledgeable, but in no way patronizing. The amazing act put on by Friedman should have netted him an Oscar. He was a base fraud. Elliot had discovered it; Frank and Dean sensed it. Friedman couldn't have cared less. He had made his bundle in Computer and would make more before he was through. It was just Wall Street pool they were playing, and Bob Friedman knew how to play.

"In answer to your question, Frank, as far as I can determine only two things have changed from what we already know about Computer. One is the market. Generally its tone is weak. The technicians are looking for a new base around eight fifty. If the Dow breaks that, my guess would be that it will go through eight hundred— that's just a guess. I am not a technician. The other is

Livermore. He's cried fire in a crowded theater and everyone is running for the exits. That's what's changed. Nothing else."

Frank looked evenly at Friedman. "What, if any, suggestions do you have, Bob, as to how this firm should respond to the slide in Computer?"

Friedman wondered why Sullivan suddenly placed such importance on his opinion.

Dean interrupted. "Frank, I think as the senior partner of this firm I would much prefer to hear your opinion rather than Bob's."

Frank knew they were coming to this. Frank was aware of the ambition that fired Dean Faulkner. He understood Dean, for the man was much like himself. He was driving, domineering, and dangerous. But Faulkner lacked Frank's charm.

"Gentlemen, I think Dean is correct. I owe you an opinion and suggested course of action as head of this firm."

Frank for some reason remembered a summer day long ago, when he was only seventeen.

It was so hot in New York that the city seemed like a blast furnace.

He remembered being dizzy from the suffocating subway car with its windows open, and the hot air from the rushing train pulled at black dirt-covered walls blowing soot over the riders as the subway careened toward a screeching stop. The station's name was spelled out in little ceramic blocks on white tiled walls and painted in black on the pillars supporting the station. It said WALL STREET.

Now it was February—cold and gray—and a hundred years later. God, it did seem like a hundred years to Frank. He brushed the thoughts from his mind. No one who had been watching his face or his eyes could have discerned that Frank's thoughts had digressed.

He wrote a few more lines on the yellow pad in front of him.

"You asked for my opinion. I'll be brief. I think we should sit tight. There's too much institutional money in this stock to let it collapse. I would guess that the boys in Boston might back up their position by a little timely buying, but that's only a hunch. It depends on how much confidence they have in their advisers."

The phone in the conference room rang. Dean picked it up. "It's for you, Frank."

The voice on the other end of the line was well known to Frank. It was Bennett Alden, chairman and chief executive officer of one of Boston's largest banks. Frank knew that Alden had helped organize the institutional and private investor group that had bought into Computer—at a substantial discount, but they had put their money down nevertheless. He could visualize the tall sandy-haired banker with the lean face and very light-blue eyes. He knew Bennett Alden to be of that Yankee group of New England bankers whose backgrounds hid behind bland smiles and unblemished manners, a shrewd ruthlessness.

"So nice to hear your voice, Bennett."

Everyone in the room became taut when Frank mentioned the name Bennett. It could only be Bennett Alden, and they all knew what that meant.

"No, the weather here is moderating a little, Bennett. Snowing like the devil up there, eh? Well, that's the price you fellows pay to be near that sailing country you're so proud of. Say, Bennett, I'm in a directors' meeting with my partners; would you mind if I put you on the speaker phone? You know most of the people here. Dean, Glen Farrell, Bill Davis—Bob Friedman is sitting in with us too—he's our senior analyst who wrote that report on Computer—fine. I'll put you on."

Frank pressed the button on the speaker phone.

"Can you hear me, Bennett?"

"Yes, I hear you fine."

By this unobtrusive maneuver Frank had suddenly involved them all in a call that he knew would be important and foreboding.

"Go ahead, Bennett." Frank wished to force Alden to begin speaking—to divulge what he had to say. It was a slight psychological advantage. Something that Frank did instinctively.

The dry, nasal voice of Bennett Alden was mellowed by the speaker.

"Frank, we intend to hold a little meeting up here in regards to Computer." Everyone in the room strained to catch each inflection in Bennett Alden's voice. "Our bank, as you know, feels a great responsibility to the investor group we helped to assemble that bought into Computer . . ." There was a long pause. "As you can imagine, our group is less than overjoyed by the stock's performance." Another pause. "Our feeling here at the bank is that if the company's technical position is sound, then we can ride out this market and wait for the stock to come back."

Frank stubbed out his cigar. Dean's eyes fixed on the speaker with intensity. Glen Farrell lit another nervous cigarette.

"We want to have your firm represented at this meeting as the investment bankers for Computer, and we would very much like to have Mr. Friedman, who wrote that report, present. We will have Ray Tittle and his people here and we are asking Dr. Karkov and Fletcher Courtney to be present as well. We hope they can persuade Dr. Nichols to come in from the coast—yes, and I might mention we hope to be able to have Dr. Eisenstadt from MIT here. I believe you know each other . . ."

"Not intimately, but we've met."

"Yes, I understand you have. We intend to get together at my house on Sunday. If Nichols can make it. I've asked him to come out Saturday and stay over. I'd like it very much if your firm was represented, Frank, by your-self if you can get away, Mr. Friedman, and anyone else you care to bring along. I'm out at Prides Crossing. If you tell me when you'll be arriving I'll have a car pick you up."

Frank looked around the room. "We'll be there, Ben-nett. How about eleven o'clock?"

"That would be fine. We can have some lunch. I re-member your craving for lobster salad."

Frank laughed. "See you Sunday." He pushed the off button on the speaker phone and turned to look at his partners.

"Well, our Yankee friends seem to be a little strained."

Glen Farrell stubbed his cigarette. "Strained. Those in-stitutions must be banging Bennett's balls together. Those fish-eyed guys in Boston aren't going to take a bath like this unless there's no way out." Glen's lips tightened. "If that Karkov isn't right—and we look like we supported the stock with that goddamned institutional report"— Glen glowered at Friedman—"we could lose a big piece of the Boston market, and those boys have very long arms, Frank . . ."

Frank put his glasses back in his pocket and took a drink of water. "I doubt if our New England friends hold their position based on Bob's report." He glanced at Dean, whose eyes he could see were far away. "If you can make it, Dean, I'd like you to come Sunday."

Dean came back. "You're damn right I can make it."

The meeting was adjourned.

The phones buzzed across the country. Fletcher Court-ney had put in a long-distance call to Nichols after Ben-nett Alden had spoken to him. But a short distance down the street, Charlie Fox had just hung up from a raving maniacal call from Angi Vittorio. Charlie stared out at the dirty brick wall across from his office window, Angi's last torrent of screaming abuse still ringing in his ears.

He sighed, put on his hat and coat, told his secretary the
number where he could be reached, and left for a much
different kind of meeting at the six-story brick apartment
house in Queens.

Angi's eyes were popping out of his head. He paced
the room like some ranting Sicilian panther. Charlie sat
quietly in a corner, his hands folded across his fat paunch,
his eyes watching Angi's every move.

"So your Irish prick friend thought we shouldn't sell.
That son of a bitch. I told you I smelled somethin'." He
whirled about, crossing the living room in four catlike
bounds. He grabbed the lapels of Charlie's suit and
yanked him to his feet. He was screaming. His eyes
showed his lost control. His lips were flecked with white,
his speech thick with fury. He shook Charlie Fox until
the little man's glasses fell off. "You fat little cocksucker.
You motherfucking little prick. You know what you cost
me? Do you? Do you? You son of a bitch!"

Charlie Fox made no obvious move to resist this hulking Sicilian. Charlie Fox had grown up on New York's
Lower East Side, where the neighborhood was a polyglot
of Italians, Jews, and Irish. You had to be tough just to
walk to school. Especially if your name was Feinberg,
which was what Charlie Fox's name had been before he
changed it years ago. He remembered a big Irish kid
who hit him in the head with a sock filled with lumps
of coal. It took twelve stitches to close the gash in Charlie's
scalp. What grew into Charlie through life on New York's
East Side was a simple inner courage that bullies every-
where recognize, and inwardly admire.

Angi Vittorio held Charlie Fox, his black eyes popping
out of his head, his voice screaming obscenities. Charlie
simply looked back at him, steady and unafraid. He
brought his small arms up quickly, forcing Angi's hands
away from his coat, and in one motion, learned on the

streets of New York, he buried his right knee in Angi's groin.

Surprise and pain crossed Angi's face as he collapsed and rolled on the thick pile carpet. He was clutching his groin moaning obscenities as Charlie rushed to the writing desk and grasped the gold-plated letter opener. He stood near Angi quietly, holding the letter opener very professionally, thumb on top of the handle, the blade extended, his fat short legs slightly flexed.

Angi crawled slowly to his feet. His face was a mask of disbelief. He looked at the little man before him and he saw the steady blue eyes following him. He began to laugh. He laughed so hard that he had to sit down on the elaborate Spanish-style sofa. He was flabbergasted. This was a language that Angi understood.

"Why you little Jewish prick. I never knew you had it in you. For Christ's sake. Little fat Charlie kicked Angi in the balls. You son of a bitch. You know, you're all right. You know that!"

Charlie's smile was thin and grim as he put down the letter opener.

Angi was still rubbing his testicles. "Okay, Charlie, let's cut out the crap and talk. What the hell are we goin' to do with this Computer thing? I still think Sullivan fucked us. The point is, what do we do now?"

Charlie's mind was on the kid who put twelve stitches in his head. He remembered putting his sandwiches in his coat pocket and filling his lunch box with rocks. The other Jews on the block were not toughs in the sense that the Irish and the Italian kids were. But Charlie had friends. One was a big Italian nicknamed Bananas because of his nose. The other was his brother Jake, who was big and strong and dumb—unlike Charlie. They found this Irish kid with some of his friends. There was one hell of a fight. Charlie had hit the Irish kid right in the balls with a lunch box full of rocks. He hit him with everything he had. Years later Charlie wondered if that kid was ever able to screw a girl.

"Angi—listen to me and listen good. When Computer started to slide, I told you we shouldn't sell in that kind of a market. I told you that there were a lot of institutions holding the stock. That if the market turned around even temporarily, they would be back in there buying; that Frank told me some Boston people, very savvy guys, had bought two blocks of the stock for eight and a half million. These guys have the best advice around."

"Then why did Sullivan sell? Answer me that. Why?"

"He said he needed money."

"That's horseshit. Sullivan needs money like a whore needs the clap."

"You don't understand how these guys live, Angi. They're not like you. Money isn't all that makes them go. They have to live in the right places, belong to the right clubs. Frank's got an apartment on Park that must be worth at least two hundred forty G's. He's got a house in Connecticut that cost him over half a million. He's got a place down in Nassau that costs a mint. These guys also have to keep capital in their business. They buy all these places heavily mortgaged. Their taxes are very high. Most of them trade in the market to help pay their overhead. I'm not saying Frank doesn't have money. Of course he does. But it is conceivable that for personal reasons—he mentioned taxes when he spoke to me—he had to sell Computer to pay off bank loans, back taxes—something. I believe the guy."

Angi scowled. "Well, I don't. I think the fucker lied to us. I still think he knows something we don't. But the hell with that. What do we do now?"

"Angi—I keep telling you. We have to wait for this market to turn and pray for some good news about Computer. If we keep selling into this market we'll get killed. It's too late and too risky to short the stock. The only thing we can do is wait."

Angi's eyes were alive with thought. "Tell me some-

thin'. Why didn't Sullivan sell his stock through his own
firm—huh—why?"

"Probably because his firm is the investment banker
for Computer and if the word got out he was selling his
position it would have been bad for the stock."

Angi went out to get a beer. When he came back Charlie
had put on his hat and coat. It was nearly five o'clock.
Outside the early darkness of February was closing in on
Queens.

"Where you goin'?"

"I've gotta get back to the office. I'll talk to you tomorrow."

Charlie got into the mustard-colored steel-walled elevator that jerked its way down six floors. By the time he
got to the street it was dark. The sky was overcast. He
pulled his collar up and held it closed at the neck with
one hand. His other held his hat against the sharp damp
wind that whirled dirt from the street at his face.

He walked to the corner to get a cab. It was a lousy
place to get one at this time of afternoon. He could hear
the planes above the overcast coming into La Guardia.
The noise of traffic from the expressway drummed in his
ears. If Charlie Fox ever thought about how forlorn this
treeless drab area of flat-topped apartments was, he was
not thinking of that now. As he bent into the chill wind
and rounded the corner in search of a cab, his thoughts,
oddly enough, were on a little chubby kid with a lunch
box full of rocks, and an Irish kid who today might not
be able to screw.

Charlie found a cab and told the driver where he wanted
to go. The tires squealed as the cab burned rubber in a
silently hostile sharp U turn.

As the cab reached the intersection of the next street the
driver slowed down, but not enough. The oncoming delivery truck, which had QUEENS LAUNDRY AND DRY CLEAN-
ING—ONE DAY SERVICE painted on its side, saw the cab and
tried to stop. But worn tires, the slick pavement, spun the

truck into a sweeping out-of-control spin and crashed it squarely into the taxi.

The cab driver was thrown to the street. Charlie was pinned inside the cab semiconscious, the blood flowing from a gash over his right forehead. Before lapsing into a coma he vaguely remembered hearing the sirens screaming and the flashing red and blue lights; the jolting of the cab as they tried to pry the door open with a crowbar to get him out.

When they got him into the ambulance he saw a chubby child's form carrying a lunch box. He smiled and passed out.

After Elliot's death, Dina had been saved from a complete collapse by one thought that kept her from falling into the abyss of dangerous depression. It was the thought of Whit Fraser's love for her, and her terrible need to cling to that love in the desperation of her confusion.

Frank had accepted Dina's collapse and her obvious attraction for Whitney Fraser, out of guilt—the guilt that sprang from having used his wife for his own purposes.

In the initial phases of Dina's recovery Frank accepted being moved from his wife's bed to the guest bedroom, and in the beginning he even enjoyed the independence of sleeping alone. But as the weeks passed and March came, Frank felt lonely and shut out from Dina's life. He became more attentive toward her; more considerate. As he watched her recover and regain her beauty, he felt his old desire for her begin to stir. But when they breakfasted together—when they sat before the fire in the living room after dinner—Frank could sense that there was a presence between them, and he didn't have to be told who this presence was. It was Whit Fraser.

Thursday night. They had planned to have a quiet dinner at home, just the two of them. They were seated on a sofa near the crackling fire. Before them on the butler's table were two half-emptied glasses of brandy. Dina looked nervous and apprehensive. Frank's face in the soft firelight looked at her with an expression of empathy that she had rarely seen.

She avoided her husband's eyes as she felt the nearness of his presence. Frank's face, with its strength, his hair still full though streaked with gray. The light-gray eyes that she knew never missed anything seemed to penetrate her thoughts. His face seemed to be reflecting some inner sadness as he watched her. His voice was husky as he spoke.

"I don't think I've ever seen you look lovelier, darling." He said this slowly, rocking gently the amber brandy he held in his right hand. She forced a smile as she tried to reply to him with her eyes. But she was feeling too confused to look at him directly.

In the large living room with its dim lights, and the fire reflecting shadows before them, she did look beautiful. Her skin had regained its color, and her eyes—those large violet-blue eyes which would not look directly at her husband—had regained their old luster. She was dressed in dark-blue wool that clung to her figure and set off her shoulder-length hair. She wore a diamond-and-emerald brooch that Frank had given her for their fifth wedding anniversary above her right breast. She reached for a cigarette and lit it.

"You know, I feel as if I have been in solitary a bit too long, darling . . ." Frank's voice was a husky chuckle. Dina smiled nervously.

"I'd like to come back if you think you're well enough. It's no fun playing bachelor, you know." He watched Dina closely and saw her mouth pull into a taut nervous line.

Though Dina was avoiding Frank's eyes, her mind was electrically alive to what was happening between them. She knew Frank, and she knew that in his own way he loved her and perhaps at times—and this was one of the times—he might even need her and be willing to acknowledge that need. But she also knew that this moment would pass and that Frank would be immersed in the next deal, the next business crisis, and that he would then become unreachable, impenetrable. She knew then it would be she who would be forced to the periphery of his life. It would be she who would be alone, with a vacuous existence which would continue to erode her life. It was this knowledge, so hard won, that kept them on opposite sides of the Sheraton sofa.

She also knew that they could not go on like this. And she really dreaded hurting Frank. It wasn't that she didn't admire and respect her husband. It was that she felt he didn't need her; for with Frank, to be needed was an experience he had only infrequently known. What Dina wanted to rekindle in her life was beyond Frank's ability to give.

Dina avoided her husband's eyes and flicked the ashes of her cigarette into the fire.

"Frank, come back whenever you like. It's been lonely for me, too. But really"—she hesitated, still avoiding his gaze—"don't expect too much. I still feel awfully shaky." She paused and stubbed out her cigarette.

Frank watched her for a moment and reached out and took her hand and held it gently in his. He drew her hand to his lips and kissed it softly. Dina turned her face toward him. He watched two silent tears curve slowly toward her mouth.

Over on the East Side at the United Nations Plaza apartments, a chill evening wind blew against the windows of Whit Fraser's fifteenth-floor apartment. He had drawn back the drapes and was looking out over the East River, at the U.N., and the steel-and-concrete spines of lower Manhattan; the lights from Queens reflecting against the windblown waves that collided with the swift-flowing current. A shadowy tugboat passed silently as he watched. Except for college vacations he occupied the apartment alone. The boys' rooms remained empty during most of the year. He kept himself so busy that the loneliness caused by his wife's death was assuaged by work. He had always been able to push himself so that he arrived in the apartment ready for a quick drink and bed. But Dina had changed all that.

Because Whit had fallen in love with Dina even before his wife's death, his Midwestern conscience had sharpened the feelings of guilt that currently plagued him; thrusting at him more deeply for being in love with another man's wife. Whit was not the usual East Sixties immigrant. His standards had not become as blasé as those other New York friends of his who had thrown off the so-called antique codes of behavior for the laissez-faire attitudes of upper-middle-class Manhattan. Whit was essentially a square. He disliked affectation and cocktail-circuit friendships. He was short on chitchat, avoided promiscuity, and inwardly longed for a love he could share with a woman; a love that was at once passionate, deep, unselfish, and faithful. Whit wanted a home again. He wanted to reawaken his life, not hide from its realities in exhausted sleep.

But there was Frank. Whit had met Frank shortly after he had married Dina. He admired Frank. He admired the man's style. He admired Frank's success, the quiet ability he had to lead men. But he also knew that Frank's purpose was to get what he wanted, and he was usually successful. It was not that Whit saw Frank lacking in human values, but rather he viewed him as one who had been formed by the environment of the jungle in which Frank had chosen to make his life. Frank's world was too compressed to permit the values Whit admired to be nourished and to survive.

Whit paced the living room with a malt scotch in one hand, a cigar in the other. He was just under six feet in height with broad square shoulders, an almost stocky frame. His hair was chestnut and his blue eyes and fair skin seemed to come to an observer as a surprise; for some reason he should have appeared more in keeping with a

darker complexion; more swarthy. There was about Whit
a certain competent gentleness and veracity that made him
quietly appealing to both men and women. It gave his
face an almost youthful aspect. But one of Whit's most
distinguishing characteristics was a moral directness which
revolted against an adulterous relationship with the wife
of one of his close friends. He felt unclean, ashamed for
himself and for his sons, should they discover, as they
eventually would, the behavior of their father.

Whit was tearing himself apart with what he considered
to be the right thing to do. Stop this affair with Dina and
get out of her life—and Frank's. But he couldn't. He felt
too strongly about Dina and he knew that she was drawn
to him. They could give each other what both of them
needed; he could even help her to have a child. That
thought appealed to him. He enjoyed being a father, and
now with his children grown up, he was alone. The thought
of having a child with Dina was enormously appealing
to him.

He walked to the stereo and flicked the switch. The
FM station to which he kept the set tuned filled the living
room with lush warm music.

Whit went over to the bar and poured himself three
more fingers of straight malt scotch whiskey, no ice.

The honey-throated vocalist was singing about love the
second time around.

Whit stubbed out his cigar, his mouth a straight line.
He shook his head silently, finished the scotch, and went
toward the bedroom and a troubled restless sleep.

Thursday had been a gray, penetratingly cold day in
Boston. When Bennett Alden had called Fletcher Courtney
about the weekend meeting to be held in Alden's house,
Courtney knew the storm signals were up. When he finished talking to Alden he walked into Karkov's office
where the scientist was in shirt sleeves buried behind a

desk covered with engineering drawings, reports, folders, technical publications; chaos. Karkov's office always reminded Courtney of a room where someone had turned an immense fan up to maximum.

Karkov's thick gray hair was disheveled. His glasses had slipped halfway down his nose. His heavy shoulders were slumped in concentration. His large head and fleshy face with darting dark eyes didn't even know that Courtney was in his office.

"I hate to disturb you, Doctor, but I think we had better have a little powwow."

He stood before Karkov, spare, sardonic, and in some inscrutable fashion, patronizing. For Fletcher Courtney held the view that Karkov was a brilliant scientist who shouldn't be allowed outside his office without a keeper. Courtney knew that he was Karkov's buffer against the world outside, and Karkov knew it too. Both realized that each supplied a function which was essential, and though they held no particular affection for each other, they tolerated one another because it served a purpose.

When Karkov finally looked up he swore.

"Jesus Christ. What the hell are you interrupting me for? Damn it, I'm going over the reports on the Potomac installation. The sensors and the line reporting systems are fine, but the goddamn computer is raising hell again. We'll have to rework some of the circuit design."

Courtney walked to a chair filled with books, placed them on the floor, and sat down.

"Karky—you'd better listen to this."

Karkov shook his head in desperation.

"What the hell is it this time?"

"It's Bennett Alden."

"Alden? What does that fish want? Doesn't he have his stock, for Christ's sake? Now what's the matter?"

Courtney was used to Karkov's insulation from the real world.

"Yes, he has his stock. And so do his friends. That's exactly the problem. They're not particularly happy."

"Why?"

Courtney shook his balding sandy-haired head in disbelief. "Karky. You mean you really don't know why Alden's crowd should be unhappy?"

"You mean the stock?"

Courtney sighed. "I mean the stock. It has slipped somewhat in price since they bought in."

"So what. Stocks go up and down. What the hell is so unusual about that?"

Courtney again shook his head resignedly. "It just so happens that Computer has dropped over twenty-one points since Alden's group bought in." Fletcher got up to close the door. He poked his head out and said to Karkov's secretary, "No calls. No interruptions." He closed the door.

"On paper, Karky, our Yankee friends have lost over five million dollars in less than three weeks. That would make anyone unhappy."

Karkov looked shocked. "Three weeks? Over five million in three weeks? Well, what the hell is wrong with the market?"

"The market is generally weak, that's true, Karky. But have you read the Livermore article on Computer?"

"Who the hell is Livermore?"

"He's a security analyst. One of the best. And, I might add, with a widely read following of buyers and sellers."

"So . . ."

"So he's written a full-length article on Computer in which he described our company as almost a fraud, very definitely a highly overpriced speculation, and most definitely a sell. His recommendation to several thousand sophisticated investors is to get the hell out of Computer."

Karkov was stunned. He jumped to his feet and walked quickly around his desk to tower over Courtney.

"What the hell does that son of a bitch know about what we're doing? Is he a physicist?"

"No."

Karkov was white with anger. "Then I'll sue the bastard. How the hell can he report on a technology as sophisticated as ours without being a physicist?"

"He's talked to a lot of technical people, Karky."

Karkov began pacing up and down the room. It wasn't the drop in value of the stock that bothered him; it was the implication of chicanery that Courtney seemed to be saying was implied in Livermore's article. Karkov had been through a lifetime of skepticism and verbal abuse for his unorthodox methods and views, but what really made him madder than hell was when someone implied that he was a fraud.

Karkov kept pacing up and down.

"It's those goddamn chips. When we can work out the reliability factors in our new circuit design, we'll have the whole world by the balls."

Courtney appraised Karkov carefully. After six years of close association with this hulking scientist he had to admit that he really didn't understand the man. Karkov's driving force was to develop and build technical products. This was his sole obsession. He didn't care about money, titles, or position. Technical creativity was his motivation, but for some reason Courtney held the private view that the man might be a quack, a technical charlatan; or he might be the abused genius he proclaimed himself to be. But Fletcher Courtney's country-boy shrewdness edged his personal evaluation more toward the quack than the genius.

"Karky"—Fletcher's voice was nasal and flat—"Bennett wants us to come to a meeting he's having at his house on Sunday."

Karkov exploded. "Screw Bennett. I've got to work here Saturday and Sunday too. I'm not going to any goddamn meeting at Bennett's house."

"Now, Karky, don't get yourself all wound up. This isn't just a casual get-together." Karkov was pacing the floor like a caged lion, his heavy face red with anger. "Bennett is going to have the group he put together who bought our stock, plus some others including Nichols and Eisenstadt."

"Eisenstadt!" Karkov exploded, taking a technical publication and throwing it across the room. It bounced off the top of a gray filing cabinet, sending a withered philodendron in a clay pot crashing to the floor.

"That no-good son of a bitch. That little runt from MIT who's never built a product in his life. You mean that prick Eisenstadt is going to be there? The hell with it. I wouldn't go if—"

Courtney held up his hand in a pained effort to halt Karkov's invective.

"Look, Karky, sit down or walk around, but try listening for a change. We have a few problems that don't have a damn thing to do with your chips or your minicomputers; they're financial."

"That's what I have you for—"

"I'm aware of that, Karky, but neither you nor Bennett's group nor anyone else knows what I'm about to tell you, so if you'll just keep quiet for five minutes I'd like to go into this with you."

"Jesus Christ," Karkov growled. "Why the hell do I have to be bothered with this crap?" He walked over to the window and stood looking out at the flow of traffic on 128. He released a long exasperated sigh, waving the unlit cigar like a baton. "Go ahead, for Christ's sake. Get it over with."

Courtney had remained seated, composed and resigned. He spoke slowly and carefully. "In the first place, Karky, you don't operate this business in a vacuum. All your brilliant ideas aren't worth a damn if you don't have the money to develop a product and market it successfully. I'm not patronizing you. I'm simply trying to tell you that

Bennett Alden represents one of the largest banks in Boston. He's this company's lead commercial banker, and you don't bite his hand unless you're in a hell of a lot stronger position than we are.

"Alden has his personal reputation and prestige to think about. He's responsible for organizing the group who bought a part of your stock and mine. These are personal friends of his. This whole Boston money crowd, the old crowd, is just one big family. He's personally embarrassed, not to say distressed, because it looks like he's dragged his buddies into a bum deal."

Karkov started to speak.

"Wait, Karky, hear me out. From his point of view as well as his friends', it's a bum deal unless the stock comes back—meaning if you can work the bugs out of the impregnated-chip technology. But even if you can, what they don't know—what you don't know—is that I've just spent the morning on the phone with one of our accountants, Steve LeDune from Fuller, Cross. They have a bit of a shocker for us."

"Those goddamn accountants—what the hell do they want now?"

Fletcher Courtney exhaled sharply, his lips compressed. "Mr. LeDune wants us to write off our research and development costs."

Karkov whirled around, his eyes blazing. "Why, that's nearly ten million dollars. That'll kill our earnings!"

"It'll do more than that, Karky. It'll give us one hell of a loss. What do you think will happen to our stock then?"

He paused. Karkov was panting with rage.

"Those fuckers. They can't do that. I'll sue their asses off. I'll—"

"Hold it, Karky. Don't pull the Russian bear act now. We don't have time for it." Fletcher Courtney's voice was annoyed. "But you now have some idea why we have to go to that meeting on Sunday. When Alden's crowd hears this they'll go through the roof." Courtney's face was a study in thoughtful purpose. "As a matter of fact, I'm relying on Alden—and I think there is just enough of the slave trader left in him—to twist Fuller, Cross' arm a bit. After all, that bank controls one hell of a lot of business. Fuller is a big firm, but they would *have* to listen to a guy like Bennett Alden if he wanted them to."

Karkov looked as if he had been poleaxed. He almost fell into his chair, his face a thick fleshy mask of disbelief.

What was happening was simple enough, but its consequences were horrific for Computer Ecolog. It had been Computer's practice to capitalize as an asset on their balance sheet the research costs the company incurred in developing new products. These costs were listed as an asset. They amounted to nearly ten million dollars. Now Fuller, Cross and Company, Computer's accounting firm, felt that the company should write off this amount, which would have to be applied against the company's earnings, and in one arbitrary accounting procedure, Computer Ecolog would go from a rather modest profit to a very substantial loss. Its stock would probably go right through the floor.

"Now, Karky, let's not go off the deep end. It hasn't happened yet, and maybe we can keep it from happening. So let's take one crisis at a time. There's another little item I think we should talk about."

Karkov held his head in his hands. His mouth clamped on the unlit cigar. This volatile Russian's moods were cyclonic. From deep despair to euphoria. The winds of his disposition blew from all points of the compass. His voice was low. "Let's have it, for Christ's sake. What other tidings of joy do you have for me?"

"You remember that gift we made to the Nichols Institute."

Karkov shook his head.

"Do you remember the timing of that gift?"

"What timing? I don't know what you're talking about."

"I'll refresh your memory. When we were negotiating for the sale of some of our stock to Alden's group—"

"You were negotiating."

"All right—I was negotiating. Do you remember that I learned that Ray Tittle's firm was going to be the consultant for Alden's group? Well, I also learned that they got in touch with Eisenstadt at MIT, who suggested Paul Nichols as another authority on impregnated-chip research. They wanted more than one point of view, and as you know Eisenstadt is not your greatest fan."

"The little Jewish prick."

"In any event, I had a quiet meeting with Nichols before he met with Tittle's group. I flattered him about his work. Told him what a great admirer of him you were."

"That's horseshit. I don't even know him."

Fletcher went on resignedly. "Told him what a great admirer of him you were, and gave him the distinct impression that we might be willing to contribute meaningfully to his Institute. I hinted that I understood he might be asked to give a consulting opinion about our company. I couched this very tactfully and carefully, I assure you. He couldn't possibly be offended. But, I felt that unlike you, Karky, this guy Nichols is hungry. He wants to build a monument to himself with that Institute of his. I just sensed that he was up for a tactful grab. When I left that meeting, there was never any doubt in my mind that Nichols would be on our side when he made his report to Tittle." Courtney paused. "You may remember that I persuaded you to make a gift to the Nichols Institute long before I learned of his positive recommendation to Tittle concerning the development and promise of your technology. This was a calculated gamble. Alden's group might have bought Eisenstadt's view, that you have some good ideas but were at least two years away from actual production."

"That Jew prick—"

"But I felt if we gave money to Nichols' Institute after we had made the deal it would have been too blatant. The whole point of all this is that Nichols will be there with

Eisenstadt at Bennett Alden's on Sunday. I doubt if anyone is aware of this, but do you begin to get a little better
idea of why we have to be there?"

Karkov shook his head wearily. He felt imposed upon
by all this spinning of webs by Fletcher Courtney. Courtney had intruded the chicanery of finance on his passion
for research and product development. True, Courtney
had made Karkov rich and himself as well, but the eccentric quack or genius, whichever view you took, was dis-
trustful of this lean accountant who was president of his
company. Odd how two men can grow to use each other
for their mutual advantage in a pact of tacit mistrust that
had endured for six years. Many marriages don't work
nearly as well.

Fletcher Courtney had placed a long-distance call to
Paul Nichols. The scientist with the rushed, almost lisping
speech had already been called by Tittle and asked to
attend Sunday's meeting. He said he would come.

Nichols knew at once what was behind Courtney's call,
and the cagey scientist gave Courtney the verbal assurances
that Fletcher needed.

As Fletcher Courtney worked his way into the rushing
traffic of Route 128, he headed northeast toward Marble-
head with the sure knowledge that things could be worse,
and if he waited around long enough he was positive they
would be. But then the thin smile of satisfaction spread
across his face. Really—what the hell did he care? He had
made his; they could all go to hell.

Dean Faulkner's ambition was to take over the firm of
Sullivan & Co. He would either do this or start his own
firm. Dean's life, like Frank's, was centered around business. He had married Chris, who came from an old New
York moneyed family, and there was just enough between
them to keep them together. His wife after her marriage

simply continued doing what she had done all her life: shop, go to the theater, entertain, attend classes. Even have an affair or two. Without a great deal of warmth or mutual admiration, they had let their marriage settle down to a basis of discreet live-and-let-live. At least they had the realities of their marriage in perspective without the hypocritical pretentions of many of their friends.

In their own way they were tolerant of each other's needs, found sexual satisfaction in bed, and each generally felt they could stay the course if the other didn't interfere too much.

This let Dean focus most of his life around the business, and he was one of the most effective corporate finance partners in the firm. He was not only technically acute, but he knew how to cultivate business. He belonged to the right clubs, entertained those he wished to promote for his own purposes, and was able to put his enormous energies into a single purpose: to become the senior partner and have the largest partnership interest in Sullivan & Co.

Dean had long watched Frank control the firm. He envied Frank's easy charm, his instinctive abilities to lead and command men. He certainly envied Frank his wife, Dina.

On this Friday night he walked toward his apartment at Sixty-second and Park, from the Hotel Plaza, where he had had dinner in the Oak Room with the president of United World Wide Utilities. They had talked about raising approximately one hundred million dollars for United. Dean had been working on this deal for several months in conjunction with United's traditional investment bankers, who by virtue of their long association with United were getting the lion's share of the fees.

Dean had been carefully cultivating a personal relationship with Ward Maudling, United's president, and Dean sensed that United might be receptive to a more vigorous and imaginative approach to their financial problems than their present investment bankers seemed to be providing.

Dean played his cards with Maudling quietly but effectively. He didn't want to overtly offend Maudling's historic bankers, as they were one of the most prestigious firms on the Street and Sullivan & Co. were syndicate partners with them in any number of deals. But it was the old Wall Street pastime of pirating another firm's account with a minimum of bloodletting and a maximum of finesse. This was a game of intrigue that Dean was made for. He had the necessary combination of intelligence, initiative, tact, and ruthlessness to be very effective.

On this Friday night as he walked east and then north up Park Avenue to his apartment he felt the chill March night wind blow against his face. The honking yellow taxis flashed by. The long line of timed lights blinked alternately red and green as they regulated the endless stream of traffic. The stainless-steel office buildings with their blaze of lights funneled the wind. Splashes of color from expensive shops caught Dean's eye as he heard the clicking of his leather heels on the pavement. His quick stride hurried him toward his cooperative apartment that he did not think of as home.

Dean's mind was preoccupied with Sunday's meeting in Boston.

From the beginning of this whole affair, when Elliot had made known his views on Computer to both Dean and Frank, Dean felt that his senior partner had not been entirely candid concerning his personal activities regarding Computer. The thought that spun its web in Dean's mind was the acknowledgment by Frank that he had authorized the release of Friedman's report right after Elliot's death, without any consultation with his other directing partners. Nagging at Dean was the suspicion that this was unusual for Frank. He had the authority as senior partner to order the report released, but Dean knew Frank intimately, and what troubled him was the feeling that Frank had stepped out of character. Why?

All Dean could think of was that Frank had some *per-*

sonal reason for wanting that report released that had nothing to do with the interests of the firm. The rationalizations that Frank had given at the partners' meeting for his action rang false. He had no way to be sure that his suspicions were justified, but he was damn well going to find out.

Dean expected Sunday's meeting at Bennett Alden's house to uncover some scurrying spiders. His dark eyes, reflecting the lights of Park Avenue, gleamed in anticipation.

Frank had called Dina from the office and asked if they could have dinner at Valjean's. It was one of Dina's favorite restaurants, just off the corner of Third Avenue and Fifty-third Street. He could hear the hesitation in her voice, but was grateful when she said she would dine with him.

Frank had bought Dina a diamond-and-emerald bracelet to celebrate her recovery. He was going to give it to her tonight. He instructed the chauffeur to pick her up and bring her directly to the restaurant. He would take a cab uptown.

As he rode uptown he felt uneasy about his wife. He felt that she was becoming more and more estranged from him; remote. Perhaps too involved with Whit and too removed from him to be able to rescue their marriage, a marriage that Frank knew was in deep trouble. But he was determined to try.

As the cab jerked its way through the seven thirty East Side traffic toward his dinner date with Dina, Frank thought about his meeting with Ray Costanza that morning.

Costanza was head of the firm's compliance department. His responsibility was to see to it that all employees of the firm, including its partners, did not violate any of the regulations of the New York Stock Exchange, the Securities and Exchange Commission, or any of the various federal and state regulatory agencies. He was also called upon to check closely into the background of new partners that came into the firm. Costanza was affectionately known at Sullivan & Co. as the Gestapo. Frank had hired him when they had a serious problem in their Chicago office, and Costanza had turned out to be the right man for the job.

He was quiet and tactful. He worked smoothly with the other attorneys in the compliance department. Costanza was a lawyer himself, although he had not practiced law in the last ten years. He was of medium height with thick dark hair, and dark skin. His eyes were so brown they appeared black. His speech was pure Brooklyn. Frank had found Costanza very useful because he was so quietly resourceful in getting things done.

Costanza sat before him in Frank's paneled corner office, large enough to hold a Duncan Phyfe dining table with six Sheraton chairs. This arrangement was used for small meetings. Against the wall opposite Frank's desk was a Hepplewhite sofa in front of which stood a butler's table. Before Frank's English partner's desk were three other chairs. The middle one was now occupied by Ray Costanza.

The office was so large that the furnishings did not crowd it. As Ray Costanza sat in front of Frank, the two men looked strangely slight in the oversize room.

Frank smoked thoughtfully as he looked at Costanza. He remained silent for perhaps a full minute without uttering a word. Ray, as was his practice, simply waited for his boss to tell him what he wanted done.

"I've been giving a great deal of thought, Ray, to a possible problem that could be embarrassing to the firm."

Ray nodded. "Yes, sir."

"It's very ticklish because it involves one of my key partners. I don't even have any solid facts to go on, but I am suspicious. Perhaps unjustly so." He looked at Costanza.

"You know, of course, of the firm's involvement in Computer Ecolog?"

"Certainly, sir."

"You are aware that even with the decline in the price of Computer's stock the firm's position is still a large one."

"Yes, sir. I am aware of that."

Frank paused. "What I am about to ask you to do I find very distasteful, and I needn't tell you I expect you to do what I ask in complete confidence—reporting only to me." He paused again, his gray eyes fixed steadily on Costanza. "And I don't want any slipups, Ray."

"No, sir."

Frank had given a great deal of thought to Sunday's meeting at Bennett Alden's. He had purposely asked Dean Faulkner to come with him. He knew that Dean could be exceedingly dangerous to him if given an opportunity. Frank's instincts sent him warning signals about Dean and the meeting in New England. Frank wanted something to club Dean with if he needed it, and he expected Ray Costanza to provide him with the club.

"Ray. I probably have too little to go on other than my own feelings, which from experience I have learned to trust. As I said, I want this held in absolute confidence between us. It's my feeling that Dean Faulkner, who as you know is a director of Computer Ecolog, has been trading the stock in a blind account without reporting those trades to either the firm, the Exchange, or the SEC." Frank paused. "Now this is only a hunch—I have nothing else to go on. But I want you to arrange for a tap on Dean's private line. I want a record of every phone call made on that line to support or negate my suspicions."

Frank watched Costanza closely. He could almost see the dark face turn several shades lighter. Ray's eyes were wide with surprise.

"Sir, that isn't easy to do. And if I may say so, sir, if you don't have much to go on, isn't that a little drastic?"

Frank cut him short. "I don't expect it to be easy. I simply want it done." He eyed Costanza severely. "I am aware, Ray, that your connections and abilities to perform such services are not exactly beyond your experience. That's one of the reasons I hired you. Now, I don't care how you accomplish this. I just want it done and done quickly."

The interview was over. Ray Costanza rose and said, "Yes, sir," and left.

The cab turned into Fifty-third Street and Frank told the driver to pull over to the blue, white, and red awning that covered the entrance to Valjean's. He looked at his watch. It was eight fifteen. He was early. He walked into the restaurant, where Valjean, complete in chef's hat and apron, met him at the door with effusive Gallic demonstrations of welcome, and guided Frank to one of the best tables in the center of the room near the wall facing the entrance.

The room's charm was in great part due to the murals of the southern coast of France that added so much to the color and atmosphere of Valjean's.

The restaurant's air was one of soft candlelit elegance: exquisite food, magnificent wines, and outrageous prices. Dina liked its intimate luxurious atmosphere. She and Frank were well known to the staff, whose superb service was even more graciously given to the Sullivans. of the staff's Gallic appreciation of a truly beautiful woman, as well as Frank's generous tipping.

Dina was late, and Frank early. He knew Valjean rated all Americans who dined in his restaurant by their knowledge and appreciation of fine food. Too much alcohol spoiled the taste of a good wine; a salad with any kind of vinegar-based dressing destroyed it. Frank was high on Valjean's list of cultivated Americans.

Dina walked into the restaurant, her eyes seeking Frank.

She wore a long-sleeved black velvet gown with a deep neckline that showed the swelling of her breasts. There was an air about her of quiet melancholy that called forth a sympathy which women as beautiful as Dina seldom receive. Every man in the room looked at her with longing. Every woman with admiration and envy.

Frank saw her and felt something within him stir. He rose to greet her as she walked toward their table. Within Frank was a blend of emotions as he watched his wife come toward him. Pride in himself for having won her. Love, his kind of love. A feeling of fear at the thought that he was losing her.

"Madame, if I may say so, you look magnificent."

Dina smiled at Valjean, who escorted her to her table. Frank stood while Valjean held her chair.

"It has been some time, Valjean, since we've seen you."

"Madame, it has been much too long. You brighten th*
life of an old Frenchman with your beauty."

"You're very gallant, Valjean, as usual."

Frank sat down, which was Valjean's signal to leave. Like any great restaurateur he knew people. He sensed that Frank wanted some time alone with his wife before the intrusion of ordering dinner and wine.

"You *do* look very special tonight." Frank reached out and touched Dina's hands. "I want tonight to be very *special* for us. After all, it's our first real date together since you've been"—he hesitated for the right phrase— "since you've been getting back on your feet."

He watched her eyes and he saw her look at him with that affectionate sadness that made him uneasy.

"Sunday I have to go to Boston to meet with Bennett Alden. It's very important. But tonight I would just like to have a long leisurely dinner with my wife, and tell her how glad I am she's getting well and how lucky I feel to be married to her."

Dina touched Frank's hand and looked at him with eyes filled with the shadows of sorrow. "Frank, thank you. It's thoughtful of you to take me to Valjean's. You know how much I enjoy it here."

"I felt we should do this, Dina. It's been so long since we have spent any real time together."

Her eyes looked away. "I know, Frank, I know."

As the dinner progressed and they had gone through most of a bottle of '67 Haut Brion they both started to relax somewhat. Frank's tone became more confiding, and Dina sensed a change in him which surprised her. He seemed to be telling her that he was trying in his own way to reawaken their feelings for each other.

Dina had never had a talent for self-analysis. Her attitudes toward Frank when they were first married were superficial. Frank was physically attractive. He was an acknowledged leader in his field and in the community. He was sought after by dozens of women after the death of his first wife. As far as Dina was concerned, Frank fulfilled her surface requirements. It had taken the tragedy of Elliot's death, and her developing love for Whit Fraser, to see how barren her life had been.

For Frank, Dina had been another victory. She was the most beautiful and exciting woman he had ever known. And because of her family background, she provided him with entrance into that Protestant world of socially desirable people and places that all his Irish money could not buy. In his own way, he loved her.

At the thought of losing his wife, Frank began to feel emotions that were new and strange to him.

"I've been away a lot, Dina, I know that. But you know how this business is." His eyes narrowed as they reflected his thoughts. He paused, filling her glass and his with the last of the wine.

"You know how hard I've worked to build the firm." He looked at her with steady gray eyes that suddenly seemed cold; that exposed the man Dina was used to. But the cold quickly passed and his eyes rested on her with a new warmth, even a look of need. Dina could not remember ever seeing Frank vulnerable before.

"It's hard to explain, but things are happening at the firm that could create difficulties for me." He took her hand and held it gently in his.

She searched his face. "Frank, what *is* going on?" The question she had just asked her husband surprised her. One of their rules was that she never asked him about his business and he never volunteered any information. It was a large part of the gulf that separated them.

Frank looked at her for a long time and signaled the wine steward for champagne.

He held the chilled hollow-stemmed glass of Dom Pérignon, watching the bubbles rise, his thoughts turning inward.

"You know, life is strange. You start out a hungry kid and if you know what you want, if you have the guts to fight for it and build, and you're lucky, sometimes you get what you set out for. But when you finally get it, it's elusive. You have to fight just as hard to hold it as you did to build it." He sipped his champagne. Dina took out a cigarette and he lit it for her.

"You know the kind of life I lead."

She waved her cigarette slightly and interrupted. "No, Frank. I don't know what kind of life you lead." She hesitated. "You've never really been very confiding."

His eyes looked at her with an acknowledged sadness. "I know that. It's been one of my greatest mistakes; not letting you in more on things. I simply didn't think you'd be interested in what I'm doing. Most women are bored by it."

Her eyes seemed to come slowly alive in the soft candlelight. "Frank, when a woman is married to a man, whatever experiences they can share, I mean truly share, bring them closer. Everyone wants to feel needed."

"I know, darling. Or at least I am beginning to know."

He drew a long breath. "Dina, there's a business problem which can be handled. I'm going to tell you about
it so that we can make a start at coming together. But it's
not the business that bothers me now as much as it is you.
I want us to be closer. I want us to start all over again and
see if I can't be the kind of husband you want." He paused.
"I've been on my own all my life, Dina. It's hard for me to
share. But I feel that you and I are drifting apart, and I
wanted this night to be the night we make a start at coming together."

He slipped his hand in his pocket and withdrew a slim,
green velvet jewelry box. "Darling, this is for you. In the
candlelit room he watched her eyes grow moist with surprise and excitement. She opened the box and the emerald-
and-diamond bracelet sparkled like a thousand tiny stars.

"Oh, Frank, it's absolutely beautiful." She looked at him
for a long time, her eyes brimming with tears. The atmosphere of the restaurant, the wine, the champagne; Frank's
obvious attempt to look at the holes in their marriage and
to begin to fill them up; her feelings for Whit—she felt so
confused and guilt-ridden.

Frank watched her as her eyes spilled over into tears of
mixed joy and sorrow.

Dina's thoughts went back a thousand years ago, to that
night when her first husband, Peter, asked her to marry
him.

They were at a discreet corner table at Joseph's in
Boston. Peter had been nervous and obviously under the
stress of some internal pressures that made his normal shy-
ness more acute.

She kept looking at his face: the finely formed delicate
bone structure; the pale almost transparent skin of his
temples laced with the tiny blue veins. She could actually
see the physical beating of his pulse. Even in the subdued
lights of the restaurant she could see the little beads of perspiration that glistened at his hairline, where the full dark

hair was neatly combed but refused to stay in place. He was constantly brushing it back from his forehead with thin white, long-fingered hands.

He looked so young, so vulnerable. They both were. She was only twenty-two, Peter just a year older.

With trembling hands he reached into his pocket and withdrew a black velvet jewel box. He placed it before her.

"It belongs to my mother." His voice was so low she could hardly hear him speak. "It's a very old family ring, darling." He hesitated, not looking at her, his eyes focused on the table.

"Will you wear it?"

She could hardly hear him. She could only listen to the dark foreboding of her own instincts. He was rich, kind, in love with her. She thought of her father, and of the terrible pressures the economics of his life was forcing upon him; upon them all. Peter would help. She would marry him, bind the promise with this family diamond she was about to slip on her finger. Love would have to wait.

She shook the thoughts from the past out of her mind and wiped her eyes with a handkerchief.

"Tell me what's going on, Frank." She slipped the bracelet on her wrist. The room was beginning to spin slightly from the champagne. Her skin and hair glowed in the light of the half-burned candles. The room seemed to become soft shadows. She heard the blur of voices. The passing of waiters and exiting diners as if in a dream. She saw only Frank's face. The thatched gray hair. The gray eyes that searched hers for an attempt at a new understanding.

As she looked at Frank, watching him light a cigar, she felt his authority, his quiet masculinity. The style the old hunter had acquired on his arduous climb from the streets of New York had always impressed her. She felt herself sexually stimulated by her husband as she watched him, saw his own eyes far away.

"Dina, when I go to Boston, I'm taking Dean with me."

Frank looked at his wife closely. He had suspected that Dina and Dean had been more than just casual friends. "I want Dean with me so that I can watch him. I don't know what he's going to try to do, but I'm an old war-horse, darling, and my instincts tell me he's up to no good."

"Frank, please tell me what's going on. Just once let me have a piece of your life so that I can feel a part of some-thing, of someone."

Frank looked at his wife for a long time. Her head was bent low, her gaze averted. The sadness in her face reached him and he began to speak.

He told her the story of his involvement in Computer, but Frank omitted, even now, the sale of his own stock through Charlie Fox. There was a part of Frank, trained in the jungle of New York, that trusted no one.

When they left Valjean's and were home in bed, they made love in a way Frank had never made love to Dina before. It was passionate, fulfilling lovemaking. And then Frank Sullivan, in the darkness of that March night, said it; for the first time in his life, he said it. His voice husky, broken: "*I need you. I need you, Dina.* I'm so goddamned alone."

The short flight to Boston in the Sabre Liner left the three passengers quiet and introspective. There was little conversation. Each seemed preoccupied with his own thoughts.

Frank's mind was focused on his wife and last night. For the first time in his life Frank felt he might know what loving a woman was all about. He knew that Dina felt the change in him. He remembered her in his arms and was determined to win her back. By Christ, he wasn't going to lose Dina. Not to Whit or to anyone else.

As the Connecticut shore slipped beneath them Dean's

thoughts were centered on the meeting and on Frank. Over and over in Dean's mind revolved the question of why Frank had released Bob Friedman's report on Computer so soon after Elliot's death without consulting the other directing partners.

Dean knew that if he could dig deeply enough into the reasons behind Frank's action he might uncover circumstances that would make Frank vulnerable. It was this vulnerability that Dean sought to exploit; hopefully to explode.

Perhaps the time had come, Dean mused, to dethrone King Sullivan. A slow sardonic smile worked its way across Dean's face.

Bob Friedman had never been in the Sabre Liner before. The luxury of the aircraft, its ability to compress time and distance, thrilled him. As the city of Boston came into view, Bob could feel the jet slow down and rapidly lose altitude as it banked sharply left toward Logan. They were swinging wide over Massachusetts Bay for an approach to runway 33L. Bob watched as the jet flew low past the sprit of peninsula that is Nantasket; over the flat polluted islands that are washed by the brine of Boston Harbor, and finally the black asphalt runway ahead and the scrunch of the jet's tires as the plane landed. Bob Friedman thought that this was a hell of a way to live. He was excited about being on the inside of a real crisis, especially when his own security wasn't threatened and he could be an observer.

As the jet taxied over to the general aviation area, the phone in Frank's New York apartment rang. The butler answered and a gruff voice asked for Frank Sullivan.

"You tell him when he gets back to make damn sure he calls me. Angi Vittorio. And tell him that his old friend Charlie Fox is in the hospital, and he don't look like he's gonna make it." The butler heard the click of the receiver as Mr. Vittorio hung up. Perplexed, he wrote the message

and left it on the hall table where he always left Mr.
Sullivan's calls.

The limousine that Bennett Alden had waiting for Frank
and his party now left the airport and drove leisurely past
the depressing areas of Revere and Lynn; headed for Salem,
then Beverly and Beverly Farms, then Prides Crossing.

Frank knew that Beverly Farms was a crusty preserve
for some of Boston's oldest families. Beverly Farms, and
Prides Crossing in particular, clung to great dark rambling
houses that faced the Atlantic with Yankee stoicism; grim
relics of an old life-style that was still followed by the
Bennett Aldens of Boston. Frank wryly shook his head as
the car swung up the curved drive to the door of the great
dark house painted a weathered red with dark-brown trim.
The house looked cold and forbidding, but then so did
Bennett Alden.

Bennett greeted them at the door dressed in a vintage
gray tweed suit. His lean figure and thin face seemed to
match the house. Bennett was the product of a New England family that had settled in Massachusetts when Maine
was still part of the Bay Colony.

The two adjectives to describe Bennett Alden were
"spare" and "reserved." Behind rimless glasses, his eyes
were the color of the sea, which Frank had glimpsed as the
car turned up the drive. Bennett's hair had darkened and
thinned with the passing years. But it was easy to see in
Bennett a tall blond young Bostonian of thirty years ago
who was, by family connection and background and by his
own cool capacity, destined to fulfill his role as the chief
executive officer of one of Boston's largest banks, one in
which the Aldens owned the largest block of stock.

Bennett's manner was cautious but courteous, his gaze
quietly appraising, his laugh forced and thin. He was a
shy man; a loner; a man of narrow views and deep prej-
udices. You didn't greet Bennett with a slap on the back,

not even if you had been his classmate at Groton. He seemed a man incapable of joy.

He escorted Frank and his party through a dark mahogany hallway into a large dining room whose wide-paned windows faced the sea. Frank noticed several portraits which he assumed were of the Alden family hanging from the walls, seeming to be looking with perpetual criticism at the long dining room table that was set for luncheon.

Frank, Dean, and Bob Friedman followed Bennett into the living room which gave a sweeping view of rolling lawns and great ancient trees, whose bare branches Frank could imagine providing cooling shade in summer when those same trees were covered with thick green leaves.

The lawn, fawn-colored in March, reached down to a crescent-shaped granite-bound beach whose sea-sprayed rocks submitted to the pounding of endless winter storms.

On this day the sea was a cobalt blue, and the horizon was clearly delineated as it met a cloudless sky.

They stood in the living room waiting for Bennett to make the introductions.

Frank hoped that this meeting would end as bright as the panorama of sea and sky, but his intuition told him this might not be.

The room in which Frank was standing was large and rectangular with the severity of the dark paneling modified by the paintings of old sailing vessels and whaling scenes. On top of a large English sideboard was a glass-enclosed model of a fully rigged clipper ship. Several comfortable chairs were placed in a wide semicircle that flanked an oversize sofa. All faced the Atlantic.

The far wall was covered from floor to ceiling with books. Scattered Oriental rugs gave warmth and color to this family room, filled with its whispers of the past; this room caressed by the eastern light reflected from the surface of an endlessly changing sea and sky.

As Frank looked about the room and at Bennett Alden, he remembered that the original Aldens were slave traders, and Frank guessed that a lot of that ruthlessness still flooded the blood of their Yankee host.

Frank surveyed the room. He saw several men he knew, and some he had never met before.

Bennett made the introductions in a broad Back Bay accent. "Frank. Dean." Bennett turned toward Bob Friedman. "And I believe this is Mr. Friedman." Bennett paused. "Frank, I think you have met Dr. Eisenstadt, Dr. Karkov, Mr. Courtney. This is Mr. LeDune of Fuller, Cross."

"Mr. Ellsworth Hatcher, of our bank. Mr. Nagahama of Nagahama Securities, and Mr. Grant Weir of Lone Star Investments. Dr. Paul Nichols of the Nichols Institute. Dr. Nichols was kind enough to come here from the West Coast for this meeting. I'm very appreciative."

Bennett turned toward Frank. "Gentlemen, Mr. Frank Sullivan, his partner Mr. Dean Faulkner, and Mr. Robert Friedman."

Bennett smiled. "Well, gentlemen, I believe we are all here. I'm sorry that Mr. Tittle will be unable to attend, but he is indisposed."

Frank noticed that each man held a drink. Bennett turned to Frank's group. "What is your pleasure? I've planned a light lunch and then we can get down to business."

A uniformed butler waited silently at the entrance of the room.

"Frank?"

"I'll have a scotch and water."

"Dean?"

"Make that two."

"Mr. Friedman?"

"I'd like a dry sherry, if you please."

"Fine. Foster, will you see to these gentlemen."

Bennett Alden turned to the other men in the room. "If I may suggest, why don't we all go into the dining room. I have a New England luncheon for our New York friends." Bennett smiled. "Let's get something to eat and then we can spend as long as we like."

Frank said little as they ate. The light from the sea caught the faces of the men who had all come together to talk about the troubles of Computer Ecolog. But the ramifications of this relatively modest investment were not the real reasons they had come together. A lot more was at stake than a small company like Computer Ecolog.

The New England clam chowder was excellent. The cold lobster salad was one of Frank's favorites. He carefully but unobtrusively regarded the men seated at Bennett's table.

Eisenstadt was merry, chirping away in polite conversation. Karkov remained silent and brooding. He hadn't uttered a word throughout the entire meal. Hatcher was the senior trust officer at Bennett's bank and Frank put him down as one of the hired hands. Skillful in his own cautious area, but a yes man for Alden. Frank was sure of that.

Fletcher Courtney was cool and controlled. Frank had met Fletcher several times and he always felt a ribbon of strength beneath that quiet exterior. In a way, Fletcher Courtney reminded Frank of his own partner, Dean. But where Dean was more obviously aggressive, the small ferret with the instinct for the jugular, Courtney was harder to read. Frank bet that he could be equally calculating and perhaps just as dangerous as his partner.

The two that interested Frank most were Nagahama and Grant Weir. Nagahama until five years ago was known only as a bright analyst of highly volatile securities. With the help of a well-known investment banking firm, he had formed a highly specialized hedge fund that bought what is known as restricted stock—stocks of companies which could not be sold until their shares were registered with the SEC. Since the risk element was so high, Nagahama sold his shares only to very wealthy indi-

viduals who stood to gain in one of two ways. If Nagahama and his group guessed right, there would be very
significant long-term capital gains for his investors. If he
guessed wrong, there would be equally significant tax
losses that his investors could wash against gains they
might have in other investments. But Nagahama wasn't
interested in losses. He had made his reputation in picking winners, and right now Computer looked like anything but a winner. Nagahama was Japanese. He was tall
for a Japanese with very light skin, and a dark full head
of hair combed straight back. His black eyes darted every-
where and he radiated an intense nervous energy that was
electric. He ate quietly; said little. Frank guessed that he
was very unhappy with Computer, and with Bennett Alden, who had led him into the stock.

Grant Weir talked to Fletcher Courtney, seated on his
right. Weir was the head of a large investor group composed of Texas oil money and West Coast real estate interests. Lone Star represented a very large pool of private
capital with wide national and international connections.

Grant Weir, president of Lone Star, was only forty-three
years old. He was of medium height, solid; inclined to
put on weight. He had strong, square features; full chest-
nut-colored hair, and very penetrating green-gray eyes.
His manner was Texas country boy. Frank knew him by
reputation to be a flint-hard negotiator who had cleaned
out many a company of dead-wood executives and sleep-
walking directors.

Frank smiled inwardly at the whole group. What a
collection of sophisticated pirates these were—including
himself. How fitting it was to have assembled in this ancestral home of Yankee slave traders men who were united
mainly by greed, except for Eisenstadt and Karkov.

They retired to the living room, where Foster passed
around a humidor of cigars. Soon the blue smoke was a
haze spinning languidly.

"Well, gentlemen, let's make a start, shall we?" It was

Bennett. He stood near the sideboard facing them, with the light from the windows on his face.

"I've asked you all here because we have a mutual problem. All of us are invested in Dr. Karkov's company." Bennett made a thin smile in Karkov's direction. "I'm sure we are all understandably concerned about what has happened to the price of Computer's stock."

"That's the understatement of the year," Grant Weir drawled sarcastically.

"Yes, I quite agree." Bennett picked up smoothly. His eyes appraised Weir carefully. "If the rest of you gentlemen think it logical, I propose that we consult the three distinguished scientists here concerning their opinions about Computer: Dr. Nichols and Dr. Eisenstadt, whose views I believe differ about Computer's technology, and Dr. Karkov, to ascertain the progress his company is making so that at least we can come to a reasonable conclusion whether or not this fellow Livermore has any substance to his very negative comments concerning Computer. Then I propose that we can discuss the financial condition of the company. This is just a suggested agenda. If any of you gentlemen have other suggestions I'd be pleased to hear them."

"No, that's fine. Let's get going on this thing, Bennett. I have a feeling it's going to be a long day." It was Nagahama. Frank watched him puff nervously on a cigarette.

"Well, then, I propose that we start with Dr. Nichols, who has come the longest way to attend this meeting. I believe, Doctor, that in a sense you are speaking for the Tittle group as you acted as a co-technical adviser for them."

Paul Nichols turned in his chair and smiled nervously. His rounded shoulders, quick stammering speech, and thick glasses made him seem halting and vulnerable.

Fletcher and Frank watched him closely.

"Gentlemen, I have been asked to give my opinion many times concerning this company." Nichols was stammering out his sentences. "I must say that presently I am not giving my opinion as representing ah—Mr. ah—Tittle's firm. My opinions are my—ah—my own."

Frank could sense everyone in the room focusing on Nichols, who stammered out his conviction that he thought Karkov was on the right track; that the difficulties Computer was experiencing were not extraordinary in research and development companies.

"I believe that's what you told us before, Dr. Nichols." Grant Weir's voice carried its drawled Southwestern accent, but there was a distinct edge of annoyance in Grant's tone.

"If Ah remember, Dr. Nichols, when Mr. Nagahama and Ah were with Mr. Alden in early February at Tittle's office, yew were there as was Dr. Eisenstadt. Yew gave us the same reassurances then—"

"So I did. And—I—I haven't changed my mind. I believe Dr. Karkov is on the right track—and I think he will succeed in building—a—not only a cheap relatively high capacity computer, using impregnated chips with IC circuitry, but I—I believe his pollution-monitoring devices coupled to such a computer would be a real contribution to help clean up our environment."

Frank watched Grant Weir get up from his chair and walk slowly toward the windows. The surface of the sea had suddenly turned gray as the sun briefly hid behind a cloud.

"You realize, Dr. Nichols, that Dr. Eisenstadt here doesn't share yo' views. As Ah understand it, he feels that the impregnated-chip technology is not fah enough advanced." Grant was talking to Nichols with his back to the scientist, an unlit cigar held between his fingers. Grant kept looking out toward the sea.

"Doctor, how is yo' Institute progressin'?" The question was asked in such an offhand way that almost everyone in the room missed its implication.

Frank had been observing Grant Weir like a hawk. He

watched Nichols' face closely, saw the surprised look behind the thick glasses and listened to the stuttered nervous
reply.

"Why, I—ah—ah—I appreciate your interest, Mr. Weir.
The Institute is coming along just fine, thank you."

Grant still remained with his back toward the room.
His tone betrayed little except to Frank, who realized
that this compact aggressive Texan was going to be the
hammer and anvil of this little get-together.

"Ah'd like to talk to yew privately about the Institute,
Dr. Nichols, befo' we leave here today."

Grant turned slowly in the direction of Fletcher Courtney and looked at him for what seemed a very long time.

Frank saw Dean lean forward with hunched intensity.
The others in the room seemed puzzled and confused.

Bennett, too, was surprised at the drift of the conversation and tried to steer the discussion back to the scientists and their appraisal of Computer's technology.

"Dr. Eisenstadt. Could you express an opinion on Computer?"

The diminutive physicist from MIT smiled at the men
whose attentions were now focused on him. Eisenstadt's
natural disposition was congenial, almost merry. He
viewed this gathering of money and power as a group
whose values were inconsequential compared to the problems and mysteries that he constantly probed as a research
physicist. His manner and speech were not condescending,
but rather expressed general amusement. Like Karkov, who
he knew hated him, he was the only other individual in
the room not motivated by money. This gave him a de-
tachment and independence that the others could not
understand but only envy.

Eisenstadt rose from his chair and began to pace about,
his hands folded behind his back as if he were lecturing
a class.

"Gentlemen. My views do not differ as much from Dr.
Nichols' as you may believe. It is rather in the *timing* of

the development of the impregnated IC technology where perhaps we disagree." Eisenstadt continued to pace back and forth. Occasionally he would stop to look out at the seascape that was becoming more bleak as low-building clouds began to hide the rays of the March sun.

"As many of you gentlemen are aware, a computer is simply a device which elicits a positive or negative response to a stimulus. That stimulus can be an electrical current, a laser, a liquid crystal, and so on. Without complicating things for you, you can think of a computer as a yes/no mechanism. Switches, if you like, when stimulated, respond either positively or negatively. In effect, gentlemen, a computer, for all its sophistication, can only say yes or no.

"Now, when you design a very simple computer, you have to ask yourself what functions you want it to perform. The more you demand from the device, the more complex must be its components, its circuitry—the ability to get *messages* as quickly as possible to your yes/no response mechanisms. The ability to store and receive information at great speed and so on. In other words, the more intelligent you want your computer to be, the more complex must be its design. What Dr. Karkov is valiantly trying to accomplish, and in my opinion in time he and others will accomplish, is to build a complex computer, which means a device whose functional applications are quite varied, using a technology that reproduces a greater number of circuits in a smaller and smaller space. And, if you will, performs more functions in a far less costly device.

"There are those who think the laser approach is an answer to increased efficiency at lower cost. Obviously, Dr. Karkov thinks the impregnated chip is the route to the solution of such problems. Where we disagree is that I think that impregnated IC technology is not sufficiently advanced at this point in time. Later, surely, but not now."

"What do you mean by later?" Nagahama turned toward Eisenstadt; his black eyes and the continual clasping and unclasping of his hands reflected his nervousness.

Eisenstadt didn't hesitate. "Two years at least."

There was a general shuffling of chairs in the room.

"That's a lot of bull." It was Karkov rising to his feet, face red with anger.

Fletcher Courtney shot him a warning glance but Karkov brushed it aside.

The two scientists stood facing each other at opposite ends of the room like David and Goliath.

"I said that was bull and that's just what I meant. Dr. Eisenstadt is a research physicist. He doesn't build products. He's the same kind of fellow who told Henry Ford he couldn't build a car or Edison that he couldn't get a bulb to light by emptying most of the air out of it and passing an electrical current through a partial vacuum."

Everyone in the room focused on Karkov.

Frank looked at this great Russian bear of a man who exuded an almost primitive vitality.

"I've got Computer Ecologs right now with monitoring sensors in the Charles, the Hudson, and the Potomac Rivers that have run for a hundred and twenty days, performing every function asked of them, with zero down time. How many office copiers do you think can do that?"

Eisenstadt was not intimidated. "Dr. Karkov, I am not denying that is certainly an achievement of the first order, and you are right, perfectly right, when you say that we theoreticians don't have to build products." He chuckled. "But I hope you agree that we do contribute something to those of you who do." Eisenstadt waved his hand. "But that is not my case, Doctor. I am simply trying to point out that a few successful prototypes do not necessarily mean you are in a position to build production runs of Computer Ecologs. These men here are financial men. All investors in your company, I believe. What they are concerned with, if I understand them correctly, is your ability to deliver in production quantities Computer Ecologs that can be sold or leased, installed and serviced, and that will contribute solidly to your company's earnings."

Grant Weir drawled out a soft reply. "Ah'll drink to that, Doctor."

Eisenstadt continued. "All I am saying is that the very good work your company has done to date, Dr. Karkov, is not yet at the level of dependable production. I would classify Computer Ecolog as a very promising research and development project."

"I don't give a damn what you'd classify my company as, Dr. Eisenstadt. I said that I would have a minimum of one thousand Computer Ecologs on the market within twenty-four months and I'll have them."

"Then you must be closer to solving the chip problems than I thought, Dr. Karkov." Eisenstadt had not lost his temper nor his elfin quality, but his geniality had been reduced by the outbursts from Karkov.

"I'm a hell of a lot closer to doing a lot of things than you think-tank pussycats know anything about."

Eisenstadt bowed low and turned a charming smile toward everyone in the room.

"Dr. Karkov, I congratulate you. I have been called everything in my day but a 'think-tank pussycat'! I must say that's marvelous."

Eisenstadt's charm broke the ice. There was a scattering of laughter. Bennett Alden used the opportunity to move the conversation away from Karkov, where he knew storm clouds were roiling.

"Dr. Nichols. I take it your position is closer to Dr. Karkov's?"

Paul Nichols twisted around in his chair to face the group, found the position uncomfortable, and rose to stand.

Frank observed Nichols intently, and as he did so he occasionally glanced at Dean, whose face was drawn in concentration.

Nichols' rounded shoulders and thick glasses gave him the unfortunate appearance of a mole seeking a hole he could run to. His stammered speech only reinforced this impression.

"Gentlemen—really—ah—I think I have made my ah—position quite clear . . ." Nichols' eyes stayed away from Fletcher Courtney and Grant Weir. "Ah—I have ex—ah—amined Dr. Karkov's tech—ah—nology at length. An—I believe he can do what he says ah—he can. The time frame Dr. Kar—ah Karkov has laid out for ah—himself may—ah vary a bit—there is ah—nothing extraordinary about this in ah—such projects. However—ah I do not sh-sh-share Dr. Eisenstadt's views that Comp-Computer Ecolog is a prototype company. I—ah—feel that Dr. Karkov is far beyond the prototype phase—"

Bennett interrupted. "Doctor—essentially what you're saying is that your views have not changed materially since you first discussed your analysis of the company with Mr. Weir and Mr. Nagahama, when we met in Tittle's office about a month ago. Is that correct, sir?"

"That is co-correct, Mr. Alden."

Fletcher Courtney suppressed the smile of satisfaction that he felt at Nichols' testimony. He had covered that base well, he thought.

"Well, gentlemen, it seems we have at least a consistency of technical opinion here. Two for, and one still against, if I may put it that way, toward the progress of Dr. Karkov's company. Does anyone wish to question these scientists any further?"

Grant Weir spoke in a quiet controlled drawl.

"Ah think not, Bennett. Fo' the moment, at least. However, Ah'd like to suggest that we discuss the financials of this company, and then Ah would like to talk privately with Dr. Nichols."

"Dr. Nichols, is that agreeable with you?"

"It is."

"Then I suggest we get to the company's financials, as

Mr. Weir has suggested. Mr. Courtney, would you like to comment on this?"

Fletcher Courtney's flat-bellied figure rose. His face was as usual inscrutable. His eyes fixed steadily upon Alden.

"Gentlemen, before I begin to go into the details of Computer's balance sheet and earnings outlook I believe we had better listen to Mr. LeDune. Mr. LeDune is a partner from Fuller, Cross, Computer's accounting firm. I must say he has presented us all with a problem that was made known to me only two days ago. Steve, will you take over?"

Steve LeDune was a senior partner in the major accounting firm of Fuller, Cross. As such his job was to smooth over the rough spots in the firm's interaction with its major clients.

Accountants like LeDune felt themselves caught in the squeeze between the demands of their profession, the governmental regulatory agencies, and their major clients, whose interest in having certain accounting interpretations made in their company's favor could mean the difference between profit and loss, a high-flying stock or a loser.

It was just such a predicament that Steve LeDune knew he was in this March afternoon. His firm was not only the accountants for Computer Ecolog but, far more important to Fuller, Cross, they were the accountants for Bennett's bank. In addition, LeDune knew that Frank Sullivan, Grant Weir, and Nagahama between them controlled scores of clients audited by his firm. The total billings they controlled ran into millions of dollars.

Since what he was about to tell these men would certainly have a very negative effect on Computer's stock, he was hardly pleased to stand before them and give them the bad news. But that's what Fuller, Cross paid Steve LeDune one hundred and seventy-five thousand dollars a year to do.

Steve's manner was a peculiar mixture of authority and

preciseness, a certain programmed geniality that seemed effective enough but somewhat hollow. When he laughed it was as if someone had punched a button which activated his mirth mechanism. Yet those who knew Steve respected him for the backbone he exhibited when his firm's arm was being twisted. It would be severely wrenched this afternoon.

Steve took off his glasses and wiped them carefully. Everyone was now focused on this thin rather short accountant with the pale face, the slender white fingers and the dark hair that had not receded. Steve's hairline looked very much the way it did in college some twenty years ago. His voice had no trace of a regional accent, although he had spent a good part of his life in the Midwest.

"I know, gentlemen, that I am about to make myself very unpopular." Steve tucked the handkerchief back in his breast pocket. "But my firm has taken a position on Computer's accounting practices, and I'm afraid we are going to ask them to charge against earnings, over a specified time period, the amount on their balance sheet that has been capitalized for research and development."

Grant Weir rose slowly from his chair and walked toward the windows facing the sea. The gray sky had turned darker in the rapidly ending afternoon. Soon night would be upon this gloomy house. Grant absentmindedly watched a pair of gulls fighting over a piece of garbage that the sea had swept upon Bennett's rocks.

Grant's voice was very level. He never turned to face LeDune. The Texas accent seemed out of place in this Yankee house with its ancestral taproot so deeply bedded in New England.

"Steve, if Ah hear yew right, an' Ah hope Ah don't, yew want Computer to write off nearly ten million in R an' D?"

"That's correct."

"Ah was afraid so." Grant's back was still toward the room. He seemed held by the sea. But Frank, who knew

Grant better than most, understood how calculating this Texan could be. Frank sensed that Grant's technique in keeping his back to everyone was essentially theatrical. It was his way of commanding attention.

"Ah am assumin' that yew are telling us yew want this little ole company to write off ten million in R an' D at one crack?"

"Not necessarily."

Grant still faced the sea.

"Yew of course realize that even if these R an' D costs were amortized over ten years it would wipe out the company's earnings and create one hell of a loss."

"We are aware of that, Grant. We certainly are not pleased by it."

Karkov jumped to the middle of the room like a brawling bear. He loomed over Steve LeDune like some murderous giant. Fletcher Courtney tried to grab him but Karkov threw him aside.

"You son of a bitch. You little prick of an accountant," he screamed. "You'd wreck my company with a lousy ballpoint pen!" Karkov's hands clutched the lapels of LeDune's jacket. He began to shake LeDune so that the man's head rolled back and forth. The others watched speechless. They were simply struck dumb by the totally irrational behavior of this berserk scientist.

It was Grant Weir who made the move, the move learned in the wildcat oil fields of Texas. In three quick strides Grant had come upon Karkov from behind. He jammed his knee in Karkov's back so that you could hear the vertebrae snap. At the same time he pulled back the giant head in one sweeping motion of his right forearm. Karkov's hands dropped from LeDune and Grant pivoted the great body over his right hip, sending Karkov crashing to the floor. He gasped for air as he lay sprawled on his back.

The spell broken, several of them ran to LeDune to see if he was all right. The others crowded around Karkov.

Grant bent over the scientist and loosened his tie. "Ah'm terribly sorry, Doctor," he drawled, "but Ah'm afraid we couldn't have you shakin' up our ole friend Steve here."

Grant's attempt to lighten the situation helped a little, but the shock of the physical violence had shattered them. These men were not used to physical violence. Their methods were far more subtle, but equally effective.

Eisenstadt was dumbfounded. The little man stood horrified with his hand over his mouth. Dean was incredulous, especially at the reaction of Frank, who seemed completely unruffled but whose eyes covered everyone in the room.

Bennett Alden looked as if he had just been told the bank had failed. He was as white as the belly of a flounder, dumbstruck that this could have happened in his home.

Fletcher Courtney looked at the prostrate form of the gasping Karkov with a malice that was lethal. His lips moved to form the silent obscenities of hatred that his self-control kept him from unleashing upon Karkov.

It was Grant Weir whose reaction was the most surprising. Grant's face held just the trace of a grin through it all—the same grin that old Jesse Hudson saw on the face of the short compactly built boy with the light gray-green eyes from the First Commerce Bank in Dallas when he first invited Grant up to the main house to look him over. That was fifteen years ago.

Jesse owned more of nearly everything than any other man in Texas and Jesse was a widower with no children. Jesse had told Claymore French (Jesse held the control block of stock in the bank) to keep his eye out for a bright, tough, hungry kid who could be put into an investment company Jesse was putting together.

Jesse had a smart bunch of New York lawyers salt a hell of a lot of money away in Swiss banks. Jesse ran that money through several European investment companies he controlled. Those investment companies not only bought cheaply into companies in Europe, but also in the United States. Perfectly legal, but with certain distinct tax advantages.

Jesse wanted to have fun "buildin' and tradin'," as he called it. But he also wanted someone he could trust. Someone like he was forty years ago. Someone who could be the son he never had.

One hot-as-hell August afternoon Claymore French sent up a young fellow of twenty-five named Grant Weir.

Grant remembered. The dust was so thick on the road coming up to the main house that his shoes looked like he had been wrestlin' calves.

Jesse's place had huge ceilings in great spacious rooms. The heat that tore at you when you stepped outside seemed to spare you when you were sitting sipping a bourbon on the rocks under the slowly revolving ceiling fans.

Grant remembered how Jesse kept looking at him all through the afternoon with those shining cold blue eyes, eyes that seemed like the ice in the glass Grant was holding.

Jesse knew more about Grant than Grant did. Jesse had French give him a detailed background on the boy. Then Jesse had his own men dig into the life of the twenty-five-year-old Texan who had worked his way through the University of Texas as a roughneck in the summer, waiting on tables and doing odd jobs.

Grant had majored in economics at the university and received a scholarship to the Wharton School of Finance in Philadelphia. He had worked like someone driven. He was silent and independent. He stayed pretty much to himself. But anyone who ever spent five minutes with Grant Weir realized that here was a man who knew where he wanted to go and what it took to get there. The most impressive characteristic of Grant's was a feeling of brooding aggression which seemed to flood from him.

Jesse Hudson knew all this. Jesse had picked men all his life. It was his gift. It was one of the cornerstones of his success.

Grant slowly got to his feet after loosening Karkov's tie. He remembered that day with Jesse Hudson as if it were yesterday. And the old man's parting shot.

"Bring your things up here to the house tuhmarrah. I'm gonna work your ass off, boy. Day an' night.

"On your own time, which is gonna be damned little, you can git laid or git drunk, but no marryin'. Mah business is too demandin' for a woman. Git married, son, an' you kin work fo' someone else. Deal?" Jesse held out his old withered right hand.

Grant Weir grinned that same grin that was on his face right now. He shook the old man's hand carefully.

"Deal," he said.

The sky was dark now and the lights that were turned on through the house cast shadows on the lawn. The occasional cry of a gull, the rising sound of the wind, and the crash of the sea on the rocks told Bennett that the tide was in.

The encounter between Karkov and LeDune had spread a somber mood over the group.

Bennett rang for Foster, who was instructed to pass brandies all around. That ribbon of hard New England resolve had returned to Bennett. He was determined to salvage the purpose of this meeting, to come away from it with a course of action. He was not about to let any ridiculous theatrics interfere with his plans.

Bennett tapped the edge of a glass several times to get the group's attention.

"Gentlemen. I feel we should get on with the purpose of this meeting." Bennett made no mention of Karkov, who was still wincing from the pain of several pulled muscles in his back, but was otherwise unharmed. Grant Weir sat quietly, his face deep in concentration. Steve Le-

Dune, who had excused himself, returned several minutes later, his dark hair neatly combed, his manner composed and controlled. A somewhat forced smile came on and off at irregular intervals.

"Gentlemen." Bennett paused. "I hardly need remind any of you that it would be very embarrassing for me personally, and not in the interest of any of us, to have this little episode get out." Bennett forced a thin smile that concealed the hostility this Brahmin felt toward Karkov and Grant.

Bennett would have disliked Grant simply because he was from Texas. Bennett could barely tolerate Philadelphians, and then only a few families from the Main Line. New Yorkers were out. As for Texans, the thought made him wince.

Bennett continued. "Steve was about to tell us of his firm's decision to ask Computer to write off their R and D, before we were"—Bennett paused—"interrupted. I assume that this has little interest to our scientific friends. To save them the boredom I know they would feel during Steve's financial explanations, I propose they adjourn to my study while we discuss this matter further." Bennett rang for Foster, who silently appeared.

"Foster, would you be good enough to escort these gentlemen to my study. See to it that they have everything they require." Bennett turned to Karkov. "Doctor, I would appreciate your joining Dr. Eisenstadt and Dr. Nichols. Mr. Courtney well represents your interests. We are all aware of that." The thrust went over Karkov's head but it was not missed by Fletcher Courtney. The Missourian caught the full implication of Bennett's remark. Fletcher made a mock bow toward Bennett, who was far less than amused. Karkov scowled at Bennett, but the thought of listening to any more of this accounting bullshit was more than he could stand. He followed the two physicists and Foster out of the room.

Frank Sullivan looked at Bennett with a long appraising glance. This old-school-tie boy had smoothly removed from the room three men who might just not know how to keep their mouths shut. Three men who didn't speak the language of money and power. Three men who were not bound by the same lust, the game that obsessed the rest of them. Adroitly, with great finesse, Bennett had helped to clear the board. The men who remained understood each other. The room suddenly relaxed. Grant Weir loosened his tie. Dean got up to pour himself another drink.

Frank looked at Steve LeDune. His eyes were hard like the rocks outside that kept resisting a crashing surf.

"Now what is this all about, Steve?" Frank shot an angry glance at Bob Friedman. "Did you have any idea of this, Bob?"

"No, sir, I did not." Through the whole violent affair with Grant and Karkov, Friedman felt as if he were watching a rather bad movie. Do men of wealth and power really behave like this? Does a senior officer of one of the largest pools of capital in the Southwest toss one of the country's leading inventor-scientists flat on his ass? Does that same scientist manhandle a senior partner of one of the largest accounting firms in the country? This just couldn't be happening. The whole thing was absurd.

It was Dean who interrupted Frank.

"Bob, it seems strange to me that as our senior analyst covering Computer you wouldn't at least be aware of the possibility of a major accounting change for the company. Especially with a company of their size logging ten million in research and development costs." Dean's eyes bore in on Friedman.

"Dean, an accounting change was never mentioned as a possibility by Mr. Courtney. Though I did not check with Fuller, I doubt if they would have been in a position to tell me anything at the time I was writing my report on Computer."

"That's right, Dean." It was Steve LeDune. He was

sitting in a straight-backed uncomfortable chair against the wall, quietly smoking a cigarette.

"Mr. Friedman is correct, Dean. Our decision on Computer wasn't reached until late last week."

Frank turned to Steve. "I would like some explanation as to why your firm would take such action. You know what it will do to the company."

Frank knew damn well why Fuller, Cross and Company had decided to blow the whistle on Computer. Fletcher Courtney had been capitalizing all of the research and development costs of the Computer Ecologs, which meant he had been listing these costs, which now amounted to over ten million dollars, as assets. What he should have been doing was expensing such costs against earnings as they were accrued. But that would have wiped out Computer's earnings and would have killed the price of the stock. What was happening now was that Computer's accounting firm would not permit this practice to continue and were ready to tell Computer that they would not give their letter of opinion without qualification if Computer did not reform its accounting practices. The effect of a qualified opinion for a company can be severe.

"Come on, Steve," Frank said, "where do we stand?"

Steve LeDune almost preferred the physical attack of Karkov to what he knew they were now going to do to him. But Steve had been through this many times before, and he was known for his agility and his spunk in these crunch situations.

"Frank, we haven't come to any hard and fast decision yet concerning Computer, but we have decided that they cannot continue their present accounting practice."

Alert attention stirred through the room. Steve was giving them some leeway, some hope. Or was he?

Frank pressed on. "Steve, I would like to know if your firm has reached a policy decision on Computer. Let's tick them off. You could decide to let their R and D stay on their balance sheet as an asset, which you are obviously not prepared to do. You could ask them to take a complete write-down, which I am sure you would consider ill advised." Steve smoked quietly as Frank talked. "Or you could ask Computer to write off their R and D over a period of time, which is what I would guess your partners have decided to do." Frank spoke very quietly. A clock in the next room struck the time in ship's bells. "I would like to know over what time period you want Computer to write off these costs."

There was a long silence. Steve stuffed his cigarette into an ashtray. "All of it in the next calendar year," he said. "And any new R and D to be expensed in the year it occurs."

It was Grant who replied first. "Do Ah hear yew right? Yew want Computer to write off over ten million dollars against earnings?" Steve didn't reply. "Do you realize what that will do to the company?" Steve remained silent.

Bennett broke the ice. "Gentlemen. It's obvious that this meeting is going to take longer than we all had planned. I would like to have this settled before we break up, so I suggest you stay for dinner. We can continue until we have come to some resolution of this problem."

Grant interrupted. "Ah appreciate yo' hospitality, Bennett, but before we go, Ah want to have some time with Dr. Nichols. Ah have some particular things Ah wish to go over with him."

Bennett smiled his chill smile. "Fine. I'll tell Mrs. Alden to have the cook prepare dinner. I don't wish to isolate the others, but I think perhaps we should continue our financial discussions without them."

There was a general nodding of agreement.

"Good. I'll see to dinner." Bennett walked from the room into a dark hallway up the carpeted steps to Mrs. Alden's sitting room.

* * *

They had eaten dinner, the men of money and power.

In a separate room they too had eaten and drunk of fine wines, the men of intellect who were without power.

Anyone looking for an honest man in that house on that windblown night might be hard pressed to find one. Only Eisenstadt, the merry little physicist who had regained his warmth and mirth, might qualify.

In that house men separated by interest and suspicion were men warring with other men. Their weapons were words, veiled threats, hidden promises. If these men were crossed, they could be as dangerous as bush adders. There was nothing make-believe about the war they engaged in. Not if you felt as they did about money.

The evening wore on. They pressed harder at Steve LeDune.

Bob Friedman was asked by Frank to join the scientists. The group now was pared down to the men who really had power. The two in that room who had the most were the roughneck from the oil fields of Texas, and the Brahmin from the playing fields of Groton and Harvard.

They were back in the great living room that now looked out upon a night-blackened sea. Grant Weir had removed his jacket and opened his tie. The others, more formal, stood or seated themselves in attitudes of belligerent impatience. Frank knew that the play had to come first from either Grant or Bennett. Then he could follow. Dean, too, knew how the game had to run. He remained silent while Grant did most of the talking.

In the hierarchy represented in that room, Fletcher Courtney was not powerless, but almost. What power Fletcher had lay in his subterfuge. They didn't know what he might do to them, these circling wolves. But they knew enough to want to prevent any unexpected surprises. With these men "surprise" was one of the most dreaded words in their vocabularies. Surprises were synonymous with problems. In their lives, problems were not in short supply.

Grant paced back and forth across the room, and finally turned to LeDune. "Steve, step out in the hall with me, will yuh. Ah want to talk to yuh privately."

They walked out into the hall and moved toward the far end that was lit by old wall sconces, a polished brass chandelier whose electrified candle holders were hooded in small silken shades that gave additional soft light.

Grant paced restlessly back and forth in front of the implacable accountant. "Ah've got one of my investment companies with a right tidy little stake in Computer. If Ah kin read the signs right, it looks as if that money is goin' to git blown right out of the water. Ah'm used to losin' a little money now an' then. Ah'm a big boy. Ah haven't been workin' for old Jesse all these years without knowin' yew can't win 'em all. But Ah do know that little ole Computer don't mean shit to me compared to mah foreign partners that Ah brought into this deal. We're in some big stuff with those boys, like a four-hundred-million-dollar pipeline deal for one. The way we operate, we don't cotton to people who make dumb mistakes. When Ah say we, Ah mean us and them. They take care of us in Europe and the Middle East and we take care of them here. Now, how the hell do you think we look if we let an accountin' firm fuck up our stake in a little piss-ass company like Computer?"

This is what Steve LeDune had been waiting for: the blows that he knew had to come. Grant was now standing very close to him, the thick almost pudgy figure with the locked-in aggressions hissing out at him like the sounds of a punctured tire.

"Listen, Steve, yew don't know these guys. If mah group had to explain that we couldn't control a lousy accountin' firm, when they expect us to influence the goddamn White House, just how long do you think we'd last overseas?"

"Now, Grant, I'm fully aware of the implications of this problem. But unlike your other investment partners abroad, we aren't so lucky. We live with Uncle Sam looking over our shoulder every day. If we don't do something to moderate the accounting practices of Computer, the SEC or our own Accounting Standards and Practices Board will. We have to do something."

"Ah'm tellin' yew what you've got to do, Steve! Yew've got to keep from cuttin' the balls off this little company. Ah'm not goin' to sit by and see mah foreign partners fucked and us made to look like suckers because some bunch of accountants don't like the way Courtney keeps his books. If we're gonna git fucked, it'll be bad enough if this Karkov nut fucks us. At least Ah can explain him." Grant lowered his voice and turned so that he was nose to nose with LeDune. "But you, Steve boy, Ah can't explain. An' if Ah have to drive your balls right up your asshole so you can spit 'em out, I'll do it."

Steve's whole body shook with rage at the vulgar impudence of this repulsive Texan. But Steve LeDune remained in control.

Frank's voice interrupted. "Is this a private fight or can anyone join in?" Frank and Dean were walking toward Grant and Steve. Their antennae had picked up the sparks from Grant's colorful monologue and they were perfectly tuned to the pressures and anger of Steve LeDune. They had come to press him harder. The pressures on Steve LeDune and the other senior partners of Fuller, Cross had not even begun.

Bennett had wanted to talk to Fletcher privately as well, and had begun speaking to him when he saw Foster come into the room. The implacable face of Bennett's butler was expressionless.

"It's a call for you, sir. Ah, on the private phone."

There was a subtle change in the expression of Bennett's eyes as if for a moment he had suddenly stepped into a pleasant sensual dream. He almost felt the smile begin to spread across his face. But from years of training,

Bennett knew the discipline of hiding one's feelings. It was a very important discipline in a banker. He nodded to Foster, excused himself from Courtney, and walked out of the room.

Bennett noticed LeDune with his tormentors at the other end of the hall. He mounted the stairs on the right which led to the master and guest bedrooms. Since Bennett did not sleep with Mrs. Alden (their rooms were connected by a private hall), he entered his own bedroom and saw a small red light glowing on the locked phone on the night table beside his bed. There were two phones, but the one that was blinking a red flashing light was locked so that only Bennett could use it. A system had been installed in the butler's pantry and in the servants' quarters, so that when this particular phone rang, a red bulb would glow in order that the servants would know that a call for Mr. Alden was on his private line. If he was not at home their instructions were to call the bank and advise him or his secretary that someone had called him on his "red phone."

It was generally accepted by Mrs. Alden and the servants that not only did Bennett have very delicate problems that required the utmost discretion regarding the bank, but it was known that Bennett had very highly placed connections in Washington. It was supposed that when the red light blinked in the butler's pantry that something important and secret was afoot. And it was important and secret, but only to Bennett Alden.

Bennet took out from his pocket the little silver key that hung on a thin chain and unlocked the phone. He sat his tall spare frame on the edge of the bed. On his face there was a look of almost drugged pleasure. His eyes sparkled as if with fever. There was a woman's voice on the other end of the phone. Her tone was friendly, very businesslike, and her conversation very brief.

"Mr. Alden?"

"Yes."

"It's Martha Aldrich."

"Yes, Mrs. Aldrich."

Bennett's eyes were now hypnotically reflecting some inner thoughts that made him appear in a trance.

"I'm planning to go away for a few days, Mr. Alden. Wanted you to know." Her tones and speech were the flat broad intonations of someone who had been born in eastern Massachusetts.

"Wanted to tell you I'd be leavin' Wednesday. 'Spect to be back Saturday night. Hope you'll look after things for me while I'm away. Be much obliged to you as usual."

There was a long pause before Bennett answered.

"I'd be delighted, Mrs. Aldrich, delighted."

"Much obliged."

The receiver clicked. The red light went off. Bennett Alden sat on the bed for a few moments, finally shook himself from his reverie, and went downstairs.

These phone calls on the "red phone," as the servants called it, came at infrequent intervals. Bennett explained to the tall withdrawn woman with the colorless hair, Mrs. Alden, that when he received such a call it was of the utmost importance. He could not discuss it with her, and she should expect that he would be gone for a few days. She had come to accept this as she had accepted their loveless marriage. It really didn't matter.

As Bennett walked down the stairs to join the meeting he thought of the last time Mrs. Aldrich had called. It had been almost two months ago. Bennett remembered the drive into Chestnut Hill. The late-night ride through that damn snow. He almost didn't make it. It had taken him nearly two and a half hours to make that drive, which normally took him less than an hour.

Mrs. Aldrich had seen to it that the driveway was plowed. She was a jewel, he thought as he pressed the automatic door opener and drove his car into the heated garage.

The lights were on in the house. Bennett could feel the excitement. He almost began to shake.

He kicked off his boots in the vestibule, hung his coat and hat on the rack, and walked into the softly lit living room that was all chintz and covered maple furniture. The room was cheery and bright and very unimaginative. It mirrored perfectly the tastes of Mrs. Aldrich.

Bennett, who rarely drank, except on these occasions, now desperately wanted a drink. He was literally shaking with anticipation.

The woman who stepped into the living room was definitely not Mrs. Aldrich. She must have been in her late twenties or early thirties. Her auburn hair was long and brushed so that it hung over her left breast. She was dressed in a lime-colored satin dressing gown, her heavy breasts moving slightly as she walked. Her hair and skin seemed to glow. She was far more attractive than the others. She had about her none of that air of subservient guilt that took some of the early edge off these evenings for Bennett. In fact, she looked at him with a sensual amused smile that nearly choked him.

The table was set as usual, candlelight, wine. Mrs. Aldrich had done a superb job this time. He knew this woman would have been briefed by Mrs. Aldrich down to the last detail.

"My name is Angela." Her voice was soft with no definable or regional accent. She seemed more sure of herself than the others; more worldly. In fact, instead of the shy embarrassed preliminary exchanges Bennett was used to, this woman was openly sensual and obviously enjoying herself.

Bennett stood before the fire that Mrs. Aldrich had set, rubbing his hands, while Angela quietly poured him a large brandy.

"God, that's good," he said; the liquid burned down his throat because he had drunk too much of it too quickly, but he wanted to feel the fire of it inside him.

He wanted something to help steady his nerves with this most unusual young woman.

Bennett looked at the table and it was set as Mrs. Aldrich had always set it, so that the two places were very close together; not at opposite ends of the table as would usually be the case.

"Mr. Alden."

"I would prefer it if you called me Bennett."

"All right, Bennett."

This girl was certainly exceptional. Mrs. Aldrich could expect a bonus for this one.

"Bennett." Again the amused smile. "Are you hungry? It's really getting quite late."

"I'm absolutely famished."

Angela smiled again and busied herself putting cups of strong bouillon on the table. They sat down, their thighs touching. A flame seared through Bennett.

Angela slipped her hand under her dressing gown and brought forth her large firm breast swollen with milk.

She turned toward Bennett. His eyes were glazed, his lips parted.

She held her breast to him and he greedily sucked the warm sweet human milk. For this was Bennett's thing. No sexual pleasure more divine to Bennett than to drink heavily of the milk of a young mother and to be spent and exhausted between her thighs.

It was this minor eccentricity of Bennett's that was building up a very substantial investment account for Mrs. Aldrich. Good woman that she was, she carefully kept her own widow's counsel, and inquired not into the life-styles of those who buttered her bread.

Bennett joined the group in the living room with the secret river of pleasure running through him, knowing that Mrs. Aldrich had arranged another rendezvous with Angela. Bennett could barely keep his mind on the events of the evening.

Bennett's call took approximately five minutes. When he descended the stairs he saw the same group at the far end of the gloomy hallway. It was Grant's voice that brought him back from the promised Wednesday.

"Ah'm gonna call your senior partner tomorrow and tell ole Spotswood that we ain't gonna stand still for any rinkydink accountin' changes at this stage of the game." Grant saw Bennett on the stairs. He motioned to him with a wave of his hand.

"Bennett. Come here, will yew. Ah'm telling LeDune that Ah'm callin' Spotswood in the mornin' and tell him we aren't goin' to take a lot of chickenshit."

"Now hold it, Grant." It was Frank. The gray eyes were bleak and cold, and the voice husky and low but full of authority.

"Grant, we all appreciate your concern about Computer. I'm sure we all share your views about any charges against earnings. But this Texas twister performance isn't going to get us anywhere." It was a bold move. Dean looked at his senior partner with reluctant admiration. You didn't blow the whistle on Grant Weir and Jesse Hudson unless you were ready to play a very tough game. But then Frank Sullivan knew how to play that kind of a game; he had played it all his life.

Grant looked at Frank, somewhat surprised that the initiative had been taken away from him. He measured Frank with those steady penetrating eyes. Frank turned to Bennett.

"Bennett. I think we have inconvenienced Steve and the technical people here long enough. I suggest that we send Dr. Karkov and Dr. Eisenstadt home. It's getting late." Frank looked at his watch. It was nearly eleven o'clock. "As a matter of fact, Bennett, I suggest that we narrow this group down to Grant, you, myself, and Dean. Mr. Nagahama is ably represented by Grant. Bennett, I think it much smarter to keep this group as small as possible, so that we can make our plans accordingly—"

"Ah want some time with Dr. Nichols," Grant interrupted.

"Dr. Nichols is not returning to California until tomorrow," Bennett said. "I'm sure he would be happy to talk to you in any reasonable manner." Bennett's face was very cold as he looked at Grant Weir.

Grant felt the chill of these Easterners all around him. Fuck them, he thought. Bunch of goddamn bluestocking bastards. But Bennett had the kind of power Grant understood and respected. Connections all over the country, and very strong in Washington. Bennett's bank was also a factor in Europe as well. In Grant's world, you didn't alienate those you might need to use sometime in the future. So Grant let them get things done their way. It really was much the same as Grant's, only it added a style and polish to a relentless purpose.

Bennett had Foster arrange for cars to take the others back to Boston; Frank, Dean, Bennett, Grant, and Dr. Nichols stayed. Foster saw to those who wished to stay over at the Ritz rather than return to New York at this time of night.

Karkov grumbled that the whole goddamn evening was a waste of time.

Bob Friedman wished he could have stayed to see how these arm twisters were going to arrange to save their tails in Computer. But he could make some very educated guesses.

Fletcher Courtney kept it all to himself. He had brought LeDune to the meeting for just this purpose— to force these men to use their leverage to prevent the collapse of Computer's stock, which would surely happen if the kind of write-offs against earnings that LeDune was talking about came to pass. He had counted on just this community of greed and purpose to pull Computer out of a very deep well. His plan could not have been more successful.

Eisenstadt was the only one who had maintained his

humor throughout the evening. He smiled as he bid them good night. On the little professor's face was a look of wry amusement.

The wind was now up and blowing about the old house so that the windows rattled and the wooden structure creaked with distant sounds of old straining timbers.

The surf had built up ahead of the wind, and the crashing spray now wet the windows in the living room as the men settled themselves in comfortable chairs. Grant poured himself another bourbon at the sideboard.

Frank began to speak. His role was unusual. His power lay not in the strength of his firm, which, although large and prestigous, was peanuts compared to what Grant and Bennett represented, but in his ability to command attention from other men who sensed his strength and respected his combination of force and intelligence.

"Now, gentlemen, our purpose is a common one. Let me see if I can summarize where I think we are and see if you agree."

Dean's mouth was compressed into a thin line; his face and hands looked very pale in the soft light.

"First of all, I don't think we need to trouble Dr. Nichols for the moment. I wonder, Bennett, if perhaps you could make Dr. Nichols comfortable in your study. As I understand it, Grant would like to talk to Dr. Nichols a little later." Frank turned to Dr. Nichols. "Doctor, we will try and be considerate of your time. I know it's getting late and you have a long flight ahead of you tomorrow."

Nichols smiled a wan, apprehensive smile and got up to leave the room.

Foster stood in the hallway. Bennett's voice sounded reedy and strained. "Foster, show Dr. Nichols to my study, would you? Doctor, I certainly do appreciate your putting up with all this inconvenience. You have been very gracious. Very gracious indeed."

"Not at all." The stooped figure with the thick glasses

and narrow tie that hung from his collar like a divining rod followed Foster toward Bennett's study.

"Now to return to what I was saying. Let's summarize where we are." Frank's voice reflected his own fatigue. "As far as I can determine, we haven't settled anything concerning the viability of Computer's technology. We've got a Mexican standoff there. But this new intrusion regarding a change in Computer's accounting; I think we can all agree that we can't permit this to happen."

"You bet your sweet ass it ain't gonna happen." Grant had completely removed his tie, which he had folded and put in his shirt pocket. He held the bourbon like an extension of his fist.

"If Fuller, Cross hits that little ole company with an adjustment like that you can just piss that stock down the rat hole."

"Hold it, Grant." Frank raised a tired hand. "We are all well aware of that. What I propose is that we decide *how* to approach Spotswood and his partners at Fuller—"

"Change the goddamn accountants." Grant's voice was filled with disgust at the lack of resolve of the others. "Fuck 'em. We can get some smaller firm that's easier to handle than Fuller."

Bennett looked at Frank. "Is that a good alternative, Frank?"

Frank shook his head. "I'm afraid not, Bennett. Any change in Computer's accountants at this stage would probably be questioned by the SEC and most certainly by the Street. The analysts would rip the company apart looking for things if Computer tried to switch firms now."

"Well, let's hear somethin' that's gonna get the job done. Ah don't give a damn how it gets done. Ah'm tellin' yew that we're gonna cut the mustard on this thing."

Grant turned to Bennett. "Now, Bennett, yew listen here. We're big boys where Ah come from and we don't fuck around." Grant paused and his eyes narrowed as he looked at Bennett. "We don't piss ass all over the place when we're in a bum deal either. We take our losses and get the hell out. But, Bennett, there are two things down mah way we don't do. We don't screw our friends. An' we don't break our word."

Bennett's eyes were ice-blue. His tall frame was a bow string. The nasal Yankee dialect hissed out at Grant like an adder. "I would appreciate your explaining the implications behind those remarks, Grant."

Grant looked at Bennett steadily. "Don't misunderstand me, Bennett. "Ah'm not implying that you screwed us in this Computer deal. Not at all. But Ah'm like a hound dog on a hot scent, Bennett. Somethin' in my bones tells me that we got fucked in this deal. You. Me. Nagahama and mah foreign partners. And Ah have a sneakin' suspicion as to who the *fuck-or* as differentiated from the *fuck-ee* is."

Bennett shook his head incredulously. Frank began to laugh. Dean was dumbfounded by this unbelievable Texan. Did people really speak like that?

"Well, Ah'm not funnin' you fellows. Ah'm dead serious. Ah think this little feller Eisenstadt has the right idea. Ah think he's right when he says Karkov is two years away on his technology. An', gentlemen, Ah think we got fucked by Tittle and his boys usin' old Doc Nichols."

"That's preposterous." Bennett's face was livid. "Ray Tittle's firm is one of the most respected management consulting firms in this country. Everyone here knows that. I personally have been a friend of Ray's since Harvard and I know the man. He's incapable of any kind of chicanery."

Grant laughed. "Jesus Christ. Here we go again with dear old Harvard. Bennett, this may come as a shock to yew, but there are more scalawags out of dear old *Harvard* than Ah'd care to add up." He took a long pull on his bourbon. "Give me a good ole Texas Aggie any time,

Bennett. He's too dumb to fuck yah!" This was a private joke which only Grant Weir seemed to appreciate, and he roared with laughter.

Bennett's demeanor was as cold as a New England winter. "Grant, if this amuses you, I am quite envious. Frankly, the thought that you perceive a situation that I suggested to you, recommended by a lifelong friend of mine, to be little less than fraudulent, hardly fills me with humor."

Grant stopped laughing and walked to the sideboard for another bourbon.

"Bennett, Bennett. Trouble with yew Yankees is yew can't see the funny side of anythin'. Ah'm not accusin' yew, Bennett. Hell, no. Why should I? You're in this too. You've got your ass burned. So did Frank. Ah'm not tellin' you that old Ray Tittle fucked us, either. Ah know Ray wouldn't do that." Grant began to laugh again. "Shit, Bennett, Ah think Ray is another one of us fuck-ees!" Grant roared. "Jesus, that tickles me."

Bennett's New England reserve was still very much intact. But Frank was shaking his head in quiet laughter. This Grant was a real piss cutter.

"Would you mind telling us, Grant, in less colorful language if you can manage it, just what you're implying by all this?" Bennett's patience was wearing very thin.

"Ah'm not implyin' anythin'. Ah'm tellin' yew. Listen. Who the hell's stock did we buy?"

They all looked at Grant with new purpose.

"We bought Karkov and Courtney's stock. An' why did we buy it? Because we checked every technical son of a bitch we could lay our hands on." He glanced at Bennett. "Yew don' think we paid up that kind of money on just Tittle's advice, do yuh? Shit, no. We talked to the boys at Palo Alto and Cambridge. We talked to the best people we could get to at Stanford. We had our partners check out this Karkov."

Frank's face showed no surprise. He knew Jesse Hudson.

Those boys didn't play hunches until all the wrinkles were ironed out.

"Yew know what we came up with?" Grant made a sweeping gesture, the bourbon spilling on Bennett's Persian rug. "Not a fuckin' thing. A whole goddamn bunch of reports that cost a bundle of money and nothin' we could really hang our hat on. Nothin', that is, until we met ole Dr. Nichols. He was the one that pushed Jesse and me over the cliff. We thought it was a crap shoot. But with Nichols' reputation we figured we could go with him. What we didn't figure was that old Nichols might fuck us."

Dean, who had been unusually silent throughout the evening, looked at Grant. "But why would Dr. Nichols do that?" Dean raised his arms in a gesture of incomprehension. "What would be his motive? How could he possibly profit by recommending Karkov's company? I don't see it, Grant. He doesn't own the stock. At least I don't believe he does. Not enough to be important in any case. I don't follow you at all, Grant."

Grant Weir walked to the window and stared out at the night hidden from the stars by wind-driven clouds and listened to the sounds of the sea. He was silent for quite some time. When he spoke, his voice was flat and tired. He spoke with his back to them as if he were addressing the night.

"It's just a hunch Ah have. But sure as shit, ole Nichols is our nigger. Some way, somehow, this bastard fucked us. An', boys"—Grant turned toward them—"ole Grant is goin' to find out."

Frank intervened. "Grant. If you suspect Dr. Nichols, which is your own business, then handle it as you see fit. But I want to settle this Fuller thing before it gets much later. I have a full day in New York tomorrow." Frank turned to Bennett. "Bennett, I think that you and Grant would have the most leverage with Spotswood. Naturally, we'll do what we can, but we—"

Bennett interrupted. "I am fully aware of how Mr. Spotswood should be approached. I suggest you leave that to me." Bennett turned to Grant. "I assume that in your own fashion, Grant, you might perhaps try and be somewhat persuasive with Mr. Spotswood?"

"Don't give it another thought, ole boy. Ah won't pussyfoot around like you guys. We're in six companies that Fuller audits. Ah'll pull everyone out of there if Ah have to. Besides, we've got a lot more clout that doesn't show. Ole Spots will feel squeezed when we get through leanin' on him."

"Then I take it the matter of Fuller will be left to you and Bennett, with us being as helpful as we can." Frank looked at them both. They nodded in silent agreement.

"Good." Frank turned toward Dean. "I'm bushed. If Bennett has a bed for me I'm going to turn in. How about you?"

Dean knew that Frank had given him the signal to withdraw. He would have preferred to stay with Grant while he talked to Nichols. But he sensed that Bennett would be very unhappy if he joined Grant in any inquisition of Dr. Paul Nichols. Dean knew that was why Frank had suggested they both leave. Bennett was too important to the firm to rub the wrong way. Dean sighed. "I'm all in too, Frank. I think I'll join you."

Bennett rang for Foster.

"Will you show these gentlemen to their rooms. And Foster. Mr. Weir and Dr. Nichols will be in my study. Would you show Mr. Weir where he will sleep and point out to Dr. Nichols his room. That will be all, Foster. These gentlemen will not need you any more this evening."

That was Bennett, Frank thought. Cold as a cod, but traditionally thoughtful of an old servant whom he would not cause to lose more sleep over a crude Texan who seemed determined to disturb a respected scholar and an invited guest in the home of Bennett Emerson Alden.

* * *

The house was left to the wind and the night, as Grant Weir walked into the softly lit study of Bennett Alden.

He looked for a moment at the figure of Dr. Nichols asleep in a deep leather chair, a book resting on his lap. The good doctor slept with his mouth open, snoring slightly. When Grant tapped him on the shoulder, Nichols awakened with a start.

"So-so-so-sorry," he stammered. "Mm-mm-must have dozed off a bit."

"Don't worry, Doc." Grant smiled. "It's been a long night for all of us. Ah don't want to disturb yew, Doctor. Ah just wanted to talk with yew a little before yew go back to the Coast."

"Certainly. Certainly. Be v-very hap-happy to."

"Yew see, Doc, it's this way. Me an' mah partners checked yew out real careful. Real careful. Before we decided to get into this Computer thing. We even took the trouble to find out about yo' personal life, Doctor. An' frankly, we liked what we heard. Matter of fact, all the reports we got on yew an' yo' Institute checked out real fahn. That's what made us decide to go in. A man with yo' standin' in the scientific community and yo' personal reputation. Clean as a whistle."

Nichols didn't know whether to be complimented or offended. He never supposed that someone would check into his personal life. But that hardly mattered. Nichols' entire life was his Institute. It was mistress, wife, and mother to him.

"By the way, Doc. How is the Institute comin'?" Grant asked that question offhandedly as he looked about Bennett's study. The high-ceilinged book-lined room, with its thin Oriental rugs and furniture that had been handed down from Bennett's seafaring ancestors, seemed to Grant like the odd corner of some musty museum. It was nothing like his own den in Dallas, whose motif was chrome,

Mediterranean and Spanish. And *new*. Not all this stuff
that looked as if it came from someone's attic.

"The Institute is ju-just fine, thank you, Mr. Weir."

Grant stretched and flopped down in a straight-backed
leather chair that felt damned uncomfortable. He yawned
broadly. "Sorry, Doc. Just a bit sleepy." Grant didn't look
at Nichols as he spoke. His gaze was up at the ceiling, his
manner deliberately disarming. Nichols knew this. And
the more relaxed Grant seemed to appear, the tighter the
knot grew in Paul Nichols' stomach.

"Ah was hopin' that things were goin' well for yew,
Doc. When we checked out the Institute we were surprised that it had the kind of financial support yew've
been able to round up." Grant paused. "Yew do most of
the fund raisin', Doc?" Nichols nodded affirmatively.
Grant smiled. "Now that's right interestin', Doc. Yew
don't look like a fund raiser." He paused, addressing himself. "Curious."

"I have be-be-been fortunate that some industrialists
and government agen-agencies have thought my work im-
important."

"Ah see. Ah guess somebody must think it is important,
Doc. Yew've got quite a plant out there at the university.
Those labs of yours and yo' conference centers and dor-
mitories. That's a real setup, Doc. Took a look at it mah-
sef before Ah first talked to yuh. Very impressive." Grant
was still not looking at Nichols, although the physicist was
watching him like a cornered rabbit.

"Doc. Ah suppose that those industrialists who lend support to yo' Institute have a first look, yew might say, at any
projects yew fellows happen to be workin' on that they're
interested in."

Nichols didn't answer immediately. Grant's head came
down from resting against the back of his chair. Those
steady dark eyes of his looked squarely at Nichols waiting
for an answer.

"It ah, it all de-pend-pends, Mr. We-eir, on the circum-

stances. Naturally we cannot disclose to them cl-classi-
fied information that may apply to their fields of interest."

"Ah'm aware of that, Doctor. What Ah meant was that
if someone gave yo' Institute say a half a million or a million dollars it would be natural for yew to share or at least
cooperate with their research people on problems of, say,
mutual interest?"

Nichols was very careful. "Y-y-yes. I g-g-guess it would."

Grant reflected for a while. "Ya know, Doc, all this fuss
about a little ole company like Computer doesn't make a
lot of sense"—Grant paused and looked at Paul Nichols
carefully—"unless yew understand the total ramifications
of the problems we're all involved in, which sort of radi-
ate, yew might say, from Computer like some kind of
chain reaction. What Ah mean is that the complications
of the problems arise from the chain reactions they set off.
Computer is only the firin' device, Doctor. It's not where
the essential destructive energy comes from."

Nichols remained silently impressed. Whatever he was,
Grant Weir was no fool.

Grant moved his hand in a motion of frustrated fatigue.
"But yew don't know what the hell I'm talkin' about, Doc,
do yuh?"

Nichols shook his head. "I'm a-a-afraid that analogy
escapes me."

Grant was so goddamned tired that his bones ached.
He wiped his mouth with the back of his hand. "Yew see,
Doc, without borin' yew with the complication of this
thing, let's make it real simple."

Grant heard the wind howl outside. Then the crack of
a large limb and the muted sound of it crashing against
the hard wintered ground.

"On the basis of yo' reputation and reports, Doc, we
put a very prominent group of European bankers into this
Computer deal with us. They are a hell of a lot more important to us than our investment in Computer."

The wind was up again. Nichols wondered how many

storms had raged across this coast and flung their furies at Bennett's trees.

"Now yew see, Doc, we don't have any kick comin' if Karkov gets his goddamn technical problems licked and starts to market those products. If they work, it will be one of the best deals we could have gotten into, and our reliance on yo' advice will have been more than justified."

Grant paused to look around to see if Bennett kept any liquor in his study. He didn't. He waved his hand at Paul Nichols. "Just gonna get me a little more bourbon, Doctor. Yew want a drink?" Nichols shook his head negatively. "Hold still, Doc, will yuh? I'll be right back."

Nichols' apprehensions gnawed at his stomach. He could feel the first streaks of pain from his ulcer.

Grant returned with a glass half full of bourbon. "No damn ice in the place. Everyone's asleep," he muttered as he walked to the chair and sat down again opposite Paul Nichols.

"Yuh see, Doc, it's like this. Anyone can make a mistake. Karkov can be right as hell and we hope he is." Another limb cracked and fell.

"Christ, we're lucky if the damn house doesn't blow away, eh Doc?" Grant smiled. He knew the house had been there for over two hundred years. "Ah guess the ole place will hold together better than us, eh, Doc. Here's lookin' at you." Grant took a long pull on his bourbon.

"What I was sayin', Doc, to stop piss-assin' around, is that if you gave us yo' best advice an' we took it, then hell, we ride or fall off with the horse, eh, Doc? But,"—Grant lowered his glass, his eyes narrowed as he searched the twitching facial muscles of Paul Nichols—"but if we didn't get yo' *best* advice, Doc, for one reason or another, then that's a whole *different* ball game. Then we have troubles *we don't deserve*. An' Ah might add, Doctor, that becomes a different ball game for yew too." Nichols watched him with increasing anxiety.

"Yuh see, Doc." Grant sensed the fear in the man,

searched the blue eyes for what he was seeking. A skilled hunter like Grant Weir sensed when he had found spoor.

"Ah'm not so untutored that Ah don't know that these research-based projects like Karkov's can develop problems. Frankly, Ah was surprised to hear that he had a hundred or more of the damn things in the various rivers bein' tested. But if Eisenstadt is right, an' he thinks Karkov is at least two years away with his impregnated-chip technology, then we have to turn around and look at yew an' hope you're right, Doc. But even if you're *wrong,* an' yew gave us the benefit of your *unbiased* opinions, we couldn't really blame yew, Doc, because science is really not that *exact,* is it? Not really an *exact science.*" He laughed as he thought of that one and took another drink.

"But jus' suppose, Doc—an' Ah'm not sayin' this is at all a possibility—jus' suppose money isn't really so easy to come by fo' yo' Institute." Grant looked at the amber liquid as he absentmindedly swirled it about in his glass. "Jus' suppose someone made a contribution to yo' Institute in behalf of impregnated-chip technological research. Ah don't suppose you'd turn it down, would yuh, Doc? No reason to." Nichols felt the pain begin to stab at his abdomen.

"Now, Doc, Ah'm not sayin' it would prejudice any opinion yew might give as a consultant, but in such circumstances Ah do feel that mah group would have every right to believe that the advice they got was a *little* less than they paid for. Unless of course yew told us that some funding had been contributed toward impregnated chips. Then we could make up our own minds if yew or yo' Institute might have any bias toward that technology."

Nichols rose in protest, his face flushed with anger. "M-m-Mr. Weir. You can hold any opinion you wish, sir. That is entirely your own affair. But my reputation and that of my Institute mean more to me than any contribution regardless of its size." Nichols stalked out of the room shaking in fury and in fear. He had seen the look in

Grant's eyes, and he knew that this redneck Texan had uncovered the track. As Paul Nichols grasped the handrail of the stairs, a searing abdominal pain made him wince in muted agony.

Grant watched him go. He sat in the uncomfortable leather chair for a long time, swirling the bourbon around, listening to the sounds of the house defending itself against the gale.

Grant finally stood up and put his bourbon down carelessly on the small Queen Anne table beside him, where the glass would leave a ring to be polished away by a disgruntled servant in the morning.

Grant finally rose, belched, expelled a large amount of abdominal gas, and walked unsteadily in what he hoped was the direction of his bedroom.

He stumbled in the darkness searching for the door he thought Foster had pointed out to him earlier in the evening. He began to whistle to himself and then to sing quietly.

Grant's face became a mask of menace in the darkness as he fell against the bedroom door; cursed, and finally opened it.

"Jesse," he said to the blackness of the room, "these Yankee bastards have fucked us again. But, Jesse, the eyes of Texas are upon them." Grant laughed softly to himself at that last one.

"The fucker," he said. "The no-good lyin' motherfucker."

Grant Weir threw himself fully clothed across the bed, and fell instantly asleep.

The great clock in the lower hall struck three sonorous chimes. The house was silent, answering only to the wind.

In front of 280 Park Avenue, March swept in like a lion. The flags in front of the building whipped against a twenty-knot breeze. The people on the street scurried in front of the huge glass-fronted structure, bent their heads low, clasped their hands on their hats and collars. Some waved desperately for one of the cabs to stop, or rushed for their individual destinations, driven by the fierce wind and the bone-chilling cold.

Inside 280 Park in the west building were three floors of the main offices of Fuller, Cross. The worldwide head-quarters of one of the nation's major accounting firms. In an appropriately impressive corner suite on the twenty-third floor was the office of E. Davis Spotswood, managing partner of Fuller, Cross and Company. Spots, as he was known only to his equals—and they were few in number—was a man of medium height, about sixty years of age, with a fine head of silver-gray hair and an appropriately tanned complexion that told of a recent visit to the Caribbean.

Spots was the managing partner of Fuller for a variety of reasons. He was a first-class administrator. He worked well with a group of diverse and very bright partners. He had just the right combination of geniality and drive to keep such a large firm headed toward increasing profita-bility, and enough knowledge and bite to help keep the firm out of trouble and get done what had to be done.

On this Thursday morning in the second week of March, several partners including Steve LeDune and the firm's legal counsel were gathered together in tight-lipped concern. Some were seated silently in chairs grouped in a semicircle around Spots' desk. Others sat on the grilled surface of the window seats that vented the controlled air circulating silently through the room. At the moment, LeDune was speaking.

"It's just a goddamn backbreaker, Spots. Hell, I knew this was going to happen when I left Bennett's house. I just didn't think it was going to happen so soon."

E. Davis Spotswood's face was hardly genial. As a matter of fact he was madder than hell. He didn't mind these smaller companies trying to twist his firm's arm because he could tell them to go jump. But the game had been turned around on Mr. Spotswood, and he didn't like it one damned bit. It was *his* firm's arm that was being twisted, and it was being twisted by a group that he simply couldn't afford to ignore. He had to admire the finesse with which it was being done.

It all began early in the week, shortly after LeDune came back from Bennett's. It started with a call from Trans Union America. Their financial vice-president called and told Dexter Harrison, one of the general partners of Fuller, that he wanted to have luncheon with Dexter.

Since Trans Union had sales of one and a half billion dollars, and paid Fuller, Cross auditing fees of approximately $750,000 annually, Dexter Harrison canceled the luncheon date he had with another client. He spent a harrowing two hours at "21" with Parker Roberts, senior financial vice-president for Trans Union. The gist of the luncheon was a series of complaints by Roberts of Fuller's auditing of his company's accounts. A strong protest at Fuller's charges for its services, and then the surprise.

Dexter didn't know what Roberts was talking about, but he could quote verbatim what he had said.

"Dexter. The big thing that worries us is the way your firm is getting the reputation of changing the rules after the ball game has been played."

Wide-eyed, Dexter looked at Parker Roberts. "Parker. What the hell are you talking about?"

Parker looked at his watch. "It's late. I've got to run. But take a piece of advice. The word *is* getting around."

Dexter came back to his office completely and utterly baffled. This was a big account even for Fuller. Naturally, he reported the luncheon meeting to his managing partner. So did all the others in the room who had similar meetings with large accounts for which each of them was responsible.

They represented a fair cross section of the country. They came from Fuller's offices in New York, Chicago, Dallas, Atlanta, Minneapolis, Los Angeles, and Seattle. They represented nearly five million dollars' worth of billings for Fuller, not counting the call Spotswood had from Jesse Hudson, which his partners didn't know anything about.

It wasn't until that call came that Spotswood had the whole thing put together. Every one of these companies was in one way or another connected to interests controlled by Jesse Hudson, or borrowed from banks with close connections to Bennett's bank.

No personal word had come from the Brahmin in Boston. Bennett didn't play that way. Just a series of lower-echelon meetings with Bennett's people. A few very carefully chosen people. Men who could get the message across but never mention the game or the players. Debtors have very sensitive antennae where lenders are concerned.

Jesse Hudson, of course, needed no such disguises. He had simply called Spotswood, asked him what the hell his firm was thinking of in changing Computer's accounting practices, and if he—Spotswood—let that happen he could kiss every goddamn account of Jesse's goodbye. "And," Jesse added, "we'll kick your ass all over this country and Europe too." Spotswood was still angry at the way the crusty son of a bitch slammed the phone down on him.

So here they were, flown in from all over the country, finally alerted to the message that was being so subtly and not so subtly transmitted to Fuller, Cross: *Lay off Computer.*

LeDune broke the silence. "Well, Spots, what do we do?" He didn't elaborate on the squeeze the firm was in. He didn't have to. Computer's research-and-development account should begin to be charged against earnings. The SEC, or the accounting profession's own rule-making body, or even the Wall Street analysts would become critical of Fuller for not being more conservative in their accounting treatment. But the real fear for Spotswood and his partners was the position they would be in if Karkov was wrong and blew the company. The thought made Spotswood shudder. It was an accountant's nightmare. Every goddamn shareholder of Computer with a lawyer would *sue them*. That's what really stared out at Fuller, Cross. And that's what frightened all of them. But how do you kick out nearly five million dollars' worth of billing?

"Gentlemen," said E. Davis Spotswood, "for the moment we sit tight and pray." There were no objections from his partners. What else could they do? When virtue is tempted by profit, it is a rare group of men who will choose virtue.

When LeDune called Fletcher Courtney, the Missourian smiled as he hung up the phone. He grinned and walked into Karkov's office.

"What the hell do you want?" Karkov bellowed. The smile remained on Courtney's face. But a thin film of genuine hate came into his eyes as he measured Karkov coolly. "The wicked have triumphed," he said, and walked out of the room.

In Dallas at offices in the First Commerce Bank Building on the tenth floor, a young thin man with neatly cut reddish-blond hair wearing a dark-blue suit sat opposite Grant Weir. Grant was in his shirt sleeves and tieless. The young man seated in Grant's office was twenty-nine years old. His name was Bryan Hastings. He listened carefully, not taking any notes; he didn't have to. Young Mr. Hastings was blessed with almost total recall. His memory was like the tape in a computer bank. Everything went in, was stored, and could be recalled at will. He was quiet. He was possessed of unimaginable ambition, carefully clothed behind an almost blank exterior. He seldom spoke. If he had not been raised as a well-educated God-fearing Methodist, Bryan Hastings had the psychic makeup to be a very successful criminal. But Bryan was too Christian and too smart to try to make it that way. Bryan wanted to be another Jesse Hudson. He had the right teacher. He was Grant's right-hand man.

Grant put his hands behind his head with his fingers

interlaced as he spoke. "Ah want you to go up to the Southern California National Bank in L.A. See Gardner Hall. As you may or may not know, he's chairman and chief executive officer of the bank. He's also on the board of the Nichols Institute. The son of a bitch is on the board of everythin' in L.A. He's a real blowhard. But he's got a lot of contacts, includin' the Republican senator and the governor of the damn state. He's a whoremaster who would fuck a snake if it would hold still long enough." Grant paused. The light from the early-morning Dallas sun played upon the face of Bryan Hastings. Grant had no particular love for this kid. It would have been hard for anyone to love Hastings, including his mother. But he was a smart, useful little son of a bitch, and Grant knew that this particular brand of sidewinder would go far.

"One thing I might tell you about Gardner. We own the bastard. We own him from his eyeballs to his asshole. So be polite, but tell him what I want him to find out. Tell him I want to know where the Institute gets its money. I want to know who contributes, especially the anonymous donors. I am especially interested in any large anonymous contributions made, say, between October and January. And God damn it, you tell Gardner I want names. I don't care how he gets them. And if the contribution should be in cash I want to know *who* and *how*. I don't want to hear any bullshit that he can't do it. You tell him if he wants to be chairman of that bank he'd better goddamn well get me this information, and fast."

Grant looked at Bryan Hastings. The young man had not moved a muscle. He now rose and looked at Grant.

"It's done, Mr. Weir." He turned and walked out of the room.

That little bastard gives me the creeps, Grant said to himself and picked up the phone.

In New York an unusually warm March sun awakened Dina as she felt the presence of its light in her room.

Frank's bed had long been empty. She glanced at the clock. She reached for the phone and placed a call to Dr. Whitney Fraser. A crisp voice answered.

"Dr. Fraser is at the hospital, Mrs. Sullivan. He will not be back in the office before two."

"Does he have any room for me on his calendar, Miss Travis?"

Miss Travis knew as only another woman would know that Dr. Fraser would always be able to work in Dina Sullivan.

"I would say around three forty-five, Mrs. Sullivan." She paused. "Is there anything I can tell the doctor?"

"I don't think so. If it's not an imposition, Miss Travis, would you tell Dr. Fraser I will see him at three forty-five."

"It's certainly not an imposition, Mrs. Sullivan. I'm putting you down in the book. Three forty-five, then."

"Thank you."

'Goodbye."

Dina hung up the phone. She hadn't seen Whit since he last examined her a little over a week ago. He had telephoned her on Tuesday and asked her if she could make an appointment with him as soon as possible.

Was there anything wrong? she had asked, and he assured her that there was not. But she had a premonition that there was something more than he was telling her. She had searched his voice in her mind and her intuition had touched a caution button. Perhaps she was imagining things. She buzzed for the maid on the intercom and told her that she would have some warm milk and toast.

As she showered she rubbed the soap luxuriously over her breasts until her nipples hardened. She became awakened sexually and thought about a lazy morning making love to a man, slowly with an almost relaxed abandon, if there was such a thing. Her mind flicked on images of Whit, of Frank, and of Elliot. She shuddered as she thought of Elliot. But she could not make herself forget the passion of that night.

Whit had helped her overcome her guilt concerning Elliot's death. In so doing he had freed her sensuality. She found herself *wanting* the kind of passion that Elliot had shown her. But she wanted that passion continued with the feeling of being loved, and loving deeply in return. A part of her mind knew that in day-to-day relationships this was a fantasy. But the desire persisted. She thought about it, as the warm water ran over her body. Slowly she began to masturbate. She had closed her eyes and concentrated on the erect penis of Elliot Thompson when the bathroom phone rang. She was approaching climax and didn't want to answer the damn thing. It stopped ringing and the light on the touch button remained lit so that she knew either the butler or the maid had answered. The buzzer in the bathroom sounded like a chain saw.

God damn Frank and his passion for phones and intercoms, she thought. She reached for a towel and stepped out of the stall shower to pick up the phone. The butler's voice, flat and impersonal, said, "It's Dr. Fraser, Mrs. Sullivan."

For some reason a flash of apprehension touched her. She clutched the large bath towel around her, brushing her wet hair from her face.

"Whit?"

"Yes. Have I interrupted something?"

"No, no, darling. I'm just standing here dripping all over everything. I was in the shower."

She felt that his tone sounded serious, although he was making every attempt to keep it natural.

"Want me to call you back?"

"No, darling. Just let me blot myself a little. Hang on." She wiped quickly at her body and took a smaller towel and rubbed her hair vigorously. Then she swept the towel about her head into a neatly fashioned turban and put on her dressing gown. "Okay, darling. I think I have things under control now. What is it?"

"About your appointment at three forty-five."

Irritation. Had he dragged her out of the shower to change an appointment?

"I thought, Dina, we might meet at my place at say five if that's convenient." He paused.

Now she felt that something *was* wrong. Whit didn't take his practice out of the office. He obviously wanted to tell her something of importance, but for some reason not in his office. She was suddenly frightened, and though her voice tried to remain calm, it reflected her anxiety and he could recognize her concern as she spoke.

"Now, darling. Don't be so mysterious. Have I got cancer or something? Am I going to drop dead for God's sake?"

He laughed. "No, Dina. You're as healthy as a horse, I'm happy to say." He chuckled. "Really in *beautiful* shape."

She laughed. "So I'm appreciated."

The hell with being discreet over the phone, he thought.

"You're always appreciated, darling. You should know that by now."

She felt relieved and flattered. She didn't respond to many men as she did to Whit. Usually her manner was diffident and aloof. Simply, she was falling in love with Whit Fraser and he was already in love with her.

"Whit, can't you even give me a hint? It's going to be a long wait until five."

"Darling. It's nothing serious. Please don't be anxious. It gives me another opportunity to see you." He paused. His voice was just slightly hesitant. "Do you have any other plans?"

She was getting cool. She turned on the heat lamp timer to twelve minutes, and stood under it.

"Not especially. Frank has been getting home around eight lately. Something's come up at the firm. He's terribly preoccupied." She paused. "I would like to be here before he gets back."

"I understand," Whit said. But she sensed in his voice a hint of depression.

"Darling, don't be annoyed. I feel I should be here when Frank gets home. He's been working terribly hard lately and he's very tired."

"I know." His voice had cheered up somewhat. "If you can make it at five that will be fine."

"See you then," she said and hung up.

She dressed herself leisurely. She was going to have lunch with Cissy Cartwright. She had an appointment at her hairdresser at two and she had a fitting at four. The whole day had promised to be a bore until Whit called. Now, suddenly, she felt alive but apprehensive. Something told her this was to be no ordinary day in her life. Her intuition, as usual, was dead on the mark.

On the fifteenth floor of the United Nations Plaza apartments, a setting sun splashed at the gray rushing East River, painting it with streaks of orange and red. The scattered clouds that were moving northeast behind a blustering wind occasionally shut out its rays and returned the river to its gray-green cast. Gulls squawked and circled in moving updrafts of air. Occasionally a tug with a cargo of barges would pass at unusually high speed, its velocity helped by the swift current.

Whit stood with an ice-cold martini in his hand as he glanced at his watch. It was now five fifteen. She was fifteen minutes late. This was unusual for Dina.

As he sipped his drink he was aware of the dull sounds of traffic on the drive below, that mass of congestion fighting its way home to mid-Manhattan, Queens, Westchester, and Connecticut.

Whit hated New York. He longed for those infrequent vacations when he could leave the city with its dirt, noise, and violence. He had thought often of returning to Wisconsin. But he had established too much here now to leave. The years at medical school in New York, and then the chance to teach at the university, the association that was offered him to assist Dr. Morrow, who was chief of internal

medicine at the hospital, the assumption of Morrow's
practice when the old fellow died. No. This city with all
of its faults and several of its very real virtues now held
him captive. Especially since the death of his wife, and the
beginning of Dina.

A siren wailed below, strident and impatient.

He sipped at his martini and looked out at the vertical
architecture of lower Manhattan, at the UN and the dirt-
embedded buildings of Queens.

The doorbell chimed. He opened it and looked at her.

"God almighty, lady, you look beautiful."

He swept her in his arms before the door had closed,
gathering in her fur coat in a massive embrace. Her lips
felt cold as he kissed her. He refused to let her go. They
stood holding each other in the small vestibule as he
rocked her gently in his arms.

"Oh, lady, I *love* you."

She laughed as she slipped from him and took off her
hat and coat and handed them to him.

"Now *that's* what I call a welcome." She was radiant.

"Come over here and have a drink. I've mixed a batch
of martinis for us."

"I'd love one. But first, I think I'd like a repeat of that
super performance you just gave at the door, Doctor. You
think you're up to another scene like that?"

He looked at her with great tenderness. "I think I might
be able to summon up the necessary enthusiasm." He held
her tightly to him again, running his hands over her back.
And then gently he cupped her head between his hands,
framing her hair against her face. He looked at her for a
very long time, and then he kissed her tenderly, with great
gentleness.

"Oh, Doctor," she said, "I love you so terribly much."

They sat down on the sofa, each with a drink. The river
was now painted over by the setting sun.

She had kicked off her shoes and sat with her legs tucked
up beneath her, facing him. She looked at Whit with eyes

filled with tenderness for him, but her expression was shadowed by concern. Dina's moods were so attuned to Whit's that she now knew he was waiting to tell her something that would upset her.

"Please, Whit. No more mysteries. Tell me *now*. What is it?"

He got up and walked to the window. He turned to her and spoke very softly. "Dina. You're pregnant."

Her mouth dropped open. Even beneath her makeup he could see her face drain of color.

"I'm what?"

"You're pregnant."

She took the rest of her martini and drained the glass. "My God, are you sure?"

He shook his head. "I'm sure."

The thoughts began to swirl around her mind like blowing dust. Frank. What would she tell Frank? A child. *Her child.* Her own child. *Her own child!*

She stood up and rushed to Whit. "Oh, God, Oh God, Whit, please be sure." She clung to him. He put his arms around her and kissed her, not wanting to take a second of this from her. "I'm sure, darling. Believe me, I'm sure."

She kissed him and moved toward the sofa. She sat down, her eyes looking at a faraway dream.

"That's what I've always wanted. To have my own baby. To bring up my own child and give it what I never had. *To always be there.* To have my child know that as long as I live, that child will have my love, my strength, my protection. Oh, Whit." She began to cry gently. "That's all I've ever really wanted. A child of my own."

He nodded silently.

"But aren't you thrilled for me, darling? You know how much this means to me."

"Of course I'm thrilled. It's just that I've had a little more time to think this through than you've had."

"What does that mean?"

He remained silent.

She put her hand over her mouth. Gone from her face was the look of maternal surprise and wonder she had shown just a moment ago. Her expression had turned to one of acute concern.

"My God, Whit. Whose is it?" It was pure Dina. No equivocation. No hysteria. No acting. As the magnitude of the problem hit, her face paled.

"My good sweet God. *Whose child is it?*"

He sat beside her, his arm around her, drawing her close to him. He kissed her hair softly.

"Darling, the important thing is that you will have a child. It doesn't matter to me whose child it is because I know how much this means to you. The real part of all this is Frank."

"Don't you think I realize that?"

It had become dusk. The lights of the city began to sparkle their false diamonds at the oncoming night, outlining the spears of steel and concrete that thrust at the sky, and would be so starkly uncovered by the morning sun.

Whit poured them both another martini.

She turned toward him with that marvelous directness of hers. "Whit. What do I do?" She didn't say what do *we* do.

How he loved her for that. For her willingness to assume the total burden *herself*. God how he loved this woman.

He looked at her quietly for a moment and then put down his drink. He took her hand and kissed it very gently.

"Dina. You don't seem to understand. This could be *my* child, our child, but that doesn't matter to me. What *does* matter is that we are going to face this together." He paused, not letting go of her hand. "Dina. My life wouldn't mean much to me without you." He said this with an inner agony produced from the anxiety he felt; a dreadful foreboding that circumstance would shatter his dream of spending the rest of his life with her. It made him feel very vulnerable and alone.

She looked at him with great tenderness. The tears welled up in her eyes and spilled down her cheeks. Her voice was choked as she spoke. "Darling. I don't think you fully understand. I am going to have a child, and I don't know if that child is yours or—or someone else's. How can I let you share this with me? Why should you?" She wiped her eyes with a small handkerchief. "You don't know Frank like I do. If—if you take my side in this, God only knows what he'll do to you if he suspects. Oh, don't you see? You have the board of directors of the hospital, the trustees, the faculty, your friends. And, Whit"—her shoulders began to tremble and she buried her face in her hands and began to sob—"oh, Whit, darling. The boys. What would the boys think if you got mixed up in something like this?" She shook her head. "No, I have to do this alone."

He sat close beside her as she sobbed. His arm around her holding her gently. She lifted her head and turned to look at him. Her eyes were filled with the love and the agony she felt at that moment. "Isn't this like my **life**," she said. "I'm finally going to have what I've wanted more than anything else, and the joy of everything is shot to hell."

She wept quietly with Whit holding her. Suddenly she sat erect, dabbed at her eyes with her handkerchief. She looked at him and smiled, her lips trembling. "I must look a mess. Let me fix my face. Then I have to be going. Really I must."

"But, Dina. What do you mean you have to be going? We haven't settled a thing." Whit's voice reflected his anxiety. It was in part his fear that she would settle on some course of action that would exclude him from her life.

"Don't be upset, darling. I just want to freshen up and then I'm going back home."

"To tell Frank?"

"Yes. When I've pulled myself together enough, and when I've figured out what I'm going to do. I'm going to tell Frank."

Whit felt the fear of her independence cut through him.

"And what about us, Dina? What about me? What about the simple fact that you could be carrying our child?"

She looked at him and took his hands and kissed the tips of his fingers. He could feel the softness and the warmth of her lips. Her voice was barely audible.

"I love you, darling Whit. I love you. I love you. But this is something I have to handle myself. I don't know what's going to happen. I only know that my baby has to grow up in a home full of love; not like I did. And I don't want to hurt you. Oh, Whit, I so much don't want to hurt you."

He wouldn't let her go. He held her to him so that her wet cheeks pressed against his. He could barely speak. He felt his own tears run down his face and blend with hers.

"Darling. I don't give a damn about anyone or anything but you. You're not just stepping out of my life. You can't."

The phone rang. They let it ring. The hell with it, he thought. Then out of force of habit he slowly separated himself from her. He walked to the strident, incessant ringing of the goddamned phone.

"Yes."

"This is Mrs. Calisher, Doctor. It's about 1402, Mr. Bloomfield. His temperature is—"

Oh, God, dear God, he thought. Will it never end? My life is tearing apart and I have to worry about—

He saw Dina at the door. She had quickly put on her coat and picked up her bag and was standing there looking at him. Somehow she was smiling. She blew him a kiss. Her voice was still strained.

"Don't worry, darling. I'll be fine. After all, I have a really *great* doctor." And before he could say anything she was gone.

"Dr. Fraser, are you there? Dr. Fraser—"

Whit's mind slowly came back to the phone he was holding in his hand.

"I'm here, Nurse."

"Oh. I thought perhaps we had been disconnected."

"No."

"Well—ah—I see. Well, Doctor, it's about 1402—"

When Frank got to the office that same morning, Miss
Finley, his secretary, had placed on his desk along with his
opened mail his weekly copy of the *Reporter*. There, staring at him from the front page under the byline of that
seer of seers Mr. Stirling Livermore, was another article
on Computer titled: *Computer Ecolog Flashes Tilt?*

That miserable son of a bitch, thought Frank. That's all
I needed was that ratcatcher sniffing around again. Frank
quickly scanned the article. It was a general knock at Com-
puter as being a very overvalued speculation. But this time
Livermore was criticizing the accounting treatment of
Computer's capitalizing its research-and-development costs.

The stock was being hit hard as a result of Livermore's
article. The trouble with the bastard was he had an uncanny way of puncturing high-flying balloons. He was
thorough, professional, and cynical. Not only had he built
his readership among the odd-lotters, those who buy less
than a hundred shares of stock, but he had a known following of very sophisticated investors. They bought when
Livermore suggested a company was a buy and sold when
he suggested it was a sale. Stirling Livermore didn't run
the Street, but he was not to be dealt with lightly.

The morning progressed. Miss Finley's console begin to
light up as Frank's partners called about the Livermore
article. Porter Conrad, Frank's trading partner, called to
discuss the firm's long position—the amount of Computer
stock the firm held in its own inventory. As of the opening
of the market the firm was long two hundred thousand
shares of the stock at $15. In other words, the firm had in
its inventory three million dollars in Computer stock, a

position with which Frank and his partners felt most uncomfortable.

Frank and Porter decided, after consulting with Bill Davis, the firm's syndicate partner, to short fifty thousand shares. This meant that they would sell fifty thousand shares at the market, or $15 a share. They would be betting that Computer would go down in price and they would cover, or deliver their short position at a lower price. The difference would be their profit. This trading mechanism was filled with risk and they knew it. It would only be a hedge against any real disaster in the stock. The firm's position was just too large for so volatile a company as Computer.

Frank's experience told him that what Computer needed was a real piece of good news that would get the word out to the little guys, the suckers who were always too late on the way up, and too early on the way down. In short, Frank and his partners needed a break. But Frank was too old a hand to believe too faithfully in the benevolence of fortune. If Frank Sullivan had a credo it would have been that of Benjamin Franklin, who expressed the philosophy that "he who lives on hope will die farting."

Across the river in Queens, Angi Vittorio rose at his customary 6 A.M. and made himself some coffee. His wife lay breathing softly in drugged sleep as a result of the Dalmane she had taken about two in the morning after finishing the paperback sex thriller she couldn't put down.

Angi was always a restless sleeper. He would awaken at odd hours of the night, prowl the apartment in his dressing gown and slippers, smoke one cigarette after another until the living room was gray and acrid with smoke.

Angi's apartment lay directly under the approach path to one of the busiest runways at La Guardia, but he had long ago learned to tune out the roar of the incoming jets.

Angi would chain-smoke and sip on a beer watching the late late movie. Finally, red-eyed and exhausted, he would take a Librium and lie down on the wine-colored crushed-velvet sofa. He would fall into a restless sleep only to stir as the morning light groped its new rays about the heavy window drapes. The noise of banging garbage cans being collected by the Queens sanitary engineers usually awakened him to the start of another day.

Angi's day was rather ritualized. He never left the house until noon. He called about the city, mainly to the people who owed him money. Consulting his collection book, which was written in a code only he knew, he made appointments to collect. As a creditor, Angi had a very simple approach to business. He secured each loan by mortgages or pledges of collateral on houses, automobiles, jewelry—whatever. Then he charged a small service fee for supplying the needy borrower with cash. This came off the top of the loan. Angi's debtors hardly qualified for normal commercial banking relationships, so unfortunately he was their only source of debt capital. Since Angi felt he was filling a particularly risky but useful role in the world of commerce, he felt his interest rates should be pegged accordingly. With Angi's service fees, these interest rates cost his borrowers up to 65 percent.

Angi was well aware that his rates of interest were illegal and sometimes prompted his clients to want to refuse payment. Angi's admonition before he gave anyone cash—he never dealt in checks—was simple. He would look at his new debtor with black menacing Sicilian violence and growl, "The only way you can not pay me is to die." They usually got the message.

As the morning progressed and the market opened, Angi's day would begin to develop momentum. He would give the market time to generate some volume. Then he would call Charlie Fox. But he would not call Charlie at Fox and Bohlen, because Charlie Fox was not there. He was still recuperating from his accident with the dry cleaning truck that had hit the taxi he was riding in almost two months ago. Charlie had suffered four broken ribs, a broken right arm, a punctured lung, a ruptured spleen, and a fractured skull.

But Charlie Fox did not die. The stubborn little man fought with an unusual tenacity to hold on to the thread of life that several times seemed to be slipping away. He was still in the Hospital of the Sacred Heart, with its dirt-blackened brick front and its ancient hallways, its antique fixtures hanging from spider-piped ceilings, green vinyl-tiled floors that had been polished thin.

The Sacred Heart Hospital had never quite had a patient like Charlie Fox, nor a patron like Angi Vittorio.

When Charlie was in a coma and it was thought he would probably not recover, Angi was plagued with the dread that his clandestine investment in Fox and Bohlen would go down the drain. Bohlen couldn't run the business. When Angi tried to sell it, his friends, whose sources of information were thorough and reliable, knew he had big trouble. They were willing to buy him out—at 50 percent less than the firm of Fox and Bohlen was worth.

Angi was caught in a bind and the thought of taking a bath of 50 percent for the kind of money he had invested in Fox and Bohlen made him frantic.

During the precarious phases of Charlie Fox's recovery, this cyclonic Italian said mass every day for a struggling little Jew who lay in a Catholic hospital, fighting every inch of the way to hold on to his life.

The masses became more frequent. To show his penance Angi tried to give up smoking. He slept less and was more restless. Then the miracle seemed to happen. Charlie Fox began to recover. The more assured Charlie's recovery, the less frequent were Angi's visits to the church. And when Charlie was recuperating and beginning to fidget from boredom, Angi helped him out. Not without a great deal of difficulty, and the pledge of sufficient cash contributions to bolster the sagging structure of the Sacred Heart, was Angi able to get Charlie Fox back to work.

One day two green-uniformed Negroes installed a quote

machine so that Charlie could watch the market from his bed. Even more impressive was the direct line to Fox and Bohlen that Angi had installed in Charlie's room.

Contrary to the fear of the doctors and shocked sisters, giving Charlie back the thing he loved most, the stock market, helped to speed his recovery. It also did a great deal for Angi's peace of mind.

Angi spent a part of each day in a solicitous pilgrimage to the Hospital of the Sacred Heart, where he would try to lend Charlie's day some added cheer with gutter humor and a mixture of thoughtful presents. He began to clutter the small private room. Boxes were piled on the gray steel clothes cabinet, and on the sills of the dirty windows that looked out on the hospital's parking lot.

Charlie and Angi understood each other perfectly. Charlie was Angi's pilot fish who cruised with the shark for the benefits they both derived. The only difference was that Charlie Fox would have preferred to withdraw from the relationship.

When the door to Charlie's room opened on one particular afternoon, framed in the doorway was no picture of benign concern. Rather this massive Italian with murder in his eye faced the now slim form of Mr. Charles Fox as he lay propped up in bed watching the New York Stock Exchange and the American Stock Exchange tape on his video screen. There was a look of concern on Charlie's face.

Angi came into the room quickly. "That son of a bitch Livermore. That cocksucker—"

Charlie raised his head. "So you heard about the article on Computer?"

"Heard about it! I got the fuckin' thing right here." He threw a copy of the *Reporter* onto the green metal chair. The paper fell off the chair and crackled against the wall. "That fucker."

"Careful, Angi," Charlie smiled. "The sisters might hear you and throw me out of here. I don't want to be the first Jew excommunicated from the Sacred Heart."

"Fuck the Sacred Heart."

"But, Angi. All those masses." Charlie was pulling his leg.

"Never mind with the wise-guy stuff. That goddamn stock is gonna hit the skids again and this time I ain't gonna sit here like some dummy while all the smart cocksuckers on Wall Street fall all over themselves gettin' out."

Charlie eyed Angi with cold steady appraisal. "Just what do you intend to do, Angi?"

"I'll tell you what I'm gonna do. I'm gonna tell that fuckin' Irish prick friend of yours that we pulled his ass out of the fire for him. Now he's gonna save our ass for us."

"How?"

"He's gonna buy our goddamned stock, that's how. And he ain't gonna buy it at no goddamn market price, either. He's gonna buy it for what we sold his for."

"You must be mad, Angi. Stark, raving mad."

"Mad, am I? You think I'm kiddin', huh?"

Angi's voice reverberated down the aseptic corridors.

"Fuck him. Fuck you. Fuck all you Wall Street con artists. This is Angi's game now, and I know how to play it. I'm gonna take the eyes out of that Irish cocksucker."

Angi had worked himself into a towering rage which spilled his profanity into the sterile tranquillity of the Sacred Heart. His back was turned toward the door of Charlie's room. He was facing Charlie, waving his arms in grotesque gestures of hostility, completely unaware of the silent presence of the sister superior, who stood with her hands clenched tightly into fists that were placed squarely on each hip.

She stood there for a moment like some great starched bird until she could contain herself no longer.

"Mr. Vittorio." It was a command straight from God. Angi spun around to confront this formidable emissary of the church. Her very appearance touched the spark of fear and respect that had been beaten into him by his parish priest in Brooklyn nearly forty-five years ago. His mouth dropped open. His face blanched. He started to stammer an apology.

The sister held up one white arm and pointed with one very white forefinger. Her lips formed the word like a bullet.

"Out. Out, Mr. Vittorio. And I don't want to see you back in this hospital on my shift unless you bring a written order from Dr. Moran."

She had reached into the psyche of this middle-aged loan shark, and dragged by the ear a ten-year-old boy, whom she was throwing out of school and not permitting back without a note.

Angi started to protest.

God's emissary raised her hand and closed her eyes as if praying to the Holy Father to let her keep her self-control.

"Get out. Out. Get out. You're not welcome here, Mr. Vittorio."

Charlie tried hard to keep his expression serious, to satisfy both the Avenging Angel in white and the humbled predator in the checked knit suit who was being summarily dismissed.

Angi stole a furtive look at Charlie. "I'll call yuh." He fumbled with his hat. "Bye, Sister. I'm—I'm really sorry if I got outta line."

Her arm was still extended with its finger pointing down the corridor. Angi passed quickly in front of her starched bosom and headed fast for the ancient elevators of the Sacred Heart.

Charlie lay in bed thinking about Angi long after he had gone. He hadn't the faintest idea what Angi intended to do. But he knew from his association with Mr. Vittorio that Angi's solutions to problems seemed to revolve around the precept that if you twisted someone's arm hard enough, applied enough pressure, scared the living hell out of whomever you were trying to affect, then they usually folded and came your way. But these techniques were successful in the sleazy lunchrooms and backwater bars of Queens and Brooklyn where Angi usually held his business conferences. Charlie could only contemplate what their effect would be when applied to the well-upholstered suites of Wall Street and Park Avenue. One thing Charlie's intuition told him was that Frank Sullivan was in for some surprises.

Charlie knew Frank from the years long ago, and he knew the toughness that had been carefully hidden behind the façade of style that Frank had so painstakingly built over the years. Frank had grown, as they say on the Street. That meant that he was a member of the right clubs, served on the right boards of directors, lived at the right addresses, summered and wintered at the right places, and had come to head his own powerful and prestigious investment banking firm.

No one knew better than Charlie how tough an Irishman there was, so carefully tailored in those Savile Row suits. Angi would be in for some surprises himself.

Outside on the street Angi's mood was one of anger mixed with a sense of penance at the violation of all propriety he had committed at the Sacred Heart. He crossed himself quickly and mumbled a silent "forgive me, Fadder" and looked for a phone booth. He found a bank of phones on the next block. The wind was blustery. Blown newspapers scurried across the street like crumpled birds. The buildings were impregnated with grime. Unwashed dented automobiles were parked bumper to bumper on both sides of the street. Broken glass glistened on the sidewalks.

None of this drab squalor impressed itself on Angi. This was where he lived, what he knew, and as he proceeded toward the bank of telephone booths on the corner, he had only one thought in mind: to get hold of that cocksucker Sullivan and tell him what Angi Vittorio wanted him to do.

He opened the door of one booth and saw the yellow sticker placed over the change slots: SORRY OUT OF ORDER. Angi cursed and looked in the next booth. A steel-sheathed cable hung loose with its phone torn off. "Those nigger fuckers," Angi growled. He automatically attributed all the woes of life in New York to Nigger Fuckers and those Fuckin' Spics. He jerked open the door of the next booth. The little yellow sticker was again pasted over the change slots. Angi took his thinly soled foot in its crinkled patent-leather loafer with the gold bit and snaffle over the instep and kicked viciously at the booth. "No fuckin' good!" he yelled. "Every fuckin' thing in this fuckin' city is no fuckin' good!" He kicked the booth again. A stab of pain shot through the toes of his right foot, "Jesus Christ." He hopped on his left foot holding the other in his hand, his face grimacing in pain. "Son of a bitch," he cursed.

He saw a tired-looking neighborhood drugstore up the block and limped toward that.

"You gotta phone?" he growled at the resigned face that watched him from behind the counter. The head jerked in the direction of a dark corner in the back of the store. There was a pay telephone on the wall. Angi grunted. He got the number of the firm of Sullivan & Co. from information and dialed the call.

"I wanna speak to Frank Sullivan."

"Just one moment, please."

Angi heard the phone ringing to another extension.

"This is Mr. Sullivan's secretary, may I help you?"

"Yah, lady. You can tell Mr. Sullivan that Angi Vittorio wants to talk to him."

A long pause.

"Does Mr. Sullivan know you, Mr. Vittorio?"

"No. But he knows a friend of mine, Charlie Fox. Tell him Charlie Fox told me to call him, it's kind of an emergency." Angi smiled as he gave Miss Finley that last one.

Another pause.

"I see. I'll have to see if Mr. Sullivan can take this call."
She buzzed Frank, who was on the phone talking long distance.

"I'm sorry to interrupt, Mr. Sullivan—"

Frank pushed the hold button.

"What is it, Miss Finley?" His voice was irritated.

"I'm sorry, Mr. Sullivan, but it's a Mr. Vittorio. He says he's a friend of Mr. Charles Fox, who told him to call you. He says it's an emergency of some kind."

At the mention of Charlie's name, the warning lights began to glow in Frank's mind.

"Tell him to hold a minute."

Frank went back to his call.

"Look, Parker, someone's on my other line. I have to take the call. Let me ring you right back. Fine. I appreciate it."

Frank got back to Miss Finley.

"Put him on."

"Hello."

"Is dis Frank Sullivan?"

"Yes, it is. You say your name is Mr. Vittorio?"

"Dat's right. Angi Vittorio. I'm a close friend of an old pal of yours—Charlie Fox."

"Yes. I have known Charlie for a good number of years."

Angi began to laugh.

"Listen, Sullivan. I'm at a pay phone in some junk drugstore in Queens. I wanna have a little talk wich ya— an' I don't like phones. So I'm gonna hop a cab and come down to your office—"

"I'm afraid that's impossible, Mr. Vittorio. I'm completely booked for this afternoon."

"I don't give a shit how booked you are, Sullivan. You can unbook yourself 'cause I'm comin' down there to talk about a little stock called Computer Ecolog. Remember? You sold it through Charlie Fox. Remember that—"

The operator cut in. "Please deposit five cents for the

next five minutes or your call will be interrupted . . ."

"Son of a bitch," Angi growled and groped in his pocket for a nickel. He deposited it. The little bell rang. "Thank you."

"Screw you."

"What did you say?"

"Not you, Sullivan. Now listen. I ain't got all day. I got a kind of interest you might say in Charlie's welfare." Angi's face broke into a grin. "Yeh, you might put it that way, and I'm comin' down there to talk to you about Computer Ecolog."

"Just who do you think you're talking to, Mr. Vittorio?" Frank's voice filled Angi's ear with restrained anger. Angi's face grew purple. His neck swelled so that his collar began to choke him.

"Listen, you Irish prick. I'm comin' down there and you better goddamn well look like bein' there when I get downtown, because you and me got some real business to talk about." Angi smashed down the receiver. He glared at the noncommittal face behind the drug counter and lunged out of the store to look for a cab.

Frank was so surprised at the whole tone of the call that his reactions other than anger were slow in coming. Vittorio. He didn't know anyone by that name. He leaned back in his chair. His eyes looked without seeing the broad expanse of the Hudson and East Rivers as they wound their way north. The air was so clear that he could see past the George Washington Bridge. The whole island lay beneath him like the bleached upturned skeletal jaws of a stranded whale. Its towers reflected the late light of an afternoon sun. Who the hell was Vittorio? He reached for the call buzzer.

"Miss Finley. Get me Charlie Fox."

Miss Finley flipped through the Rolodex and found the number for Fox and Bohlen.

Frank spoke to Mr. Bohlen and learned that Charlie was

still in the hospital. When he asked if a Mr. Vittorio was associated with the firm, Bohlen's tone became noticeably defensive. His reply was not at all convincing.

"No, Mr. Sullivan. We have no Mr. Vittorio associated with this firm. No, sir."

Suspicions began to form in Frank's mind.

"Could you tell me if Charlie is still at the Sacred Heart?"

Bohlen's voice was even more wary.

"He's still there, Mr. Sullivan. Supposed to be discharged sometime this week."

"I see. Thank you very much, Mr. Bohlen." Frank hung up. His next call was to Charlie Fox.

Charlie's voice was mixed with the genuine pleasure of hearing from an old friend and the realization that Angi had contacted Frank.

"Frank. It's good to hear your voice."

"I didn't realize you were still in the hospital."

"Yeh, Frank. I think they're getting ready to let me out of here sometime this week. I've been here so long I think they've finally converted me."

Frank gave a hoarse chuckle.

"I don't think this is a particularly good time to come over to our side, Charlie. The church is going broke."

They both laughed.

"Say, Charlie. I just received a rather peculiar phone call from a fellow who claims to be a friend of yours." Frank paused. "Charlie. I don't want to impose. Am I tiring you in any way?"

"Hell, no, Frank. I'm going nuts in this place. I'm glad to talk to you."

Frank hesitated. "Do you know a Mr. Vittorio?"

There was an audible sigh on the other end of the line. "Yes, Frank, I do."

"I see. Is he in any way associated with your firm?"

Another pause.

"Frank. I'd rather not go into that one over the phone."

"I see."

Frank thought for a moment.

"He's coming down here to see me on some matter. I gathered from his conversation that you were somehow involved. He said something about my sale of Computer stock. How would he know anything about that?"

Charlie sighed audibly this time.

"Frank, it's a long story. I can't talk about it on the phone."

Frank paused. His voice was husky, with a trace of annoyance and concern. "I've known you too long, Charlie, to believe that you would disclose to a stranger a personal transaction of mine that I asked your firm to execute." His voice carried a distinct chill. "I won't disturb you further, Charlie. I hope you're up and about soon." Frank hung up. He buzzed Miss Finley.

"There will be a Mr. Vittorio coming to see me. Let me know when he arrives. I want to see him as soon as possible. If I'm in a meeting, I'll break it up."

"Yes, Mr. Sullivan."

Frank looked out at Manhattan Island sprawled below him. A large white ocean liner was steaming slowly down the river on its way to the open sea. It was one of the Swedish ships. Frank sighed. He wished he were on it. He felt tired and depressed. The market was lousy. His firm's profits were down. His partners were restive and tense, as was almost everyone he knew. He needed very much to get away from it all for a while.

The Street did that to you. After a time the incessant tension simply sucked you dry of vitality and perspective. You had to get away to refresh not only your body but your mind.

He watched the white ocean liner slip out of his vision. His thoughts wistfully followed it.

He flicked back to the time he was a boy. When he

didn't have a dime. It seemed to him he was happier then. The thought occurred to him that he should simply quit, liquidate his investments in real estate and securities, and tell everyone to go to hell. Maybe he and Dina could find their way back together again. That's what she always seemed to want: to spend more meaningful time together; and she was right. He didn't give her the time she needed. This goddamn business wouldn't let him. But he knew he would never quit. The pulse of the Street was part of the beat of his own life: the pressure, the action, the deals, the challenges. The whole jungle was the only place where Frank was truly at home.

The social side of his life was just an extension of his business. He entertained people who were useful to him in one way or another, so that even in his relationships with most other people, Frank never left the office. The more he achieved, the more remote seemed to be his ability to enjoy what he had won.

One of Frank's more intriguing qualities was his ability to understand this. A part of his mind was able to stand aside and philosophically appraise the other part: his motives, his drive, his hypocrisies, his rationalizations. Frank knew when he was kidding himself, and from long training he knew it didn't pay. He had learned to look at the bottom line of everything, including the net net, as the Street would say, of his own life. He understood in large measure why he did what he did, but that didn't keep him from doing it. Frank Sullivan was astute enough to know that he might be building sand castles that could be washed out with any incoming tide, but this was part of the fascination of the game, the *risk*. Simply put, Frank wouldn't change because he didn't want to.

As he thought about this, Miss Finley buzzed.

"It's Mr. Faulkner, Mr. Sullivan."

Frank sighed. He lit a cigarette and exhaled the smoke. "Put him on."

"Frank." The high-pitched voice grated on his ear.

"Yes, Dean."

"I want to talk to you about Trans Union. Have you got some time?"

"I'm expecting someone shortly, Dean. Can it wait?"

Dean paused.

"Frank. These things can always wait, but I thought you might be interested in knowing that Joe Feldman called me about ten minutes ago concerning those Sierra bonds we sold his pension fund."

Oh, Christ, Frank thought. Not those goddamn bonds again.

"What did he want?"

Dean's voice was edged with sarcasm. "Not very much. He simply said that he wanted us to buy the bonds back from him at par."

Frank's stomach sent him a warning jab.

"How many did he buy?"

"Eight hundred thousand."

Frank didn't respond for a moment. His thoughts were on those goddamn bonds. When he did answer, his voice was traced with fatigue and annoyance.

"Come on in," he said and hung up the phone.

Frank's firm had underwritten a bond issue to help finance Sierra Resorts, a year-round golf and skiing development in the Berkshires in Massachusetts. The bonds were backed by the state of Massachusetts. Thus the rating services gave the bonds their second highest rating: AA. Frank's firm headed a syndicate that sold ten million dollars' worth of bonds. If one read the prospectus carefully (which few people did), he or she would have noted that the AA rating was given subject to the on-time completion of the projects contemplated by Sierra Resorts, Inc., such as the building of an initial ski lodge, ski tow, clearing several new slopes, artificial snow-making machinery, an eighteen-hole golf course, restaurant and lounge, sauna, a hundred condominiums, an Olympic-size swimming pool and so on.

The builders and developers were less than professional. The projects were not completed on time. They remained uncompleted.

The state of Massachusetts withdrew its guarantee. Sierra Resorts, Inc., went into bankruptcy, and everybody with a lawyer was suing Sullivan & Co. and its syndicate partners in the deal, as well as the accountants; even the rating services and the state of Massachusetts. It was a hell of a mess.

To make matters worse, Joe Feldman, Chairman of Trans Union, had just called Dean and told him that he expected the firm of Sullivan & Co. to buy back eight hundred thousand dollars of his bonds at his cost, or he would sue them to their eyeballs. But what was even worse, Joe would cut the firm off from every dime's worth of business that Trans Union gave to Sullivan & Co. He would use whatever weight he had—and that was considerable—to see that friends of Trans Union would not do business with Frank's firm.

Frank waited for Dean to come in with all the enthusiasm that Mary Stuart had while waiting for the ax.

Dean walked into Frank's office, his face grim.

Frank never thought of Dean without likening him to the ferret.

To Frank, Dean represented a malignant but highly talented partner whose ambition it was to unseat him and become the senior partner of Sullivan & Co. No one knew better than Frank that, given the opportunity, Dean Faulkner would use any means to get him out of the way.

Why did he tolerate this? Dean's capital position in the firm was second only to Frank's. More important, Dean was a highly effective producer of substantial corporate business. That business would be hard to replace if Frank fired Dean. He had the power to do so. It was written into the partnership agreement of the firm. But it would be necessary for Frank to have grave reasons for effecting so serious a move. Dean might very possibly be able to gather enough of the younger partners together to walk out en masse if it came to a showdown. This was improbable because of Dean's personality. He had the charm of a hungry snake, and this reflected itself within the firm in a certain lack of warmth and affection for him. But it was always possible that Dean could become Frank's Cromwell. Frank not only expected Dean to create problems but had taken certain precautions to see that if trouble came, Dean would eventually meet with Cromwell's end. At least that was the way Frank had planned it. God alone knew how it would turn out.

Frank and Dean looked at each other without affection. Frank spoke first. He already knew the answers to the questions he was about to ask but wanted those answers confirmed by Dean.

"When did you speak to Joe?"

"About ten to fifteen minutes ago."

"How unhappy was he?"

"You know Joe. If he didn't have something to cry about it would ruin his day. Only this time he's bleating like a shorn lamb. I can't say I blame him."

"Is he giving us any way out?"

"No."

"What are our alternatives?"

"Two. Let him sue us and take away his business or buy back the bonds."

Frank stubbed his cigarette into the heavy glass ashtray. For some peculiar reason he thought of Elliot Thompson and Dina; he thought of Whit and Dina. Jesus, he felt old and tired. Between Sierra and Computer, and Faulkner trying to steal his firm, and Fraser trying to steal his wife, Frank was beginning to feel pulled just a little thin.

"We'll have to have a meeting of the partners on this,

but personally I don't think we can afford to antagonize Joe."

The buzzer squawked. Frank's voice snapped back at Miss Finley.

"What is it?"

"Mr. Vittorio is here. Wait, Mr. Vittorio! You can't go in there! Mr. Vittorio! Mr. Sullivan! Mr. Vittorio!"

The door to Frank's office opened and there stood the menacing dark Sicilian in the checked knit suit glowering at both Dean and Frank. The helpless Miss Finley looked imploringly at the back of their uninvited guest.

Dean had stood up. His body seemed to vibrate like a tuning fork. His dark eyes flashed their malevolence at this intruder. His high-pitched voice hissed out at this unbelievable interruption.

"Who the hell are you?" Dean said, and looked wonderingly first at Frank, then at Angi blocking Frank's doorway. Dean's reaction was as if someone had thrown an overripe fish into the room. Angi caught the inference and glowered at Dean.

"I'm Angi Vittorio. Now, which one of you two is Sullivan?"

Frank stood up slowly, with great dignity. His voice was very firm.

"I'm Mr. Sullivan, Mr. Vittorio. This is one of my partners, Mr. Faulkner."

Frank looked over Angi's shoulder at Miss Finley, who caught his signal and silently closed the door.

Frank turned to Dean. "I was expecting this *gentleman*, Dean." There was no missing the sarcasm in Frank's voice. "Perhaps not quite so dramatically, but he was expected nevertheless. Dean, you had better let Mr. Vittorio discuss his business with me, whatever it is, privately."

Dean looked first at Angi and then at Frank. He was absolutely incredulous that this swarthy Italian had forced his way into the office of the senior partner of Sullivan & Co. Dean couldn't believe it.

Frank motioned to Dean. "I'm sure whatever Mr. Vittorio's business is I can handle it."

Dean shook his head still in disbelief and started to walk from the room; Frank stopped him.

"Would you round up the boys say about four thirty or five. I want to get back to Joe no later than tomorrow. Call him and tell him we'll have a decision for him on those bonds before noon tomorrow."

Dean walked out of Frank's office and stopped at Rose Finley's desk. He was still incredulous. His eyes accidentally drifted to Rose's dictation pad. Rose watched him with silent dislike.

Rose Finley had fallen in love with Frank almost twenty-five years ago.

After her first interview she knew that he was going to be the man in her life; the only problem was that Frank had other plans.

Frank was not about to marry a pretty Irish girl from New Jersey with no money and no social position. Even if he were attracted to Rose, he would have turned it off; Frank could do that. So the attraction that had matured over the years was very one-sided. Frank was aware of it, and he was particularly thoughtful to Rose, but it ended there.

"Do you know who this Vittorio fellow is?"

Miss Finley viewed Dean with carefully concealed suspicion.

"No, sir, I don't."

Dean paused. "Do you know who he's with?"

"No, sir."

Dean had long ago learned to read upside down, and glancing at Miss Finley's dictation book he noticed after the name Vittorio, another name, and then some shorthand symbols. The other name was Charles Fox.

Small acts often precipitate large events. Miss Finley's open notebook did just that. The first thing Dean Faulkner did when he got back to his office was to call in Charlie Butterworth, who was a staff assistant to Dean. Butterworth was affectionately and somewhat unkindly referred to by his contemporaries at Sullivan & Co. as Marsh, a contraction for *marshmallow*. Marsh was Dean's pilot fish. He swam morosely with his shark, quiet, depressed, controlled, unhappy. His function was to keep his shark happy. He did grunt work that Dean assigned to him. He hopefully followed Mr. Faulkner about in the unfounded belief that devotion and loyalty would be rewarded by Dean.

"Marsh."

"Yes, Dean."

"I have a special job for you that I want carried out with the utmost discretion."

Marsh was instantly elated: an opportunity for his subservient soul to serve.

"I want you to find out who a Charles Fox is, and what if any relationship he has to a Mr. Angelo Vittorio, and I don't want a soul to know about this."

The hound-dog face of Marsh Butterworth was almost reflecting joy.

"Right, Dean. I'll get right on it."

"Remember. I don't want any leaks on this. If you want to call me, use my private number. Don't go through my secretary."

"I've got it, Dean."

And with that brief conversation, Mr. Frank Sullivan's considerable troubles would be multiplied, and his joys most certainly divided.

Frank looked at Angi Vittorio, the gray eyes meeting the dark brown. The winds of time swept back to the gang fights Frank had when he was a kid. The Irish against the wops and the Jews. The old generalization that all wops were yellow moved about at the back of his mind. It was a boyhood maxim that experience had long dispelled. But Frank had an uncanny ability to read men. He read this one to be dangerous but without real courage. The gray eyes never flickered from the brown.

Angi became uneasy. He looked about Frank's office, obviously impressed.

"Nice spot ya got here, Sullivan."

Frank didn't reply and didn't offer Angi a seat. He slowly sat down himself, lit a cigarette, and waited without saying a word. It was a tactic Frank had learned to employ skillfully, and its effect on Angi was readily discernible. He was clearly unnerved by this cold Irish prick who didn't say anything but never took his eyes off him.

Angi had been through the gang wars as a kid himself. He was in a business where bullying and threats were as much a part of his routine as another man's morning coffee, but he sensed the strength in this Irishman. He knew instinctively that Frank was tough, a gut fighter regardless of all the trappings of civility that his office and the man himself portrayed. Angi knew from experience that a guy like Sullivan went for the jugular if he had to. A little shiver of fear spread around the edges of Angi's mind.

Frank smoked slowly, never taking his eyes off Vittorio, never uttering a word.

"Look, Sullivan. I came down here because Charlie Fox and me—well, we pulled your tit out of a wringer with this Computer Ecolog. Now we got our tit caught and we want *you* to get it out."

Frank remained silent, smoking quietly. Angi had never had an experience quite like this before. Angi was like a blowfish: when he sensed danger he puffed himself up by bellowing and threatening.

"Listen, Sullivan, don't give me that silent treatment. That may work around these punks you've got here, but it don't mean shit to Angi Vittorio. Now, listen to me, Sullivan, and listen good. I told Charlie at the time that you must have known somethin' was wrong with the company when you sold, but he wouldn't listen. He said that Frank Sullivan wouldn't do that. He gave me a lot of bullshit about what a *big* man you were, a high and mighty Irishman." Frank's lips tightened. Angi watched him like a hawk. "Yeh. Some big goddamned Protestant Irishman who was holier than the Pope. I told Charlie he was a jerk; not to believe that bullshit." Angi's eyes began to bulge and his voice turned to gravel. "I let Charlie, that dumb Jew shit, take you out of Computer, an' keep us in, an' I ain't playin' sucker to no Irish Protestant because everyone tells me he's a big man—screw that. You copped out, Sullivan, why I don't know. But that bullshit Charlie gave me about you bein' squeezed for dough, that's a lot of crap. You sold because you know somethin' we don't, an' I'm not lettin' you get away with it."

Frank sighed, an indifferent, patronizing sigh.

He lit another cigarette carefully, slowly, always looking directly at Angi. Finally he spoke. His voice was low and very controlled, but the threat of menace was in every syllable.

"I am assuming, Mr. Vittorio, that your connection with the firm of Fox and Bohlen is not something casual or unimportant to you. Is that correct?"

Angi was very wary. "What the hell is that supposed to mean?"

Frank exhaled blue-gray smoke in Angi's direction.

"It is not *supposed* to mean anything, Mr. Vittorio. You have special knowledge of a perfectly legal securities transaction between myself and the firm of Fox and Bohlen. And you intimate to me that you personally have a stake in Charlie Fox's firm; that you are suffering financial hardship due to the fall in Computer's stock. Is that a fair approximation of your position, Mr. Vittorio?"

Angi was flustered. His face seemed to turn gray, his eyes popped at Frank in undisguised hostility.

"Speak English, Sullivan. I ain't one to screw around with a lot of fancy words. Lay it out, whatever the hell it is you're sayin'."

Frank remained implacable, inscrutable, smoking slowly, always looking at Angi with cold hostile purpose. Frank read the fear in Angi's eyes and he knew this *was* a yellow wop. He was a kid again on the East Side. He was in an alley with a bunch of wop kids. They circled him slowly until he found the piece of two-by-four with the rusted bent nails lying near the wall of the tenement house. He remembered the look of surprise and fear in their eyes as he picked up the board and began to move at them slowly, carefully. They started to back away and then suddenly, he was only fifteen at the time, he let out a savage cry, a bloodcurdling scream that summoned all the Gaelic warriors of his ancestral tribes and he rushed at those wops swinging wildly with the vicious weapon that fate had put in his hands. He remembered how they broke and ran from that mad Irish kid. The thoughts made him smile as he looked at Angi Vittorio. The Sicilian *knew* that he was facing a merciless opponent. It almost made Angi shiver as he looked at Frank.

"What I'm saying, Mr. Vittorio," said Frank, "is that I believe you have a special connection with Charlie's firm. Is that correct?"

Angi was very uncomfortable.

"It's none of your goddamn business, Sullivan."

Frank exhaled more smoke in Angi's direction.

"Mr. Vittorio, I'm afraid you've *made* this my business. Somehow you intimate that I caused you and Charlie some financial hardship. That tells me you must have an interest in Charlie's firm. I'm sitting here wondering, Mr. Vittorio, if your interest is known to the Securities and Exchange Commission and the Internal Revenue Service." Frank paused and stubbed out his cigarette. The ashtray was getting pretty full. "I don't have any idea what your business interests are, Mr. Vittorio, but I think I could make some educated guesses."

Angi was a cornered wop.

"Sullivan. I got friends who don't fuck around."

Frank's face never changed expression. He was still the kid in the alley with the two-by-four with the nails in one end of the board, rushing a bunch of wops. He was as deadly as a bush adder and Angi knew it. This kind of Irishman didn't scare. Besides, Angi never really went in for rough stuff. He had stayed out of trouble because he worked alone. He hollered and blustered and frightened, but when it came down to it, as far as Angi went was to hire a couple of goons to work someone over. Nothing permanent, no crippling, just a last resort to remind his debtor that his bill was overdue.

"Are you threatening me, Vittorio?" It was the first time Frank had dropped the Mister.

"I ain't threatenin' nobody. I'm just interested in your long life an' good health."

"That's very thoughtful of you, Vittorio. I'm most appreciative. Now, suppose we get down to business. What is it exactly that you want me to do?"

Angi eyed Sullivan for a long time. When he finally spoke he spit the words at Frank.

"I want you to buy our stock at the price you got for yours."

Frank smiled. "I'm positive that a man of your experience wouldn't expect anyone in his right mind to subscribe to such a proposition."

"Well, think again, you Irish prick." Angi was on his feet advancing toward Frank's desk. Frank remained seated while Angi's temper raged so that his lips became flecked with saliva and his dark eyes seemed to pop out of his head. His speech was almost incoherent.

"You fuckin' Irish prick. You bailed out while that

fuckin' company was fallin' apart and everybody got their balls knocked off but you. You're sittin' there smellin' like a goddamn rose, and we got shit all over us. Well, not Angi Vittorio, Sullivan. I'm gonna grab you by the short hairs where it hurts." He leaned over Frank's desk, both arms spread wide.

"Sullivan, you cocksucker. Either you buy that stock from us or I'm goin' to Livermore and give him the whole story. You'll be finished. Those white-shoe phonies will eat you alive. I'll nail you to the goddamn wall, Sullivan."

For the first time Frank slowly got to his feet. His voice was so low and filled with menace that Angi's bellowing and roaring stopped immediately.

"Sit down, Vittorio." It was a quiet command. Angi backed up hesitantly, very slowly, and then sat down.

Frank looked at Angi silently for a long time and then turned his back on him and moved toward the windows overlooking Manhattan.

Frank was most effective when he was under pressure. And Angi was forcing to the surface all the guile and cunning, the tenacity and strength, the will and drive and guts it took to build on Wall Street the kind of firm Frank had created from nothing.

Angi was dangerous, but his opponent was deadly.

Frank, as he looked out over Manhattan, saw for a brief flash the face of that German officer in the farmhouse at Horb. The perplexed pleading look as he started for his P-38, then stopped. His mouth and eyes looking at the impassive face, and the gray eyes; those implacable gray eyes of the American major. Frank's Colt .45 jumped in his hand. The heavy slug hit the German full in the chest, sending him crashing over the chair, his body sliding backward away from Frank, the look of surprise and horror still on his face as if he had suddenly realized just before it happened that he was going to die. Frank remembered the others, their arms with outstretched hands raised high toward the ceiling, their faces struck with terror.

The picture slipped from his mind as he began to speak to Angi, only half turning toward him, not looking at him. Frank coughed. His voice was strained. Have to give up those damn cigarettes, he thought.

"Vittorio. Let me tell you a little something about our business. The sale of a portion of my holdings of Computer was a perfectly legal sale of registered stock."

Frank continued. "I couldn't care less whether or not a columnist like Mr. Livermore is informed of such a sale. Mr. Livermore's column doesn't interest me, nor does Mr. Livermore." Frank was bluffing. He was a master of this type of poker playing.

Angi watched him closely and couldn't tell if this cold Irishman really meant it. But Angi was no fool. His instincts told him that Frank was more than a little concerned.

"Furthermore, Vittorio." Frank moved to turn and regard Angi with menace. "Since you came in here and disrupted my office, and personally threatened me, I'm going to interest myself in *your* affairs. I don't have the distinction of knowing your friends, Vittorio, but I do happen to know the heads of the Internal Revenue Service and the Securities and Exchange Commission. It occurs to me they might very well take an interest in your affairs."

Angi laughed. "Sullivan, you kill me. I got nothin' to hide. I file a clean return. I ain't even been audited."

Frank was backlighted by the large glass windows. The light emphasized his flecked gray hair. "I'm sure you've been quite careful, but the government can be very thorough and very patient. It has nothing but time and money —and, I might add, some very competent investigators." Frank coughed again. A slow smile spread across his face but his eyes didn't smile. "Would you like to trade a Livermore for the IRS, Vittorio?" Frank chuckled. "Now, if you'll excuse me, I've got a meeting to attend." Frank pushed his intercom.

"Yes, sir."

"Will you show Mr. Vittorio out, Miss Finley, and tell the others that we'll hold the meeting I had called at four thirty in my office." It was now five fifteen.

Angi for the moment had little to say. As the door to Frank's office opened, and the figure of Miss Finley stood in the doorway, Angi turned to Sullivan, his face a mask of frustrated determination.

"Okay, Sullivan. If that's the way you wanna play, we'll play. I'll trade your friends for mine. The IRS for Livermore. Let's see how you like that."

Frank watched him in the double-knit coat and matching narrow-brim hat storm past Miss Finley, down the corridor toward the elevators.

More than a little anxiety hung in the back of Frank's mind as he sat down at his desk. If Vittorio went to Livermore he could cause Frank a lot of embarrassment. The unseen mists of trouble that shrouded the rocks upon which Frank's life might be smashed could very well be spread by Vittorio. But on the other hand, Frank was gambling that the hook of fear he had planted in Angi, threatening to direct the IRS's attention toward Angi's affairs, would call his bluff. Frank had fought and bluffed all his life and he was used to the risk, but he was getting older and more tired, and the game which he couldn't stop playing was beginning to wear him down. Jesus Christ, he was tired.

After the meeting with his partners, in which they decided to buy back Joe Feldman's bonds and take a loss of nearly six hundred thousand dollars, Frank slumped exhausted in the back of the limousine as the big car moved up the East River Drive.

It was nearly eight thirty. The traffic had thinned so that they made good time. Tony handled the big car skillfully. Dean Faulkner sat beside Frank; silent, lost in his own thoughts. Glen Farrell was in the front seat beside Tony. The three partners were dead tired. The day had wrung them dry. They would each return home to wives that expected their exhausted husbands to kiss them out of habit and reach impulsively for the first of several martinis that would help them unwind from the trials of another day on the Street. But Frank's evening was to be wholly different. It would completely change his life.

They sat together in the large living room after a nearly silent dinner. Frank could not shake the events of the day. His mind jumped from one problem to another until the four martinis began to affect him.

Dina hardly touched her food.

"Is there anything wrong, Mrs. Sullivan?" The butler was concerned.

She smiled at him. "Not a thing, Bevan. It's delicious. I'm really not very hungry, that's all."

Frank looked up. He didn't want to hear about another goddamn problem. He sensed that Dina wanted to talk to him about something serious; but he wanted to relax, forget about anything of importance and just enjoy drinking. He was beginning to unwind. That was why the dinner was so strained. Frank just didn't have the strength to listen any more.

They sat facing each other in the living room like two strangers. They toyed with their drinks in silence. Finally, Frank spoke.

"Well, Dene. What's happening in your life today? Anything new?"

The question struck Dina as being so preposterously banal, considering the events of the day, that she began to laugh. She laughed until her laughter became uncontrolled, almost hysterical. Her body convulsed with racking spasms until the tears streamed down her cheeks.

Frank remained seated. He looked at his wife incredulously.

"What the hell is so funny?"

Dina waved her hand at him in a gesture of surrender.

"Wait. I can't"—she held up her hand—"oh, God. It's so

damn hilarious—my sides. Oh, they ache, Frank." She was trying very hard to stop laughing. She saw the expression on Frank's face, which was anything but sympathetic.

She finally stopped. "Oh, Frank. I *am* sorry. It just struck me so funny, I don't know why. I guess when your whole life has changed in one day and someone asks you what's *new*. It just struck me as hilarious." She looked at the set line of Frank's mouth and watched his eyes search her face.

"Oh, Frank, Frank. It's all so completely wild." She shook her head. "It's just incredible."

Frank's face was grim and unpleasant. His voice was cold as ice.

"Just describe to me, if you can, without all the hilarity, just what is so damn funny. Do you think you can manage that?"

Dina felt the cut in his tone and it annoyed her. She looked at him directly, her voice very level and steady.

"I'm pregnant, Frank." She said it flat out, her eyes meeting his.

He let her statement come at him slowly like developing mist. It surrounded his mind in amorphous cerebral shapes not impacting immediately; rather building in intensity until, like mist, the damp began to penetrate. The impact of what she had just told him was so completely unexpected that he lacked for the moment the ability to comprehend.

"What did you say? You're—you're pregnant?"

"That's right, Frank. I'm pregnant." She looked directly at him, her chin slightly raised, her whole body taut with a stubborn purposeful pride.

Frank shook his head. "Jesus Christ, I need another drink." He got up and walked to the sideboard and very carefully, slowly, stirred the rest of the martinis chilling in the cocktail shaker.

Dina watched him with his head slightly bent trying to cope with the implications of what she had just said.

He turned toward her with a wry smile.

"You'll have to forgive me, Dene, but it did come as a bit of a surprise."

He took a long swallow of his martini. Dina noticed that his hands, those strong well-shaped hands she had always admired, were shaking slightly.

"Do you want another drink?"

She shook her head, a look of compassion in her eyes.

"So I'm going to be a father. Well, God damn it, that ought to give me some points with the boys downtown."

She forced a smile.

Frank walked over and sat down opposite her, turning it all over in his mind. Dina interrupted. "Frank, one thing you and I have never done is lie to each other." He stared at his drink. "I'm telling you I'm pregnant, Frank, and we both know what that might mean."

He didn't look at her. He couldn't. His mouth became set, his lips compressed. He suddenly looked old to her; almost beaten, but Dina knew Frank.

"Frank. I want to talk about this. I've had a good part of the day to think about it; you haven't; so please listen to me." She watched him as he toyed with his drink, lost in his own thoughts.

"You know this is what I have always wanted more than anything, to have my own baby. Now I'm going to have that baby, Frank. This child could be ours, but, darling, we both know that it might not be."

Her words tore into him like a burning iron. That god-damned Elliot, he thought, that son of a bitch. But then he remembered that he was the one who brought Elliot and Dina together for his own purposes. The thought cut at his heart. His mind picked up Whit. That bastard was always around. Whit was drawn to Dina, obviously. He could see that.

"Frank, I've done a lot of thinking in the last few hours. I don't really know what I'm going to do." She hesitated. "But I *do* know what I am *not* going to do. I'm not going to bring my baby up in an atmosphere where my child is not loved. I want my baby to be really loved, Frank, really wanted. I'll do anything for that."

He was looking at her now with the antagonism gone from his face. She continued to speak. "I'm not going to have my child—"

He interrupted her. "Couldn't you just say our child?"

She looked at him squarely. Her eyes welled with tears. She just sat there watching him; her heart nearly breaking; knowing what she was doing to him, to her husband who was no longer young. He seemed vulnerable to her for the first time, and she was stirred with a compassion for him that showed. It spilled down her cheeks in silent tears.

"Well, for God's sake. Couldn't you just say it?" His voice grew louder. He stood up, unsteadily advancing toward her. He towered over her as she remained seated.

"God damn you. God damn you to hell! Say it! Say our child! Say it for Christ's sake! Can't you just say it! Say it!" He began shaking her violently. He slapped the back of his hand across her face so hard that her upper lip cut against her teeth. A thin trickle of blood ran down her mouth. He looked at her in horror at what he had done. He was half drunk; crazed with the agony of the truths his mind found unbearable.

"Oh, God, Dina, I'm so sorry. Oh, sweet Jesus, I'm sorry." He knelt beside her, taking his handkerchief from his breast pocket and dabbing at her lip.

"Oh, God, I didn't mean to do that."

She hadn't said a word. She looked up at him, her eyes filled with tears. She searched his face and then slowly put her arms around him and drew his head to her breast. She patted the back of his head as she would a child. She kissed him gently, holding him tightly.

Her mind flicked back to her sixteenth birthday. The party was over; it was late at night. It was in the big old house on Chestnut Street in Boston; the house they could no longer afford.

She lay awake listening for her father; waiting for him to come home. It was almost dawn before she heard him.

She threw a dressing gown on and rushed out of her room to find him holding onto the bannister. He was so drunk he couldn't climb the stairs. She saw him sit down on the steps, his face wet with perspiration.

She went to him, putting her arms around him. She was afraid of waking her mother; of the scene that would follow.

She remembered the wild bewildered look of the blue eyes as he stared at her; his eyes seemed focused on her hair. She remembered him trying to brush something out of her hair with trembling fingers. It was a little piece of confetti that the girls had thrown which she had missed when she had brushed her hair.

"Your birthday—oh, my God, your birthday."

She remembered the tears running down his cheeks as he held her to him. They were both crying quietly in the gray light before dawn.

Frank's voice wiped away the pain of the reminiscence.

What stood between them was what Frank so desperately wanted to hear. They both knew that what he had wanted Dina to say was probably a lie. They knew too as she pressed him against her that their mutual torment had momentarily brought them closer together than they had ever been before. Each understood that in time it would tear them apart.

The night passed slowly. Frank had taken off his jacket and removed his tie. Dina lay on the sofa, her head resting on his lap. He stroked her hair, his face a montage of suffering; both their thoughts were far away.

"Do you think you understand why I feel the way I do, Frank?"

"I think so. I'm not so sure you're not selfish. You don't seem to include anyone but you and the baby."

"I am selfish, but I'm selfish for the child, Frank. There

will come a time when the question of this baby will kill any love you might have for the child. Sooner or later the baby and I would lose any real meaning for you. We would just get in your way."

He knew it was the truth. She had spoken from an inner strength that made Frank apprehensive. He realized she had the self-reliance to leave him; the courage and independence to break away. This awareness made him afraid at the thought of losing her.

"You know I'll never give you a divorce."

"I know that."

"So what are you going to do?"

"I don't know."

Frank grappled with his own thoughts. He fought not to ask her what hurt him so much to verbalize, but it was too late for that now.

"Dina. Is Whit in the picture?"

Her voice seemed far away. "Yes, Frank, he is."

If Frank had anything left that the years of clawing and fighting hadn't broken, Dina had just shattered that now. When he spoke his voice was so strained she could barely hear him.

"Do you love him?"

"Yes, Frank, I believe I do." It broke her heart to have to say that to him. "But I love you too, Frank. It *is* possible to love two people in different ways."

"I guess it is. I'm a little too old and I suppose too stuffy to understand that, especially when I happen to be your husband. I find it a little difficult to accept. What does Whit plan to do?"

"I don't know."

"You realize what I can do to him, don't you?"

"I told him that, Frank. I told him that any relationship he might have with me could only hurt him."

"Then for Christ's sake, Dina, what the hell are you going to do? Are you going to walk out on both of us?"

"I just don't know yet. I really don't. Look, it's so late.

You'll be exhausted in the morning. We won't solve anything tonight. Let's go to bed."

She started to rise and he stopped her. They looked at
each other for a moment. She could almost see the shadows
of depression enveloping him.

"You know something, Dina?"

"What?"

"I've never felt so alone in my whole life."

She turned in his arms and raised herself up so that she
could kiss him; so gently. She felt the stubble of his gray
beard. A siren wailed the night cry of the city. They got
up and silently turned out the lights.

Gardner Hall sat in his office on Wilshire Boulevard and
remarked to himself that the air outside was delightfully
free of smog. Driving down from Beverly Hills the sun was
bright and inviting as its morning rays reflected off the
white-faced buildings. The leaves of the palm trees glistened from an early-morning rain. All in all, to a displaced
Chicagoan like Gardner Hall, L.A. seemed like a fine place
to live. He had been out here now for nearly fifteen years
but he still had the Midwesterner's appreciation for warm
sunshine. He had no desire to return to Chicago. He had
built for himself, at least outwardly, a prestigious and
pleasant life by the shores of the Pacific.

Of course, all was not as it seemed to be. Mr. Gardner
Hall did not smoke nearly three packs of cigarettes a day
because he was blessed with internal peace. Far from it.
He was one of those contemporary corporate phenomena
who existed and prospered not by talent but by his ability
to *seem* talented. He was a big good-looking man, affable
and charming. He had a full head of handsome gray hair,
an expansive waistline that was not unbecoming; a pair of
china blue eyes set in a thick somewhat jowled tanned face
that gave him an authoritative and distinguished appearance.

Gardner's real ability was in making contacts. He knew

everyone worth knowing, at least as far as his evaluations went. He and his gregarious wife entertained constantly. They were thought of as great additions to a party and were in continual demand. Gardner, as chairman of Southern California National Bank, was considered a solid pillar of the community and this enhanced his social attraction.

But in the long hours of the night when Gardner's preoccupation with personal problems would not let him sleep, the real Gardner Hall came to life.

Gardner's biggest problem was simple: he couldn't afford to live the way he did on his after-tax income. He had made several quiet investments, one of which had really bombed, and Gardner's personal net worth was getting very thin. He had some large loans coming due and he didn't know where he was going to get the money to repay them. He bluffed his way through each day, and shivered and shook each night.

On this day in April, Gardner was waiting for a visitor. He had had another visitor earlier in the month whom he could have easily lived without seeing. That had been Bryan Hastings, the right-hand man of Grant Weir. Jesse Hudson and Grant owned Gardner Hall. He was their front man in California. They let him in on just enough deals to live the precarious economic existence his ego called for, but they cut him mighty thin.

That was why Gardner was so affronted when that skinny kid from Dallas came into his office the first week in April. That little Texas shit sat right across from Gardner's desk and just as nice as pie delivered Grant Weir's message. It was a simple message: find out fast if any important contributions were made to the Nichols Institute during January or February. That little Texas sidewinder enjoyed Gardner's discomfort; having to receive Grant's instructions through an aide. It was humiliating.

His thoughts left Bryan Hastings and centered on Allan Rose, the financial vice-president of the Nichols Institute. Allan was a bright CPA who had the backbone of a stuffed doll. Allan had left the world of business because his analyst suggested that he find a less pressurized calling. When a spot at the Institute opened, Allan grabbed it. It was less money than he had been making, but he enjoyed the academic environment.

Gardner had called Allan shortly after Bryan's visit and told him that under no circumstances was Nichols to know anything about this. Allan was unnerved as usual; caught between the conflicting loyalties to a member of the board of trustees and the founder of the Institute.

Gardner assured him that he was not being disloyal. He told Allan that he was on the trail of a major donation and he needed the information he was asking for as part of his plan to secure the additional funds. He didn't want Nichols to know, so if the thing fell through he wouldn't be disappointed.

On this particular day Allan was flying down from San Francisco aboard Pacific Airlines, furtively eyeing the young hostesses; silently wishing he could have a wildly passionate night with the redhead whose breasts and legs made him have an erection under the newspaper spread across his lap.

Gardner was on the phone when his secretary announced that Mr. Allan Rose was waiting. He handled the call quickly and asked to have Mr. Rose sent in.

The short, somewhat portly accountant with thinning dark hair and hazel eyes that never quite looked directly at you extended a clammy hand to Gardner.

They got down to business quickly. Allan had been able to come across an unusual contribution. It was from an anonymous donor, issued through a bank in Racine, Wisconsin. The gift was a certified check for three hundred thousand dollars, and it was dated December 15. He had called the bank but they were not very informative. That was all there was to it.

Gardner drummed his fingers absentmindedly on the

desk; then he buzzed his secretary. He and Mr. Rose would
be lunching at the Pacific Union Club, he said.

It had taken more time and energy than it was worth to
trace the donor of that check. But Gardner was the boy
with the contacts, the network of cronies spread across the
country. Finally, he was able to get to the president of the
Farmers Bank and Trust Company of Racine. When he
had what he wanted, it didn't mean a thing to him, but
when he called Dallas and gave the information to Grant,
there was a long pause at the other end of the line.

"Say that name again, Gardner."

"William Le Pointe of the Computer Ecolog Company."

Grant gave a long whistle. "Well, I'll be a turkey-trottin'
son of a bitch."

Gardner could never understand Texans. They were all
a little crazy, but if you were crazy like Jesse and Grant,
maybe that ought to be contagious.

"You did a right smart job on this one, Gardner. Believe
me, Ah won't fogit it. Much obliged to yuh." Grant hung
up.

Grant's next call was to Bennett Alden in Boston. It was
4 P.M. when Grant called. It was nearly 5 P.M. in New York
when Bennett called Frank Sullivan.

"I appreciate your difficulties, Bennett, but I don't see
how we can be helpful to you."

"Frank, this whole thing is beginning to become very
distasteful to me. It's placing me in an embarrassing position with some of my more important associates. Your firm
is the investment banker for Computer. You sold two stock
issues for the company. I'm sure you would share my embarrassment if this stock fell much further, especially if
there is any hint of chicanery; that would reflect on the
reputations of all of us."

"I agree, Bennett, but just what is it you want us to do?"

"The stock is going to need a few friends." There was a

pause on the other end of the line. Frank let it sink in; his whole body seemed bent with fatigue.

"We'll be as friendly as we can, Bennett."

"I hoped you would."

They each hung up. Frank shook his head wearily. "Jesus Christ," he said. "When the hell does it stop?"

What Bennett was suggesting to Frank was that his firm step into the market to halt the slide in Computer by buying stock. Frank knew this would at best be only a very temporary remedy and would wind up costing his firm a lot of money.

The battered old warrior leaned back in his chair and closed his eyes. They were irritated from cigarette smoke and fatigue. His thoughts roamed the spectrum of his problems. He thought of Dina and he yearned for her. He longed to be rid of his burdens and go away someplace; any place. His thoughts returned to Dina. They had reached a silent understanding. They each acknowledged they would not try to penetrate the protective layers they had built to insulate themselves from hurting the other further.

Frank thought of Computer. He wished he had never heard the name of the goddamn company.

As he gazed out the windows, he saw a Boeing 727 making a wide swing over the beginning of Long Island Sound on its way into La Guardia. The plane seemed suspended in air, losing altitude so gradually that it was hard for Frank to remember the jet was probably doing over 150 knots on its final approach. Frank thought of his own plane, in the hangar for its one-hundred-hour inspection. The idea began to form in his mind. He was physically and mentally exhausted. Asking Dina to join him would hurt too much; it would hurt both of them. No, he'd go alone. His excuse would be Paul Nichols, but that was really just an excuse; it was what he would tell his partners. In reality, he just wanted to get the hell away from everything and everyone, at least for a little while. He wanted to drink; he wanted to gamble a little, and he wanted to meet a woman who was interesting and attractive; someone who would help him lose himself even for only a couple of days. He wanted to say fuck you to everyone and everything.

Grant had called Paul Nichols and asked if the physicist could see him. Nichols was terribly busy, but Grant assured him it was of the utmost importance. Paul Nichols still remembered the tail end of the conversation before Grant hung up.

"Ah strongly recommend, Doctor, that yew see me. Yuh see, Ah think yo' Institute may be in for some real problems." Grant paused. "An' if mah information is correct, Doctor, yew may have a few real problems yosef."

Grant told Nichols he would fly to San Francisco and meet him at the Fairmont tomorrow evening. They could have dinner together. Nichols reluctantly agreed.

Paul Nichols at the age of sixty-one was like most men: not what he seemed to be. He was stooped with thin graying brown hair. He walked through life peering out from behind thick lenses. His thoughts flowed so profusely that he could not verbalize clearly; his mind always ahead of the words. His speech therefore was slurred; he stuttered. At times, when racing to express his thoughts, he occasionally sprayed saliva at his distressed listener. His face would light up frequently with a quick smile, and just as swiftly it could become somber, reflecting some thought he found distressing.

He was considered one of the world's authorities on impregnated chips involved with the integrated circuitry of computers. What really lay hidden behind the stumbling cranelike façade was a fierce competitive drive motivated by an immense ego. Paul Nichols was an academic prima donna. He was a displaced Easterner, who had his aca-

demic roots in Princeton and MIT, as well as a graduate
fellowship at Cambridge, where he had become an Anglo-
phile. It was while Nichols was in England that he attracted the attention of Sir Hartley Johnston Trevel, one
of that country's leading theoretical physicists. Sir Hartley
discovered in Nichols an extremely rapid mind that was
not afraid to tackle an occasional consulting problem in-
volving nontheoretical research.

It was in this capacity that Nichols was brought into
contact with Thorton Wheeler, executive vice-president
for foreign operations of Trans International Industries.
Through Wheeler, Nichols met Guy Harrington, chairman and chief executive officer of TII. It was through
Guy's sponsorship and interest that the Nichols Institute
received its original financial support.

Nichols had remained unmarried, though he was not
immune to the attractions of women. But the monkey on
Nichols' back was his acute need to prove to others, but
mainly to himself, that he was a very important man. To
Nichols, whether he chose to admit it or not, the very
physical presence of the Institute—its grounds and buildings—were incontrovertible evidence that Paul Nichols
was someone of importance; had really accomplished something significant in his lifetime. Anyone that threatened
his Institute threatened him. Tomorrow evening, something told him, in the person of that obnoxious Texan, a
threat to his Institute existed. His intuition could not have
been more accurate.

The night had come slowly to San Francisco. From
Grant's room in the Fairmont both he and Paul Nichols
watched the lights begin to wink on across the Bay. The
haze of evening was enveloping the Golden Gate Bridge,
which is painted rust-red. An occasional freighter bound
for the Pacific steamed slowly away from this magical city.
The beauty of the coming night was lost on Grant Weir.

Unfortunately the tension of this evening's meeting also helped to distract Paul Nichols from the esthetics of the softly pressing darkness.

Grant had ordered a bottle of bourbon and a bottle of scotch. Grant never drank anything but bourbon; the scotch was for Nichols, who hadn't touched it. The bottle of bourbon was about half empty.

They had eaten dinner in Grant's room. Nichols had picked at his food, his appetite lost to the anxiety caused by Weir's presence.

Until now Grant had been ominously polite; his voice, couched in its Southwestern drawl, was suspiciously low. Grant had eaten with the authority of the hunter. Nichols reflected the unfortunate plight of the hunted.

Grant had removed his coat and tie. He finished the apple pie à la mode and poured himself another half glass of bourbon and water. He wiped his mouth quickly with his napkin and stood up. Nichols watched him with uneasy concentration.

Grant moved to the window and looked out at San Francisco Bay; the splashes of light seemed like luminescent stars reflected from the surface of the dark water.

"Right purty, Doc. Yes, sir, this is one hell of a town. Had a lot of fun in this town, Doc.

"Ya know, Doc, life is sure funny. You wonder some-tahms how yah git to a certain stop on the road. Know what Ah mean, Doc?"

Nichols shook his head negatively and remained silent. He kept watching Grant with furtive concentration.

"Well, take yew an' me. I reckon there aren't two more different people on the face of this earth, Doc, than yew an' me."

Grant turned and pointed his hand holding the bourbon at Paul Nichols. The motion of his arm was too rapid and the bourbon spilled over his hand and wrist onto the beige carpet. He exchanged hands and drew the back of his whiskey-sodden right hand across his mouth, licking at the bourbon with his tongue. "Goddamn, Doc, that's a waste of good whiskey."

Grant Weir was now nearly drunk. Nichols became even more apprehensive.

"What Ah mean, Doc, is, think of the roads yew an' Ah took to meet here in this room in San Francisco. Did yah evah think of that, Doc?" Nichols shook his head again.

"Well, now, Doc." Grant began to pace up and down in front of the windows looking out at the distracting magnetism of San Francisco Bay. It would not let him go.

"Well, Doc, Ah've given that one hell of a lot of thought." Grant paused. "Yuh see, ole Jesse an' me, well, sir, we dirt-scratched for every dime we ever made. Jesse didn't have two beans to say grace over when he started. An' when Jesse found me Ah was jus' a skinny-assed kid out of school with a thin belly lookin' to git movin'. So we come to appreciate the gut-bustin' it takes to build the kind of empire ole Jesse Hudson has put together." Grant cocked a sharp dark eye at Nichols. "Yah beginnin' to git the drift of what Ah'm sayin', Doc?"

"I'm afraid not, M-m-m-Mr. Weir."

"Well, lemme continyuh. Yuh see, ole Jesse an' me ain't no goddamn Harvard Business School stunts. We're Texas traders. We don't always expect to be top dog. Shit." Grant took another drink of his bourbon and waved his glass at Nichols. "We win a few an' we lose some, but we sure as hell are bad losers, Doc, you know what Ah mean?"

It was a rhetorical question. Grant narrowed his eyes as he looked at Nichols. He walked over to the sofa and put his drink down on the glass-topped table. He took off his shoes and put his stocking feet up on the table. He expelled a long very audible quantity of gas, which he followed by several hiccups and a loud burp.

Nichols visibly winced.

"Sorry, Doc. To get back to what Ah was sayin'. Jesse an' me don't like to lose—especially when someone's pullin' our prong. Know what Ah mean?"

Paul Nichols was feeling ill. Grant's not particularly subtle hints plus the incredible crudity of the man upset Nichols physically. He felt that he had endured enough for one evening. He looked at Grant, at that compact chunky figure with the round full face, the dark chestnut hair, those cold gray-green eyes. Grant's face was perspiring. There were little beads of sweat just beneath his hairline and around his mouth.

"Mr. W-W-W-W-Weir. I'm afraid I really must go. I-I-I-It's been quite ah—ah—un—un—well, shall I say ah —quite an inter-interesting evening, but I'm v-v-v-very tired."

Grant waved his arm. "Hell, no, Doc. You cain't go now. Why, shoot, Doc, we ain't even begun talking about what Ah'm here for."

Nichols protested and started to get up to leave. Grant didn't move. His voice was menacing. All attempts at even pretended cordialities were over.

"You git your ass into a chair, Nichols." It was a barely audible order, but the threat implied in the repressed violence that Paul Nichols knew was surfacing within Grant made him return silently to his chair.

Grant eyed him with cold contempt. He rose slowly to his feet, walked over to the table, and poured more bourbon into his glass. Nichols was incredulous. The man had finished nearly three quarters of a fifth of bourbon in under three hours. Grant swayed back and forth and fell to the floor, spilling the rest of his drink. Nichols moved to help him.

Grant waved him back. "No—no. Shit, Doc. Ah've just had me a li'l too much bour—bourbon." Grant staggered to a chair and fell into it. His face was dripping wet. Beads of perspiration rolled down his cheeks. His breath was labored. He could speak only with difficulty.

" 'Sall right, Doc. Jus' a li'l too mush"—Grant gave a giant belch—"bourbon. But shit, Doc, Ah didn' come all the way up here to git drunk. Fuck it. Ah came up here to git *you*."

Paul Nichols watched Grant carefully. Nichols was stone sober. The fear of physical violence that had haunted him all through his boyhood and his undergraduate years at college had been with him all evening, but Nichols was beginning to see that Grant was in no position to hurt him physically. Nichols watched Grant with furtive, expectant concentration.

"Doc—yuh fucked us. Yew skinny prick, yew fucked me an' Jesse, an' we're gonna git your ass for it." Grant forced himself to sit up in the chair. He pointed his hand at Nichols.

"Yew son of a bitch. Yew took money from Computer fo' yo' fuckin' Institute, an' then yew tol' old Tittle that Computer was okay." Grant's face poured out sweat. His chest heaved as he struggled to his feet. Paul Nichols watched him carefully. He realized that he could always stay out of Grant's reach with the Texan in this condition. The thought almost made him smile.

"M-M-Mr. Weir. I did, as you say, accept a contribution to the Institute from Computer, but that was long before I was called on to give a con-consulting opinion, and besides, that would not have influenced my recommendation."

"Yew lyin' cocksucker. Yew fucked us an' Tittle. Yew cost ole Jesse and me a bundle, an' yew embarrassed the hell out of us with our partners. We're gonna cut yew a new asshole. Yes, sir—we sure as shit are."

Nichols watched Grant, who was now on his feet, his eyes protruding, his lips frothed with saliva. His face was almost purple. He kept pointing at Nichols, mouthing obscenities and swaying so wildly that Nichols was sure he had to fall.

Paul Nichols, for the first time during this nightmare

of an evening, was no longer afraid. He was no longer the terrified fraternity pledge who stood atop the twelve-foot wall while his student tormentors kept screaming at him to jump. He just couldn't do it. He clung desperately to the top of the wall and began to cry. His shame and his terror were only relieved when the pledge master of the fraternity with unexpected insight and compassion guided him down from the wall. Never again until this night did Paul Nichols ever allow himself to be placed in a position where his physical courage might be tested.

"You know what Ah'm gonna do to yew, Nichols? Ah'm gonna git yo' ass thrown out of that Institute. We're gonna tell the board what a thievin' son of a bitch their director is, an' then we're gonna turn off your contributors. An' we can do it. We'll git yew through the banks." Grant advanced toward Nichols, falling, stumbling, reaching out for him with wildly flailing arms, his face contorted with hate and frustration.

"Yew cocksucker." He lunged at Nichols, who silently backed away. Grant stumbled over a coffee table and fell face forward onto the thickly padded carpet, his body striking the floor with a muffled thud. He rolled over on his back unable to rise, his chest heaving in great rhythmic convulsions; his lungs gasped for air. He lay looking up at Nichols, the dark eyes damning the physicist with cold fury. He raised his arm, his finger pointing straight at Paul.

"We gonna cut yew a new asshole." His body shivered. He had rolled partially over on his left side. His right arm was still extended; the forefinger of his right hand pointed accusingly. His speech had now degenerated into unintelligible gibberish. His body had become rigid. He lay there like some fallen gladiator, his finger pointing in rigid aimless accusation.

Paul Nichols could feel his own heart pounding so rapidly that he was sure that its beat must be audible. He felt the perspiration on his face, the terrible need of his lungs for fresh air. He rushed to the window and fumbled for the stainless-steel handle that would let in the cool of this San Francisco night. He rushed back to look at Grant, who was still lying there, breathing more evenly now.

Paul Nichols felt the damp air from the Bay creep into the room. He knelt beside Grant, who was able to follow him only with his eyes. He tried to move Grant's arm that was locked in muscular spasm. The arm would not move. Grant lay there like a living piece of sculpture. Nichols put his ear to Grant's chest and heard the irregular heartbeat.

He rose slowly to his feet, took out his handkerchief from his breast pocket, and wiped his face and forehead. He was smiling; the hunted had become the hunter. The change in circumstance filled Nichols with a wry vicious pleasure. He walked to the telephone and dialed the operator. His voice was serious and concerned, but his eyes were bright and flushed with revenge.

"This is Dr. Paul Nichols in Suite 1224. I need a medical doctor up here quickly. I believe my friend"—he paused, almost beginning to laugh, but he was able to control his voice—"I believe my friend has suffered a stroke."

"We'll send someone right away, sir."

"Thank you." He hung up.

He looked down at Grant without compassion.

He walked to the window and breathed deeply of the mist-laden air. A gust of wind moved the curtains so that they seemed to spread toward him like rustling empty cloaks. A great chill filled the room. He opened the bottle of scotch and took his first drink of the evening. The lights across the Bay seemed to flick off and on as patches of fog and mist blown by the night winds swept across them like some spectral hand.

Nichols walked back to the coffee table and poured himself another scotch, a very modest one. He sat down in the chair looking critically at the prostrate form of

Grant Weir lying on his back, his eyes focused on the ceiling, his right arm still raised, his right forefinger still pointing upward.

Paul Nichols began to laugh. He laughed until the tears came to his eyes. It was a merciless tormented laugh. It was a long way down the road for Paul Nichols, who had spent his lifetime protecting his own physical vulnerability, masking his own anxieties, and disguising behind a benign façade, an unpitying heart.

Only Grant Weir, who could hear every sound quite clearly, and the night wind were privy to the shadowy soul of Dr. Paul Nichols.

Frank needed an excuse to get away from the pressures that were building all around him. He had done this all his life. It was the only way you could survive on the Street. He got into the habit of taking short frequent vacations so that he was never away for long, but it gave him the breaks he needed.

He used Stirling Livermore and Nichols as an excuse. He told Dina and his partners he wanted to persuade Nichols to give some interviews to certain carefully selected members of the press who might be a little more friendly to Computer than Stirling Livermore; it seemed logical.

Nichols was not happy at the telephone call advising that Frank was going to see him when he was on the West Coast, but there was very little he could do but agree to meet him.

Faye Stein sat in the Red Carpet Club of United and tried to ignore the rather brazen examination she was getting from the man in the blue blazer and open-neck shirt exposing a hairy chest which Faye found repulsive. She could not understand this macho preoccupation with décolletage. They hung beads around their necks, or gold chains, and as far as she was concerned they all looked like fags. She pretended to go back to her book.

Faye was used to having men look at her; in fact, she was used to men. She was a three-time loser, having married and divorced three husbands; the last one was a well-known realtor in California who had found his marriage to Faye somewhat expensive. With community property law staring him in the face, and the fact that he had been caught by Faye not once but several times with other women, he settled quickly but expensively, by turning over to Faye two prime office buildings in the heart of downtown Los Angeles. He could afford it, and in the process he had made her a wealthy woman. That's why Faye Stein was waiting for United's midday flight to Los Angeles. She was going out to meet with her attorney and her accountant on her quarterly examination of the buildings' finances.

She sensed that the hairy chest was making his move to come over and sit beside her. She was hardly concerned.

She had spent the last four years after her divorce in intensive Freudian analysis. She was tired of the banality of her life, and had decided to find out who she was. It was a painful trip, but it had been worth it. Now at forty-four she was relaxed, ready to take what life offered her; her values adjusted; her objectives realistic and obtainable.

All she really wanted was to find a man she could give herself to; one whom she liked, or loved, but *very definitely respected*. She didn't care if it resulted in marriage or just living together. As a matter of fact, she would prefer the latter. She had had it with marriage, and she was no longer very impressed by that little piece of paper.

The receptionist came over with her ticket.

"We have you in 4B, Miss Stein, by the window. Your flight is boarding, so I suggest you give yourself plenty of time for security check." Faye smiled, and thanked her and gathered up her things to leave.

Hairy Chest was evidently not on this flight. She

breathed a sigh of relief as she left the club to walk to the gate.

When Frank seated himself comfortably next to the attractive woman on his right, he couldn't help thinking the flight might prove interesting.

She had removed her shoes. Her stocking feet were pressed against the seat in front of her. She had already started on a glass of champagne.

Frank noticed that she was probably in her forties. She had long red hair and skin that had seen too much sun. She was attractively dressed in a black sweater and carefully tailored white pants.

She seemed at first glance mature and theatrically attractive. There was about her an air of confident appeal; an almost diffident languor.

She smiled readily at Frank and went back to her book.

The lumbering 747 was in a steep climb. The ribbon of the Hudson River slipped behind while the giant plane gained altitude, rapidly passing over New Jersey and turning west to chase the sun.

"Something to drink, sir?"

Frank looked up at the stewardess.

"Yes. I think I'll have some champagne as well."

He smiled at the woman on his right, who seemed only mildly interested in the book she was reading.

"We're going to be together for nearly six hours. I might as well introduce myself. My name is Frank Sullivan."

She closed her book and smiled at him.

"I'm Faye Stein."

"It's my pleasure—ah, Mrs.—" Frank couldn't see anything but a baroque pearl-clustered ring.

"It's just Faye, Mr. Sullivan."

"Well, then, I would be flattered if you called me Frank."

She put her book down and turned toward him. She moved her body slowly. Faye Stein was indeed a very arrestive lady.

She was attracted to Frank. She sensed that he felt disquiet; perhaps even troubled, but he seemed strong to her and almost courtly. He certainly wasn't the usual airplane romeo looking for a quick score. He looked distinguished, significant; someone who had accomplished something.

"Frank it is, then," she said.

"Would you care for more champagne?" The stewardess was back.

Faye turned to her.

"As a matter of fact, that would do nicely."

"And you, sir?"

"I think I'll switch to a Bloody Mary."

Frank's first impression of Faye Stein was positive; he liked her. She seemed mature and attractive, with enough refinement to be appealing, yet without the coyness that he found so annoying in many women. She was worldly but not tarnished. Her sense of humor was intact. His initial impression was that this woman had somehow found a way to handle her life. She seemed sure of herself, not cocky, no fake bravado, just a quiet feeling that Faye Stein had done it, had seen it, and now she wasn't working too hard at maintaining an image of herself. She was Faye Stein and you either liked that or you didn't. She couldn't have cared less.

They had reached cruising altitude.

Frank and Faye; he decided they sounded like a vaudeville team.

She laughed loudly at that one.

They had both switched to Bloody Marys.

The intimacies that only traveling strangers seem to share so easily began to flow between them. Occasionally he felt her leg touch his as he brushed accidentally against her.

When he lit her cigarette she held his cupped hands sheltering the flame just a little longer than necessary. It wasn't a game. They liked one another in a way that was easy and natural.

They didn't bother with the movie. They were lying back in their reclined seats looking at each other; she quietly smoking and talking; Frank listening.

She said she had a reservation upstairs for lunch; could he join her? Frank didn't like to eat in the lounge. Usually it was noisy, and he used these long flights to work. He hadn't bothered making a reservation and now the lounge was full.

"I get so bored on these flights. I like the change of eating upstairs, but if there's no room for you—"

"We'll check the stewardess again and see."

There was no room.

Faye decided it was unimportant. They would eat together in their seats.

"Are you married, Frank?"

He smiled. The inevitable question.

"Isn't everybody?"

"I'm not."

"I'm sure you were at one time."

"Why are you so sure?"

"Because most people do seem to marry sooner or later."

"Well, I fit both categories. I got married *sooner* and *later*. Three times, to be exact."

Frank laughed, his voice again husky from the cigarettes and alcohol.

"You don't disappoint me, Faye, but you seem too smart a woman to have taken three trips—"

"The first one I was just a kid, right out of Sarah Lawrence. My parents thought it was a great match. He had money. We had money. It was a merger, not a marriage. He was weak. I was young and we knew—at least I knew—it would never work."

The flight attendants were adjusting the window screens to further darken the cabin for the movie.

They were close to each other; not touching, but feeling an intimacy growing between them.

"Number two was a real bastard. I caught him fooling around with the mother of one of my daughter's friends—a close friend of *mine*, I might add. I thought I would try to make it work—for Dot's sake—but he was just no good. He was one of those men who need the constant gratification of knowing they are attractive to women, and they need the mothering some women will give a good-looking man."

"Faye. You don't have to go into this with me."

She smiled. "When you've been through what I've been through it doesn't make any difference." She looked at him searchingly.

"And you, Frank. I'm sure life hasn't been a bed of roses for you."

He laughed. He laughed so hard that he began to cough. He raised his seat, but he couldn't stop coughing. She signaled for the stewardess, who brought him some water. She looked concerned. Frank saw it in her face.

"Sorry, Faye." He breathed heavily. "Really caught me. Sorry." He touched her hand. "Faye. You would have to know this period of my life to know how funny that was. No, I think you might say that life has never been a bed of roses for me."

His eyes looked wistfully away.

"I've had to fight for every damn thing I've ever had." He almost whispered it. He was not looking at her. His mind was a thousand miles, a thousand years, away.

"I'm tired of it, Faye. Damn tired."

He said it in such a way that it touched her. Their hands reached for each other, just briefly.

"Do you want to tell me about it?"

He shook his head slowly.

"Faye. No one is interested in someone else's troubles. If there is one thing I've learned over the years it's that."

She moved closer to him. Her eyes never left his face. He could feel her warmth, smell her perfume. He yearned to touch her; to hold her.

"Faye, believe me. You don't need my problems."

"Try me." She said it quietly, looking right through him; her two hands held his. "Try me, Frank."

He looked at her. His lips compressed, just the hint of a smile at the corners of his mouth.

The great plane had crossed the Rockies and was beginning a slow letdown for the L.A. area.

"Faye. It would take me a month to go into everything. It would sound like the worst kind of soap opera."

She withdrew her hand and began searching in her bag for another pack of cigarettes.

They were approaching L.A. The layer of pollution hung its buff-colored pall over the city. The tops of the crescent of mountains that ring Los Angeles seemed to reach desperately for the clear sky.

"Where are you staying, Faye?"

"At the Beverly Wilshire."

"I'll be at the Bon Air. Will you be busy tonight?"

"I do have plans, Frank."

"Anything you can break?"

She looked at him carefully. Her eyes were kind. She had been born to indifferent parents, living the better part of her life without purpose. Her marriages like her life had brought her nothing but pain. In middle age, through analysis, she had been able to awaken; to gain a hard-won awareness; a second chance.

"I think I can make a few calls."

The thought warmed him. He pressed her hand. His face showed an enthusiasm she hadn't seen during the flight.

"That's wonderful. Really." He sighed. "You know.

You may be just what I need right now."

She smiled. "A friendly shoulder to lean on?"

He looked at her, the lines of his face hardening. "I'm afraid I don't know how to do that. To lean on other people. It's been the other way around. Most people usually lean on me."

She exhaled a cloud of cigarette smoke. "I've been different, Frank. I never leaned on anyone because there was never anybody around. My whole life up until a few years ago had been a series of beautifully furnished empty rooms, and no one ever leaned on me. I wouldn't allow it. I was too selfish; too preoccupied."

They fastened their seat belts, moved the backs of their chairs upright, and in a few moments were on the ground.

"Are you being met?" His voice was hesitant.

"Yes. I am."

She saw his look of disappointment.

"What time shall I pick you up?"

"About eight?"

"That's fine." He paused. "Faye. I'm looking forward to tonight."

"So am I."

When he had unpacked he ordered a drink. He sat on the edge of the bed feeling tired but a little more relaxed.

He thought of Faye. He could see her red hair, the soft brown eyes, her full mouth. He thought about her body, that long lithe body that even at forty seemed firm and inviting. He felt himself slowly aroused by his thoughts of her.

She was Jewish. His friends would get a kick out of that. Screw them, he thought. Better still, screw her. He shook his head. Frank, Frank, he thought to himself. He smiled.

Another thought crossed his mind and the smile faded.

He picked up the telephone and dialed Paul Nichols. Nichols' secretary put him straight through.

To Frank's surprise the scientist seemed glad to hear from him.

"Yes. A pleasure, Mr. Sullivan." Even the stammer seemed reduced. "The Bohemian Club. About twelve thirty. Th-that would be fine, Mr. Sullivan. See you then."

Frank hung up. The thought nagged at him that for some reason Nichols had changed direction. Why wasn't he being defensive? Frank shook his head. He would find out soon enough.

The night was soft. Covered with stars.

Frank left the limousine and sought the desk clerk. Faye was in suite 503-4.

He knocked on the door. For some reason he felt uneasy. Suppose she wasn't there. He felt a small ache of anxiety.

Later, they were in a corner of the dining room, sitting close together. The candlelight from the table glowed on their faces.

"The best way I can put it, Faye, and I can only say this to you because we don't know each other very well"— he paused and turned to her, his look questioning—"perhaps that's not accurate. Perhaps we do know each other; even in so short a time. Do you believe that's possible; that two people can understand each other in a day or a week; more so than others who have spent a lifetime together?"

"I not only believe it's possible, Frank. I'm the living proof. I've been married to three men. I don't think any of them ever understood me, and I can't say I understood them. I didn't even understand myself until my analysis; that was a little over four years ago." She paused and stubbed her cigarette.

"I do think two people can know each other in a short period of time, Frank, but they can also fool themselves a lot too."

Frank looked away from her. His face reflected fatigue, a look of resignation.

"Faye. This really is one hell of a time for me. My whole life seems to be caught in cross currents that are trying to drown me." He whispered an aside, not to her but to himself. "But I don't drown very easily." His jaw hardened as he said it.

"My business, my wife—the two things in my life that I suppose are most important to me. It's possible I could lose them both."

Faye had not missed the fact that he had unconsciously mentioned his business first.

"Do you love her, Frank?" She asked this with genuine compassion.

Frank was a long time in answering. He inhaled deeply. The smoke curled out of his mouth.

"I do, Faye. I do love her." He held up his hand.

"But God, Faye, we have a hell of a problem. I don't think we can hold it together."

"Does she want to?"

He sighed. "I think if there was a way—she would like to, but as far as *she's* concerned, I don't believe there is."

Faye nodded, her lips pouted in thought.

"Frank. Stop me if I'm being too personal."

He shook his head.

"Don't worry, Faye. You're not the type."

"Is there another woman?"

Frank began to chuckle softly.

"No. It's not another woman."

"Another man?"

"In a way, but—"

"I'm sorry, Frank. Let's forget it."

"Let's."

He pushed back his chair.

"How about a walk?"

They walked arm in arm, slowly, around the narrow confines of the grounds.

They stopped in a darkened corner underneath the trellis.

Faye looked up at the velvet sky. The warm air caressed them.

Frank turned her gently to him and held her. He kissed her face very tenderly. He felt the richness of her hair between his fingers.

"I would like to make love to you, Faye." He said it quietly, almost sadly. "I'm no good at playing games."

She wasn't coy. She kissed him, her generous soft mouth on his. He could taste her lipstick.

When they were in Frank's suite they held each other quietly in the darkened living room. He began to move his hands over her body, gently stroking her breasts.

She kissed him quickly and slipped away.

"Wait. Let me get out of this thing."

He undressed while she was in the bathroom, and got into bed.

The light in the bathroom went out. He could see her coming to him; his dressing gown around her. She slipped in bed beside him and kissed him hungrily.

"Let's just lose ourselves in each other, Frank. Let's just say to hell with everything. Let's have this night if nothing else, not hoping, not promising, just tonight."

Her hands were experienced and sure as she reached for him. She used her nails and her tongue, licking him like a hungry cat. She gave him her breasts with their distended hard nipples.

"Suck on that, Frank. Suck." She clawed at him with her nails. "Oh suck me, Frank. Suck my tits while you fuck me. Suck me, Frank. Suck and fuck. Oh, Frank, Frank, Frank."

He could feel her grow rigid beneath him as her breathing crescendoed in climax, in great gasping sighs.

"I'm coming again, Frank. Oh, God, Frank, hard. Push hard."

* * *

They had breakfast. The night had not worn out their intimacy or their interest.

She knew he had to fly to San Francisco, but he would be back in the evening. They could have another night together. She would take it hour by hour if necessary. She had learned to do that.

She didn't think in terms of love. She wasn't sure what that word meant any more. She was too experienced to ask for commitments, and she was strong enough now not to need them. She had matured emotionally so that she was able to let go. She had learned not to contrive hope, for she knew that where hope was limited, sorrow got little sun.

Frank had reserved a corner table at the Bohemian Club. It was twelve forty-five and Nichols was late. This annoyed Frank. Why were the academic types incapable of keeping an appointment? He would never be able to understand that. The only ones worse were the damn doctors.

Frank took out a cigarette. He thought of Faye. He felt something for her. He didn't know what it was. He didn't think it was love. Frank wasn't sure if he understood love. He thought that as much as he understood that emotion he felt it for Dina. The thought of Dina burned through him with an almost physical pain. He shook it off. His mind turned back to Faye.

He needed that woman. Both of them seemed to understand this. He was honest enough to ask himself if he would still feel the same if circumstances were different and if he didn't need her. He shook his head slowly and put out his cigarette. He couldn't answer that.

Where the hell was Nichols? Why was he wasting his time here instead of being with Faye in L.A.?

He caught the figure of Paul Nichols being directed to his table. Frank's annoyance plainly showed. His greeting to Nichols was cold and formal.

"I-I-I ap-apologize, Mr. Sullivan. Got tied up in traffic.

It's getting worse all the time. Had to park quite a distance."

"That's all right, Doctor. No harm done."

They ordered. They both picked the stone crabs and drank a well-chilled bottle of a California Chardonnay.

They talked about the meeting in Boston. Their conversation was forced.

Nichols dabbed at his mouth with a napkin. He sat back comfortably, pushing his chair away from the table.

Frank sensed a confidence in the man that was clearly absent on the two previous occasions they had met.

Frank talked about the problems Computer was having in the market as a result of Stirling Livermore's articles. Would it be possible for Nichols to take some of the sting out of those attacks in a series of interviews arranged with a "friendlier" reporter? Frank watched Nichols squirm slightly at this suggestion. Frank's manner became distinctly colder.

After much evasion, Nichols insisted he had no objection to discussing his views for a technical publication, but he stuck by his guns in rejecting an attempt to have him speak to the public press.

The fatigue had momentarily left Frank's face. His eyes were the cold of a winter sea. He reflected concerted cold anger.

"Doctor. From my point of view I can't accept that; neither will Mr. Alden or Mr. Weir."

When he mentioned Grant Weir, Frank saw a peculiar light pass across Nichols' eyes.

"I can assure you, Dr. Nichols, this matter will have to be reviewed with Courtney and Dr. Karkov as well."

Nichols was a lousy poker player. Frank had observed the twitch that ticked at Nichols' face when he spoke of Grant. Nichols tried to disguise his anxiety but it was useless. Frank had sensed where he was vulnerable; Nichols knew it.

Nichols finally came to the point. "I believe Mr. Weir

th-thinks I supported Dr. Karkov because of M-Mr. Courtney's interest in my Institute.

"You see I f-feel Mr. Weir's judgment is un-f-fair, and quite inaccurate. I simply re-refuse to be b-bullied by Mr. W-Weir, or by anyone. I'm n-not responsible for what's happened to C-Computer's stock."

He looked at Frank, who was stubbing out his cigarette.

Nichols needed help to handle Grant Weir. If anyone could help him he felt it was Frank Sullivan. He made his move.

"I did not d-discuss your first visit here, M-Mr. S-Sullivan, with Mr. Weir."

Nichols thought he saw just the faintest reaction.

"I d-did n-not m-mention your v-visit to Alden, either, w-w-when he c-called."

Frank began to smell the first wisps of smoke. "I have no objections to your telling Weir or Alden anything you like, Dr. Nichols." He said it evenly, coldly. Nichols wasn't sure if Frank was bluffing.

He was bluffing. The last thing on earth that Frank Sullivan needed was Grant Weir or Bennett Alden to have even the slightest suspicion that he might have had any inside knowledge concerning Computer, or had acted covertly in his own self-interest without sharing that knowledge with Alden and Weir, and the rest of the insider group. What really bothered Frank was how Bennett and Grant would interpret what he had done, and most of all, how they might react. They had the kind of influence that could seriously hurt Sullivan & Co.

Frank signaled the waiter for a brandy. Nichols declined. Frank lit a cigarette, and sought a way to play this academic charlatan.

"Dr. Nichols. We feel you can be helpful to all of us." Frank lowered his voice. His eyes seemed to reach far beyond Paul Nichols.

"Mr. Weir left us—I should say left *me* at least—with the impression that there was something less than *satis-*

factory"—Frank emphasized the adjective—"with the relationship between you and Courtney."

Nichols started to object. His blue eyes flashed with anger.

Frank held up his hands.

"Wait, Doctor. I didn't say I agreed with Grant. I simply meant that he left that impression with all of us. I'm sure it wasn't lost on Mr. Alden." Frank indicated he wasn't finished.

"This isn't your kind of a game, Doctor. It's my impression that you're not conscious of the damage that can be done to an institution like yours by alienating people with the connections of an Alden or a Grant Weir. They can hurt you enormously, and you won't even know it's happening. It will take many forms. Directors will resign. Contracts will be lost. Old contacts that you relied on for financial help will disappear. Rumors will start among your colleagues which will affect your professional reputation and that of the Institute."

Nichols needed some time to pull himself together. He excused himself on the pretext that he had to make a phone call.

Frank nodded. He watched Nichols walk quickly out of the dining room.

Frank smoked quietly as he waited, sipping his brandy.

When Nichols returned, he had regained some of his composure. His manner was still furtive, nervous, but he was back in the game.

"Mr. Sullivan. Sup-p-pose we a-assume that we m-might have a m-m-mutuality of interests." He looked questioningly at Frank.

Frank's face remained glacial.

"Mr. Weir has threatened me. I d-don't know wh-why. I fe-feel he has d-drawn some mistaken conclusions. I c-c-couldn't seem to reason with him. I can't have him s-slandering me. It's un-f-f-fair. C-c-could you try and reason with him?" Nichols paused, his eyes looking down at the table.

When he spoke, his voice was barely audible. "It would be just as unfair to ac-cuse *you* of h-having some k-kind of nefarious relationship w-with me."

There it was. The little bastard had finally said it. The good doctor was feeling pressed. If pushed too far he might go to Bennett. If Bennett started to probe it could get back to the firm and to Dean. It would arm Dean with a powerful weapon, one that Frank didn't want to have to face.

He looked at Nichols, his voice not betraying his thoughts.

"I can see no reason why I couldn't talk to Grant for you when he's recovered sufficiently." Frank looked at Nichols with an expression of cold distaste. "That's, of course, if you agree to help us with the interviews."

Nichols nodded his head in agreement.

Frank looked at his watch. It was two forty-five. It had been a long lunch.

On the way to the airport as the driver left the city for the expressway that wound around the light industrial area, past the low hills with their precarious rectangular houses, his thoughts became a montage of his problems.

He was in grave danger of losing his wife, the only human being he really cared about. She carried a child that might be his; the paternity of that child ate cruelly at him. If Dina left him, he would most certainly lose the child. He found himself increasingly torn with the desire that the child *be* his. His mind turned to Elliot. His face became grim as the pain of Elliot seared his consciousness. Then Dean's face came. He began to think about the problems of the firm.

Perhaps this was the time to take a part of his capital out and retire. Why not? Why not just toss in the sponge and say to hell with it? Why not do it?

The car was moving into the general area of the airport. What kept him from following his own logic and getting out? As he thought about it, there were some good reasons for not throwing in the towel.

If he gave up the firm could he spend the rest of his life with only Dina and the child? He knew he couldn't. If he lost Dina *and* the firm, what reason would he have for living?

Frank needed the pressures of his life. Leisure led to introspection and any insinuation of self-analysis made him uneasy. He had just enough awareness for him to realize that if he lifted the edge of the curtain of his life he would see nothing but a vacant room.

They were having dinner in the dining room of the Bon Air. She was looking at him intently as he spoke; her hand occasionally sought his. His thoughts were far away.

She was dressed provocatively. She hungered for him. She was a very sensual woman, especially when she met a man like Frank, with his masculinity, maturity and charm. There was also the perverse attraction that was almost masochistic. She knew that Frank could combine any relationship with cold purpose. He could hurt, and would if it were necessary. This excited her.

As she watched him, listened to him, ran her long nails gently across his palm, she wanted him. She wanted him to take her to bed. She wanted to suck him and fuck him until she shrieked with pleasure, but she sensed he was far away.

He had to leave tomorrow, she knew that. She had to remain on the Coast for a while but she would come back to New York. She was going to see this man again. She would make him her man. Not just with her body. She sensed he needed her. She didn't give a damn if they lived together just as long as they *were* together.

Three husbands were enough; she wasn't looking for more. But Frank Sullivan was a man she could spend the rest of her life with, she was sure of that. She sensed he might not love her, and she was aware that what she felt for him was probably not love, but whatever it was she wanted it. Like Frank, she usually got what she wanted.

Frank turned to her; the gray eyes now sought hers. His voice was huskier than usual. "I've been very inattentive, Faye, to such an exciting woman. I'm really sorry. I'm just so damn tired lately I don't know what's wrong with me. Up until a few years ago I could work the tail off any young fellow we had in the firm, but now"—his voice trailed off—"I must just be getting old."

She squeezed his hand slightly. "Frank. Do I look like the kind of woman who's attracted to an old man?"

Frank started to smile; then he began to laugh. He looked at her and laughed so heartily that he began to cough; he couldn't control it.

The other guests were looking anxiously at their table. He put the napkin to his mouth and stood up.

An anxious headwaiter moved in their direction. Faye took his arm as they walked out of the dining room, Frank clasping the napkin to his mouth. Faye noticed when he took it away that it was speckled with drops of blood. She helped him to his suite.

While he was in the bathroom she called the front desk for a doctor. When Frank heard this he protested vigorously, but she paid no attention to him. She helped him undress and sat beside him once he was in bed.

The doctor came promptly and examined him quickly but professionally. He prescribed a mild medicine to relax the muscles in Frank's throat and administered a sedative so that he would sleep soundly.

When she saw the doctor to the door he motioned to her to follow him into the hall where they could talk.

"Mrs. Sullivan—"

Faye interrupted. "Miss Stein, Doctor."

"Yes. Well, Miss Stein, of course it's difficult for me to be sure; I certainly don't like the looks of that throat. When he gets back to wherever he lives, I suggest that he have a thorough examination. You have to get him to stop smoking immediately. That throat of his looks terribly raw."

Faye thanked the doctor and went in to Frank. He smiled at her as she sat beside him holding his hand.

"Frank. The doctor says you have to stop smoking. He was very serious about that. He also said you have to have a thorough checkup when you get back to New York." She looked at him tenderly. She saw he was already responding to the sedative.

"Frank. I'm coming back to New York when I've finished what I have to do out here, and I'm going to make sure you take care of yourself."

He smiled up at her and touched her nipple, which almost instantly became erect. He laughed very softly. "Faye dear. I had such a marvelous evening planned for us."

"I'll bet you did."

She smiled and leaned over and kissed him.

He fell asleep. His face relaxed and seemed at peace for the first time since she had met him.

She undressed and turned out the lights. Only a faint shaft of light came from the bathroom door that she had left slightly ajar. She looked at Frank for a long time. He was snoring lightly. She felt chilled at the forebodings of her mind as she thought of what might lie behind the doctor's suggestions.

Was this rational to get herself involved with a man who admitted he was in love with his wife, who seemed harried by so many problems, and now this?

Didn't it make sense to walk out of Frank Sullivan's life, now? What did she need it for?

She got into bed beside him and lay staring up at the ceiling. What was she doing here? Was she going to take on the problems of another man for the fourth time in her life? Didn't her analysis teach her anything? This time she *knew* what she was doing, and for the most part why she was doing it.

"So nu, Faye," she said to herself. "What do you need

this for?" She punched the pillow as she turned over on her side.

"Who knows," she said, and tried to fall asleep.

Marsh Butterworth was sitting in Dean's office. It was 10 A.M. Dean had left instructions to hold his calls.

Outside, the weather was not behaving as if spring was less than two weeks away. It was bitter cold. Gale-force winds blew the grime of the streets with stinging effect against the faces of those who valiantly bucked the wind.

Dean paced back and forth in front of Marsh. This always made Marsh nervous. Almost everything Dean did made Marsh nervous. Their conversations were the joke of the firm.

When a visitor sat in Marsh's office and the phone rang, Marsh would leap at it, muttering a brief apology. He was as excitable as a flushed quail.

If Dean were on the other end, the visitor would be treated to a series of "You're so right, Dean. Yes, sir. Absolutely. I couldn't agree with you more. Absolutely."

Marsh did everything but kneel.

Around Dean Marsh felt alive. He absorbed Dean's savage vitality and made it his own. He was at the center of power when he was with Dean, and he felt that power vicariously. As far as Marsh was concerned, it was what he wanted. It was excitement without risk. He didn't have to stick his neck out.

Now, he sat coiled with anxiety waiting for Dean to react to what he had just told him.

Dean stopped pacing and turned to face Marsh. His sharp pale face was a mask of concentration.

"Now tell it to me again, Marsh; slowly."

"I did as you directed, Dean. I found out who Charlie Fox is, and I think I have an idea about this Vittorio fellow."

Dean nodded.

"Fox is a partner in the firm of Fox and Bohlen. They're a small firm as far as I can tell. Just barely hanging on. This Vittorio, I'm not sure, but I have a strong feeling he's one of those Mafia types who has some inside connection with the firm. He lives out in Queens near La Guardia."

Dean thought for a moment. "I want you to arrange a meeting between myself and Vittorio. Make it someplace where no one is likely to know me." He thought for a moment.

"I still belong to a club in midtown. Our crowd never goes there. It's mainly for artists and writers, or midtown business people. Get me a quiet room there. It's the Lotos, off Fifth Avenue on Sixty-sixth. Set that up as soon as you can, Marsh."

On the day of the meeting Dean waited for Vittorio in the club lounge. He was engrossed in a copy of *Antiques* when a club steward directed Vittorio toward him.

"Mr. Vittorio to see you, sir." Dean nodded. They shook hands.

"I've a private room where we can talk. Would you follow me?"

Dean liked to get whatever exercise he could. He always walked stairs if possible. Without asking Vittorio if he would like to use the elevator, Dean began to walk quickly up the beautifully curved staircase with its superb carvings and its view of a superior stained-glass skylight if one bothered to look up. It was three flights to the meeting room they would be using. Dean could hear Vittorio breathing hard behind him.

They entered the room. Vittorio was obviously ill at ease. He was still puffing from his exertion on the stairs. He looked around.

"Don't they have no elevators in this place? What is it, anyway?"

"It's a private club."

Vittorio was puzzled. "Whadda ya do here?"

Dean laughed. "Sometimes I wonder about that myself."

Dean motioned to a chair underneath a large window. A small table had been set in the opposite corner of the room. Angi seated himself on the sofa while Dean moved a straight-backed chair opposite him.

"How about a drink? I've taken the liberty of ordering a bottle of wine for lunch."

"You gonna have one?"

"Yes, I am."

"Then I will."

"What's your pleasure?"

"Chivas on de rocks."

Dean picked up the phone. "Would you send up two Chivas on the rocks, and two sherries." Dean turned to Angi. "It saves time."

Angi's face seemed to relax slightly.

Dean walked over to the table and picked up a menu. He handed it to Angi. "Just check whatever you like."

The meal went slowly, awkwardly.

"You guys sell stocks 'n' bonds?"

"Yes, we do."

"You gotta few tips, Faulkner, on how I can make a bundle?"

Dean smiled. "I'm not in that end of the business, Angi. I'm in the banking end. My partners and I help arrange long-term capital financings for companies, either privately, or in the public marketplace."

Dean watched Angi carefully.

"But you're no novice to the business, Angi. My sources tell me you're interested in Charlie Fox's firm."

Angi was instantly on guard. "Yah. I buy an' sell a few shares now and then."

Dean decided to probe further.

"I'm told that your interest in Fox and Bohlen isn't quite that casual."

Angi's face became an angry cloud. "Whadda you tryin'
to say, Faulkner? Get it out. I don't like a lot of screwin'
around."

"I appreciate your directness." Dean paused. He
wanted to phrase this very carefully. "Angi. I wanted to
talk with you because I admit I was disturbed when I met
you in my partner's office. You seemed sore as hell about
something and I have been wondering why." Dean fin-
gered his napkin, his eyes averted from Angi's.

"You see, Angi, we are still a general partnership. That
means, as I am sure you know, that we are *jointly and
severally* obligated and liable for each other. Frank's problems are my problems, and vice versa."

"Well, then, you got yourself a problem."

The lunch had made Angi less belligerent.

"I am afraid I don't understand."

"Whadda ya mean you don't understand?"

"Just that. That's why we're here. Just why would we
have a problem that would involve you, Angi?"

Angi got up from the table, his face glowering.

"Because I don't stand around and watch one of my
friends getting his balls knocked off by some con artist
like Sullivan."

Dean still didn't understand. "You'll have to explain.
I'm afraid I'm lost."

Angi whirled at him, his face flushed with anger.

"Are you kiddin' me? Whadda ya think I am, some
goddamn dumb bastard who don't know what's goin' on?

"You just got through tellin' me how buddy buddy you
guys are. Everybody's got his cock up everybody's asshole.
Ain't that right? An' now you're tellin' me you don't
know what Sullivan done to my friend Charlie Fox?
That's a lot of bullshit."

Dean held up his hands. "I'm afraid I really don't
know what you're talking about, Angi."

Angi glowered at him. "He sold seventy-five thousand
shares of Computer at forty-nine, the son of a bitch. An'

you know what he told Charlie when Fox wanted to know if he should bail out too? He said the company was okay. Some mumbo-jumbo shit about their being different technical opinions or crap like that. He said your company was puttin' out some kind of report about the goddamn company. It would show everything was okay. Well, that was a lot of shit. An' I told Charlie. I said, 'Charlie, that Irish fucker ain't levelin' with you. You're gonna get your tit in a wringer.' I warned the little bastard, but he wouldn't listen. So I told him I don't like wiseguys like Sullivan who would stick it to a pal of mine. I told him the only way to handle a cocksucker like Sullivan was to play rough. That's why I was in his office when I bumped into you. I told the prick he had better buy Charlie's stock back at the price he got for his, or I would tell this guy Livermore, the guy that's bangin' the balls off this company. You know who I mean?"

Dean listened with rapt attention, his face masking the pleasure that was surging inside him. It was marvelous. It was beyond his wildest imagining. *He had the firm!*

Dean made a valiant effort to control his excitement.

"Angi. That's a very serious accusation to make against my partner. I have nothing but your word to substantiate these charges, but even if they're true I can assure you my partners won't repurchase Mr. Fox's shares at any price. What Frank Sullivan does as an individual is up to him." Dean paused for a moment. "Angi. This is the first time I've heard of this, and I'd like to be constructive. Frank's in the hospital undergoing some tests. Let me talk to him and get back to you."

Angi looked at Dean suspiciously. He picked up his narrow-brimmed hat and held it for a moment. "I don't stand anyone fuckin' one of my friends. You get back to me." His charade, now so transparent to Dean, was laughable.

Angi missed the slight change in Dean's eyes; they were

again the eyes of the ferret. "I'll get back to you, Angi." Dean held out a surprisingly strong hand.

Angi left.

Dean could almost feel the response of his partners when he assembled them to hear what Angi had told him. *Frank would be through.*

Dean's timing couldn't be better. Frank was ill. He looked terrible when he came back from the Coast. Dean knew he would never have a better chance. He'd have to move carefully, but quickly. He picked up the phone and called Marsh.

"Get hold of our pilot. I want to know if Frank used the plane to go to the Coast anytime last month. And find out if he took anyone with him. If possible, see if the pilot knows who he was going to see." Dean hung up.

When the answers came back Dean knew he had won. He knew Frank could be a brutal adversary, so that nothing could be left to chance. Frank had to be deposed, cleanly and quietly.

Slowly, his mind cautioned; *carefully*.

How to begin. That's what he needed to think through. How to begin?

That evening when Dean returned home he told his wife he particularly wanted to be by himself tonight.

Chris understood her husband too well. The years had revealed to her a man whose skills she could admire, but whose character she found flawed. It had separated them, but it hadn't destroyed their relationship. They had, figuratively, learned to live in separate rooms.

On this night Chris sensed a mood in her husband she didn't understand. She knew better than to pry.

Dean sat in his study; the red, black and chromed lair where he chose to seclude himself to work and think.

He was searching for a way to begin. He mixed a martini, dimmed the lights, and let his mind roam. It floated over a variety of machinations. He needed an ally. He needed someone respected and admired by his other partners.

He stood up. Glen Farrell. By God, that was it! Farrell. And Farrell was close to Frank. He would be perfect.

He thought about this carefully, pacing back and forth in tense concentration. If he could only persuade Glen Farrell he would have them all.

He picked up the phone and dialed him in New Canaan. Farrell answered.

"Dean? No, it's all right. Jane was just getting the kids in bed." He paused. "Are you okay? You sound uptight about something."

"I am."

"Is it serious? Do we have a problem?"

Dean sighed resignedly. "When don't we have problems?"

Glen laughed. "I'll buy that." His voice became serious. "What's up?"

"I can't go into this on the phone; it's too important."

"That doesn't sound good."

"It isn't."

Glen hesitated. "Well, you've ruined my evening. What do you want to do?"

"I hate to be this obscure, but I don't want to go into this at the office either."

"Can't you give me a clue?"

Dean thought for what seemed a long time.

"It concerns Frank."

"Is he all right?"

"As far as I know."

"Dean, I hate these guessing games."

"I'm sorry. Could you meet me somewhere tonight?"

"Is it that urgent?"

"I'm afraid it is."

"I sure hate to come into town this late—"

"You don't have to. I'll come up and see you."

Glen was impressed now with the urgency of this call. Dean was senior to Glen in both capital position and length of service. He was second only to Frank. Dean was also very much of a prima donna and he prized his place in the pecking order. He didn't make trips to visit partners junior to him unless something really was up.

"No, I'll come down."

"Suppose we split it. I'll meet you at the Candlelight in Greenwich."

"That's hardly splitting it."

"Let's leave it that way, Glen. I'll have to order a limousine. It's seven thirty now. Suppose I plan to see you about nine or nine thirty. It depends upon how quickly I can get a car."

"Don't worry about it. I'll be there. You take your time."

Dean hung up. The first nail in the coffin of Frank Sullivan was being hammered home.

Glen arrived at the Candlelight at nine o'clock. The tables were crowded, but the manager knew Glen and made a special effort. He found a table in a far corner where they would be better able to talk. Glen ordered a drink and waited.

Glen Farrell had come into the firm right out of Boston College. He was of medium height. He was rapidly losing a good part of his sandy hair, which had become flecked with gray. His face was round with light-blue eyes and his manner was quick and decisive. His accent still contained the long flat a's of his native Massachusetts.

Frank had spotted Glen early as a hot young salesman. Frank put him in charge of their Boston office, and Glen did a hell of a job—so much so that Frank brought him to New York and put him in charge of national institutional sales.

Glen was a combination of the ingratiating and the aggressive. He had the drive and the intelligence to make him, at thirty-nine, a directing partner in charge of *all* sales for Sullivan & Co.

He stood up and motioned to Dean as he saw him being directed toward his table.

Dean apologized for intruding on Glen's evening.

"Forget it. Tell me, what's so hot that you came all the way up here to your poor country cousin?" Glen's face was smiling, but his eyes probed Dean's.

"Don't give me that poor country cousin stuff. I know the price of real estate in New Canaan."

Glen laughed. "Come on, Dean. What's up with Frank?"

Dean avoided Glen's eyes. He toyed with the silverware absentmindedly.

"It's hard for me to begin. Frank and I have never been in agreement as to how the firm should be run, you know that."

The smile had left Glen's face. He knew what went on between Dean and Frank.

"It's difficult to say what I have to, because I'm not so sure how unbiased it sounds coming from me." Glen nodded.

Dean's face was sharp and intense.

"Frank is almost out of Computer. He sold his stock, seventy-five thousand shares that I know of, through a firm called Fox and Bohlen—at forty-nine, I might add. Then he released that institutional report of Friedman's. He's left us all, the whole damn firm, high and dry. I don't know why he sold. He must have had some kind of information he didn't want to share with us." Dean shook his head in a gesture of resignation. "I figure he cleared almost $2.3 million before taxes."

"I don't believe it." Glen's face was white.

Dean's voice was very controlled. "You'd better believe it, partner. I can substantiate every word I've told you."

"It can't be. It simply can't be. Not Frank."

"I'm afraid it's true."

Glen was ashen. There was a special bond that he felt with Frank. Frank had made it the hard way. He was an Irishman who had made all the white-shoe bastards make a place for him on top of the hill. Glen admired that. He wanted it for himself. He always felt that Frank was a man of integrity. But to screw your own partners, to risk exposing the firm to the kind of publicity which could only hurt it; *his own firm.* It was totally unbelievable.

Dean called the waiter over and asked Glen if he wanted a drink.

"You're goddamn right I do. Give me a Gibson. Second thought, make it a double."

Dean masked a smile. "I'll have a martini. Not too dry."

"Dean. Are you absolutely sure of this?"

"Absolutely."

"Jesus."

They both remained silent for what seemed a very long time.

"What do you propose we do?"

Dean pursed his lips and shrugged. "I really don't know *what* to do."

"Does anyone else know?"

Dean shook his head negatively.

"Have you spoken to Frank about this?"

"No. What do I do? Face him with something like this when he's ill? I can't do that."

Glen thought for a moment. "You have to confront him with it before you tell the other guys. That would be a hell of a thing to do."

"I can't, Glen. I've never seen Frank look as worn out as he did when he came back from the Coast. I simply can't face him with this until we know how seriously ill he is."

"Well, then, what do you propose we do? This goddamn Computer thing can blow up on us like a bomb."

Dean nodded. "Frank says he persuaded Nichols to give some interviews to some of our friends from the financial press. That could help."

"Yeh. It could. But this damn stock has been on a Nantucket sleigh ride for weeks. If it keeps going the way it has, the thing will be off the board." Glen shook his head.

"I'm afraid the only conclusion I can draw is that he didn't want us to know," Dean said. "We probably would have joined him in the sale. That would have created problems in the market: the key partners of the managing underwriting firm bailing out . . ." Dean paused. "No. I'm afraid that's what Frank was trying to avoid. He wanted to sell without our getting in the way. He certainly must know something we don't."

Glen had to agree. It was the only rational explanation.

"You heard that Grant Weir had a stroke, didn't you?"

"Yes. There's been some rumor of that around the firm."

"Did either Frank or I mention to you that at the meeting in New England Weir made some very broad insinuations about Nichols?"

"I never heard that."

"He did." Dean paused. "A curious thing: where do you think Grant was when he had his stroke?"

"Haven't the faintest idea."

"With Nichols."

Glen's eyes widened. "Has anyone spoken to Grant?"

"You can't."

"Why not?"

"His speech has been affected."

Glen thought for a moment. "Can he write?"

"Perhaps he can, but from what I've heard his doctors want him under complete bed rest. No visitors. Not even Jesse."

Dean waited, then finished his martini. "An even more curious piece of news. Frank made two trips to the Coast. On the first one he took with him Dr. Eisenstadt, a physicist from MIT, one of the world authorities on impregnated-chip technology. Who do you think they went out to see?"

Glen shook his head in confusion.

"Dr. Paul Nichols. They met with Nichols shortly before Frank sold his stock—about a week before that report went out."

Glen was simply astonished.

Dean viewed him quietly for a long time before speaking.

"I'm afraid we've all been hung out to dry, partner." His voice sounded fatigued.

"What do we do? What the hell do we do?"

Dean hesitated. "I've given that a lot of thought. I think our main concern has to be the firm. It's sure to get out one way or another. There's this fellow Vittorio—"

"Who's he?"

"I think he has some interest, I don't know if it's legitimate or not, in Fox and Bohlen. I met with him today. He wants us to buy their long position at the same price Frank got for his stock. Vittorio claims he warned Charlie Fox to sell when Frank did, but Frank told him his reason for selling was he needed the money. Now, Vittorio is threatening to go to Livermore and tell him the whole story. Under the circumstances I think we better call a meeting of the directing partners."

"Without Frank? Shouldn't we wait until he gets out of the hospital?"

"I don't know. I've thought about that. Frank's ill. He may be sicker than we know. Rather than have him at a meeting that could get very hectic, I think we should lay this out for the boys and see what they want to do. At least that way we can face him with a decision."

Glen thought about that for a long time. He wasn't sure.

"Frank could be in the hospital for a couple of weeks. I just don't think the firm has that kind of time."

Glen shook his head in reluctant agreement.

They were both exhausted. Glen took the check from his protesting partner and both rose to walk to Dean's car. Glen's face was a mixture of sorrow and concern.

The night had become colder. The wind had risen and

spurred the clouds across the face of a pale moon.

Dean turned to Glen seeking a commitment. "If we start this thing, it could become very unpleasant."

"That's what concerns me. I hate to have to face Frank like this."

"So do I. But I don't see any alternative. Do you?"

"I wish to hell I did."

"So do I, friend. But even if we could bury this it wouldn't stay dead."

They shook hands. Glen watched the black limousine pull away. He walked to his car feeling very vulnerable and unsure.

Dean had called for a meeting of the directing partners to be held on Friday. He deliberately picked the start of a weekend so that his partners would not be in the firm walking around with long faces the following day, letting the employees know something was up. They sensed it anyway. Dean knew from long experience that every organization had a grapevine, and Sullivan & Co. was no exception. It picked up rumors almost as soon as the directing partners were out of the boardroom. Dean didn't understand how things leaked, but they did. He was going to make damn sure this time they didn't. He wanted to take over a firm, not a corpse.

He had carefully planned this meeting with every detail thoroughly considered. His approach would be the same he had used with Glen. He was doing this for the firm, for its customers and employees, and for the partnership. He smiled as he thought of it; it was like motherhood.

How could he be opposed on the issues? What he wanted to achieve was an informal authorization on behalf of the partners to ask Frank to step down. It would even be in Frank's interest. He was seriously ill, or at least it seemed he was. Frank could keep his interest in the firm. He could even retain his title of chairman, but Dean would become chief executive partner. It all seemed so natural, and

Frank's illness was a great cover. It allowed the Old Man to move aside gracefully in a shift that would make sense to both the Street and the press.

He had called the meeting for two o'clock in the boardroom. He had decided that there would be no minutes taken. He didn't want any written record of this meeting. Dean had spent a lifetime making sure that most of what he did in business had some record to substantiate his actions, but not this time.

The boardroom, sometimes called the senior partners' conference room, was that windowless arena where the direction of the firm was decided. It had been designed by Frank with a large round walnut table that was supposed to do away with any seating by rank. There was a numberless clock on the left wall as you entered, and a large oil portrait of Frank Sullivan on the rear wall over a seventeenth-century English sideboard.

The portrait of Frank was a good one. He looked down on all of them with vigor and authority. It was a far cry from the Frank Sullivan that lay in the hospital only a twenty-minute cab ride away.

As they filed into the room, Glen Farrell's eye caught Frank's portrait. He felt guilty being here. He was the only one present other than Dean who knew what this meeting was all about.

They took seats haphazardly around the large table. The clock showed two fifteen. Dean was seated opposite the door, all eyes focused on him.

He had waited years for this moment. He was so close, and now it was beginning.

Because of Dean's and Glen's manner the other partners were subdued. There was none of the light banter that usually preceded the opening of one of these meetings. They all knew something was up.

Dean's voice was quietly controlled.

"Gentlemen. I've asked you here this afternoon to discuss something of the utmost importance to this firm. Without doubt this is the most unhappy day of my life, to have to bring this to you. I have already discussed this with Glen; I simply had to. I could not continue holding all this to myself." He paused. "I know of no other way to do this than to start at the beginning."

Dean told it just the way he had repeated it to Glen. They were all stunned. There wasn't a sound in the room except Dean's voice. The shock among the group was almost physical.

Seated around that table were seven men who were in their late thirties or early forties. Frank had hand-picked every one of them. There were close personal bonds to him.

Besides Dean and Glen there were Dan Terrell, directing partner, corporate finance; Bill Davis, syndicate; Roger Aiken, operations; Bob Isaacs, planning; Wilbur Royce, administration. Although each owed his place around the table to his own abilities, he owed it more to Frank Sullivan. What they were hearing, however, was rapidly making them forget those personal obligations. Frank's stock within the firm was falling almost as rapidly as Computer's.

The clock on the wall showed exactly three o'clock.

Wilbur Royce, the most senior partner in rank after Dean, was the first to speak.

"I have never heard anything like this in my life. It is totally out of character for Frank. Dean, if I didn't know you wouldn't have called us all together if you couldn't back this up, I'd refuse to believe it."

"So would I," Dean said. He turned to Glen. "Do you have anything you would like to add to what I've just said?"

Glen was as troubled as the rest of them. There was something about this meeting that smacked of a kangaroo court. He didn't like it. It was too conspiratorial without Frank here.

"The whole thing is so completely wacky I can't believe it either," Glen said. "What bothers me are the practical ramifications. We simply can't let Livermore get his hands on this kind of information. It would be the juiciest scandal about a major Wall Street firm in years."

It was Bob Isaacs. "And how do we stop Vittorio or whatever his name is from going to Livermore? We're not the Mafia. We can't dump him someplace in Jersey."

Dean spread his hands flat on the table. "I don't know the answer to that. My own inclination is to talk that over with Frank. He got us into this thing. He may have to get us out."

There were several voices who echoed, "Amen."

The room had begun to be foul with smoke. Ties were loosened. Jackets opened. The air of nervous concentration could be felt as a material presence.

Dean thought that the time had finally come to make his play. He wanted someone else to lead into it. He tried Glen Farrell, but Glen wouldn't touch it. Dean wondered if he had misjudged Farrell; if Farrell was going to be of any help at all. If he wasn't, Dean would have to do it alone. It was too late now.

Wilbur Royce gave him what he needed. He looked carefully around the room. "I think we have to decide how we are going to approach Frank, and what we're going to tell him."

"I agree," said Terrell.

Wilbur turned to Dean. "I think this is your baby, Dean."

There was a general murmur of agreement.

Dean didn't respond immediately. He waited what seemed a long time before he spoke. He wanted all their attention. The room became quiet.

"It seems that what you're asking me to do is to confront Frank without deciding how I can respond to him."

"I don't understand that," said Terrell.

"What I mean is that Frank isn't going to accept my accusing him of jeopardizing *his* firm. He could very easily ask me to resign, deny the whole thing."

There was a general sense of agreement.

"What are you suggesting?" It was Farrell at last, Dean thought. Maybe the son of a bitch was worth a late night ride to Greenwich after all.

"I'm not suggesting anything. I'm simply stating that I believe we have to move. If I'm to take on that responsibility I need the authority to do it."

"You already have that, Dean. You're executive partner."

"He means, I believe," said Terrell, "that he needs Frank's authority. Am I right, Dean?"

Dean nodded his head affirmatively.

"But we don't have the authority to give you that," Wilbur Royce said. "Only Frank can do that."

"I realize that," Dean said. His eyes were averted from them. He was looking at the table.

"But we do have a negative authority," Dean said. He paused, looking around at each of them. "It depends how strongly we feel about the survival of this firm."

"What do you mean by a negative authority?" said Isaacs.

Dean seemed morose; resigned. "I mean that *we* make up the firm. If I go to Frank I have to go with the knowledge that we are all willing to resign if—"

"If what?" said Terrell.

"If Frank doesn't step aside."

"Jesus Christ." There was a general hum of comment. Their faces were worn with concern and doubt—doubt about their careers, about the future of the firm. Each man around the table was twisted in a knot of fear and indecision.

"Holy shit," said Davis. "You want us to be ready to resign if Frank doesn't step down. That's a pretty tall order, Dean."

"Gentlemen. I don't want you to do anything. I brought you together because it was my duty to bring this situation before my partners. We can wait for Frank to come out of the hospital, whenever that may be. We can wait for him to recover, however long that takes. It's a question of what sense of urgency you place on all this. If this hits the press we'll be up to our necks in litigation. I'm pretty sure we'll be in for disciplinary action as well. We'll have the Stock Exchange, the NASD, and the SEC all over us. But that's up to you. I simply will not take on the problems of trying to turn this firm around without the authority to do the job." Dean leaned back in his chair looking at all of them. He had made his case.

They began to talk to each other in small groups. Some got up and walked around to release their tensions.

"I think Dean has a point." It was Farrell. "If we agree on the seriousness of this as Dean has outlined it, then I think it's unfair to tie him down so he can't function properly." He looked about the room. You could almost feel the anxiety. "We have to move on this or the shit's really going to hit the fan. I think Dean needs the authority to get the job done."

"I agree," said Davis.

Those who were standing took their seats. All eyes were on Dean.

"Then I have your word that each of you is ready to submit his resignation if Frank doesn't agree to move over?"

There was a general nodding of heads.

"You realize," said Dean, "that what we are asking Frank to do is probably in his own best interest and the firm's. He simply won't have the day-to-day pressures. If we are absolutely discreet about this and it doesn't leak, it will seem very natural to the press and the public; after all, he's a sick man."

There was a murmured consensus. It sounded logical.

Glen Farrell finally spoke. "I have to tell you guys that my salesmen are getting killed on this thing. When you see the institutional figures for this month you'll know what I mean. We've worked like hell, all of us, to build this into a major-bracket firm, and I can tell you that I for one don't want to see my capital pissed down the drain." Glen surveyed each of their faces. "Something has to be done and Dean is the logical guy to talk to Frank. I don't think we can expect him to do that unless he has our backing. I suggest we make it unanimous."

Dean remained silent, his eyes focused on the table.

Glen turned to the rest of them. "What do you say?"

There were murmurs of troubled doubt, but finally with great reluctance they all agreed.

The son of a bitch had paid off, Dean thought.

Dean remained with his eyes averted. He waited a very long time before responding.

"Gentlemen. I want to ask each of you not to discuss this until I have spoken to Frank. Not to your wives. Not to your secretaries. Not to anyone. For once let's see if we can keep something in this room before the secretaries hear it."

There was one secretary, however, who knew that something portentous was taking place, and she was rapidly putting two and two together. Rose Finley had always guarded her boss from unnecessary outside stress; now she would act to protect him from the wolves within.

Frank lay resting, his door closed. He only half heard the muffled sounds of a busy hospital. It was Tuesday, four days after the partners' meeting. Frank knew nothing of what had taken place downtown. His doctor was to see him tomorrow morning to give him the results of the tests.

Frank's common sense told him that he was seriously ill. He felt resigned. He had packed into his life enough living for three men. If it was his time, he had regrets, sure; but he wasn't a complainer. Long experience in life had taught him that if his time had come, no doctor could do a damn thing for him.

The bronchoscopy had left him very tired. He had been sleeping, aided by sedation, for almost forty-eight hours. Dina had been with him most of the day. She had left him only a short while ago to return to the apartment.

As she entered she heard the phone ring and Bevan's voice as he answered: "No, Mrs. Sullivan is not here, Doctor—just a moment, I think she's come in. Let me check. Yes, Doctor. I'll put her right on for you." Dina took the call before removing her coat.

"Dr. Rogers? Yes. Is everything all right?"

"Yes, Mrs. Sullivan. I'm sorry to disturb you at home. I understand I just missed you at the hospital."

"Yes. I just this minute got in. Are you sure Frank's all right?" There was a pause on the other end of the line.

"Mrs. Sullivan. The reason I'm calling is that I am absolutely jammed tomorrow. I'm going to speak to your husband in the afternoon but I wanted to make sure we had a chance to talk first. I would have preferred to do this in person, but I thought with my schedule tomorrow I might miss you—"

"I appreciate your thoughtfulness very much, Doctor."

"I feel I should come straight to the point, Mrs. Sullivan, if you are agreeable—"

Dina felt a shaft of anxiety. "Go ahead, Doctor."

"I want you to understand that our prognosis for your husband is not as ominous as his condition may sound to a layman. He's a sick man, but I think we may have caught things in time. He has a fair chance if he allows us to help him. He's a very strong-willed individual, as I'm sure I don't need to tell you." He could hear Dina's rapid breathing over the phone. "Mrs. Sullivan, we believe your husband has carcinoma of the right lung. Our X-ray and bronchoscopic examinations indicate this. We are going to recommend the removal of that lung."

Dina sat down holding the phone with both hands. Her coat had slipped half off her shoulders. Her hands began to shake so that she could hardly keep the phone to her mouth.

"Mrs. Sullivan, are you there? Mrs. Sullivan—"

"Yes, yes, Doctor. I'm here."

"I'm particularly sorry to upset you, but let me assure you that we have had great success with this kind of procedure."

"I understand, Doctor."

"I'm going to talk to your husband late tomorrow afternoon between four and five o'clock. I assume you will want to be there."

"Yes, of course."

"One other thing, Mrs. Sullivan. It's been my experience that a patient prefers to hear this kind of news from his doctor, rather than a member of the family. If I may suggest, I would rather you not visit Mr. Sullivan until shortly before I arrive." He paused. "It will be difficult for you to act naturally and I think it would be easier on your husband if we handled it this way."

"I understand, Doctor."

"I'll see you tomorrow then."

"Yes. And thank you for being so considerate, Doctor. Goodbye."

She hung up the phone and sat there, confused and distraught. She had been preoccupied trying desperately to resolve the problem of the child that was growing within her and the course of action she would take regarding the child and Frank—and Whit.

As she sat with Frank during these last five days she felt a renewed compassion and tenderness for him; also a growing sense of obligation. When she left the hospital and occasionally met Whit and they commiserated together, her feelings for Whit were of a different kind; a plaintive longing. A desire to let him wrap her in the emotional security she knew he could give her and relieve the pressures that were crushing her life.

As she sat by the phone, her thoughts a maelstrom, it rang again. Its sound startled her so that she almost jumped out of the chair. She still had not removed her coat.

"Hello

"Dina?"

"What? Oh, Whit. Let me take this in my room." She saw Bevan mixing a cocktail for her as she walked to her bedroom. She picked up the phone. "Whit. I'm so glad you called. I just hung up from Dr. Rogers." Her voice shook. "Whit, he says Frank has cancer. They're going to have to take out his right lung. Oh, Whit, he looks so awful. I don't know if he can stand an operation like that. Whit, I'm so afraid for him."

"Dina, can you meet me for dinner? We'll go down to the Village. It will do you good."

"I don't feel like it, Whit. They're going to tell Frank tomorrow."

"Dina, I think I should be with you tonight if only for just a little while. Darling, thousands of people have had perfectly good results from this kind of operation. If they have caught it in time, Frank can live a very normal life if he's sensible. It's serious, but it's not the end of the world." He paused. "Darling—tonight's one night I think we really should be together. Why not come over to my place if you don't feel like the Village?"

She waited before replying. "Bevan has my dinner here, Whit. I'll eat here, and maybe join you later, but only for an hour or so. I need some time on my own tonight. Things seem to be falling down all around me. I have to find something to hold on to."

"Isn't that where I come in?"

"Oh, Whit, if it were only that easy. I just wish to God it were." She fought to keep from crying. "Darling, let me go now, please. I'll try to see you later. Good night, Whit." She hung up.

Dina's instinctive forebodings were more comprehensive than Whit's and more accurate. For tonight Dina was not going to see Whit. Tonight Dina would begin to grow up, and her teacher would be of all people, Miss Rose Finley.

Dina ate alone; Bevan served her with solicitous concern. She ate without appetite, her mind jumping from one distressing thought to another. As she finished her meal, the phone rang.

Bevan came into the dining room to tell her the call was from Miss Finley. Dina thought that very odd. What would Rose be calling her for? She knew Frank was in the hospital.

"I'll take it in here, Bevan," she said.

"I'm sorry to disturb you, Mrs. Sullivan, but I felt I had to talk to you. I didn't want to talk to Mr. Sullivan before I discussed this with you."

Dina could sense the urgency in Rose Finley's voice. "Is there something wrong, Rose?"

"I'm afraid there is."

Dina was now concerned; this was most unusual for Rose Finley. She had been with Frank for over twenty years. She knew more about him than anyone else; far more than Dina.

"Is it something you wish to discuss with me on the telephone, or do you want me to see you at the office in the morning?"

A long pause.

"Mrs. Sullivan, I don't think it can wait until morning. I thought if you didn't mind, I would come to see you tonight."

"But it's a long trip from Short Hills, Rose—"

"I'm not home, Mrs. Sullivan. I'm still downtown."

"In that case, if you think it's so urgent come up. I was going out, but I'll cancel it. I'll see you when you get here."

She called Whit to tell him what had happened.

"I don't have the faintest idea of what she wants, but Rose is like Frank's right arm. She's as loyal as a Scottish nanny. Darling, something's up. If Rose is coming to see me it's serious. Whit, darling, I'm exhausted. I'm going to freshen up and wait for Rose. I'm sorry about tonight —I did want to see you if only for a little while. Please call me tomorrow night, darling. I've got to go." She hung up.

Rose Finley found a cab near Delmonico's. As she sat

absentmindedly watching the darkened buildings of the financial district give way to the brightly lit East River Drive, she thought about the events that had brought her to this evening.

Rose was fifty-three years old. In September she had been with Frank Sullivan twenty-four years. She lived in Short Hills, New Jersey, with her widowed mother, whom she helped to support and take care of. Men had infrequently found their way into her life, but there was no time for them. Frank was demanding, and as his small firm grew she found herself on call almost perpetually. At first she objected. She became testy and at times actually unpleasant, but Frank knew her worth and saw to it that she was compensated. He made her get her registered representative's license so that he could run trades through her and she could collect the commissions. In addition, she had built up a small brokerage business of her own, and traded for her own account in the market, following what Frank bought and sold.

As a private secretary and R.R., she had built up over the years through investments and savings a capital account that was very close to two hundred thousand dollars. Her income plus commissions came to about forty thousand. All this she owed to Frank Sullivan.

Rose Finley may have admitted falling in love with her boss, but with Mrs. Sullivan in the picture Rose had gradually turned her affections toward protecting and serving Frank rather than showing any signs of overt affection. Her life had settled into a relatively satisfactory routine, at least as far as she was concerned. Her family regarded her as a spinster aunt, but she was respected for her character and her independence.

Around the firm there was a suspicion that Rose wore a wig. Her hair did seem a little unnatural for a woman of her age. She wore it short, without a hint of gray, but if Rose was able to put her hair in a drawer every night it was her own secret.

Her manner was courteous but somewhat formal. She smiled easily, but if you watched her hazel eyes carefully you found them calculating and appraising. She was addicted to tailored print dresses and an occasional suit. If you met her on the PATH trains going back and forth to New Jersey she always looked trim and pulled together, no matter how harried the day had been or how crowded the train. The most important part of Rose Finley's life was her job, and, very simply, her job was Frank Sullivan.

As the cab stopped in front of Frank's apartment house, Rose's face wore a grim and determined expresssion. Her life was about to come apart because her boss was threatened. Rose Finley had her Irish up.

The two women sat in Frank's study, a contrast in life's roulette. Rose held a cup of tea on her lap while she quietly but earnestly told Dina what was happening at the firm.

"So you see, Mrs. Sullivan, I believe Mr. Faulkner has rounded them all up in favor of him. He's going to see Mr. Sullivan in a day or two, and then I think it will be too late—"

"But what exactly has Frank done that's so terrible? I still don't understand that."

"After Frank came back from a meeting in San Francisco with Nichols, he sold some stock in a company we're having problems with. The word is that Frank acted on inside information without telling the rest of the partnership—or the customers—of the firm. That's a serious matter if it's true."

"But what am I supposed to do about that?"

Rose Finley looked away from Dina's inquiring gaze. Her voice dropped so that Dina could hardly hear her. "I'm afraid, Mrs. Sullivan, you'll have to tell him."

Dina was incredulous. "Tell him! Are you serious, Rose? Do you know what they're going to tell him tomorrow? They're going to tell him that he has cancer and they have to remove his right lung. And you want me to bring him problems of the firm. That's impossible, Rose."

The two women sat facing each other, Rose's mouth now a determined line. Dina looked at her with sympathy but also with impatience.

Rose put down her cup gently; she had tears in her eyes. "Mrs. Sullivan, this is going to be hard to say so please accept what I tell you as being in the best interests of your husband. After all, I've spent nearly a quarter of a century with Mr. Sullivan." She lowered her eyes. "You might say that in some ways I know him better than anyone." She paused. "I don't mean to sound presumptuous, but most wives don't get the time to spend with their husbands that we do. We see a different side of them. We know their business problems, and many of their personal problems far better than a wife." She looked at Dina with a good deal of understanding. Her voice softened. "That's why I'm here tonight. Because if you don't tell Frank what's going on downtown and he's forced out of the firm as a result"—she looked away—"you'll kill him as well as any cancer." She turned to Dina. "Mrs. Sullivan. We both know what kind of a man Frank is. He's a gut fighter. He built this firm with his intelligence and his drive and his courage. You don't know what it's like downtown. It's a jungle. Every day is survival day. Many of the men are lucky just to be alive. Decisions are made downtown, Mrs. Sullivan, where twenty percent of the capital of the firm can be committed in a ten-minute meeting. It's like no place else on earth. The pressures, the pace—the whole game. It becomes a part of you. It takes a particular kind of a man to survive and be successful in that kind of life."

Dina had the incredible feeling that if Frank had ever stopped to tell her about his life this is what he would have said, and all this was coming from a middle-aged matron who was her husband's private secretary.

"The real thing, though, is what this means to Frank. His life *is* downtown." She hesistated. "I don't mean that the way it sounds. I just mean that there's no use saving him from cancer if you let them really kill him by destroying his firm."

Rose Finley was visibly shaken from the feelings she had released to Dina. Dina was positive that Rose had never unburdened herself to anyone the way she had this night.

She stood up somewhat hesitantly. "Mrs. Sullivan, you've got to tell him. I apologize for saying all this to you—especially under the circumstances. I do hope you appreciate why I felt I had to see you and say these things."

Dina nodded. She was so stunned by the unexpected visit of Rose Finley and by her uninhibited conversation that she walked her to the door in a trance.

She sat in the living room, her face covered with her hands. Oh, sweet God, she thought, what do I do? Her inclination was to call Whit and ask him. She had always been advised by men: by her father, by Frank, and now by Whit. This time she was on her own.

She walked to the bedroom and caught a glance of herself in the mirror: she looked awful. She had decided that Rose Finley was right. She owed it to Frank to put him on guard. It was his life, and his firm. The final decision as to what to do should be up to him.

She undressed and turned out the light. Normally, she read for a time before she went to sleep, but tonight she was exhausted. Her entrance to sleep was hastened by the fact that she had made a major decision, and she had made it alone. Tonight was her beginning. She was growing up.

She decided to see Frank early. She was in the hospital before 10 A.M. She told him everything Rose had told her. She sat by his bed holding his hand as she spoke to him. He had outworn the night's sedation and was alert. He listened to her with grim attention. When she had finished he took her hand and kissed it. His eyes were now bright with challenge. He asked her to dial Miss Finley for him. She handed him the phone. His voice was huskier than usual.

"Rose? Dina's here." It was the first time Dina had ever heard him call Miss Finley by her first name.

"I certainly appreciate what you did last night. I'm very much obliged." He coughed. "I want you to get Ray Costanza and send him up here. Tell him I don't want anyone to know where he is. I'll make arrangements here so that if Dean comes he won't be admitted. And, Rose— I'm very appreciative." He hung up.

A nurse came in with some pills and a needle. Frank waved her away. "No more of that stuff, Nurse. Not for a while, anyway." She smiled and started to ready him for his injection. "Look, Nurse. I know you're just following Dr. Rogers' orders, but I'm not taking any more medication for a while. I've got things to do and I need a clear head."

"But, Mr. Sullivan, I have to give you this medication. I have no choice."

Dina tried to intervene. "Nurse. Couldn't we wait until we see Dr. Rogers this afternoon? I'll take the responsibility."

Frank looked at his wife with admiration. Was this Dina? Normally she would be pleading with him to follow the doctor's orders.

"It's most unusual, Mrs. Sullivan. I'll have to report this to my supervisor and she will contact Dr. Rogers." This was upsetting hospital routine. The young nurse took her equipment tray, and shaking her head left the room.

Frank turned to Dina. He smiled at her. "It seems to me that the women in my life are the only ones supporting the old man." The smile faded and his face became hard as his thoughts reflected upon what was going on downtown. She looked at him tenderly. The full head of flecked gray hair and the heavy gray brows were all that hadn't changed about Frank Sullivan. His face seemed thinner and the lines of age more apparent. His skin was pale and hung more loosely about the straight planes of his jaw.

Now that Dina knew what was wrong with Frank, she understood the huskiness of his voice. As she held his hand looking at him with a clearer insight than she had known during any period of their marriage, she understood a lot more. She saw the light that had come back into his eyes. She recognized it; it was the light of battle. She understood too that he enjoyed it. Lying there with cancer of the lung, her husband had regained his vitality because he was back in the game. Rose Finley was right. She understood him better than anyone: what was the use of saving this man's life if you killed the thing that made him live?

She bent over and kissed him, and for the first time he knew that she understood.

"What can I do, Frank? Just tell me, and I'll do it."

He smiled at her and drew her toward him. He stroked her hair and kissed her lightly on the forehead. His voice was barely audible. "I'll holler if I need help." He patted her hand and closed his eyes to rest.

She stayed with him, as an hour passed, trying to be unobtrusive. She knew his thoughts were on the struggle to hold on to his firm. But how? He looked so weak. What could he do against all of them? Her mind turned to Dean. That miserable bastard, she thought. I'd like to scratch his eyes out. It was hopeless. The best Frank could do would be to step aside gracefully and let them have what they wanted.

As she looked at her husband lying there, she knew that would not be his response. Frank Sullivan wasn't stepping aside for anyone. Not under these circumstances.

There was a soft knock on the door. She turned to see the silent presence of Ray Costanza. Frank, who was again alert, gave a brief smile to Ray as he motioned him to come in the room.

"Ray, you know my wife, Dina."

"Yes, indeed. Nice to see you, Mrs. Sullivan."

Frank pressed the electric button that elevated his bed. Costanza remained standing; awkward at intruding.

"Dina, I wonder if you could let us talk for a while. Why don't you get a bite of lunch and I'll see you later." She nodded, picked up her bag and walked over to her husband and kissed him.

"Please don't overdo it, Frank." She looked at Ray Costanza, who met her eyes with understanding.

"It's been nice to see you again, Mr. Costanza."

"My pleasure, Mrs. Sullivan." They both watched her leave the room.

"Well, Ray. I guess you know why I asked you to come up here."

"I think so, sir."

Frank looked at him with determination. "Before I go any further, maybe I'd better ask whose side you're on."

"I didn't know there was a side, sir."

Frank's eyes flashed. "I don't have the time or the strength to play games, Ray. You know what I'm talking about. Whose side are you on?"

Ray's eyes were steady. He stood there impassively. "I'm on your side, sir."

"All the way?"

"Yes, sir."

"Even if it costs you your job?"

Ray paused. "Yes, sir."

"Good. By the way, now that we have that settled, how do you like the odds?"

"I don't."

"Neither do I." Frank's voice became concerned. "Have you got anything?"

"Yes, sir, I have."

"What is it?"

"You were right, sir. Mr. Faulkner has been trading Computer in a dummy account away from the firm."

Frank's eyes came alive. "Can you prove that?"

"Yes, sir. I have tapes of phone calls he's made to an attorney we've been able to trace. The orders have been given in code. I didn't want to alert Mr. Faulkner, so I've made no move to contact the attorney."

"Then I don't understand. What good is the information if it's in code?"

"If I can explain, sir. What I did was to call on an old army buddy of mine. He was head of cryptography for our outfit. He's one of those guys who's a puzzle freak— even now they have some kind of international association—" He saw the impatience come into Frank's eyes. "In any case, sir, I had Tom go over this code of Dean's. It was ridiculously simple. He called it a Boy Scout code. Anyway, it clearly reveals Dean's trading instructions to his attorney on Computer. I have the only transcribed copy of the tapes in my safe at home."

Ray Costanza paused. "Sir, I took the liberty of having the tap removed from Mr. Faulkner's phone. I felt I had what you wanted. I did this on my own authority—you weren't available."

Frank motioned weakly. "Forget it, Ray." Frank paused. "Would you mind sitting down? I want to think for a moment. Can I get you something—a cup of coffee or tea?"

"No, sir. I'm fine."

Ray sat in the white vinyl club chair in the corner quietly leafing through a copy of *Town & Country*.

Frank pushed the button to lower his bed and lay quietly looking up at the ceiling. An observer just walking into the room would have thought him resting. He wasn't. He realized that his biggest problem was his lack of strength. He was weak from whatever it was that was wrong with him, and he was debilitated from the tests, especially the bronchoscopy.

"Ray, I very much appreciate what you've done—and I might add the loyalty you've shown me. I won't forget it. I want you to do something else for me. I want you to get hold of Charles Fox; he's a partner in Fox and Bohlen. Tell him you are going to go to the SEC and the IRS and disclose the association between a Mr. Angelo Vittorio and his firm. Say you're doing this on my instructions— that you have to proceed unless Charlie can guarantee to keep Vittorio in line. Tell him that I have no wish to hurt an old friend, but if I have to, to protect the firm, I have no choice. Oh, one other thing, be sure to bring the transcripts of those tapes on Faulkner with you to the meeting."

"To the meeting, sir?"

"Yes. I'm coming downtown Monday for a meeting at three."

"But, sir—"

Frank held up his hand, his face haggard but grim.

"Just do as I tell you. Have my secretary call a meeting of the directing partners for three. I want them all there. Every goddamn one of them. And I want you there too."

Ray was stunned, but knew better than to question the old man further.

"Now, if you don't mind, I'm going to doze off."

He started to turn over in preparation for sleep when he thought of something else.

"Wait, Ray. Make sure you pass the word that the doctors won't permit any visitors. I don't want to see Dean until I'm ready for him."

Ray got up to leave. As he did so the telephone rang. Frank picked it up and waved Ray off.

"Is that you, Frank? Are you alone?"

"Faye. It's good to hear from you."

"Darling, I've been so worried about you. Do they know what it is yet?"

"I don't know. Rogers is coming to talk to me this afternoon."

"I'm going to be back in New York tomorrow, Frank. Can I see you?" There was a pause. "Is anything wrong?"

"No, not really. It's just that there's that problem at the firm—"

"Is it bad?"

"It's what we've talked about. It's coming to a head. And then there's Dina." There was a long pause on the other end of the line.

"Will I be able to see you at all, Frank?"

"I don't know, Faye. I want to see you—but I'm so damn tired and with all the complications here—"

She understood what he was telling her and it hurt. "You rest, Frank. We'll keep it loose and see how it goes. I'm not going to add to your problems—"

Strange how he felt about these two women. One he loved as much as it was within his capability to love anyone, but they couldn't seem to reach each other. With Faye, it was so easy. They could talk about anything. She seemed interested in most of what he was doing. She took pleasure in just pleasing him. This was his attraction to Faye Stein, and it had become a strong one.

"Faye. When you get back, let me get in touch with you. That will be the best way. I don't know what they're going to tell me here—or even what I'm going to do about the firm, but I'll be in touch."

Her voice sounded strained. "I'll be waiting, Frank."

Frank had slept most of the day. He would not take medication of any kind, and would only allow the nurses to record his temperature.

It was now four fifteen and Dina had come in. She looked at him with a teasing expression of reproach.

"Have you had a chance to rest? Are you doing what they tell you? If the reports I've been getting about you are accurate, you're not going to get their Favorite Patient Cup this year."

"I take the fifth, Madame Chairman."

He looked at her for a very long time as he held both her hands in his.

"How's our baby doing?"

She was surprised. "I guess fine. I really don't even feel pregnant. I'm as healthy as a horse."

As she held her husband's hands, both looking into the eyes of the other, there was a knock on the door. It was Hugh Rogers.

Hugh Rogers tried to strike the right tone between information and empathy. He told Frank in a quiet undramatic voice that the diagnosis was carcinoma of the right lung and their recommendation was a right pneumonectomy; the excision of the right lung.

When he had finished explaining to Frank what they had found, Frank waited several moments before replying.

"When do you want to operate?"

"As soon as it can be arranged. Dr. Bellows, who does most of our thoracic surgery, will operate."

Frank thought for a moment.

"Doctor, I understand what you've told me and I will go with your decision, but I'm afraid I have one or two things to clear up in my business before I let you fellows get a crack at me."

Dr. Rogers was confused. "I'm not sure I follow you, Mr. Sullivan."

"Let's just say, Doctor, that after I've cleared up things downtown, I'll be in a better position to go into this with a clearer mind."

Dr. Rogers looked at Dina. She shook her head in resignation.

"Surely you're not telling me, Mr. Sullivan, that you place any greater priority on your business than you do on your own health—especially after what I've just told you."

Frank looked at his doctor with a cool, almost patronizing glance. He remained silent.

The doctor turned to Dina. "I'm not quite sure I understand what's going on here, Mrs. Sullivan."

Dina started to reply but Frank interrupted her.

"Doctor. It's not such a tragedy. I assume I'm not going to die within the next few days. I'll be ready for your operation after I've done what has to be done at my firm."

Dr. Rogers was dismayed by his imperious patient. "Have you considered how weak you are, Mr. Sullivan? I have no idea what it is you wish to accomplish, or its importance, but I can assure you, that once you get out of this bed, you'll hardly want to go to your office."

Frank realized his attitude must seem capricious.

"I'm sorry, Doctor. I'm afraid I have no alternative—at least from my point of view." He smiled. "Doctor. I'll make a deal with you. I'd like to rest here for a few days with no medication. No sedation. Then I want to go downtown and do what I have to do. If I'm still alive," he smiled as he said it, the gray eyes flashing a cold humor, "then I'll come back here and let you fellows have me. Is that a deal?"

Dr. Rogers looked at Dina. He was plainly annoyed. Not only was Sullivan subverting his authority, which rankled him, but he seemed determined to pursue a course of action that would drain him of what little strength he had and would make a pneumonectomy—which was a physiologically traumatic surgical procedure—even more difficult. As he looked from Frank to Dina, Dr. Rogers thought seriously of dropping the case. It was Dina who spoke.

"Dr. Rogers, may I talk to you alone, please?"

He nodded and they moved into the hall.

"Doctor, I know my husband may appear to be stubborn to you," she smiled. "I must confess he is at times, but not this time." She looked at him with eyes that seemed filled with some inner pain. "My husband is not an ordinary man in almost any sense of the word. He is the kind of man who builds things. He built his firm.

I'm afraid I can't go into the details with you, but there is a serious problem at his firm, and he is the only one who can do anything about it—if anything can be done at all. I believe I understand what you must think of all this. No one wants him to stay in this hospital and have this operation more than I do, but I have come to understand something else, Doctor—only very recently, I might add. My attitude toward this was the same as yours until someone said to me, 'What's the use of saving his life through surgery, if the loss of his firm, which really has been his life, would kill him?' What I'm saying to you, Dr. Rogers, is in the strictest of confidence, of course. Frank would be terribly angry if he knew I was confiding this much in you."

Hugh Rogers studied Dina carefully. "Mrs. Sullivan, of course you know what your husband is asking me to do is not at all in his best interest medically. I might add, if I do what you and he are suggesting, I could—and very probably should—be criticized by this hospital. This is a teaching facility, Mrs. Sullivan, and I would hardly be acting as an example to either the staff or the medical students if I permitted Mr. Sullivan to walk out of here with carcinoma of the lung and have him come back after he has cleaned up his affairs at the office." Rogers shook his head. He watched Dina carefully. Her eyes were downcast, her face disappointed and resigned.

Hugh Rogers shook his head in a gesture of resignation.

"I could never refuse a beautiful lady, Mrs. Sullivan. If you'll promise to find me another hospital to go to when they throw me out of this one . . ."

She smiled. Her face was worn with fatigue.

"Thank you, Dr. Rogers. Both Frank and I are very grateful to you."

The afternoon had become evening. Dina had left. Frank was alone with his thoughts, his mind conceiving a plan.

He knew physically he was very weak. This was his biggest problem. It was one thing to talk bravely about going down to the office, it was another to do it. He needed an ally. Someone he could trust absolutely. But which one? Ray Costanza he knew was with him, but he preferred someone from the board of directing partners. Every son of a bitch on that board was there because of him, and now he was lying in bed with cancer, and the bastards were trying to steal his firm. After all these years of watching these young bastards develop, was he saying that he couldn't put his finger on *one* man he could count on to go down the line with him?

Screw them, he thought. This was not the way Frank Sullivan was going to make his exit. If he was going to be thrown out then they would literally have to do it over his dead body.

He was the Irish kid swinging the two-by-four. Frank smiled bitterly as he thought of that day so long ago.

But whom could he count on? There had to be one. One goddamn man out of the bunch of them, but who? His mind went down the list:

Glen Farrell, sales. Glen was a possibility. He was well regarded, and Frank had always felt close to him. He was aggressive. He'd be good to have on your side in a fight like this, but was he loyal? Would he stand with a sick man if it cost him his career should Frank lose? Frank couldn't answer that one. He tabled Glen Farrell for the moment.

Bill Davis, syndicate. Frank dismissed him quickly. Bill was a good man, but he didn't carry the weight with the others.

Roger Aiken, operations. Not Roger, for the same reasons as Bill.

Bob Isaacs, planning. Not Bob. Bob's job was too far removed from the daily crunch of market decisions. He was a good man, but not the one Frank needed or wanted to go into the pit with.

Dan Terrell, corporate finance. Dan was strong and aggressive, but he rubbed people the wrong way. A contentious ally was the last thing he needed right now.

Wilbur Royce, administration. Wilbur, Frank thought. Could he be a possibility? He was third after Frank and Dean in the hierarchy, and on an equal basis in partnership interest with Glen Farrell. Wilbur Royce. Frank's mind went back to the first time he had interviewed Wilbur, who joined the firm after having spent four years running the Philadelphia office of an old Main Line Stock Exchange firm that had become a victim of the attrition of Wall Street. What was there about Wil that made him hesitate? Frank probed the thought.

Wil was too much of an administrator, that was it. This was going to be a knock-down drag-out fight, and he needed someone who didn't mind a little blood on the floor. No. He wouldn't use Wil, he'd stick with Ray Costanza. Ray wasn't a partner, but he was the *only* senior officer of the firm Frank felt that he could absolutely trust.

He thought of Ray. No Ivy League schools; no button-down collars, but a first-rate mind; someone who got things done quickly, and quietly; and the guy had *moxie.* He was also a lawyer. It was the combination he wanted. To hell with the fact that he wasn't a partner. When Frank got through with all this he would *make* Ray a partner. There were only two conditions: he had to live, and he had to win.

That same evening Dean had remained at the office until 6:45 P.M. He was about to leave when his phone rang. His secretary had gone and he answered it himself. It was Angi Vittorio.

"Faulkner?"

"Who is this?"

"It's Angi Vittorio."

Dean was annoyed. He had made up his mind to call

on Frank tomorrow, and all his concentration was centered on that visit. The last thing he needed was the intrusion of Angi Vittorio.

"Angi. Nice to hear from you. I assume you're calling about my partner."

"You're goddamn right I'm calling about your partner."

"I told you, he's in the hospital."

"Tough shit."

"I'm seeing him tomorrow, Angi. I'll have a chance to talk with him then. I haven't seen him since you and I had lunch."

"I don't give a damn, Faulkner. It's been nearly two weeks since I spoke to you on that fuckin' stock, an' the son of a bitch is down anodder eight points. Now you listen to me good. I'm goin' to nail your firm's balls to a fuckin' mast. My friend Charlie Fox is almost outta business on accounta dis ting, an' you bastards ain't gettin' away with it."

"Look, Angi." Dean's voice was cold but alive with awareness of the threat of this punk hood. He was about to tell Angi of their plans to bring Nichols in from the Coast for a series of interviews, but thought better of it. Perhaps, Dean thought, it was time to play Frank's game. Dean's voice became menacing.

"Angi, I think I've had all the threats and intimidations I need from you. We're doing our best with a difficult situation and if that's not good enough for you, then I'm afraid you'll have to pursue whatever course of action you think best." He paused. "Just one more thing. I have a suspicion that your affairs may not stand up to examination quite as easily as our own. I told you when we had lunch together that my partners would never redeem your friend Fox's stock, which I clearly believe you share an interest in, so I'm afraid the only place we can look forward to seeing you is in court."

Angi's voice hissed back at him over the phone. "Listen

hard, prick. I'm gonna take your eyes out, ya hear me?
When I'm finished with you cocksuckers you'll be eatin'
stale bread. Nobody fucks Angi Vittorio—"

Dean hung up. He sat there for several minutes running the alternatives in his mind. Any deal with this
maniac was impossible. Frank would probably have an
idea. If he didn't, they would have to hire an investigator
to get the goods on the son of a bitch. Someone like Angi
Vittorio should be easy to intimidate. What worried Dean
was the trouble he could cause before they nailed him.

In the limousine going back to his apartment, Dean
stretched out his legs and let his mind roam freely over
the full spectrum of his problems and his opportunities.
Tomorrow was Thursday. If Frank would see him, he was
determined not to wait any longer. This last call from
Vittorio made speed even more important. It would be
devastating if this got to the press.

He decided to make it short. Frank didn't like long-
winded discussions, and once Dean confronted him with
a request for his resignation, he knew damn well the rest
of the meeting would be very short indeed. Frank would
have to be made aware quickly that Dean had the support
of the entire board. When he understood that, and especially in his physical condition, Dean felt Frank would
have no alternative. He would have to resign. Dean
probed for the holes. Frank was seriously ill. He was sixty
years old. He had committed, if nothing else, a brazen
breach of trust with his partners, and had subjected them
and the firm to potential publicity and loss of business
that might prove fatal. What better way to mend some of
his personal fences than for Frank to retire gracefully? If
Dean could hold the boys together, he had the final
weapon of a mass resignation by the board. He had Frank
by the short hairs. No matter how he turned it over in
his mind, Frank had to lose.

Tony was threading the big limousine through the

heavy traffic of Park Avenue. Dean knew that tomorrow would be one of the most important days of his life. He was wrong. He had miscalculated by two days.

Thursday was to show certain signs of spring in Boston. The day was unusually warm with a clear sky in which a light breeze aloft pushed an occasional cumulus cloud.

Fletcher Courtney, the eternal pragmatist, needed help in the matter of Computer's stock. Another two weeks of this kind of selling and the stock would be beyond recovery. A chance meeting with Karkov during the previous week found the Russian in an unusually good mood. When Courtney asked what could possibly cause such a change in spirit, Karkov took him over to his desk and showed him an integrated circuit chip smaller than the size of a fingernail.

"What's so new about that? Those damn things have been giving us all the trouble."

"You dumb bastard," Karkov growled. "This isn't what you've been looking at. This is a new wafer the boys in Santa Clara have been working on. This chip is made from an ion implanter—it's like a miniature version of a particle accelerator. It's a fast and accurate method of firing impurities into silicon. Magnets then bend the impurities in the right direction. Even you should know by now that these impregnated wafers can carry thousands of more bits of information on something as small as this." Karkov held the tiny silicon chip on the end of his finger. "This one contains our new circuitry. We've tested them in three Computer Ecologs in the Charles, and the goddamn things haven't missed a tick!"

Courtney was flabbergasted. "You mean to tell me the thing is actually working? The sensor monitors in the rivers—the computers—the whole system?"

Karkov's face was a huge grin. "It looks that way, Fletch. It sure as hell looks that way."

Fletcher was almost speechless. His mind was working like lightning.

"Look, Karky, don't interrupt me. We've got to hold a press conference."

"But I haven't had time to evaluate the system properly. It looks good, but we've had that before and fallen on our asses."

Fletcher's eyes pleaded with him. "Don't fight me now on this, Karky. This could be the thing to save the damn company."

Karkov was subdued. "What do you want me to do?"

"I'll take care of the details, you just show up and explain to the investment analysts, in as simple language as possible, what these new chips are doing for us. Be relaxed. Be confident and cheerful, and if we have any good news, for Christ's sake, don't qualify it by saying we haven't done sufficient testing—they'll know that. But any good news we can get to the analysts, *let's get it out*. The only thing I want from you is a promise you won't go off the deep end if somebody gives you the needle. Just shake it off; roll with it." Fletcher turned to Karkov, who for some time now had been following the Stock Exchange quotes. He knew where Computer was heading. "Karky, please—this is the last chance we've got. Make it good. This chip thing could turn it all around for us."

Fletcher went back to his office and got on the phone. He called each of the security analysts on his list. The ones who were out were told to get him at home tonight. Calls went out to Jesse Hudson, and Bennett Alden; to Sullivan & Co., and to Paul Nichols. He smiled as he guessed with what relief Nichols would receive this news.

A press conference would be held in the Sheraton Plaza at noon Friday. Fletcher knew it was very short notice. He also knew that he was going in on a wing and a prayer, but he didn't give a damn. What could they lose? Their asses were dragging now. The stock was quoted at five in a very thin market. Any buying or selling would move it quickly up or down. Fletcher was praying he could move it up.

On Friday promptly at noon, Fletcher Courtney introduced Dr. Martin Karkov to the small group of security analysts. It was not only what Karkov said but how he said it that seemed to help dissipate the atmosphere of cynicism that hung in the room like heavy smoke.

He told them what Computer Ecolog was trying to accomplish, to measure pollutant effluents in rivers, streams, in the soil, and in the air, by placing sensors in those environments and tying those sensors via long lines and microwave to a cheap but efficient computer that could be placed in a plant, an office, anywhere. The government alone was a potential market for hundreds of Computer Ecolog systems.

The new IC technology that was changing almost daily had come up with a silicon wafer that could be artificially impregnated with impurities which enabled it to store more bits of information on an incredibly small surface, and whose circuitry though quite complex could be contained on a chip the size of one's nail on the little finger. The chip manufacturers had at last given Karkov what he needed. He had never had a problem with the sensors or the means of sending the information back to his computer —it was the damn chips that had given him the most trouble.

Karkov spoke to them quietly but sincerely. He came across not as an eccentric scientist or greedy promoter, but as a pioneer working on a product line that not only could have broad commercial appeal, but one that would make a positive contribution toward the environment.

The small audience scattered in the oversize conference room had started out as cynics who at worst would get a free lunch. At the end of Karkov's presentation there were several obvious converts. They were all aware of Computer's accounting practices and had discounted them in their earnings projections for the company. They knew that Computer would probably be showing losses until it could get itself into volume production. They knew all this and yet there were a few among them who were intrigued by what Karkov was trying to do. They were willing to reexamine their attitudes toward the stock and possibly even recommend a little cautious buying.

A pale young man circulated quietly among the others seeking their opinions. No one knew that he had arrived in Boston from Dallas as the sole passenger of a Lear jet. He didn't mention what firm he was with. No one would have recognized it anyway. It made very little difference to the young man, whose name was Bryan Hastings.

When Karkov finished his talk at 1 P.M., Bryan Hastings didn't wait for lunch. He immediately called Jesse Hudson in Round Mountain, Texas. Jesse's response to that call was one of the reasons he was considered a desirable partner in a deal, and it also was one of the reasons Jesse was very rich.

He hung up from Bryan after grunting his acknowledgment and sat back to think. With Grant still laid up in the hospital Jesse was doing a lot more than a man of eighty should be, but he loved every minute of it.

The stock had dropped to 4⅞, the first time it had broken 5. If he tried to buy a hundred thousand shares he would obviously bid the price up, but he would still get the stock for one hell of a lot less than the $34 it had cost him originally. And this was registered stock. He was free to sell it without any restrictions.

Jesse smiled. He would be willing to go up to $750,000. That would be his limit. If the goddamn thing went up, he would declare his foreign partners in. It was a gesture that would go a long way with the Germans. It would be talked about in the clubs and offices in Dallas and Houston, in New York and Zurich, in London, and no doubt in Jidda and Riad. It was cheap publicity. Hell, if the son of a bitch bombed, he'd eat it and take it as a tax loss. Yes, sir, it was cheap at half the price. Old Jesse's rheumy ice-blue eyes held the light of inspiration. He slapped his skinny thigh and reached for the phone. The word would go out: *Buy Computer.*

Jesse sat back in the rocker to do some more "thinkin'." He placed his head with its wisps of uncombed white hair against the worn embroidered pillow that was tied to the back of the rocker and let his mind wander. The wide-bladed ceiling fans circulated the air in the large room, whose broad windows were protected from the scorching sun by a wide veranda. Old shade trees looked out upon a wide expanse of lawn that sloped gently down to the narrow river that ran through his land.

Jesse sat and rocked and thought. Dressed in a white shirt with a detachable collar, his sleeves rolled up, and the narrow suspenders holding up his shiny dark trousers, his feet in white cotton socks and old leather slippers, he looked as frail as corn silk. But Jesse Hudson was as sharp and tough as cactus.

Jesse's whole life was the *game.* He didn't play it to make more money. He was worth over a billion dollars and was as tight as a tick. What kept Jesse young was the game itself; money was just a way of keeping score.

What he was rockin' and thinkin' about was Sullivan & Co. He had heard that Frank was ill, probably with cancer.

Jesse had often thought of the benefits of owning a firm like Frank's. Hell, he was involved with deals all over the world, and was payin' fancy fees to investment bankers like Frank for raisin' money, findin' him companies to buy— shoot; why not own his own bankin' firm, then he could keep all the deals in the family.

Jesse knew that Frank owned the majority interest in Sullivan, and Frank was sick, wasn't he? Maybe damn sick. Might be just the tahm to give him a way out. Wouldn't hurt to ask. Jesse thought about that for a minute. He didn't like to approach people directly. The ice-blue rheumy eyes looked inward. Suddenly he cackled to himself, sat straight up in the chair and reached for the phone.

"Ah'll git that Yankee bastard to do it fo' me." He put down the phone, realizing he didn't have Bennett's number. He got up and poked around his desk for the worn blue diary where he kept the numbers of important people he wanted to call.

"Here's that son of a bitch," he said, and gleefully dialed the phone.

Bennett Alden was not looking out of his office window seeing the blue sky of this May afternoon, nor did he notice the clear light of the lengthening day that sparkled off the surface of Massachusetts Bay. His mind was on other things.

He was thinking about tonight; a night that he had anticipated with increased excitement ever since that good widow Martha Aldrich had called and told him that she would be away again for a few nights, which to Bennett meant only one thing: Angela.

This would be the third time Bennett had been with Angela. He had never been so completely captivated by a woman in his life.

Angela seemed to Bennett the living embodiment of his erotic imagination. She seemed to understand his need for "creative" sex, and she satisfied this hunger by introducing him to the kind of excitement that was so intense, so prolonged, that more than once Bennett heard himself actually screaming from sheer pleasure.

Bennett always paid for performance, and Angela was being paid handsomely, especially after her husband had moved out when the prospect of becoming a father proved too confining for his free spirit. For the first time in her life Angela felt secure financially. She was no fool. Angela knew the time would come when her breasts would stop feeding the insatiable Mr. Alden. She also knew that she could not satisfy his hunger for the erotic indefinitely; Bennett would one day ask Mrs. Aldrich to find him another girl. But she realized, under the tutelage of the ever practical Mrs. Aldrich, that Bennett also paid handsomely for silence and discretion. That was Angela's real annuity, and it was as good as money in the bank—Bennett's bank, to be exact.

The delicious thoughts of Angela's body and mouth were occupying Bennett when his intercom buzzed and his secretary announced that Jesse Hudson was on the line.

At the sound of Jesse's name, Bennett's reverie was cruelly interrupted.

"Bennett, Ah'm right sorry to disturb yew. How yew feelin'?"

Bennett's voice was coolly polite.

"Fine, Jesse. I assume you're well."

"Hell, Ah gotta be. Grant's comin' round, but he ain't back full tahm yet." To Jesse "full tahm" meant at least an eighteen-hour day. Grant was barely able to put in six or seven hours, seven days a week.

Grant had been lucky. The clot that had at first paralyzed the right side of his body had apparently dissolved, leaving him weak, with a slight twist to the right side of his mouth, and a limp in his right leg. But the ferocious drive of Grant Weir was helping the physiotherapists to speed his recovery, and he was making remarkable progress.

Bennett was not good at small talk, and he was in the habit of coming to the point.

"What can I do for you, Jesse?"

Jesse was slower; cagier.

"Suppose yew heard the news about Computer?"

"Yes, I did. I'm quite relieved. Frankly, I was concerned that I might have gotten you and your partners into something that looked as if it was going the wrong way." Bennett paused. "You might tell Grant that I believe this vindicates Paul Nichols."

Bennett simply had to get that one in.

"Ah reckon it does."

Both men knew that Grant would always think Nichols

a liar, who had his hand out, but for the moment it looked
as if Paul Nichols' luck was still holding.

"Say, Bennett. Ah'd like tuh ask a li'l favah of yew."

"I'll try to be helpful."

Bennett disliked nothing more than to have to do something for this crass Texan, but he knew that Jesse had
very influential partners and contacts worldwide, and a
commercial banker learns quickly to smile blandly, and
swallow hard no matter how much it hurts, when a Jesse
Hudson asks for a favor.

"Ah hear that Frank's in the hospital. Sick pretty bad—"

"Yes, that's right."

"They think it's cancer?"

"I don't know, Jesse. That's what I hear."

A long pause.

"Bennett. Me an' Grant have fo' some tahm now talked
'bout buyin' control of an outfit like Frank's. We think it
would fit right nicely into our setup."

Bennett thought quickly. Jesse was right. An investment
banking firm like Frank's would make a lot of sense.

"Yew know Frank a lot better 'n we do, an' Ah would
be right 'preciative if you would give him a call an' feel
him out." Pause. "Ah think the tahmin' would be good for
Frank; Ah surely dew."

Bennett hesitated a moment, could find nothing negative in what Jesse was asking and agreed to broach the subject with Frank.

Fate is like the shadow of a hawk, and that afternoon
when Bennett hung up from Jesse, he picked up the phone
to call Frank in the hospital.

It was Friday. He might have put off his call until
Monday, but he didn't. If he had, things would have been
different for Frank Sullivan.

When the call came in to Frank, he had been asleep.

Bennett apologized for disturbing him, but excused his
thoughtlessness by telling Frank he felt his conversation
with Jesse important enough to warrant calling him.

"I appreciate your getting right back to me, Bennett."

Frank hung up and lay staring at the ceiling, thinking about Bennett's call. As he lay there an idea began to take shape in his mind, and the more he thought about it, the more he felt it might work.

Ever since Frank had learned of Dean's plan to get him out of the firm, Frank's anger had become an almost consuming hatred. The firm had been his real life. It had been his child, that he had nurtured and protected for over thirty years, and Faulkner was trying to take it away from him. Not while Frank Sullivan was alive.

What he needed now was the strength to get through that meeting on Monday, and some help. Some very important help.

He reached for the phone and dialed Jesse Hudson.

That was just the moment when Faye Stein tried to call Frank; when she tried again she was told that he had temporarily requested no more calls.

When Fletcher Courtney called Paul Nichols it was 8 A.M. in Palo Alto.

The early sun had broken through a high thin overcast of cirrostratus clouds, and was beginning to cast the first long shadows of a new day.

Paul Nichols listened to Courtney, a slow smile spreading across his face. It was the best news he had heard in a long time.

"So K-Karkov s-seems to have v-vindicated my p-position." He wiped his face with a towel as he pulled the long extension cord from the bathroom to the bedroom. He sat down on the edge of the bed.

Courtney's voice seemed to carry a distinct touch of irony.

"Looks like you were right, Doc. A lot of people will feel better about that."

Nichols could almost see the smile of this cool Missourian three thousand miles away.

"I ah ap-preciate your calling, Mr. Courtney."

"No trouble, Doc." He paused. "I imagine your friend Eisenstadt will be surprised."

"N-n-no doubt he will. Thank you ag-gain."

Paul Nichols remained sitting on the edge of the bed, his eyes bright with pleasure. He had been right, by God. He was once again the fraternity pledge being led down from atop the high wall—only this time he wasn't crying, and his terror had fled.

It was Sunday. When Dina knocked softly on Frank's door and walked into the room she found him asleep. He looked even more haggard than he did yesterday. She knew nothing about the phone calls he had been making nor about his plans for going downtown on Monday for a three-o'clock meeting. She went over to the one comfortable chair in the room and sat down looking out the window, her mind not focused on anything in particular. She was waiting for Frank to awaken. These days, except for her baby, whom she felt growing within her every day now, her thoughts centered around Frank. She was fearful for him. She had no idea what he intended to do, but she knew her husband, and she knew he was going to fight for his firm if it killed him. She looked at him as he slept and a wave of melancholy came over her. Not just for Frank, but for herself and Whit as well. She felt that Frank's illness had created new circumstances in their lives that removed, at least temporarily, any chance for her to make decisions affecting her own life and that of her child. She was torn between a sense of obligation to Frank and an even stronger desire to create a life for her child that would be without the loneliness and pain that had been so much a part of her own life. Then there was Whit. She knew he was going through hell being separated from her. Her love for Whit was tormented and confused because of her genuine feelings for her husband, and the guilt she bore because of Elliot. Her life had become a maelstrom of conflicting currents that were tearing her apart. She began to weep silently, fighting unsuccessfully to keep back the tears. She wiped her eyes as Frank began to stir.

He focused in on her slowly, a smile spreading across his face as he saw her get out of the chair to come to him. Frank, who never missed anything, noticed that she had been crying, and he reached out to touch her face with a hand that looked surprisingly thin.

"Dina. Is something wrong?" His voice sounded even deeper and more strained than usual.

"No, Frank. Really." She bent down and kissed him.

He looked at her carefully and thought that perhaps her tears were for him, and in a way they were, but in reality they were for all of them caught up in this nightmare from which they couldn't seem to awaken.

He held her hand and then pulled her toward him very gently, kissing her cheek and her hair.

"Dina, sit by me. I want to talk to you. I'm going to need your help." One more day, he thought. God, where would he get the strength? His mouth turned grim.

She pulled the small straight-back metal chair to his bed and held his hand, waiting for him to speak. He looked wretched. Her eyes searched his face with compassion. She stroked his hand as she would a child's.

"I don't have the strength to argue with you, so please just do as I ask."

She nodded her head silently, her face mirroring fear and surprise.

"Take my pen." He motioned to the night table. "There's a note pad in the drawer. Better write this down." He was almost whispering now, trying to conserve his voice.

"I'm going to the office on Monday for a meeting at three."

He motioned away the objections she was about to make. "No. Let me finish. I'm going down there, Dene." He said it with such finality she knew there was no arguing with

him. Her heart broke for him. She squeezed his hand so
hard she hurt him.

"Oh, Frank." She rose from her chair and put her arms
around him and burst into tears. He stroked her hair softly
as she wept, her body wracking in uncontrollable sobs. She
was weeping for the tragedy that was all their lives.

She raised her head, her face wet with tears. She began
to smile, then to laugh softly. He looked at her curiously.

"It's just that you're the one that needs help, and you're
comforting me." She got up for her bag to comb her hair
and repair the damage to her makeup. A few deft touches
and she turned to him with a determined but trembling
smile. "There we are. No more of that. Now what do you
want me to do?"

"Call Rose and tell her to remind Ray Costanza I want
him to stand by ready to come into that meeting if I need
him. Get a private Cabulance to take me downtown and
arrange for a doctor if you can." She looked at him. He
knew what was in her mind. "No. Not Whit."

"But he may be the only doctor I can get."

"Then I'll do without one." He paused. "Better have a
wheelchair to get me up to the floor. I'll walk from the elevator to the conference room. I'll need you to help me
dress, Dene. Bring a blue shirt and pick out a suit and a
tie for me. Make it a gray suit. And buy me some of that
Sudden Tan. I don't want to look like a complete corpse."
He thought for a moment. "I guess that does it."

She had been writing his instructions quietly. She knew
she couldn't get another doctor to accompany him downtown on such short notice, and she was determined that
there be one standing by. If he was going to kill himself
she would at least do everything in her power to prevent
it. She made up her mind that her first call would be to
Whit.

She stood up and looked at him, resigned to help him
accomplish what she knew he had to do. A thought flicked
through her—perhaps if Frank did what he intended he

might solve some of her problems—but she pushed it out of her mind as sick and depraved.

"One more thing. Talk to them here and have them give me whatever they can so I can talk. If they have any pep pills or something to keep me going until I can get back here, I'd better have them."

She could see that he was exhausted and she had a lot to do before she came back here. She brushed back her hair and forced a smile.

"Well, Frank. I guess we go into battle together. That's a first, anyway." She bent over and kissed him. "I'll arrange everything to be ready for Monday by about two fifteen. If we leave here by two thirty or even two forty we should be downtown in plenty of time." She looked at him tenderly. "Don't worry, Frank, I won't let you down. Now, I'd better get started." She blew him a kiss. He waved after her with a feeble motion of his hand and closed his eyes. He was asleep almost instantly.

She called Whit at his hospital from a phone in the lobby. He wasn't available. She left a message that she would call back at one. She took Frank's list out of her pocket to decide how she should begin. When she put in a coin to dial Rose she found her hand was shaking so that she dropped the dime on the floor.

Rose Finley's voice was welcome support. The two women quickly decided on how to cooperate.

It was ironic that in forty years in business, dealing almost exclusively with men, in the most critical hours of his life, Frank Sullivan had to rely on two women. These women were helping him because they loved him, each in her own way, and were only too aware that by carrying out his wishes they might be killing him.

Unknown to Frank, Dina had been able to get in touch with Whit. She pleaded with him to drop what he was doing Monday afternoon and help her. Nothing would satisfy her until he agreed to come down in a *second*

Cabulance and stand by if he were needed. She could hear his frustration and annoyance over the phone.

"Do you realize I have a full schedule of patients of my own to see? I just can't reschedule my day at the last minute to sit around waiting for Frank because he's too damned hardnosed to listen to anyone. If he's determined to kill himself I can't stop him."

"Please, Whit. Please do this for me. I know what a terrible imposition this is for you, but I'm begging you—please help me."

He could hear the desperation in her voice and all the pain of his longing for her flooded back to him. He had spent two of the most miserable weeks of his life without her since Frank had gone into the hospital. Except for their calls to each other in the evening or early in the morning they had nothing. Dina at least had Frank, as crazy as that sounded. He had no one. He was alone. He was miserable, and there wasn't a damn thing he could do about it. He loved her. He had from the first day he met her, and he did now. He always would. He knew that *never* was a long time, but he felt that there would never be another woman in his life but Dina.

"All right, Dina. I don't know how I'll manage it, but I'll try and cancel tomorrow afternoon."

"Oh, bless you, Whit. Bless you, darling. God willing, if everything goes right we may not need you. But if we do I want you there."

She heard his long exasperated sigh.

"I must be crazy."

"We're all crazy, darling. Bless you." She hung up.

Rose Finley had made sure that most of them were in the senior partners' conference room not later than two forty-five. Dean was the exception. It was nearly three and he had not yet arrived.

Dean was still toying with the idea of not coming at all. He cursed himself for not going to Frank sooner, but he had considered carefully and felt it would not look right if he pushed too quickly. When he was ready to see him, Frank couldn't have any visitors—or so they said—and now this lunatic who was supposed to be half dead was getting out of a hospital bed to hold this crazy goddamned meeting? He was beside himself with frustration and rage. But if he didn't attend then what? What could he accomplish by staying away? Nothing. He had a lot more to lose than gain. He didn't realize it, but Frank had preceded him by just five minutes. He was being wheeled into an elevator by a paramedic. Dina was with him.

The atmosphere in the conference room was one of troubled silence broken only by occasional attempts at conversation to relieve a feeling of general embarrassment. The doors opened and Frank walked in. They greeted him warmly, but Frank's expression was glacial. He seated himself at the end of the table facing the double walnut doors. There were the muffled sounds of chairs being pulled up to the table. All conversation had stopped. They sat looking at Frank, and he at them. They were all there except Dean. Glen Farrell, Bill Davis, Roger Aiken, Bob Isaacs, Wil Royce, and Dan Terrell. Frank surveyed the faces of each of them carefully. They were all young enough to be his sons.

Glen Farrell observed Frank. He looked much thinner in street clothes. The pallor that Glen expected wasn't there. He didn't realize that Frank had particularly attended to this with a careful application by Dina of Sudden Tan before he left the hospital. But it was the gaunt angular planes of Frank's face that told the story. When he began to speak his voice shocked each one of them.

The doors opened and Dean Faulkner came in to take his place beside Frank. His face was tightly drawn into lines of compressed anger.

Frank's voice was little more than a harsh whisper.

"I'm not going to do a great deal of talking because I

can't. But I am going to get some things cleared up around here." He looked at each of them but carefully ignored Dean, who was sitting directly on his right.

"You held a meeting here nearly two weeks ago which I was not privileged to attend. I was in the hospital, as you know." His lips tightened and his eyes seemed focused on some invisible spot in front of him. His two hands were folded on the table occasionally clasping and unclasping as he spoke.

"I believe the meeting was called by Dean to discuss a personal transaction of mine which came to be construed as my selling shares outside the firm." He put his hand to his mouth and began to cough. Glen Farrell started to light a cigarette, but Frank signaled him not to. There were quick glances around the room.

"I believe you came to the general conclusion that I had done this on the basis of inside information that I didn't share with my partners. Is that correct?" The gray eyes swept each of their faces. There was a general nodding of heads.

Dean pushed back his chair and looked at Frank, who still did not turn in his direction.

"I called the meeting, as you know, Frank, and that is the general conclusion we came to." The tension within Dean seemed to strike those in the room with an almost physical force. He stood up and began to walk slowly as he spoke.

"Frank. It's incontrovertible that you did sell your stock through Fox and Bohlen, and that you did visit Dr. Nichols with Dr. Eisenstadt. None of us knew of your visit, and none of us knew of the sales of your securities; especially away from this firm."

Dean turned quickly to face him. "What the hell were we supposed to think? You're the only one in this room who's made any real money in the stock—"

Frank held up his hand. He still was not looking at Dean. "Not quite."

Dean stopped. "I'm afraid I don't get that, Frank."

"I said, 'Not quite.' "

"I don't understand."

"I'll be glad to enlighten you." Frank raised his head to look at Dean. They all followed his eyes that were now the eyes of a wolf. "You've done pretty well *trading* Computer, Dean. And, I might add, *away* from this firm." Frank paused. It was becoming increasingly difficult for him to speak.

"What are you talking about?"

"I'm talking about trades in the stock that you've been making in a dummy account that you have not reported to the SEC or to the directors of Computer." Frank smiled sarcastically. "Last time I looked you were still a director. That right, Dean?"

Dean's eyes flashed in rage. "That's a damn lie! Where the hell did you ever get a story like that? I demand to know!"

"Take it easy, Dean." It was Wil Royce. "Let's keep this thing civilized. Frank's under great physical strain."

"I'm aware of that—and I'm sorry. But I'll be damned if I'll stand here and listen to accusations like that from anyone."

"It's not an accusation. It's a statement of fact. If you force me to embarrass you further by bringing in proof, I'll do so."

Dean stopped as the gray eyes looked at him unwaveringly.

Frank turned to the rest of them who were now looking between Dean and Frank with their mouths open, absolutely amazed.

"I didn't get out of bed to come down here to talk about Dean. You fellows have in effect accused me of using inside information, and I want to tell you factually, with absolute conviction, that when I sold that stock I knew no more about Computer than any of you—"

Dean interrupted. "That's sanctimonious nonsense, Frank. You went to the Coast with an acknowledged expert in IC technology and you talked privately with one of the consultants who advised Tittle and Alden. If that's not access to inside information I don't know what is. And then you released Friedman's report. Why, Frank? Don't you think these circumstances were a little unusual, to put it mildly?"

Frank could sense that Dean was defusing the revelations concerning his own trading in the stock.

Frank was beginning to feel the pressures of the ordeal. He felt pains in his chest and throat and he was rapidly running through what little reserve of strength he had. He began to feel flushed and beads of perspiration were beginning to glisten on his forehead. He felt dizzy and he had to fight to preserve his ability to concentrate. Glen Farrell was watching him closely.

"My purpose for going to the Coast was to find out whether or not there *was* any information I could get on Computer that might help us, but there wasn't. I learned no more than we were told at Bennett's house in New England."

"Then why did you sell, Frank, and away from the firm?" Dean's high-pitched voice hissed in anger.

"For personal reasons which I don't intend to discuss here."

"Isn't that a little cavalier? You've got the brass to accuse me of *illegally trading* the stock, but your sale, which if not illegal is certainly a breach of Stock Exchange regulations, is sure as hell a breach of trust as far as your partners are concerned."

Frank was losing ground. He didn't have the strength for this kind of fight. If he could only hang on until—

Dean saw his weakness and bore in. "Well, come on, Frank—why did you sell?"

They all saw Frank fighting for control. He held up a thin hand, and Dean out of reflex backed off. He shouldn't have.

Frank's voice was hoarse and very strained.

"You all must have heard the news by now of Karkov's press conference."

There was a general murmur of agreement.

"Why would I sell my stock if I had any knowledge that Karkov had finally licked his technical problems? That's simply absurd."

He had scored and Dean knew it. Dean started to speak, but Frank again stopped him. Just the memory of his authority, and their sympathy for his physical appearance, made them all defer to him.

Frank pushed back his chair. He smiled weakly at them. "Gentlemen. So much for your inside information."

Some of them had begun to stand to release their tensions.

He began to cough and motioned for them to sit down.

There was a knock on the door and Ray Costanza entered. There were no empty chairs, so Ray stood impassively in front of the double walnut doors.

Frank was trying hard to control himself. He felt so weak that he was afraid he would pass out. His face was now wet with perspiration. He turned to Dean, his eyes merciless. His voice was barely audible. "Ray has proof of your illegal trading in Computer, Dean, and if you force me I'll have him produce it."

"What kind of proof?"

"Taped conversations in code between you and your attorney. We've taken the trouble to break your little code."

Dean was supremely indignant. "Do you mean that you have the gall to sit there and tell me that you've tapped my phone? One of your own partners?" He looked around at the other men in the room, then back to Frank. "How many of their phones are tapped, Frank? Or is that something you'd rather not discuss?"

Glen Farrell turned to Frank. "That's something I'd like answered, Frank. Are there any other phones being tapped in this place? Because if there are, you can have my resignation as of now."

There was a general murmur of approval. Frank motioned feebly. "No." His voice was so weak that he wasn't really speaking now, just making sounds and gestures so that he could be understood. His body was beginning to sway slightly.

Dean sensed that this had become a battle for survival, and in a very real sense, if he were going to win he would have to destroy Frank; physically.

Frank understood this as well. He was using every ounce of that iron will to hang on. He had to hang on if his plan had any chance of succeeding.

"Holy Mary, mother of God, have mercy upon me."

He was praying silently; his early Catholicism flooding back behind his eyes; eyes that were burning with salt from the sweat pouring down his face. He was unable to see clearly those around him; those faces which were now a blur, from whom voices seemed to come as if in a dream.

"That's the damnedest piece of nerve I've ever heard of in my life." Dean got up and began walking rapidly back and forth, his face flushed with rage; his dark eyes were malevolent.

"Do you realize what that maniac is doing? We've caught him selling out his own firm, and now he's accusing me of illegal trading." Dean whirled facing them. "Do you know what will happen to this firm if that human wreck continues to run it; or if I take my capital and my accounts—yes, I said *my* accounts—out of this place. You'll be able to set up a bowling alley here—that's about all the damn thing will be good for."

Glen could sense the fear that swept through the rest of them. Every one of them knew the importance of Dean's contributions to the firm. His capital position was second only to Frank's, and with Frank out of the picture it was very possible Dean *could* take significant business with him.

These were young men. They were bright, tough, and opportunistic, but their loyalties could not be strained much beyond their self-interest. They were being pushed to the breaking point. They wouldn't stand idly by and watch their capital disappear in a firm heading for the rocks.

Glen held up his hand.

"Now hold it, Dean."

"I will like hell." Dean pointed to Frank. "Look at him. Why, the man's barely rational. He's going to fall over. Look at him, for Christ's sake!"

"I said hold it, God damn it." Glen was standing. He looked at Frank, wondering if he should break this up and get Frank out of here or end the meeting.

Dean had recruited Glen to support him in just this kind of bloodletting, but the sight of Frank, the viciousness of Dean's attack, the old loyalty Glen felt for his senior partner, and not in the least the knowledge that these two could irreparably shatter the firm beyond any salvation and ruin them all—these considerations were forcing Glen to become an impartial referee.

Glen knew what Frank had gone through to get here, and though the sight of him tore at his heart he knew that Frank wanted to finish this fight or die, or maybe both.

"Dean, I don't want to hear another outburst from you or anyone else in this room."

"You don't. Well, just who the hell do you think you are, Farrell?"

As Dean looked at Farrell with an expression of rage and betrayal there was a knock on the door. Rose Finley opened it and introduced the two men in the doorway.

Rose looked at Frank and her heart nearly stopped beating; her voice was barely audible.

"Mr. Sullivan. Mr. Jesse Hudson and Mr. Grant Weir." She silently closed the door behind them.

They were all stunned; poleaxed. They could have been struck by lightning and not have been more surprised. Dean stood there with his mouth wide open. Jesse and Grant surveyed the room. They sensed what this was all about immediately; one look at Frank was enough.

Jesse stood there bent and feeble, an old worn blue coat hanging away from his shoulders; it looked at least two sizes too large for him. He held a battered gray Stetson with a stained sweatband, his wisps of silky uncombed white hair defying direction. But it was those rheumy ice-blue eyes of Jesse's that galvanized everyone in the room. They all knew who he was, and the power he represented. What they couldn't understand was what he was doing here.

Grant stood leaning on a cane, the right side of his face slightly twisted, his body at least thirty pounds lighter. But there was no mistaking the savage threat in those dark-brown eyes.

The room was electrified.

At the sight of Jesse and Grant, Frank slumped in his chair with an audible sigh of relief. Thank God, he said silently to himself.

Grant helped Jesse remove his coat.

There was the sound of chairs being pushed back as they made room for the two Texans.

"Here, sir, take my chair." It was Wil Royce.

Dan Terrell, who was sitting beside Wil, stood up. He didn't know Grant, but he knew he was with Jesse; that was enough.

Ray Costanza was still standing near the walnut doors.

As Frank's eyes moved toward Ray, he was silently grateful not to have had to depend upon the tapes to fight Dean.

He realized now that it wouldn't have worked. Dean could have claimed the tapes were faked and he simply didn't have the strength to refute that. No, this had been his only real play. He had needed to hang on until they arrived. It had taken every shred of his will, but he had done it.

"Ah'm right sorry, Frank, that we're so late, but our plane was held up for forty minutes over La Guardia."

Jesse settled himself in his chair, his shirt far too large
for his scrawny neck, and his dark-blue tie, wrinkled and
spotted, hung askew, its knot at least two inches from his
collar.

"Might I ask what these gentlemen are here for?" It
was Dean; his face was pale, his black eyes darting and
anxious.

Jesse looked at Frank, paying no attention to Dean.

When Frank had called Jesse from the hospital after
talking to Bennett he had made a deal with Jesse over the
phone. He had told Jesse that he would sell him his majority interest in the firm under three conditions: a fair
price to be agreed upon; his retaining his role as chairman
if he was physically up to it, and the attendance at this
meeting of Jesse or Grant or both, with the purpose of
utterly destroying Dean.

This was the kind of game that excited Jesse. He could
get what he wanted, and it gave him a chance to use his
power. This was a game these wolves knew how to play.
They knew how to stalk, how to wait, and how to move
in for the kill when they sensed vulnerability.

"Yew lookin' a mite peak-ed, Frank. Yew sure you're
all right?" It was Jesse.

Frank nodded, smiling for the first time since this horror began.

"Ah think we both looked better the last tahm Ah saw
yew, Frank," said Grant.

Frank's voice was now nothing but a strained whisper.
"Glad to have you both here," he said.

Jesse looked around, realizing that Frank was in no condition to conduct the rest of this meeting. Jesse was twenty
years older than Frank, but he was still the lead wolf.
His eyes glowed at the thought of another battle, another
kill.

"Mah name is Jesse Hudson," he said needlessly. "Ah'm

goin' tuh ask all of yew to remain 'cause you're all partners, and yew should hear this."

Jesse looked around the room, his lips smiling, his
stained crooked teeth making him look like the village
clown—that is, of course, if you didn't know about Jesse,
and if you weren't watching his eyes.

"Frank an' me have struck a deal regardin' this firm of
your'n. Ah suppose yew'd all like to hear it?"

There were murmurs of bewilderment; quick glances
of dumbfounded confusion and disbelief.

"Well, now, boys, evahbody jus' ree-lax. It's all vury
simple. Ah've had a mind to have a piece of ah firm like
yo's fo' years. It's a natural fo' both of us."

He looked around the room at the stunned faces.

"Boys. It's the best thing that could happen to all of us.
Our investments 'round the world and the companies we
own or control, give us assets of over two billion dollars."

Jesse started to sneeze. "Sorry, boys. Now, we got a
hell of a lot of cash and yew fellers don't. Also, we're
doin' deals all over the map an' payin' fellers like yew
fancy fees for helpin' us raise money, buyin' companies—
hell, yew know the game. Ah don' have to tell yew fellers
nothin'."

Jesse started to laugh; it was more of a cackle.

"Shoot, boys, we kin put capital into this firm an' feed
you enough captive business to double what yo' doin',
an', boys, we kin keep it all in the family."

It was too much of an initial shock for them to react as
affirmatively as Jesse's logic would warrant, especially considering the current state of the market, and of Sullivan
& Co.

Jesse was too experienced not to understand that they
needed time, but still he sensed a latent hesitant reaction,
an initial lack of approval.

"Natur'lly Frank will remain as chairman, if he's up to
it, an' we want each of yew to stay on, if you're a mind to.

Boys, there's a lot more money in this for all of yew with the strength we can bring to yuh."

Jesse looked around. "Ah'd like tuh talk tuh yew fellers fo' a while in another room." He turned to Grant. "Why don' yew have a li'l talk with Dean here an' Frank, while me an' the boys git acquainted."

Jesse was a smart old fox. He knew that a firm like Frank's depended upon two things: its partners and its clients. He wasn't about to buy Frank's interest and be left with a firm whose principals were unhappy; unproductive.

Jesse rose, hunched over. He waved a skinny hand to the group. "Come on, boys. Show me where we can sit an' chew fo' a while."

They looked at each other with quick, furtive, perplexed glances, but they followed Jesse out of the room.

Grant turned to Frank. "Yew got any bourbon aroun' here, Frank?"

Frank forced a smile and picked up the phone. He dialed the kitchen extension and asked Goulet to bring up some bourbon.

Grant turned to Dean, his eyes hard and direct. He seemed to be looking right through him.

"Yew gonna join me in a drink?"

Dean shook his head. "It's a little early for me."

"Dean, Ah'm afraid Jesse an' Ah can't quite see yew as part of this new setup."

Dean's stomach turned into a hard knot, but he didn't let it show. He was still tough and dangerous. Grant knew this; he wasn't Jesse's hatchet man for nothing.

Dean's voice was strained but his manner was defiant. "Do you think you can come up here and walk into this firm and not consider me? My partners have voted unanimously to resign if I don't head this firm. You'll be buying a vacuum without me, Grant."

Grant started to reply when there was a knock on the door, and Goulet came in with a tray bearing a crystal decanter of bourbon, a small pitcher of spring water, and an ice bucket; there was only one glass.

Grant got up and took off his coat and opened his tie. He poured a straight four fingers of bourbon, which he wasn't supposed to drink at all, and took a very long pull.

His eyes moved back to Dean. They were menacing. He wiped his lips with his fingers.

"Now we didn't fly fifteen hundred miles up here to talk a lot of bullshit."

Dean started to speak but Grant cut him off.

"Ah mean to make this quick, cause yo' partner don' look like he kin take much more of this."

Grant glanced apprehensively at Frank, whose face was now covered with glistening rivulets of perspiration. He was holding on to the edge of the table to keep from collapsing.

"I don't give a damn what you've come up here for, Grant, and if you think you can abuse me with that Texas tornado stuff you can forget it. Frank has sucked you into this deal. You don't know our business. Without those men who just walked out of this room, this firm is simply *office furniture;* and I've got those men."

The sound was like the crack of a rifle: Grant had brought his cane down sharply on the table. Dean almost jumped out of his chair, but his face, although startled, was still not intimidated.

"Now let *me* tell yew somethin' about *yo'* business, yew little fucker, 'cause when Ah get threw with yew today, there ain't goin' to be enough left of yew to shit on.

"First of all, who the hell do yew think yo' talkin' tew, one of yo' fancy partners, who maybe if he's lucky, has got half a million dollars in his capital account?

"Shit, man, Jesse can take this whole goddamn firm, includin' yew an' Frank, an' buy it like we do paper towels. We could buy ten firms like this an' furgit about them—but what's a hell of a lot more important, Dean, is *what we kin do to yew—*"

Dean was still the ferret, but Dean knew the game. Jesse and Grant hadn't come up here unprepared; they didn't operate that way.

"Now, Dean, boy, Ah'm tellin' yew that Jesse an' Ah are goin' to cut yo' fuckin' balls off—"

Dean stood up, his face white, his eyes blazing with fury.

"I don't have to listen to this kind of crap, Grant. You're not talking to Paul Nichols now, you're talking to me—"

The cane cracked the table again like summer lightning. Grant was on his feet, his face furious, contorted with rage.

"Sit still, yew li'l cocksucker, an' listen to me.

"We know *who yew are,* who *yo' contacts an' clients are,* and we're gonna cut yo' nuts off, boy; an' when they fall yew ain't even gonna hear them drop—"

"You can't threaten me, you hillbilly hoodlum—"

They stood facing each other on opposite sides of the table. Their hatred was a physical force.

Frank, almost forgotten by them, was still seated, his eyes closed, his face terribly pale. His body began to sway slightly.

"Ah'm not threatenin' yew, Faulkner, Ah'm tellin' yew! If you had the brains God gave geese, you'd a' known how to play this game, but maybe yew don' quite know how *we* play—cause when yew leave this room, Dean boy, *financially you're a dead man.* It may take us a little tahm, but we'll fuck up every client, every bankin' connection, every contact yew got. Yew'll be livin' off your capital, 'cause you're through in this business—"

Dean's voice was a high-pitched scream of fury. "Are you mad? Do you think you're in some Texas barroom, you son of a bitch? I'll sue you if it takes me twenty years to get you! I don't care what it costs! You goddamn hoodlum cowboys think you're a law unto yourselves. Well, this is New York, not Texas. We know how to handle shits like you."

Grant had been assigned the role of Dean's remover by Jesse as a result of his deal with Frank. He had come up here prepared to take Dean out, and he usually enjoyed such an encounter. But Dean had punched a psychic button with Grant. Nothing enraged Grant more than this denigrating attitude which thrust at the self-consciousness of his country-boy origins. Grant took the rest of the bourbon and threw it in Dean's eyes.

Dean was momentarily blinded by the alcohol. He screamed in rage, throwing aside chairs, reaching for Grant in uncontrolled fury. Grant raised the cane, which contained a hidden steel shaft that made it a deadly whipping stick.

"Come on, yew little fucker, come on, Ah'm just dyin' to crack yo' fuckin' skull."

Dean stopped dead facing the cane in Grant's hand; something in his mind warning him of the lethalness of the slim weapon. The savageness of Grant's rage told him that this was not some incredible development in a grade B movie; this was real. Grant would use that weapon; in fact he seemed to *want* to use it. Dean stood looking at Grant, his whole body quivering in desire to destroy this malevolent Texan, but a spark of caution kept him from completely losing control.

Dean knew the real threat to him was not the wicked-looking cane in Grant's hand, but what Grant had threatened to do to him financially.

Dean knew that these were not just threats. He knew that Jesse and Grant could make things difficult for him, but most of all Dean knew that it wasn't Grant who was really cutting away his legs; it was Jesse Hudson talking to his partners.

Dean knew how his partners felt about him; it was not a feeling that filled him with great confidence. Dean also realized that the proposition Jesse had offered them made sense.

He knew that his partners would not be long in coming to the same conclusion. Dean was enough of a product of the Street to know that self-interest was the primary motivating force for these men; it was for him; and without his partners, he had no cards to play. But Dean would learn more. In the months to come he would learn the savage whip of Jesse and Grant when they were crossed.

They stood facing each other, these two predators, Dean knowing the game was over, when they heard what sounded like the thud of a heavy melon being dropped a considerable height onto the table. It was Frank's head. He had collapsed.

Grant dropped the cane and moved quickly, pushing the chairs aside as he thrust himself toward Frank.

"Go git some he'p, fuh Christ's sake." Grant started to loosen Frank's tie and push his head back to give his lungs more air.

"Fuck him! Let him die!" It was a shot from a gun.

Grant looked at Dean incredulously.

"Why, yew li'l motherfucker, this man is yo' own partner!"

Grant saw the wild irrational hostility in Dean's eyes as his thin taut body vibrated with uncontrollable rage.

Grant knew that if Frank didn't get help in minutes he would probably die. He didn't want to leave Frank to the malevolence of Dean, but he had no choice. As he looked at the blind hatred in the wild dark eyes Grant hesitated. "Shit," he said, and rushed limping out of the room to look for help.

Dean's breathing came in great labored gulps for air. He looked at Frank, who had slumped again onto the table, only the back of the gray head visible; almost as if he were asleep, resting his head on his forearms. Dean saw the narrow line of white skin at the collar that Frank had not quite concealed with Sudden Tan.

The furies that raged within Dean wanted to strangle
Frank; to cut off that last vital link of air and kill the Irish
bastard who, nearly dead, had beaten him. The small
spark of rationality that was left to Dean kept him on the
knife edge of sanity.

He stood close to Frank; hovering over him, his mouth
almost touching Frank's ear. He began to scream at him
in a strange high-pitched voice that was filled with the
agonies of his own frustrations.

"You Irish prick. You sold out to those bastards just to
get me!" He was almost weeping; screaming in broken
half-choked sobs.

"You sold the firm to those two whores who would suck
their own mothers' blood if there was a dime in it. You
goddamn half-dead bastard! You couldn't let me have it,
could you? Do you know what I could have done with this
firm?" Dean was foaming his rage at the back of the gray
head that heard every word.

"I've got more brains than the whole goddamn firm
put together. You know that. Those whores don't know
this business. They'll screw all of you. They'll milk this
firm and grind every ball in the place. But you don't give
a damn about any of that, you bastard. You only wanted
to get me!" Dean didn't see the doors opening. His rage
made him oblivious.

Dina rushed in, followed by the rest of them. She saw
Dean bending over Frank, screaming at him. She could
smell the hatred in the room. Her mind suddenly uncovered some dark primitive protective area that made her
a tigress. Her only thought now was to protect her husband. She moved awkwardly, but quickly. Forgotten was
the weight and treasure of the child she carried. She rushed
at Dean, clawing at his face with her nails, leaving long
deep scarlet slashes in his pale white skin.

"You bitch," he screamed and whirled around to smash
her face.

Wil Royce grabbed him.

"For Christ's sake, Dean," Wil shouted, "get hold of yourself."

Wil was tall and powerful and he wrestled Dean to a position against the wall near the doors, pinning his arms to his side as Dean gasped from the strength of Wil's grip and from the crescendo of his own emotions. Thin rivulets of blood welled into the wounds on his cheek.

Dina raised Frank's head. "Somebody go down and get Dr. Fraser. He's waiting in a Cabulance in front of the building on the Broadway side."

"I'll go." It was Glen. He ran from the room toward the elevators.

Dina's face was white, but she acted quickly and surely. She forced Frank's body back in the chair and further loosened his tie and collar. She felt for the pulse in his neck. It was weak and erratic, but there was a pulse.

Dina turned to Roger Aiken, who was standing nearest her.

"Get me my bag, Roger. There's some smelling salts in it."

He hurried from the room to Frank's office.

It seemed an eternity before Whit came. He had a wheeled stretcher with him and a paramedic.

Whit immediately directed the medic to apply the portable oxygen unit and with the help of several of the men standing about they placed Frank on the stretcher and adjusted the flow of oxygen.

"Someone get an elevator and clear everyone out. Hold it until we get there."

"I'll do it." Bob Isaacs.

Frank felt the oxygen flowing into his lungs. The room had reduced itself to a montage of colors and voices. He had the strange feeling that he was falling through an infinite black void. Yet there were rose-colored hues and violet. Soft corals and pinks. He thought of Dina and of Elliot and his mind groaned with his guilt. He felt a soft hand on his forehead. He prayed that it was Dina's, but he couldn't see. He kept falling down, down, down. A part of his mind still held the shrieks of Dean. Now the colors were changing from corals and pinks to purples and dark blues. His thoughts were of death, and his mind sought the comfort of his long-forgotten Catholicism. He wanted a priest, but he couldn't tell them. He couldn't move, his body was so weighted with fatigue.

They were pushing him somewhere now. He felt them wheeling him onto something; turning him around. He heard a dull metallic thud and felt himself going down. There were voices all around him.

He heard the sounds of the sirens and felt something being pushed against his neck, then his chest. He felt a soft hand brush his forehead, and he felt something wet drop lightly on his face.

Glen Farrell watched the Cabulance turn down Wall headed for Water Street and the East River Drive. His eyes followed Frank, Dina and Dr. Fraser in the Cabulance as it fought the city traffic. But he had his own interests to protect. He walked back into the building, anxious to get back and find out where they all stood with Jesse Hudson and Grant Weir.

When Glen returned to the conference room he could tell by their faces, by the depression and tension in the air, that the whole atmosphere was explosive. It was like a room filled with methane gas in which one spark would blow up everything.

It was Jesse who turned it all around.

"Now, boys, Ah know evahbody is right sorry to see ole Frank carried out like that. Ah suggest we all sit down an' cool off, an' maybe a li'l prayer might be in order fo' Frank. Why don' we jus' have a minute of silent prayer."

The sophisticates from New York looked at these cowboys in embarrassed disbelief, but they took their seats, and for a moment, with heads bowed, they prayed for the life of Frank Sullivan.

Wil had relaxed his hold on Dean who was still in front of him near the door, his eyes glazed, his chest heaving in great gasps; his lungs starving for the oxygen needed to feed the energies his mind and body had so violently expended.

Jesse prayed too. So did Grant, only Jesse's spiritual philosophy was particularly his own: he felt the Lord always helped those who helped themselves; that's why as he prayed with bowed head, his eyes quickly searched the faces of Frank's partners to get a better handle on their collective mood.

When those ice-blue eyes got around to Dean's, he saw the ferret looking at him with dark implacable hatred.

Jesse raised his head. His tone was serious but business-like.

"Now, boys, Ah know yew've all had quite a shock, but Ah'm almost twice as old as any of yew here. Ah've seen a lot of storm clouds in mah day, but Ah've also seen the sun come out too." Jesse turned to Grant.

"Yew've had a chance tuh talk a li'l wif our fren' Dean hyear. What's he had to say?"

It was ludicrous, but it worked. Jesse's total disregard of the theatrics that had just taken place seemed to bring them all some perspective.

Grant glowered at Dean. "He says that his partners have all agreed to resign if he's not voted to run the firm."

Jesse looked at Dean carefully, and then just as carefully at the rest of his partners, whose eyes and faces were trying desperately to avoid Dean.

Dean's mind was returning to the point of rationality where at least he could understand what was going on. He felt as if he were suspended in a void; weightless and without the ability to control his own motion. As he heard Jesse's voice, Dean felt that the old man was actually death. For Jesse was constructing Dean's death—his financial death, which to Dean was the same thing. If you took away his money and power you extracted his essence, and that was exactly what Frank had Jesse come to do.

Jesse allowed himself a little smile.

"Well, Ah reckon, boys, Ah've told you 'bout all Ah ken 'bout what we think we kin do fo' this firm. Yew'll jus' have tuh make up yo' mind. Frank an' me, we got a deal, but Ah ain't interested unless yew boys are willin' tuh come along. There's jus' one thing mo'. Frank has persuaded me that Dean here has to go, so Ah'm goin' tuh ask yew all to gimme yo' answer right now. Ah'm too ole to be spendin' mah tahm runnin' aroun' buyin' up li'l biddy investment bankin' firms." Jesse paused to let it sink in. "Ah'm goin' tuh ask each one of yew if yew want Frank an' mah deal, or if you want tuh ride with Faulkner here. But remember, whatever yew decide, yew got one shot. We're either leavin' here with a deal, or we're out."

The old man was amazing. He turned his eyes to Glen Farrell, whose mouth was compressed; his jaw muscles working rapidly.

Glen knew what this meant to Dean. If they voted to go with Jesse and Grant, Dean was a dead man; Glen could see that in the threatening eyes of Grant Weir.

Glen was concerned, too, about how much authority to run the business they would still retain if Jesse bought control. But Jesse's arguments had made sense. He had the capital and the contacts on an international level, and God knows they could use both in the shape the Street and the firm were in.

With the exception of a few firms, the Street was becoming a tougher and tougher place in which to operate profitably. Jesse was giving them a chance. Glen's loyalties to Dean were very thin. Dean wasn't the kind of man who inspired loyalty, and the sight of him standing there desperate and confused, with the dried gashes from Dina's nails on his face, didn't add to Glen's desire to see Dean take over the firm.

"Well, Glen, let's have it—Frank or Dean?" The old man was incredibly shrewd.

Glen's voice was barely audible. "Frank."

Jesse wrote Glen's name down on the back of a crumpled envelope.

"Bill Davis; Frank or Dean?"

Bill's reasoning and motives were similar to Glen's. "Frank," he said without looking at Jesse.

Dean was caught in this circle of wolves, but his ability to comprehend, to seek a way out, was returning. Some enormous vitality was pumping back his will and determination not to let these Texans destroy him. He seemed to visibly pull himself together. His eyes had lost their glaze. He stared directly at Jesse, who was no longer Death, but a wizened old man that he had to crush. He pointed first at Jesse, his dark eyes snapping out the sparks of his hate. He turned slowly to each of them like some accusatory fury, his finger wavering, his voice shaking.

"I have the pledge of every one of you to resign if I am not elected head of this firm." He paused and looked searchingly at each of them. "This has always been a business where a partner's word is his bond." Dean pointed to Jesse and to Grant. "These people don't know anything about loyalty or integrity. They're whores who don't know our business. Once they have control of this firm they can do anything they want, and they will; you know that." He was trying hard to keep his voice and body from shaking with emotion. "Look what happened when that other Texas hot shot came up here to teach the Street how to run its business; he bankrupted three firms. Is that what you want; to have your careers in the hands of two men like . . . like these?"

Jesse's eyes were two ice-blue orbs. He totally disregarded Dean.

"Roger Aiken?" Roger's face was ashen. He was damn worried about throwing in his lot with these two pirates. His only hope was that Frank would somehow make it back to the firm. He looked at Dean, who stared at him with undisguised contempt.

"Frank," he said.

Jesse nodded and jotted Roger's name down with the chewed pencil stub on the crumpled envelope.

"Bob Isaacs?" Bob's face was grim. He looked at Dean and was seriously torn between the alternatives of these Texas predators and the partner he had worked with and knew, but for whom he could not feel the pull of loyalty that those years should have commanded. "Frank," he said.

"Wil Royce?" Wil didn't have to be told which way it was going; he could count. He shared all their fears and reservations, but for now he could only go one way. The choice between a demoniac Dean and these two buzzards was a cruel one after the years Dean had given to the firm. "Frank," he said.

Jesse wet the tip of his pencil with his tongue. Incredibly, this eighty-year-old man was calling off each of their names from memory.

"Dan Terrell." Dan was almost as crusty and ruthless as Jesse and Grant. "Frank," he said, his voice terse and clear. He looked at Dean with disgust.

Jesse sat back in his chair and stuffed the pencil and the envelope in his side pocket. He turned to Dean. "Ah wonder if Ah could have a word wif yew alone." He touched Grant on the sleeve. "Yew stay." He turned to the others: "Boys, Ah want tuh clear up a few things wif Dean heayer."

They all looked grimly at Jesse, then at Dean, and with a shuffling of chairs and murmured voices they left the room.

Jesse had lived too long not to know that if you mean to destroy a man, do it right. Don't leave any cripples flapping around. They could be dangerous and come at you when you least expected it, and when you were unprepared.

"Why do'n yew jus lite somewhere, Dean, an' we kin git this ovah wifout a lot of fuss. Ah'm sho' yew do'n want no mo' of this kind of thing than we do."

Dean remained standing. Jesse and Grant were seated beside each other at the opposite side of the wide circular walnut table. Dean still stood near the double doors. There was a sense of exhaustion in the room that seeped from the filled ashtrays with their smell of stale tobacco that hung mixed with the traces of faded cigar and cigarette smoke that moved slowly in the currents of the ventilation system. The hands of the numberless clock moved inexorably onward.

Jesse sighed. "Gimme the list."

Grant flipped several pages and handed the heavy clamped folder to Jesse.

Jesse began to read quietly a complete list of Dean's major clients. These were not just names on a piece of paper, they were the sum total of Dean's business life; the product of years of work and worry. In a very real sense these names were his life; they were all he really cared about.

Jesse looked up from the folder. "Son, what's the sense of goin' on wif all of this? We kin git to every one of these people—"

It was all over. Dean was a dead man and he knew it. Dean moved. Grant saw Dean as if he were watching some impossible grade B movie; one in which the sound had been suddenly turned off. He saw Dean in slow motion, the taut projectile of his body; Dean's arms outstretched for Jesse's throat; the two men tumbling backward; the momentum of Dean's lunge temporarily driving him over the chair of the fallen Jesse Hudson. Grant seemed only to be able to hear the muffled gasps that came from Jesse.

The sound suddenly came on in Grant's mind. As Dean grasped for Jesse's throat Grant hit him with the sharp edge of his right hand squarely on the back of the neck. Dean collapsed like a discarded marionette.

Grant pulled the body of Dean Faulkner off Jesse and

rushed to help the old man to a sitting position.

"Yew all raht, Jesse?" he gasped.

Jesse shook his head. For a moment he was unable to speak.

Grant stood helpless before him, waiting for Jesse to recover. Slowly the blood returned to Jesse's face. Jesse rubbed his throat with his thin hands. He coughed several times, his breath coming back to him in quick convulsive heaves of his thin chest. He held up a skinny hand.

"Water."

Grant looked about the room and saw a carafe of water and some glasses on the sideboard. Jesse drank slowly, carefully.

"Git that son of a bitch on his feet and git him outta heayr. An' Grant, Ah wont that li'l fucker dead in every way that counts. Ah wont him broke, ruined, an' disgraced." Jesse was again the lead wolf. "If Ah should die tuhday, tuhmorruh, whenever it comes, Ah wont tuh go tuh mah grave knowin' that li'l bastard has suffered the tortures of the damned!"

Grant looked into the ice-blue eyes. "It's done," he said, and as he said it his mind flicked to Frank. That Irish fucker is one of us.

The first week in May in New York was the beginning of an undecided spring. The weather alternated between unusually warm summerlike days, and the gray blasts of February.

Frank was slowly trying to make his way back from complete exhaustion. Almost no one could understand what kept him alive those first days following his collapse. But Dina understood that it was his sense of victory that kept him going; he had savagely crushed Dean, and had saved his firm. She sat with him daily, knitting quietly or reading. They never spoke. He was too weak. The hospital had given up any thought of operating until they could rebuild his strength. Each day that passed, his body was denied the treatment that could save his life. It was almost an equation, with death the unknown factor.

Dina was five months into her pregnancy. Because she was tall she carried well, but she was now continually feeling the life within her. As she sat with Frank each day, watching him while he slept, not knowing if he was going to make it, but aware of his will to live, she tried to come to some conclusion about her own life, but she couldn't. She had to see Frank through this, that was certain. She would stay with him until he either recovered or died.

Her life with Whit was no life. They saw each other occasionally, and they yearned for each other constantly. In this period of lonely longing it was she who proved to have the strength and the determination, not Whit.

While the days passed, unable to see their future together, Whit became more depressed. His friends saw it; so did his patients and his colleagues at the hospital. He worked as late as he could, arrived as early in the morning as possible so that he kept himself in a state of semi-exhaustion. He began to lose weight and to drink more heavily. Dina was very concerned about him.

She looked at Frank, who awakened momentarily and saw her. She watched the light come to his eyes and his faint smile. He attempted a feeble motion of recognition, but the effort was too much. His eyes closed and his body sought the sleep he so desperately needed.

She looked at her watch; it was three thirty. Whit would be in his office. She decided to call. She went down to the pay phone in the lobby and rang his office. She was quickly put through. He was with a patient, but he excused himself to take her call.

"If you can put up with a fat lady, darling, I'll let you treat the two of us to dinner."

She could almost feel his sense of joy and relief.

"Oh, Dina, that's marvelous. I've missed you so damn much."

"I'd prefer if we made it at your place, Whit. Send out for something. I don't care what it is, even pizza."

He laughed. "I can't feed the two of you pizza, but I'll think of something." His voice dropped. "Dina. It's been unbearable."

"I know, darling." It was a wall booth and she was trying to talk to him discreetly. She cupped her hand around the phone. "I feel the same way, Whit. It's been so very hard on me too." She tried to put some joy in her voice. "Now go back to your patients. You've probably got some shivering woman wondering what's happened to her doctor. I'll see you about seven thirty. Bye, darling." She hung up.

She was in his thoughts all day. He found himself so preoccupied that at times he was embarrassed in front of his patients.

He called up Marelli's and ordered a dinner for two including a bottle of Verdicchio. Marelli's not only served some of the best northern Italian food in New York, but they catered, if you gave them enough notice and didn't mind what it cost.

He had ordered dinner for eight thirty. It would give them some time before a waiter would intrude, and even though Whit would send the waiter back in a cab and they would serve themselves, he wanted every available minute alone with Dina.

At home that evening, he wanted a martini, badly. He walked to his bar and mixed himself a couple of drinks. He put on some records and sat looking at Manhattan; at the Secretariat of the UN; the occasional seaplane with its wings reflecting the fading afternoon light; the helicopters, like giant dragonflies, criss-crossing the sky over the city; the tugs with their barges either fighting the current upriver or moving swiftly with its flow toward the bay. His eye took in these accustomed sights. He drank slowly, feeling relaxed for the first time in weeks, because he knew she was coming.

He saw a really yar-looking ketch coming downriver. Her hull was white as a gull in the setting sun. She was under full sail reaching before a westerly breeze with the current at her stern. She moved like a water bird. His very soul wished to be on her with Dina; with Dina's baby or his baby or Frank's baby or Elliot's baby—he didn't give a damn. He wanted to be with *her*. He could practice medicine anywhere in the world. What the hell did he care? He could buy a boat. He knew exactly what he wanted: a ketch rigged double-ender, with lots of keel and beam. They could cruise the oceans of the world together; it would be paradise. A cloud momentarily darkened the river and he knew it was fantasy.

He loved this woman beyond the bounds of reason. He thought he had loved his first wife—and he had—but his feelings for Dina were a completely new experience for him. He yearned for her so that he felt he would be unable to continue if he couldn't have her. But some awful dread roamed the attic of his mind with the terrible foreboding that this might not be.

He finished the last of his martini and decided to shower and change. He wanted this evening to last forever. He tried to shake the mood of gloom that surrounded him.

They embraced in his hallway. He held her tightly, aware of her swollen body pressing against him. He kissed her softly on both cheeks; on her lips and hair. He held her back from him slightly.

"Hey, fat lady, you're getting hard to get close to."

She laughed. Really laughed for the first time in weeks. She reached for him again and held him tightly.

"Let me hold you, Whit. Oh, God, it's been so terribly long." She stroked the back of his neck and kissed him tenderly. They hadn't moved from the vestibule of his apartment. They simply stood there holding each other in desperate longing. He felt his eyes begin to mist. He had to keep some control. He moved her back slightly.

"Let's see how you look, mamma; a professional opinion, of course."

"Of course."

Her face was thinner and he saw the circles under her eyes; the shadows of anxiety that hovered about her.

"You look absolutely marvelous, mamma, both of you do."

"We do? That's refreshing to hear, Doctor, but don't you think your prognosis is a little premature?"

"The lady has been hanging around strange medical men, picking up that fancy mumbo jumbo."

"Indeed the lady has, sir." She made a mock curtsy. "Do you think the good doctor might have a lemonade or some orange juice for the fat lady?"

He was no longer kidding. "Jesus, Dina, do you know I forgot you couldn't drink? I think the only thing I may have is some tomato juice."

"Suits the lady fine, Doctor. You go ahead with whatever you're drinking."

She was wearing a cool dark-blue maternity dress with red piping.

He could see the fatigue in her face and yet she looked more beautiful to him now than ever.

"It isn't polite to stare, Doctor."

"The hell with being polite. I just want to look at you, to hold you and be with you. Dina, these past weeks have been an absolute nightmare. I can't tell you what kind of hell I'm going through."

She put her arms around him and kissed him with great tenderness. She spoke softly. "I think I know, darling."

He held her back from him a little so he could look at her face. His voice was somber. "I really don't think you do, Dina." He paused. "You have the baby and Frank. You have an end perhaps and a beginning, but I have only you—and yet I can't have you." He paused. "Even my work has given me very little satisfaction lately."

She looked at him a long while before speaking. "Don't

you think I would give my soul if things could be different? Do you think I enjoy going back to that apartment every night alone, knowing that you're here and I'm separated from you? How do you think I feel with my baby coming? I don't know if Frank will live. If he does, I don't know what my life will become—"

He held up his hand. "Darling—let's forget about all this if we can. Let's spend the night or at least part of the night just enjoying being together. Let's forget about the rest." He took her in his arms and kissed her, but their melancholy would not hide.

The clock had moved to ten thirty. They had eaten dinner quietly, watching the darkness come to the city. Their conversation inevitably got around to Frank.

"The doctors simply don't know themselves, Whit. They have to build him up first. They've even stopped any further tests. He's just too weak."

They were on the sofa looking out at the night. She lay with her head in his lap. She had removed her shoes. She looked up at him and patted her swollen body. "Seems to me a good-looking widower like you could get girls a lot prettier than I am right now."

He slapped her thigh lightly. "Cut that out, fat lady, or I really will go looking for some lithesome wench—"

"You really would?"

"Not on your life. I don't give a damn if you look like the Goodyear blimp and have triplets."

"Please, Doctor—not triplets."

He stroked her hair. His voice became anxious, almost desperate. "Dina, what are we going to do?"

She looked up at him with more maturity and control than he was showing at the moment. She pressed his hand and then kissed it softly. Her own voice seemed far away. "Nothing, darling. I'm afraid that's the hell of it. Whit, Frank does love me, at least as much as he is capable of loving anyone." Her voice softened. "I don't mean that the way it sounds. He can be sweet and attentive and very dear at times, but there is a part of Frank that prevents him from giving fully and completely to anyone. He can be terribly cruel and vindictive too. There is an implacable side to him that even I couldn't influence. He needs me now, Whit. My feelings for him are so mixed up. If it were just the two of us, Frank and I, and if the baby wasn't coming, then it would be so much easier to make a decision about us." She hesitated. "But with the baby, my first duty must be to this child"—she looked up at him, her eyes filled with tenderness—"oh, dearest Whit—please understand that. I don't mean that I don't love you with all my heart. I do, but—"

"Shush." He said it gently and bent over and kissed her. "I know what you mean, darling."

"I just mean that there is no way that we can possibly know what we can do until we know what is going to happen to Frank. Until then I suppose you and I will just have to go on. We can see each other occasionally—if we're careful—and we'll just have to hang on somehow." She looked up at him. His lips were compressed. She could see the mist in his eyes. "That is, if you want to go through all this, Whit. You don't have to, darling, and I wouldn't blame you if you didn't."

He was so choked with emotion that he couldn't answer her. He had to fight to keep back his own tears. He bent over to kiss her and she felt his torment. She held his head in both her hands and kissed him with all the love and the tenderness that she felt for him. He couldn't fight it any longer. He began to sob quietly, his tears falling gently on her face.

A siren wailed with its air of emergency, and a flight of gulls rose from the black river squawking into the soft night air.

Faye Stein had thought about Frank far more often than she would care to admit to herself. She had resumed her life as usual after returning from the Coast and from time to time called the hospital to see how he was.

She had fought the impulse to go to him. The whole thing was idiotic. Why should she get mixed up with a man who might be dying of cancer and was in love with his wife? But for some reason she found herself continuously preoccupied with Frank Sullivan. She made an appointment with Dr. Hugh Rogers. His office was in the hospital, and the only way she could get to see Rogers was as a personal favor from one of her friends who happened to be a well-known internist at Mount Sinai.

On this particular Wednesday during the first week in May at four thirty in the afternoon Faye Stein found herself waiting in the none too spacious anteroom of Dr. Rogers' office. She had been there since three, and was furious that she had been kept waiting for an hour and a half. As she was deciding to leave, the door opened and Dr. Rogers walked in with a resident physician. The two seemed to be disagreeing over the diagnosis and treatment of a patient. He saw Faye sitting there and stopped.

"Are you Miss Stein?"

"I certainly am." Her tone was more than just a little annoyed.

"I'm terribly sorry, Miss Stein, but it's just the usual chaos around here. One more minute and I'll be right with you."

The two white-coated physicians disappeared into Rogers' office and Faye went back to a magazine she had thumbed through for the tenth time.

Finally the young resident left and Dr. Rogers asked Faye to come in.

"I apologize again, Miss Stein. My secretary's out sick today, and that just complicates the normal confusion." He looked at her quickly but thoroughly. "Now let's see. I had a note about you someplace." He began leafing through the papers on his desk.

"It's from Dr. Abrams at Mount Sinai, Doctor. I'm here about Frank Sullivan."

"Oh, yes, yes. Now I remember. You're a friend of Mr. Sullivan's."

"That's right."

He looked at her meaningfully. "And you want to know about his condition?"

"That's right."

Rogers leaned back in his chair and pushed his glasses up on his forehead. He rubbed his tired eyes and sighed loudly. He pursed his lips and gazed out of the window.

"Normally, Miss Stein, I don't give out information to anyone who's not a member of the immediate family, but in view of Dr. Abrams' letter—and my assumption that you will be completely discreet about this—"

"I will, Doctor."

"In that case, I can tell you that Mr. Sullivan's condition is quite serious. He has carcinoma of the right lung. Unfortunately he complicated things both for himself and for us by following a course of action that we totally disapproved of, and advised him against. Now, he is so weak that we can't operate on him. We can't even give him any more tests until he has regained some strength." Hugh Rogers paused. "He is gaining strength slowly, but our problem is—and we have no way of knowing or combatting it in his present condition—the degree of damage that is being done by the carcinoma that's affecting him."

Hugh looked at Faye Stein's face and he could see the concern in her deep-brown eyes. He realized that the relationship between this attractive redhead and his patient was more than casual, but his compassion and his instincts responded to her genuineness—to the sense of the straightforward which *was* Faye Stein.

Hugh Rogers leaned on his desk and looked at her attentively. "Miss Stein. As in so many things connected with medicine, we doctors have to depend on just plain luck. You can call it God if you are a religious person or chance if you're not. I call it luck. If Mr. Sullivan is going to live through this ordeal, he's going to have to be lucky. I can't tell you any more than that at the moment. I'm sorry."

She had guessed as much herself. Her face was somber as she looked at Hugh Rogers.

"There's just one thing, Doctor. A favor if you would."

"Anything I can do."

"When Mr. Sullivan is able to see any visitors, either before or after the operation, I'd like to see him."

"I think that can be arranged."

"If you can just tell your secretary, Doctor, I don't have to bother you. I'll check with her from time to time."

"I'd be delighted."

"Thank you."

Faye left. She could hear the muffled sounds of her heels on the vinyl-tiled floors. She would come late some night, when he was well enough.

Faye, what the hell is wrong with you? she asked herself as she walked out into the bright sunlight of York Avenue and Sixty-eighth Street. She didn't know.

On this night long after Dina had left, Frank was lying awake, his thoughts a mixture of the firm and of his problems with his wife.

As Frank began to rebuild his strength for his operation, he found himself more preoccupied with Dina. He was torn by the desire to reach a more fulfilling accommodation with her, and the jealousy and hate that was building inside him as his mind dwelt on the paternity of her child.

Frank was agonized by the guilt he felt for having put Dina and Elliot together, and also the maddening possibility that this child could be his; his logic doubted this, but it couldn't be ruled out. It was not knowing—not ever being able to know for sure—that was driving Frank crazy.

His feelings for Dina were changing in another way. The sale of his interest in the firm to Jesse, and the punishment his body and mind had taken in the fight with Dean, had more than exhausted him; it seemed to take from him the drive to fight to win. In a sense he had won, and now he was exhausted.

He knew enough about himself to know the old desire for the game might return. But now he wanted to forget about problems. He had solved the problems of his business, but there didn't seem to be any way that he could rid himself of the problems of his wife.

He stared at the ceiling, alone with the muted late-night sounds of the hospital, only half heard by one who had long grown accustomed to them.

When she first called his name he thought he was dreaming, but when he saw her standing in the doorway smiling at him—that same wry smile that seemed always so provocative—he knew it wasn't a dream.

"Faye! For heaven's sake!"

"May I come in?"

"You'd better."

"Frank. I know I probably shouldn't be here, but I just had to see you. I've been keeping tabs on you."

He smiled. "So you've been following my progress. I'm glad to hear it. I had given up on you; thought you'd forgotten me."

She looked at him for a long while, then bent down and kissed him softly. "It's been a long time, Frank."

She turned around and looked for a chair to put beside his bed. She sat next to him, her brown eyes showing her compassion and her concern.

"When are they going to operate? Do you know yet?"

"Not yet. But my guess is soon."

She held his hand.

"You look marvelous as usual," he said.

"Thank you, sir."

He looked at her for what seemed a long time.

"I certainly wish we were back in California, Faye."

"So do I."

She was longing to ask him about Dina, but she knew better.

"I'll have to get well just for you, Faye."

"You're damn right you will." She looked at him for a long time without speaking. She shook her head in that habitual gesture of hers that kept her long red hair in place.

"Frank. I really have no right to be here, but I had to come." She was saying more than she intended because it occurred to her that she might never see him again. Her eyes began to mist, but she fought back the tears.

"I don't know why, but you've meant more to me in the few days we've had together than you should." She squeezed his hand. "You're going to make it, damn it."

His response to her was what it had been from the first. As sick as he was she excited him, but more than that, for some strange reason she comforted him. She seemed only to want him fully and completely, and he wanted her in the same way.

If he felt as he did about her, how could he tell himself that he loved Dina? He did love Dina, of course, but with his wife there was nothing but problems. Perhaps Faye's attraction was that with her there were no problems. He felt that with her, their lives would be less restricted. But then these thoughts were ridiculous. He didn't believe in divorce, and even if he did, he was about to become a father. The thought of the baby seared through him. He turned to look at her.

She was wearing a white linen suit. Just a jacket and silk scarf tied about her neck. He raised his hand and reached for her breast, touching her nipple.

"You are definitely too much, Frank. Really you are." Her eyes were smiling, but the hint of concern was still there.

He chuckled. "Don't worry about me. I intend to come

out of this thing just to be in California with you again."

She laughed. "Then I'm glad I can do something to contribute to your recovery."

"Probably a hell of a lot more than the doctors can do."

He looked at her, still smiling. "There is something you can do for me."

She leaned forward, her eyes reflecting her eagerness to help him.

"What is it? What can I do for you?"

He was still smiling. He began to chuckle.

She was puzzled but amused.

"Come on, Frank, what is it?"

His eyes held that old light that was one of the things that first attracted her.

"Frank. Don't be a tease. What is it?"

"I'd love you to suck me."

She started to laugh, her eyes pleased at his response to her.

"Are you crazy? What if someone should come in?"

"No one will come in." He was still smiling. "It's all your fault, you know. You come in here looking so damn attractive, you get a fellow going."

She couldn't stop laughing. She reached for both his hands and held them.

"You are absolutely too much, Frank. You've got to be out of your mind. You're not well enough for that. Oh, God, Frank, that's funny."

"Well, I don't think it's so damn funny."

She leaned over to kiss him, her lips soft and full; her tongue probed his mouth.

"Now, look, Faye, if you keep that up, God damn it, you're going to have to do something."

"You just get back on your feet, Frank, and I'll do anything you want, for as long as you want it, anytime you want it."

Jesus Christ, this woman excited him. Why not turn his life toward her if he lived through this thing? They had something going between them, whatever it was. The best part about it was that neither of them cared if they understood it or not. They were simply willing to take the other as is; no quests for improvement; no strings.

She brushed her hair away from her face with her hand. She felt she shouldn't be bringing it up, but it just came out. She simply had to know how things stood between him and Dina.

His face tightened and she was sorry she had mentioned it.

"No. Don't be. I can talk to you." And he did. But the subject of Elliot, and the question of the paternity of the child, was too wounding for him to discuss with anyone.

"All I know is that if I live through this Dina and I have to make a decision. I simply don't know what that will be."

She knew he wasn't telling her everything, but she didn't care. All she wanted was to see him well again. She had enough faith in their mutual attraction to know that Frank Sullivan was going to be a big part of her life.

She looked at him for what seemed a very long time. "I'd better let you get some rest."

She kissed him softly, and he held her just for a moment as she bent over him, and kissed her in return.

As she was about to leave his room she turned in the doorway and looked at him. "When you get well again I have a feeling we'll make quite a team."

He smiled and winked and blew her a kiss.

Dina was at the hospital at 8 A.M. They would take Frank up to the operating room at nine.

She busied herself, trying to disguise her nervousness. His mood was somber and reflective. She sensed he wanted to say something to her and was struggling within himself to get it out.

"Dina, sit beside me for a minute; there's something

I've got to tell you before they take me up there."

Frank was saying his confession to her. The simple but overpowering remnants of his early Catholicism would not let him go with this secret that had been locked within him for so long. It *had to be revealed to her* if he was to have any peace.

His voice was heavy with emotion as she sat beside him looking into the gray eyes which were now averted from her own.

"That night when you first met Elliot." He hesitated, his voice now almost a whisper. "I planned that meeting, Dene. God forgive me, but I brought the two of you together to buy the time I needed to do something at the firm. It was no accident that brought you and Elliot together." The pain of telling her this was tearing at him, overwhelming him with guilt and shame. He felt a surge of pathos roar through him like some thundering sea, but he couldn't cry. He wanted to. He needed the release, but as he looked at her, he saw only the beginning of understanding. Its impact had to come upon her more slowly.

She looked at him with the developing awareness that her husband was capable of such an act, but she had not had time enough to analyze her own reactions.

A nurse had come to prep Frank for his operation. Dina stepped out into the hall, her mind absorbed by what Frank had just told her.

Dina now began to realize that she was really on her own. She had Whit, but Frank she knew could be very ominous when it came to losing his wife to another man. Frank didn't like to lose—anything. And she knew he would reveal that streak of Catholicism that had a stronger hold on him than he realized. This would complicate things for all of them.

These thoughts crowded her mind as the nurse left Frank's room and told Dina she could go in.

Frank looked at her with concern and asked her to come sit beside him.

He held her hand looking into her face, knowing that her eyes were not focused on him; that her thoughts were far away. His voice was a husky whisper.

"Dina, for God's sake say you forgive me."

He looked at her pleadingly. "Dina—forgive me." He wanted absolution.

She looked at him, her eyes not really seeing him. Her voice was flat and toneless. "I forgive you, Frank. There's really nothing to forgive. You brought Elliot and me together, then I took over from there. If there's a fault to find we can both share it. It's not just yours."

He watched her as she said it, not sure that she meant what she was saying. His heart broke for what he had done to her.

They were interrupted by a nurse who came in with the sedation that would take Frank to the edge of anesthesia.

Dina stayed with him after they had given him Demerol, and sat by his bed watching him slowly drift into a deeply sedated rest. He was still conscious when they came for him and lifted him on the rolling stretcher. They wrapped a blanket around him and started to wheel him out.

He raised a hand to stop them until she came to him. She saw he wanted to kiss her and she bent over him and kissed him and touched his brow.

"I'll be here as soon as they let me see you, Frank."

When she left the hospital and walked out into the sunlight of York Avenue, she looked for a cab, still inwardly searching for the direction her life would take if Frank recovered. She had a lot of sorting out to do, but Dina was becoming aware of her own strength, and she had one unalterable resolve: she would follow whatever course would be best for her child.

Frank had won his biggest battle. Through some incredible combination of luck and will he had survived the physical trauma of a pneumonectomy against grave odds.

When he first came home he looked like death. But Hugh Rogers was right. He said that everything depended upon luck, and the nursing care Frank would receive.

Slowly, day by day, this battle-scarred old warrior healed.

Toward the middle of June they were able to move him to the house in Connecticut, where he was now accelerating his recovery.

It was a large white clapboard house approached by a tree-lined drive. It faced a small cove that looked out on the Sound, facing the western shore of Long Island. The southern crescent of the cove held a point of land where a stand of slender white birches bent to the winds that came from the sea.

Frank had spent a good part of this recuperative period lying on a couch in the sun porch, a many-windowed room that looked out over the lawns and gardens to the cove and the Sound.

It was the third week in June, on a particularly beautiful day, when the fading afternoon light touched the splashes of color of the gardens with a richness and contrast of shadow.

Frank had been watching Dina, who was reading and pretending not to be aware of his searching gaze.

Dina was now in her sixth month and as she came nearer to the time of delivery, Frank became withdrawn, his thoughts building upon an inner frustration that made him bitter and contentious.

Dina had developed a resolve; a plan for her life that affected her attitude toward Frank, an attitude that had become one of self-imposed but temporary obligation. It gave her at least purpose and stability. It drove Frank to distraction.

Whit was the most troubled. He had been unable to

see Dina since she had gone to Connecticut, and their
lives together had been reduced to scattered telephone
calls placed by Dina from the village.

Whit had begged her over and over to leave Frank, and
to come and live with him, but she wouldn't; not without the formality of a divorce.

They each longed for the other, and their frustration
at being separated affected them differently. Whit had become morose, bitter, drinking more than he should, and
Dina began to be concerned about him. But she couldn't
leave Frank—not yet.

Faye had to fight off the temptation to phone Frank,
but she couldn't deny herself all contact with him.

She wrote him occasionally, typing the letters on the
letterhead of her real estate corporation, so that it was
unlikely that Dina would become suspicious.

Faye's letters were restrained. Frank's admiration for
her judgment was increased by that. Frank had often
thought that she knew how to play her game, and he liked
that.

Now, on this day, with the shadows of late afternoon
reaching across the lawn, Dina had decided that Frank
was well enough to confront him with what she had decided to do.

She put down her book and looked at him, aware that
he had been watching her intently. His face was taut; the
lines of his mouth compressed; there was no warmth in
the gray eyes.

"Frank, I think it's time we talked."

"What about?"

She was very calm, regal, sitting very erect.

"Let's not make this more difficult than necessary,
Frank. I want a divorce."

He looked at her coldly. He hated the word *divorce*.
It meant loss, defeat; it went against that stubborn Catholicism of his which seemed to surface on convenient
occasions.

"What do you want a divorce for? Are you unhappy? You're going to have *your* baby soon. I would have thought the last thing an expectant mother would want would be a divorce." He smiled coldly at the irony.

"I'm glad you find it amusing, Frank; I'm afraid I don't. You're well enough now, so—"

"So what? Is that what you've been planning—to get rid of me when I'm *well enough*?" He glared at her angrily.

She sighed. "Frank. Let's try and at least be civil about this. Yes. I had planned to ask you for a divorce if you recovered from the operation, and thank God, now, you have." Her face showed the anguish she felt for both of them.

"Oh, Frank, let's stop doing this to each other. Whatever we have left of our lives, let's not waste it by cutting each other up with bitterness. That's what would happen to us, Frank, if we stayed together. I see it happening now. I've watched you looking at me; looking at the baby. I can almost see the question going through your mind. It will always be there. That's why I want this divorce. Not because I don't love you. I do. I love you in a very special way, but this child will tear us apart. It's doing that now; I can see it in your face."

Her words cut at him deeply. He loved her too, that was the damnedest part of the whole thing; and she had just told him that she loved him; even if she had qualified that in her own way. It seemed to be the old story of two people who loved each other but couldn't live together. But he knew that it was far more complicated than that.

"Frank. If you won't give me a divorce, then I'm going to leave anyway—"

"To go where—with him? With that two-bit doctor you're so goddamn fond of—!" He was furious. He stood up and walked to the windows looking out on the Sound, his back to her.

Her voice was low and very calm. "No, Frank, I'm not going to Whit; not unless you and I are divorced. That's not the kind of start in life I want to give my child."

He exploded. He whirled to face her, his eyes blazing fury.

"God damn it, did it ever occur to you that that baby could be *my* child too; that you might be taking *my* child away from *me*?" He really didn't believe it, but there was always that possibility. That was one of the things that drove him crazy—the impossibility of ever being absolutely sure.

"Are you telling me you wouldn't run to your dear doctor friend if I gave you a divorce?"

"I'm telling you, Frank, I'll raise the baby alone if I have to, but I won't inflict the damage of bringing my baby up with a father whose love for him—or for her—is torn by his own vanity—"

"Vanity—Jesus Christ, is that what they call it now—when a husband doesn't know who the hell is father of the child he is supposed to love and support through life—*Vanity!* You've got one hell of an idea about vanity."

She looked at him as he stood glaring at her from the opposite end of the room.

"Frank. It's no good going on like this. I'm going back to the city tomorrow to look for an apartment. If I can't find one I'll stay in a hotel until after the baby is born."

She hesitated, knowing how much this was hurting him; it hurt her too, but she was younger, with a new life inside her; and it was she who was leaving him. Her life now had purpose and direction; for the moment his did not.

"I'd like you to transfer my securities to a bank. I'll need the income to live—"

"Are you crazy? What the hell are you talking about—income. God damn it, you're *my wife*. You don't need any income. Jesus Christ, Dina, what's come over you?"

"I'm not going to take your money, Frank. I don't need it; not if I'm careful, and I don't want it."

Her eyes misted as she saw the pain come into his.

"Oh, Frank, I'm not trying to hurt you. I don't want to be vindictive or unkind—but can't you see, this is the only way. It really is, Frank."

He sat down, his face white. He was confused, frustrated. He didn't want to lose her, but he knew now that he would, and that fact struck him with the impact of a bullet. He felt abandoned; his life shattered.

She got up and came to him and touched his cheek lightly with her lips. Her eyes were filled with anguish for him. She could barely speak.

"I'll be leaving in the morning. I'll let you know where I'll be." She kissed him with great tenderness. He could taste the salt of her tears. Her voice was strained with emotion.

"It will be better this way, Frank. You'll see. We don't have to lose touch with each other. I don't want to, and I hope you don't either."

He looked at her, his heart breaking. He couldn't speak because everything was stuck in his throat.

She kissed him again softly and turned to leave the room. He stood there watching her go, with the shadows lengthening on the lawn, feeling more alone than he had ever felt in his life.

Dina had telephoned Whit and told him she was back in town; that she had left Frank. They were going to have dinner together. For the first time in a month he felt as if he could breathe again; as if he were alive. Whatever time it took—whatever agonizing decision Dina had come to—Whit knew his love was strong enough; all that mattered was that his life be brought together, finally, with hers.

Frank couldn't stand the solitude of the house in Connecticut any longer. He had come back to New York just two days after Dina had left.

The old warrior had lost his most important battle, and in the silence of the apartment he searched for a way to ease his loneliness and heal the savage wound that had scarred his life.

The first stirrings of the call of the Street were beginning to make themselves felt, but it was too soon. He still had a way to go with his physical recovery, and he was, at least for now, too preoccupied with his personal problems to give serious thought of returning to the firm.

He called Faye Stein.

Faye's apartment on Central Park West was what he would have expected.

It was large, expensively furnished, with a contemporary lavishness that didn't appeal to Frank but which didn't offend him either.

As he walked into the large living room, he could see her face light up with joy, but he also saw the swift understanding in her eyes as she came to him.

She kissed him and guided him to the sofa.

"How about a drink?"

"I'd love one."

She walked to a high black lacquered cabinet that stood against the wall and opened it, revealing, under the lights that went on automatically as the double doors opened, an assortment of bottles and glasses that would have done justice to a small restaurant.

She quickly poured both of them two glasses of a pure malt scotch and added a splash of spring water.

They were seated on a long soft-cushioned Lawson sofa facing three draped windows that looked out on the new green of the trees bordering Central Park.

He had drunk heavily for him; especially in the afternoon.

She listened to the outpouring of his anguish, which burst from him like a ruptured boil.

It was uncharacteristic of Frank to share his feelings with anyone, and his pride still prevented him from telling Faye about Elliot, but as the afternoon wore on and the scotch relaxed him, he began to notice Faye; really see her.

She had dressed carefully for him, selecting a dress that would do the most for her body and full breasts.

She sat beside him, sharing drink for drink; skillfully loosening him up, until at last she saw the tension fade away and could see his eyes looking at her; just the hint of a smile, the first she had seen since he walked in the door.

"You know, Faye, this is the first time I've felt like a human being since I got out of the hospital."

She stroked a long red nail from his ear down the line of his jaw.

"Darling. I think you need Faye Stein's nursing care now." She was smiling at him provocatively.

"I think you'd be about the best damn medicine in town." His face clouded.

"Why would a beautiful girl like you want to get mixed up with a battered old fellow like me?" He paused. "You can do a lot better than Frank Sullivan, Faye, he's all washed up."

She took his face in her hands and looked directly into his eyes. Her voice was even and very firm.

"Frank. Don't ever degrade me as a woman again by telling me that my man is a has-been. I've had my fill of losers, and God knows you're no loser. You're a winner, baby, that's had a bad break; but damn it, you're lucky—you should thank God you're alive, and stop this old-man nonsense. I said it to you once before and I'll say it to you again—for the last time"—she guided his hand to her breast—"do I look like the kind of a woman who wants a has-been for a lover?"

He could feel her nipple extend and he knew the passion that lay within this woman. He was enormously attracted to her.

"Listen, Frank. The only thing that's wrong with you is that you don't know how lucky you are. I mean that, darling. You know, I once read somewhere that a portion of wisdom is to know when fortune is being kind. That makes a lot of sense if you think about it. Why not for once in your life *relax?* You've been a success in your business; you've got a woman who loves you—*Frank, for God's sake, just relax and enjoy it."*

He looked at her, his face and eyes smiling. He couldn't help it. Faye wanted him for himself, and he wanted her.

Why not? he thought. She was right. There comes a time when you're too tired to keep on fighting. He had fought and clawed his way for forty years. Why not spend the rest of his life with a woman who only wanted to give? Jesus, that would be something different. Why not?

He turned to Faye with a smile and a light in his eye.

He raised his glass of scotch to her in a toast. They looked at each other for a long time, and then started to laugh like hell.